PRAISE FOR *Graveside Politics*

Steve Tenore has been a class act in every season of his remarkable life. He has excelled in public service and built several successful businesses right in the heart of the Eastern Establishment. But who the hell knew he could write so brilliantly and so well! The first book by this gifted and able fellow is marvelous! Steve Tenore is very well begun in his new career.

William O'Shaughnessy
President & Editorial Director
Whitney Radio
WVOX/WRTN

GRAVESIDE POLITICS

GRAVESIDE POLITICS

STEPHEN P. TENORE

TATE PUBLISHING & *Enterprises*

 TATE PUBLISHING
& Enterprises

Published in the United States of America

ISBN: 1-5988678-5-7

07.04.02

To Karen, who redefined the word *courage* for me.

They are always there – the funeral chapel, the politicians, neighborhood offices, the pharmacy, the police station – all these local places we know only when we must but not inside out. They always seem beyond mystery – closed in on themselves and hard to explain to the citizens walking into their reception area.

Steve Tenore, with a firm but skillful hand has pulled away the curtain shielding them from view and lets us step inside their back rooms. There we hear the jargon of these specialists: we catch the odors of the embalmers labs, the schemes of public officials, half public-minded and more than hungry for private gain, the plots of those who search the stock market. We feel as though we are part of their clubs, their daily agendas, and even though forbidden to join them each page of the galloping story makes it necessary that we know now. After all we say, these characters live in our town; and even if they run our town they tell few secrets about its inside maneuvers. Now is our chance to know what webs they have spun and who weaves them and who gets caught.

Steve Tenore makes his characters so familiar to us because we know them from our towns. He tantalizes us into thinking that we can really see inside them and follow the forces that drive them, and get them to confess all to us mundane citizens.

None of these "hometown people" may be interested in us; that's how we feel about them. We need them when the crimes, the deaths, the public good call us to attention. But do they need us? We doubt it. That's the reason for poking our nose in their business. We want an open look into public life and private schemes; their sealed secrets annoy us.

He takes us from one "precinct" to another. He makes us aware of their paper-thin curtains of concealment. There he illustrates the walls they build to fend off the snooping of their peers – the other schemers who run the town – each for his or her own gusto or reward.

I enjoyed this book because I could find in these very "rock-of-Gibraltar" town leaders just so much appearance of strength, but not such that a good hard hammer couldn't crack open to reveal their soft center. This is a story every village, hamlet, town and every city tells, but few have heard it until now. You won't ignore the funeral home, precinct, pharmacy, a councilman's office from here on in. As a matter of fact you might even stop in for a visit of such inner sanctums, get a tour, and really be at home and "in the know" in your own home town.

—Rev. Msgr. Patrick Vincent McNamara,
Pastor of St. Gabriel's Church in New Rochelle.

INTRODUCTION

*T*omaas *frowned as, standing on the stone terrace of his parents' villa overlooking the harbor and marina of Fontvielle in Monaco, he glanced at the gray van still stalled on the road high above the principality. It was blocking the road's left lane. He felt a sense of unease as he continued to stare. Should he call the local police? Wasn't it his civic duty? Normally placid and easy going by nature, and physically courageous to the point of recklessness, Tomaas could not account for the anxiety that was twisting his nerves into knots. Maybe it was his high anticipation of having Janice back, having her in his arms again. He was full of anticipation. Since he'd begun dating Janice he had found full happiness for the first time in his life. But "dating" was hardly the right word; it was so much more than that. Maybe they would make up their own word one day. Janice had just called him on her car phone to tell him that she was not more than 20 minutes away. She always phoned him after an absence to tell him that she couldn't wait to see him. She always continued by reminding him to have her drink ready – a very dry martini – before she arrived and to get rid of any young girl he might be entertaining. Tomaas, in turn, would jokingly counter with, "But she wants to meet the woman I talk so0000 much about." They would laugh ciao bella and hang up.*

Tomaas' parents had been furious with him for becoming involved with a married woman – not only married but at least 30 years his senior – and, to make matters worse, the wife of a friend of his father's. Finally, though, Henri LaCroix had started to accept his son's relationship. Likely, Tomaas thought, knowing his father, he would use the relationship to somehow get to the esteemed U.S. Senator, Frank Rodino – Janice's husband. It was even Henri's idea to let Tomaas use the villa for his affair with Janice. "Your mother will come around," he said with a conspiratorial grin. "Just don't flaunt this affair in the streets of Paris."

The night grew darker. Tomaas checked his watch. His Janice would be with him any minute now and his life would take on a new intensity. Maybe it was too many margaritas. Maybe it was nothing, but he could not shake the feeling of unease. He pressed his body against the railing, watching the gray van, wondering why no one exited from it. How long had it been there? He had first noticed it nearly an hour ago. Something was not right.

He stood beside the three dozen roses from Sorasio florist. They overflowed the table abutting the terrace from which the LaCroix family enjoyed a panoramic view of the Mediterranean. Roses were Tomaas' favorite flowers, and their scent, his favorite scent, but he was not aware of their sweet smell now; his full attention was riveted on the van. He drew in a sharp breath as the gray van started to move. It crawled slowly forward at no more than five miles an hour as Tomaas watched intently, his hands balled into fists. He then noticed a white Range Rover heading up the hill from the opposite direction. He tensed as he squinted into the gathering darkness below. The van began to veer toward the middle of the road as it headed for a hairpin curve. Tomaas held his breath, staring unblinkingly as the scene unfolded. If the van didn't correct itself, he knew it would enter the right lane and go straight over the cliff. But then the van stopped short in the middle of the road. The Range Rover disappeared behind the ridge of a hill and Tomaas lost sight of it.

The scene then suddenly turned surreal. Tomaas later would swear that the van intentionally sped up as the white car reached the turn. The van swerved from the middle of the road to the right, leaving the Range Rover nowhere to go but over the cliff. The Rover, given its considerable weight, survived the worst of the impact and slid about 30 to 40 feet down the steep decline, teetered for a second and then rolled over onto its roof.

The darkening dusk had now turned to night. Tomaas could barely make out any details, but he did recall later that the van stopped and one of the passengers got out and climbed down the side of the cliff. Squinting determinedly, Tomaas could make out a dark figure against the white car; he was checking the driver's side. Tomaas blinked with confusion as he watched the figure smash in the Range Rover's driver's side window with a thick object that Tomaas couldn't identify. The dark figure then crawled inside the car, stayed for a moment, then backed out.

What the hell was going on? The scene was growing more surreal by the moment. There didn't seem to be any attempt to pull the driver from the car. The dark figure stood up next to the caved-in car, put something to his ear and mouth, then sprinted up the hill and jumped into the van. Within seconds it made a screeching U-turn, speeding toward the French town of Cap D'Ail.

An uneasy feeling crept over Tomaas. He was neither superstitious nor intuitive yet he could not shake the feeling that what he just witnessed had something to do with him. Where was Janice? Tomaas asked himself, feeling a sudden chill spread through his stomach and chest. Why hadn't she arrived by now? She was late and Janice was never late.

CHAPTER I

Day One, Wednesday, June 30, 3 AM

Three AM phone calls are never good. For Paul Arrone, they tended to be deadly. The first ring jolted him from the depths of rare deep sleep. His first semi-conscious thought: *After 20 years running the family business, I should be free of this crap.*

"Protocol," he muttered through clenched teeth. "They're supposed to follow protocol. Any night duty – hell, *all* night duty – I see belonged to Paul's on-call funeral directors, not him. He had paid his dues. For crying out loud, he was the owner. So what if he had little else to do."

The protocol was clear. After 10 PM, his expensive answering service was supposed to get the vital statistics of the deceased, then reach the on-duty director who would speak to the family. If the on-call funeral director was out for a pickup or transferring a client to the embalming room, and if someone had died in a house or a family needed immediate assistance, the call went to a tradesman.

In funeral home protocol – at least in Paul's – the tradesman caught everything that fell outside the usual, "convenient" death. If the tradesman was unavailable, he had to arrange for another freelance embalmer to take care of the first-call information and response. For this, he, or sometimes she, was paid well.

Short of the President of the United States dying in southern Westchester County, there virtually was no reason that Paul, in his haze, could imagine why his private line would be ringing at three in the morning.

The phone blared again but Paul's mind was elsewhere. He had not fallen back asleep, but was in a deep reverie, transported back some 30 years in this exact same apartment, which spanned the second and third floors of the Georgian-style funeral home started by his grandfather in the late 19th century. Thirty years ago, as now, the phone ringer would be set on high. Paul's father had told him, as his father before had dictated, "In order to be alert, in order to *sound* alert when a family needs you, you had better make sure you *are* alert. The phone has to be as loud as possible. Collect your thoughts before you pick up that line. Whoever is on the other end is going to need your help, your compassion, your comfort." That was grandpa's protocol. That was Paul's protocol.

As kids, whenever that phone rang in the night so loud it could wake the "deads" down in the reposing rooms, Paul and his four brothers would try to out-yell each other.

"Hurry, Pop, someone *needs* you," one would call down the long hall-way of the apartment.

"Quick, Dad, answer it before the dead guy on the other end comes back to life," another would shout, collapsing in guffaws.

The free-for-all would end abruptly after their father had taken his belt to all five boys or at least the awake ones, guilty or not. Dominic Arrone would then calmly weave the same belt through the waistband of his funeral director's black suit before heading out on the call.

Even now, Paul's lower buttocks twitched at the memory of the strap. *Amazing*, he thought as he dragged himself upright, *the stupid crap that surfaces when you've been sleeping only an hour.*

He neither would nor could move faster. If the caller knew the number of the private line, then he also knew it was going to ring for some time before Paul would pick up. He hadn't grown less sympathetic to the families, but 40 was 40. And 41 wasn't looking much better. Paul was tired and well aware that he was more out of shape than in. His once-athletic body now carried some extra pounds around the middle; *probably*, he thought gloomily, *around the brain too.*

Worst of all, increasingly in the last year or so, sleep came slow as a dirge. Sometimes he would get no more than an hour and a half a night. "Professional hazard," he remembered his father saying way back, soon after Paul joined the business. "These guys are hitting the wall," he would confide to his son as they watched colleagues unwind after some industry trade show.

And then later, long after his brother John was gone: "Most of us do well for years. Then one day, it all piles up. You end up a hopeless alcoholic or strung out on drugs or committing suicide. There is just so much grief a person can deal with and stay sane."

Gee, thanks, Dad, Paul would think. *Thanks for insisting that I go into the business.* Actually, family circumstances had dragged Paul in. And he went uncomplainingly. Not to witness grief, the grief his father talked about, but because of it. His long legs were now dangling from the king-size bed. He ran his large hands over his face and through his hair. Third ring? Fourth? *Go away.*

The ringing phone faded as his mind roamed back almost two decades, a lifetime. His first middle-of-the-night call. It was 3 AM then too. Back then, he got to it before the second ring.

"Digger," Sergeant Cullan had barked from the other end, "We got a jumper for you. Male Hispanic. Header off the Division Street Bridge. Landed smack in the middle of I-95."

Paul groaned, inwardly.

"How quick can you get down here, Digger?" his former police academy superior asked in a falsely concerned tone. "Unless and until your candy ass shows up, all traffic on the Thruway is at a dead halt in both directions."

Paul "Candy Ass" Arrone, the newest and youngest director of the 100-year-old Arrone Funeral Home of New Rochelle, New York, had let the sergeant's disrespect slide. In his own weird way, Paul knew that Cullan was trying to get them past the awkwardness – trying to start fresh. Trying to move past their mutual disappointment at a lot of things; like Paul, the most promising cop in New Rochelle, maybe the region, leaving the force for good to become a "digger." Trying to get them past the last major crisis they had faced together – past John.

Paul felt the silence more than he heard it.

"Come on, candy ass, snap to it," Cullan barked. "We're going to be stuck here all night if you don't get your sweet cheeks down here. Or do you have a better idea for me?"

"I expect you to walk it off, you sissy," Paul had answered calmly. "I expect you to call someone who gives a crap, but most of all, *Sergeant*, I expect you to send a police car up to the Westchester County Country Club and drag the ass of that alcoholic medical examiner out of bed and insist that he do *his* job for once."

The silence was so complete at the other end of the line that for a second Paul thought Cullan had hung up. Paul heard only the continuous clicking of the tape recorder at headquarters, where the call had been routed from the sergeant's police car to the Funeral Home. When Paul realized that Cullan was still on the line, he said, "I'll be there in five minutes, Sarge."

"Thanks," his mentor said, biting off the word. Paul started to hang up.

"By the way, Paul, you'd better bring a couple of extra disaster pouches and several pairs of gloves."

Paul swallowed.

"I have a police car waiting to escort you off Exit 15," Cullan added. "You'll have to travel northbound by escort in the southbound lane – there is no other way to get you down here."

Paul finished shrugging into his clothes, but the phone cord was still up his sleeve.

"Oh, and Paul, I should tell you that Johnson is here and it ain't pretty."

Paul was sure it wasn't. Johnson and Paul had trained together as rookies. Without a doubt, Johnson was what his father called "a gagger."

It may have been his first solo night call, but Paul knew the drill: Whenever you had to go to a house removal or crime scene that was sure to be gamey, there was always a gagger. You had to spot him immediately and try to hustle him off the premises. It was the nature of the beast. It went with the territory. The odds of getting a gagger were directly proportional to how bad the situation was. If a body was found in the dog days of August – dead, say, two weeks – you knew that when you got to the scene at least one cop would be a gagger. If, in the same situation, the body was oozing with fluids from decomposition (what insiders called a "floater") and maggots were crawling from the nostrils, then the dictums of the funeral industry invariably meant there were two gaggers, usually after one or both had eaten a lunch of tacos.

Funeral directors there for such removals had to be able to handle the dead and the living. You had tools – Vicks or Noxzema smeared under your nose and into your own nostrils and then you went to work. Of course, the dry-heaves also could break the chain of control. If you weren't able to get the gagger out of the room, you had to divert the attention of the other officers to avoid the domino effect. If a second officer fell prey and started to dry heave, or if anyone really was throwing chunks, the funeral director had a single question: "Can this guy make it to a bathroom bowl or garbage pail? Any size will do."

As Paul drove the hearse from his funeral home in the Neptune Park section of the city, he figured Johnson's gagging was likely just the beginning.

Paul headed the hearse off I-95 and down the Exit 15 ramp. The lights and siren of the waiting police car snapped on. He couldn't see who was driving in front of him but he noted the slow pace. It was something he and his father would smile about when they talked in the morning. No matter how fast the world was moving, it was a universal fact that a hearse had to move slower. It was close to 4 AM and there wasn't a single vehicle in any of the three southbound lanes. The hearse was being escorted by New Rochelle's finest, and yet they were traveling no faster than a cortege destined for Arlington National Cemetery.

People really feel they can avoid death, Paul had marveled. *Stall it at least by slowing down the vehicle that would carry it.*

What a kid he had been on that first night call. Paul stared blankly from the bed, unable to move, fixed in its memory. He was vaguely aware of the slow cold drip from the outside of his window air conditioner, the blood pulsing in his neck. Why had he found driving north down the middle of the southbound lanes so exhilarating? It reminded him of the first time he had ventured into the middle of the road to retrieve a precious baseball, Johnny egging him on. Paul had been powerful then, going where the others were too scared to go. Paul, the invincible.

Once, when he was maybe eight years old, he was standing in the middle of the street and had turned to see the family Funeral Home. It was a new vantage point for him. For the first time he saw it not as his house and the family business but both as a shelter and a beacon, standing out from the other businesses and converted mansions, the dignified *padrone* of the old city neighborhood. The Arrone Funeral Home was no neighborhood storefront conversion. It had been built to be what it was: a stately mansion, a family's sanctuary. Later, as the region's foremost family Funeral Home, it took on the dimensions of an estate – welcoming clients and families alike, shepherding them gently but firmly to where they didn't want to go, but must.

Fifteen years later, Paul found himself driving I-95 the wrong way, with an audience of maybe hundreds. Johnny wasn't watching, but anonymous night drivers and their passengers peered from the black windows of their vehicles immobilized on the other side of the metal road divider.

Paul noticed several eighteen-wheelers on the shoulder. Why was the police accident team gathered so far away, maybe a mile from the bridge? As his hearse approached, Paul counted at least ten NRPD cars and a couple of unmarked detective cars between him and the distant Division Street Overpass where the jumper apparently pulled his half-gainer.

He stopped the hearse in the middle of the roadway. He and the escorting officer got out of their vehicles at the same time. He recognized a familiar face, Brian Grady, classmate from New Rochelle High where they had spent many a boring economics class swapping porn.

"Hey, Brian, what the heck happened here?"

Grady faced him and started to answer, not looking directly into Paul's face but just over his shoulder at some black hole in the night sky. "Hi, Paul, how you doing?" he said, mumbling the words. "I've been meaning to call you since the funeral, but, you know …"

Paul recognized it. In fact, he knew it well from his earliest days at the Funeral Home – as a toddler, a boy, and then a teen overhearing the talk. Just as you needed Spanish or French or some other language for an overseas career, for the funeral industry you had to learn to speak fluent "Dead." It wasn't just the jargon, the careful phrases, the composed face. It wasn't merely gauging whether someone wanted euphemisms or blunt words. It was timing, knowing exactly what to say, and when; knowing when to be somber, when to touch the sleeve, the shoulder, when to comfort, when to let the truth about life and death show in your eyes. Or when to lighten up a bit, change the mood, let the grieving and sometimes the embarrassing ones off the hook.

"Don't worry about it, Brian," Paul said. "Call me sometime; we can catch up at Dudley's. I'll bring the Ouija board, we'll contact John, and then together we'll show your ass we can still drink it under the table." Relieved, Brian had blurted out, "Great, Paul. How ya been doing?" This time the language was English. Paul turned as Cullan approached, his boots squelching. "Hey, Sarge. What the hell happened here?"

"The best we can come up with at the moment," Cullan said, "is that a young Hispanic jumped from the Division Street Overpass. Seems he landed in front of an eighteen-wheeler that must have severed him in two. After that, we have seven other truckers who thought they'd hit some sort of animal. That last guy over there, he realized what had happened when a sneaker with a foot in it landed on his windshield. He used his CB to raise the others and us, and here we are."

Now Paul understood the large number and scattered positions of the police cars. "How did you know he was Hispanic, Sarge?"

Ian Cullan, about 50 back then, was tall and almost too thin, his honey-red hair starting to darken. His freckles fooled everyone into thinking he was a pushover.

Cullan regarded Paul thoughtfully. It was too bad, he told himself. Not only was the kid built like a cop, he was sharp and handsome, the perfect detective's entrée. But he had something extra – a maturity, Cullan guessed, that came from being around death. And now Paul no longer seemed afraid of much and that worried Cullan the most.

His long fingers made a theatrical gesture to the I-95 sign backlit by the West End Bakery's neon sign. The bakery was located just on the other side of the wire mesh fence that, along with the Thruway, separated the west side of New Rochelle from the rest of the city. Near the fence, Paul could make out what looked like the bottom half of a body.

"I found his green card in one of his pockets," Cullan said.

"So why didn't you call Alverez?" Paul asked.

Alverez Funeral Home was a chain of homes throughout the Bronx. Its closest Westchester location was in nearby Mount Vernon. It had started in the Fifties, serving a burgeoning Colombian population that had settled in the Bronx and was only then, in the mid-Eighties, making its way into southern Westchester. Juan Alverez had seen a niche opportunity and ran with it. In 20 years he created a solid business that took most funeral homes several generations to pull off. Alverez subsequently sold his firm to a funeral home syndicate, LaCroix Worldwide Shipping, one of several corporations trying to bring the economics of scale to dying.

Once dominated by mom-and-pop independents, most of which had been around for decades, the funeral market became just another consolidated industry. Houston-based Service Corporation International had led the pack in the drive to expand, raking up thousands of funeral homes, cemeteries, and crematories across the United States. The syndicates had changed the face of death in America. Paul and his father frequently bemoaned the way they were elbowing out the family homes, or scooping them up like Easter eggs, while cleverly retaining the names.

Name recognition was what the corporate suits wanted and needed along with the family homes' longevity. With the expanded base and volume discounts for themselves, they initially provided cheap services. They also provided more of them, like grief counselors and even a video production of the deceased's life. Of course down the road, once they became a mini-monopoly in a region, the conglomerates could raise prices, and did.

In opting to sell out to LaCroix, an international chain started in France that specialized in the shipping of international remains, Alverez had made a smart move, in Paul's view, especially given the number of Colombian day laborers beginning to pour into, and seasonally out of, Westchester. They had no permanent stake in the New York community. Chances were, if they died here, their families would want their bodies shipped home, high cost or not.

"Come on, Sarge." Paul was pissed. "Why did you drag my ass out here tonight? You know this family isn't going to use our Home."

"Don't bust my stones. You know how hard it is to get those local chains out here. Headquarters don't open till seven AM. If I had to deal with Europe, the damned traffic would be backed up to Boston."

Paul looked quickly over each shoulder, and then his body did a 360 degree turn. "You talking to me, Sarge? I thought you were talking to someone who gives a rat's ass."

Both men knew this removal was going to be made. Paul wouldn't leave a dog on the highway, much less a human being. Cullan knew it. Paul knew it. Both men also knew that Paul had to start building up a cache of IOUs for a later date. It was to be expected. It was how business, especially favors between cops and diggers, was done.

What Paul didn't expect was this situation, far worse than anything his father or grandfather had warned him about. He turned, walked, stopped. Two feet in front of him were entrails and blood, smeared across the road in a bizarre pattern. It was just like the pinwheel paintings he and Johnny used to do at Playland Amusement Park as kids. They had loved pouring squirts of brightly colored paint onto a spinning palate, creating wonderful pictures, uniquely theirs.

Paul said, "Is the medical examiner coming out here?"

"No," Cullan replied avoiding Paul's intent gaze. "The NRPD will secure and document the scene for the M.E."

State law required the M.E. to be called on every apparent homicide, suicide, or accident. *Crap,* Paul thought. This scene could qualify under all three. It wasn't uncommon around New York State for the local medical examiner to OK by phone the death of, say, a 90-year-old woman in her bed at home. *Yet there was no other county except Westchester,* Paul thought bitterly, *where the medical examiner would dare not to present himself at a scene like this. After all, he was supposed to be the final legal arbiter, the person who would determine the cause of death. That act alone would have far-reaching ramifications for just about everything – from how to comfort the family, to how to conduct criminal investigations, to how huge insurance claims got adjusted.*

The contrast was worse, Paul thought, because of Westchester's proximity to New York City. The Bronx County line was just three miles down the road. The New York City medical examiner held up every case where the victim died outside a hospital without a doctor's supervision until he, or a designated assistant, arrived at the scene. It defied logic that two so diverse interpretations of the law could exist side by side.

He stared at the entrails. With no M.E. on the scene and the odds that there wouldn't be one soon, Paul knew he had to take charge of the situation. He turned to Cullan. "Sarge, I need you to call DPW and get some shovels and some pails. We're going to have to start at what you, the officer in charge, determine to be the beginning of this mess and work our way to what you will determine will be the end."

Before Cullan could answer, Paul snapped, "And I need you to get Johnson and that other guy out of here." Paul pointed to the back of two hunched police officers vomiting near the lower body. For a second, Paul had considered leaving the cops there. He would love to send buckets of guts and muscle up to the M.E. mixed with the vomit from Paul's former colleagues. But knowing Dr. William Haywood, the odds of these buckets moving anywhere out of his funeral home for proper analysis were nil.

"Move the puking cops," he muttered under his breath. After all, letting them stay would only add to the smell in Paul's hearse.

Waiting for the DPW bucket brigade to arrive, Paul thought he would start by putting the bottom half of what had once been a young man onto his stretcher. "Sarge, is it okay to consider this the beginning of the scene?"

"10–4" came back from somewhere in the darkness.

Paul smeared Vicks under his nose, then handed the jar to officer Brian Grady and said, "Let's go." Paul positioned the stretcher next to the mangled lower half, then lowered the stretcher so that it was even with the body part. He opened a disaster pouch, laid it on the stretcher, and put on a double pair of rubber gloves. He ordered Brian to do the same. With so many fragments of bone lying around, the gloves might offer them another layer of protection against a skin pierce.

Paul then leaned over and said firmly to Grady, "I will take the part by the belt. You grab the one remaining leg. On three, we'll shimmy him onto the stretcher. One. Two. Three."

As Paul and Grady lifted, fluid and globs started pouring from the backside of the corpse, like stewed tomatoes and their juice flowing from cheesecloth. When Grady saw the gelatinous mess fall over Paul's shoes and pants, he dropped the leg he was holding and vomited all over the stretcher. Paul held onto the top half of the pants but since Grady had dropped his end, gravity took charge. Within seconds everything pulverized in those pants by a herd of eighteen-wheelers had poured out of the fallen pant leg. Paul vomited on the pavement.

The phone had stopped mid-ring, jarring Paul back to reality. His head snapped up. Had he been dozing or hallucinating? Whatever it was, he was still upright and his stomach churned. Whichever asshole on his staff had made the mistake of calling him at this hour must have regained sanity and hung up.

He rose and plodded across the apartment above the Funeral Home. The familiar acid regurgitated from his stomach into his throat in what he was sure would be the longest relationship of his life: he and his ulcer.

He settled into the green tufted, winged-back chair that had been his father's and looked around the room. The apartment above the funeral home was furnished with all of his parents' and some of his grandparents' things. The exceptions were a Mark Levison sound system that he had installed throughout the upper two floors that was his home, and the 50-inch LCD flat screen TV that he now sat in front of.

Two months after his brother's death, his parents had decided to move out of the Funeral Home into a condo. They chose the largest duplex in a condo complex in the north end of the city. It, too, had two floors and even a studio where Norman Rockwell had once lived and painted. While no decision had yet been made as to whether Paul would go into his father's business full time, he had agreed to move into the apartment above the Home to help his dad with his business.

His mother left every piece of furniture and china. She left every dish, spoon, and fork. She left every glass, towel, and even her sewing kit. This was done in part because it was a particularly Italian thing. She wanted to help her youngest son get "started," she would say. Paul knew it was done partly for that reason, and partly because it was *her* way of dealing with the death of her son. Paul had decided that he would accept this gesture for a few months until he saved up enough money to make the apartment into what he had always wanted, a contemporary bachelor's pad. The fact that today everything, except the TV and stereo, was exactly as it was 18 years ago, was the way *he* had dealt with his brother's death.

He reached to the Chippendale end table beside him for the Waterford crystal decanter bought by his grandmother on her 40th wedding anniversary trip to Europe. His hand moved instinctively, as had his father's before him and his grandfather's before him. The only difference: instead of 12-year-old Scotch, the decanter was now filled with Paul's own concoction –

three parts Maalox and one part Pepto Bismol, his numbing drink of choice. Occasionally, for variety he added a tonic water chaser.

He set the decanter down, put his head in his hands and let it come. He pressed his trembling fingers into the small muscles at the base of his skull. His thoughts turned to John.

CHAPTER 2

Protecting the living, not the dead, was supposed to have been Paul Arrone's life work. Later, after he stopped being a cop, Paul would say that he had gotten into the family business by chronological default. Come to think of it, he had done too many things by default.

He had three older brothers and a twin, John. The older Arrone boys had reaped the benefits of the lucrative family funeral business by being educated at Ivy League colleges. They moved on and up, returning to New Rochelle only for family visits – certainly not for the family business. The eldest, Dominic Arrone III, became an attorney and moved to Manhattan. Paul's second brother, Anthony, was a successful stockbroker now living with his second wife and kids in Easthampton. Tim, the third-born, had long ago moved out to Silicone Valley where no one was quite sure what he did for a living other than make money as easily and naturally as most people make conversation.

Of the "away sons," Anthony kept in touch the most. He and Pop still loved to talk money.

It was left to one of the fraternal twins to carry out the family tradition. Paul and John went to college together, just as they had done most every-thing else. They chose Farmingdale University out on Long Island because it offered both state-approved funeral courses as well as a decent amount of forensic science, which intrigued Paul. After graduation they took their national boards. Each earned his funeral director's license but bragging rights went to John, who scored significantly higher than his brother. That was okay. Paul wanted to go on and study criminal justice. His ambition was to be a cop.

Paul, they all agreed, was the more handsome of the two, although

John was taller by an inch or more. Gregarious, John was the kind of young man who attracted people of all ages. Children adored him and his respect for elderly people was genuine. John would have laughed at the description and said, "Of course it is. They'll be customers shortly." John was the real deal.

Both he and Paul had dark, smooth complexions, the shade that a few generations ago would have been called "swarthy," but today is considered a deep year-round tan. While Paul tended to be seen as dignified and somber, the twinkle in John's eye helped lighten the load. Whether it was the smart college women looking for far more than a distraction from their studies, or the bereaved back at the Funeral Home trying to look past shock and forward to a better day, they all went to Johnny first.

After college, John immersed himself in the Funeral Home, loving everything about the business. Watching John and his father direct funerals together, Paul realized ruefully, was like watching a crown prince in his tutelage. Father and youngest son would work side by side in the preparation room, embalming the loved ones of local families, talking in hushed tones, expertly exchanging cotton and ligatures and advice, creating an impenetrable bond between themselves, and with the "deads."

John liked to drive the hearse every chance he could get. He started to dress in nothing but dark blue, black, or the occasional glen-plaid suit. "You know," Paul would tease John, "you are dressing like an old-man funeral director."

"Thanks," John would say, nodding.

"Seriously,' Paul would protest, "you are one funeral director's convention away from being a cliché. All you need is a freaking diamond pinky ring and a cheap whore on your arm, and you can be the head of the county Funeral Directors Association."

And every time, from John, would come a fervent "From your lips to God's ear, Bro."

John was not only Paul's twin but also his best friend. Unlike most siblings, Paul understood the depth of their relationship. He had known it early, before they could barely talk, just as he knew today that it was John who taught Paul how to be a funeral director.

It was the hardest lesson of his life, Paul reflected. The hardest, he thought grimly, of John's, too.

John had stopped by the IHOP on Main Street on the way home from, naturally, a funeral. He had loved parking the hearse in places where no one expected to see it. "Advertising, man, advertising," he would pronounce with a big grin.

There was nothing extraordinary about that morning other than the fact that John ordered a three-egg omelet instead of his usual blueberry stack. The sun was shining, and business was humming in the city's downtown. Everything was usual except for the fact that there was a robbery in progress at the Barclays bank next door. It was only 400 dollars that was taken. It was only a kid from the projects. And it was only one stray bullet that found its way smartly from the chamber of a kid's illegal handgun through the window of the International House of Pancakes, and into the right temple of Paul's brother.

Paul had been on the job with the NRPD only three weeks when the call came in. Responding to the robbery/gun-shot call at the IHOP, the first thing Police Officer Paul Arrone saw as he pulled up was the parked hearse.

Christ, he thought, stretching his legs out of the patrol car, *Dad and John must really want to get to that Vegas convention – getting to the scene of a death before the police have finished. It was just like John*, he thought, striding toward the entrance, *to park the hearse right out front, in a handicapped space, so anyone driving Main Street can see the family name displayed in the hearse's window.*

Why is Sarge coming out to me? he thought, as Cullan walked toward him. Three of Paul's fellow rookies trailed. The sunlight changed. Paul slowed. They were in slow motion. He felt confused. They – all of them, the cops, the onlookers – no longer were in color. They appeared to be in black and white, a few shades of gray, like old TV westerns. His fingers flinched, and he resisted the urge to reach for his holster.

Cullan's mouth opened. He struggled for speech but failed. His eyes shifted painfully to meet Paul's. Instead of the usual "Candy Ass" salutation, Cullan said quietly, "Son, we have a situation here."

Paul would remember nothing the sergeant said that sunny morning as they stood on Main Street in downtown New Rochelle, home to four generations of Arrones. He fixated on the watery eyes of the toughest cop he had ever met. He knew who the victim was. In fact, he knew a lot of things simultaneously, including his immediate duty. Just like his brother, like his father, like his grandfather, Paul Arrone would have to comfort the parents of a dead young man. And they would be *his* parents.

He urgently needed to see his brother. And then he had to get home to tell Mom and Pop in person before they heard it from anyone else.

And no one – *No One* – would touch his brother. Only Paul.

His mouth had filled with bile at the thought of his brother's body, cold, waiting. Waiting in any one of a dozen local funeral homes that had been scheduled for the next police call. Then waiting some more, waiting for the largess of the fat-assed county medical examiner who would take his sweet time sending out staff no matter who was dead.

Paul would not have John's life – or his death – reduced to a rotation removal by another funeral home. And he absolutely could not stand the thought of his brother lying on a stretcher somewhere for what could be hours while medical examiner William Haywood golfed at the nearby Wykagyl Country Club, laughing with the local head of the Republican Party who had anointed him.

Westchester County, after all was a great supporter of the arts – but political patronage was perhaps the most deftly crafted and practiced art of all.

Westchester County's medical examiner is appointed, not elected. Nevertheless perfecting the job is not so much about qualifications and experience than about obtaining and then maintaining political advantage. This requires, in no particular order, extensive campaign contributions, back-slapping and consuming huge quantities of liquor. And playing golf, often.

Paul turned to Cullan, but before he could ask him to call the M.E. for permission to take his brother's body to his family's Funeral Home, he felt the sergeant slip a piece of paper into the breast pocket of his new police uniform.

Cullan leaned toward Paul and whispered, "Haywood will send someone over to your funeral home this afternoon. The M.E. release number is 1985—304. "You're okay to take John."

Cullan had started barking out orders. Word had spread; it seemed the entire department had shown up.

"I want this crowd moved back across the street. Henderson, go get anybody left in the IHOP and move them out of there into the hardware store for questioning and reports. I don't want to see any gawkers or press within a hundred yards of this place. Johnson, get the stretcher out of that hearse and meet us inside."

Paul and Cullan looked at each other. "Now move it," Cullan said hoarsely to the others.

He awkwardly tried to put his arm around Paul's shoulder, but Paul had moved on. He entered the restaurant as patrons were being escorted out. They were crying or ranting, some were doing both. All but the children turned their heads to avoid looking him in the eye. One black-eyed boy stared into Paul's face, then at his gun, and smiled.

The adult witnesses hustled them out. It was a small city, New Rochelle, and, yes, practically everyone knew practically everyone else. This was tragedy, and it was thrilling. Even so, this was too much – a shooting, John Arrone dead? – too much for people to digest, let alone find something to say to his surviving twin brother.

Paul smelled bacon and maple syrup, and found it oddly comforting. He lifted his head and looked around, surprised at how enormous the room was without patrons in it. Two, maybe three-dozen fellow officers had formed a blue line around the far corner of the restaurant. Shoulder to shoulder, completely covering the north and west windows, they were a curtain of decency, blocking the view of outsiders at the windows. They too averted their eyes, both from Paul and the corner booth.

As he got closer, Paul's legs started to buckle. A humming began in his ears. And the room, not he, was moving now. Queasiness, vertigo. He knew it well, a feeling imprinted from childhood, from earlier requests by his father to help out on removals or in the embalming room. He felt ashamed at his own reaction. Paul wanted his father here. He needed him desperately.

To short-circuit the sensations, Paul began to concentrate on the minutest details of breathing. He forced himself to pick up his feet, counting backwards from 100 in increments of threes as he did so. He found himself praying for the first time in years. He would spare his father this agony. Eyes half-closed, Paul moved. 100, 97, 94, 91. He begged God to get him through these next few moments, and then it happened. He heard crying first, then uncontrollable sobbing. Again, he felt shame. But it wasn't coming from him. It was coming from over Paul's left shoulder. Behind him stood four rookies, roommates from the academy, carrying the stretcher that would take his brother home. Tears streamed, noses oozed, but each kept his hands on the stretcher.

He felt it then. The policeman and protector dissolved, ; the funeral director and comforter were suddenly revealed. "It's all right," he said firmly, to no one and everyone. Just like Johnny would have done it, just like he always did on the worst days of other people's lives.

The strength returned to Paul's legs. He sat down gingerly in the booth next to his brother. John's face was on its side in a plate of eggs. The toast he had been eating at the moment of impact lay in his lap. Coffee from an overturned mug was still trickling down the side of the Formica table. Paul put his arm around his brother and leaned over to kiss him.

It hit him then. The bacon and syrup smell that had lingered in his nasal cavity was gone, replaced by an all-too-familiar smell, heady and salty. It was the coagulated blood of his brother which had poured onto the plate of eggs like ketchup from a bottle. And it was the smell of ammonia coming from the urine that had leaked out of his brother's bladder as his muscles went limp.

Paul went into funeral mode. No longer policeman, not even grief-stricken brother. He was the funeral director. It was clinical now, not personal. Paul was in the family business. Paul now *was* the business. The amount of blood was not significant, which provided at least some comfort. His brother had not suffered. He had died instantly. After death, a body doesn't bleed, bruise or swell.

There was no exit wound, Paul noted with relief. As long as they used a reverse-view casket, to show the left rather than the usual right side of the face, his mother, father, family, and friends would be able to view John.

Paul lifted his brother's face out of the eggs and swung his body flat onto the booth's long blue cushion. He turned, reached, and removed one of two towels from a pouch on the nearby stretcher. He wiped off the smear of eggs and blood from John's face. He stood and removed the cover from the stretcher, unzipped a body pouch, opened it and laid it back flat on the stretcher before him. With the help of two other officers, Paul lifted John and placed him into the pouch. He slowly, and carefully zipped him in. He did not pause even as he pulled slightly up and over the nose so like his own, even as his brother's face disappeared.

Paul stood. The burgundy stretcher cover with "AFH" embroidered in light green rested in his hands. Cullan approached him and said, "Paul, the news helicopter is hovering above. Do you want me to have Johnson pull the hearse around back? The overhang will give you some cover."

That would be the easiest decision of the day. Even with the fog of the morning thick in his mind, Paul could hear John's voice: "Out the back. Are you kidding me? Go out the front, Bro. And make sure the stretcher cover is straight so the chopper can see our initials."

Paul turned his head slightly, as if listening to someone the others couldn't see or hear.

"Ten thousand dollars of free advertising for the firm, bro. Ten *thousand*. And don't move too fast. You may never get this chance again."

Paul moved forward. "Go out the front," he announced to no one in particular.

Now almost twenty years later, frozen in his father's chair, Paul could still hear the slap of the helicopter blades above him. He remembered John's voice as well as his own. But he could not recall any other sounds from that time and the days that followed. Yes, he could remember snippets of scenes. His parents' mouths opening together as he told them, like fish gasping. He had caught his mother as she had pitched forward. He had looked up to see Pop walk away, straight as ever. But he could not remember any sounds.

He searched his mind for sounds from John's funeral. It was a silent movie. Nothing. But Paul was certain of one thing: It had been perfect.

He looked around at his parent's former living room, his own for so many years now. He scooped up the TV remote. A *Law and Order* re-run. It broke for a commercial.

Paul stared blankly at the screen and heard "Hallmark moment." He slammed the remote down, the TV went black. He thought of John's face in the eggs. He thought of his legs across the blue cushion. He thought of a leg spilling its guts on the New York State Thruway.

"No, asshole," he said aloud, "*Those* were Hallmark moments."

As he threw his head back, trying to get comfortable, he felt the long base clock in the entrance foyer to the Arrone Funeral Home downstairs ring half the Westminster chimes. It is 3:30 AM Paul thought. *All is well.* He closed his eyes.

CIA *Headquarters, Langley Va. June 30, 3:30 AM*

The chatter reports sat in front of a head analyst, who was marking his first month under the newly formed Homeland Security Department. The question confronting him was what to do with the report's information. It was no longer enough just to obtain information as it had been years earlier. Now if you hoped to succeed, or for that matter even keep your job, you had to know when the information was pertinent. Even though the chatter that had come across his desk was 7% greater than normal, was that enough to kick this information up to his boss? As he sipped his black coffee, he tried to weigh all the options and rationales for what would be his ultimate decision. Yes, there was the death of an elected official's spouse, and that along with the slight increase in chatter could mean something. On the other hand there was no clear connection between that death and any reported terrorist activity. If he started the "chain reaction" of an alert, he could cause official embarrassment and lose his job. After all, the only place higher his boss could appeal to was the director of the CIA, who in turn answered only to the President. No, he said to himself, I can't let the terrorist fever cloud my judgment. He decided to e-mail a CYA memo to his boss which would be reviewed in the morning. After all, the 4th of July weekend was coming. He knew he would have to speak with his boss several times before this high alert weekend had ended.

CHAPTER 3

Wednesday, June 30, 3:35 AM

About 10 miles west and north of New Rochelle, Millie also was awake and appeared to have an upset stomach. While Paul's home town sat on the Long Island sound, Millie's was west of the central line of the county in the Town of Mt. Pleasant. Even though the wealth of the county was spread to just about every corner, acreage was not. Traveling north in Westchester along the Taconic or I 684, the properties generally became larger. The crowded wealth of the suburban southern communities like Scarsdale, Larchmont and Pelham Manor, all of which bordered New Rochelle, gave way to a more New England feel as you traveled north. If you traveled north of Millie's home the landscape gave way to large country estates and occasional country farms many of which were inhabited by corporate CEO's and movie stars who needed the proximity to New York City but wanted the privacy provided by privilege. Millie's home was in the section called Valhalla. Not the mythical land, but a place of hospitals and prisons. This "reservation," consisting of large tracts of undeveloped land, was purchased by the county over a century ago.

Paul used to marvel that this was one of the few good decisions that Westchester County government ever made. The land was acquired at a time when wealthy families were making their move to the then bucolic land north of the city. Just a few miles south and west of Valhalla John D. Rockefeller built his family's country home, Kykuit, in Pocantico Hills, in the Hamlet of Sleepy Hollow, in the early 1900's. Rockefeller purchased not only approximately 7,000 acres in the heart of Westchester County but also the opposite land across the Hudson River in New Jersey so that he would not have to look at anything unpleasant from the balconies of his estate. Amassing land was then, and it is today, more about power and control than it is about money. People then, as they do now, moved to Westchester to be able to control their lives in a way that New York City living just didn't allow. Even the small Union Church of Pocantico Hills was largely shaped by donations from the Rockefeller family. It contained stained-glass windows by Marc Chagall and Henri Matisse, two of the family's favorite artists.

The control today isn't as overt as in the early days of Westchester's premier Republican family, but it is there nonetheless. Paul knew that the politically correct way to assure one's neighbors were all white and all wealthy was to control the zoning laws. In Westchester they did just that. Many of the northern tier communities enacted a minimum of 4-acre zoning. To this they added several "environmentally sensitive" local laws, assuring that if you purchased a large tract of land, the chances of your subdividing it into something unsightly were near impossible. Thanks to these laws, towns and villages were prohibited from creating multiple family residences. Or in Paul's words, minorities were inhibited from crossing their borders. Those communities in the southern tier of the county that were already too developed to re-zone, put in place "Architectural Review Boards" that would stymie the building of the homes of the undesirable and the unrich for an infinite period of time. Paul would think to himself that Westchester citizenry was to wealth, power and arrogance what the Rockefellers were to the oil industry – the founding fathers.

In the middle of the town of Mount Pleasant, the county fathers purchased the reservation that held Millie. It was more the result of good luck than good planning. The county supervisors, as legislators were called years ago, needed property to build a county hospital and a small jail. In order not to annoy the nearby gentry, they acquired enough property so that no one would ever know who or what was being nestled in the hills off of route 100. Now a century later, the land was among the most valuable in the metropolitan area. It had been carved up into several public/private ventures, allowing the county's closest friends and biggest political donors to reap huge profits while the county, its landlord, receives large lease payments to defer the tax burden. On face value it would seem to an outsider to be a good arrangement for all. It was in one of these buildings on the reservation that Millie lived.

That same Wednesday morning, well before dawn, Millie, a one-year-old baboon, was more anxious than usual. She was used to being caged with others of her species. This morning, though, she perched in a Plexiglas cubicle suspended from the ceiling of Containment Room No. 3 at Cardin Biotech Group. It nestled between the Westchester Medical Center and the county jail on the Valhalla Grasslands.

Room 3 was one of about three dozen that had been built for dual uses. One was to quarantine any person from the hospital or jail with a potentially infectious disease. The other was to house up to 36 people in the event of an "event." Specifically a biological attack – a prime concern since Sept. 11, 2001.

Dr. Philip Cardin, president and CEO of Cardin Biotech Group, had received a very large federal grant to provide the facilities, participate in emergency preparedness and evacuation planning and conduct research into the most likely public-health threats. There were any number of such threats, but the federal Centers for Disease Control and Prevention had identified six diseases as the highest priorities because of their potential for easy person-to-person transmission, panic by the public, widespread social and civic disruption, and the high percentage of death among those infected. The six diseases identified were: Tularemia, caused by a bacterium found in animals, most commonly rodents; Anthrax, a spore-forming bacteria; Botulism, usually food-borne; Plague and its sub-form Smallpox; and Viral Hemorrhagic Fevers, caused by several viruses affecting multiple organ systems. The latter was Philip Cardin's specialty.

A gurney stopped next to the sealed, bullet-proof, one-way window. Cardin – equal parts CEO, politico and physician – watched from the other side. Balding, he had a prominent forehead, sunken cheeks and thin lips. His skin seemed to stretch tightly over his skull. As the four masked and garbed Hazmat workers stepped quickly into the adjoining airlock room for decontamination, the solid door locked electronically behind them. They passed under Millie, whose chattering escalated to shrieking. Her agitation was clear.

Warden Walker appeared next to Cardin. Patrick Miller, the chairman of the county Board of Legislators, hovered in a corner.

"Should I call in the D.A.?" Walker asked.

"No, not yet," answered Cardin. He stepped up to the window and slipped his hands through Kevlar-lined rubber gloves attached and sealed to the special glass. Next to prisoner 3285 was a container labeled "1." Cardin carefully removed the needle from the container and injected its contents into the prisoner's arm. A bee-sting welt formed immediately. Cardin maneuvered the gloves, opened a hatch labeled "Medical Waste" and dropped the needle in. He turned to Walker.

"This should take about twenty minutes. Now you can call the D.A."

Walker did and then summoned the medical examiner. Downstairs in the lobby Haywood arrived only five minutes ahead of District Attorney Rosemarie Diaz. Although it was just before dawn, the call from Cardin did not wake the District Attorney. She had been out cavorting with some of her contributors at Zinc. Zinc was a restaurant in White Plains that each night turned into the hottest after hour's club in Westchester. The District Attorney held court there. Ever prompt, she showed up fifteen minutes after she was called. Haywood eyed the Latino beauty as she walked towards him. He could tell by the black leather Prada dress and high heels that Diaz was not coming from home. And while she had a reputation for running her office on the cutting edge, Haywood figured that even she would not introduce this as the new wardrobe for her office. Too much breast showing for the conservative party, he mused to himself as he took the liberty of staring at them.

"Do we have another death here, Doctor?" Diaz asked her breath heavy with the smell of gin.

"No," he replied, "Not yet."

They whisked passed Security and headed toward the East Wing, home to the containment rooms and Bio Level 3 experiments.

Cardin Biotech Group was the only laboratory in the metropolitan New York area certified to do Bio Level 3, or higher research. Besides the regulatory hurdles for such research, there were always local zoning ordinances that prohibited such labs. But Cardin had entered into a public-private venture with the County of Westchester, with federal backing. In such partnerships, the zoning ordinances of the Town of Mount Pleasant were circumvented. Cardin Biotech Group answered to few.

At the entrance to the East Wing, a security guard picked up a phone and announced, "One Dr. William Haywood and one District Attorney Rosemarie Diaz to see Dr. Cardin."

"Follow me," he said to the pair.

The guard stepped up to what looked like a bank vault door, entered a combination into the keypad, and swiped his identification card through the lock. The massive door swung open and the three of them stepped into an ante-room. The door behind them thudded closed and they heard the locks bolt. Vents started to hum.

The guard turned to the officials: "I know you have heard this before, but I have to do my job." They nodded.

'The humming you hear is the sound of air sensors searching for any known biohazard element or contamination that you may have on your person when you entered. The door behind us and the one in front of us leading to the East Wing are now dead-locked. Should sensors detect any contaminants programmed into their memory banks, we will be denied access. Should you be granted access to the East Wing, and sensors go off upon your departure, you will be held in quarantine for an indefinite period of time, as prescribed in the Federal Homeland Security bill passed after 9/11. This chamber is under 24-hour surveillance by video and audio tape. Do you understand everything I have explained to you?"

They nodded.

The guard stepped up to the second door and put his eye against a retinal scanner. Recognized and authorized, he entered another set of numbers into the keypad and swiped his identification badge. The large stainless steel door opened electronically.

Dr. Cardin, Warden Walker, County Executive O'Brien, and Board Chair Miller stood before them.

"What is the situation?" Diaz asked.

"We officially have a prisoner who was taken to the infirmary three days ago with what looked like a routine flu" Cardin said. "The fever and cough got worse on the second day. By day three the infirmary doctor noticed blood in the cough discharge and blood in his vomit and diarrhea. This followed the same pattern as the others, so I called in Dr. Weinstein. He's the hospital's head of infectious diseases. He ordered this isolation."

"Where is Weinstein now?" Diaz asked crossing her arms in her hallmark prosecutorial stance.

"He is being suited up in the next room and should be in there with the patient in a few moments. If you want to speak with him while he's getting ready, just press the red button on the wall."

Diaz went to the intercom box. "Dr. Weinstein, this is Rosemarie Diaz. I'd like to ask you some questions."

"Go ahead," came the voice through the speaker.

"What are your first impressions of this?"

"At first blush," the disembodied voice answered through the speaker, "the patient presents similarly to all the other cases. We see red itchy eyes, rashes, high fever, obvious head pain, muscle ache, vomiting of blood, and blood in the stools. While this can be indicative of several ailments, the fact that four prisoners died in the last two years under similar conditions with similar symptoms leads me to believe we may have an infectious agent that causes a type of Hemorrhagic Fever."

Diaz snorted her disbelief. "Are you talking Ebola?"

"No, I don't believe so," Weinstein answered calmly. "Ebola in all four known forms has the ability to spread via airborne particles under research conditions. However, an aerosol spread has never been documented among humans in real-world settings such as hospitals or households."

"Couldn't prisoners have infected each other through more intimate contact?" Diaz asked.

"Not possible," Weinstein answered. "If you look at the "outbreak" for lack of a better word, in its entirety, there is no link among the prisoners in question – no common denominators. This prisoner, for example, wasn't even in prison the last time someone was infected. We are dealing with an infectious agent that might be airborne."

"Then why hasn't the entire prison population been infected?" the D.A. persisted.

"That is why we are here, Madam D.A. Either the Cardin Group is doing one hell of a job of containment or we are on the verge of facing an epidemic of monumental scope and consequences."

Weinstein had finished suiting up, grunting from the effort. "We had better not be looking at the genesis of a mutation of the Ebola virus that makes it possible to be spread by air or casual contact. If we are, and this virus is able to survive outside the host on, let's say, a prison cot, well then I am afraid that ..."

His voice went quiet, contemplating such a scenario. Prisoner 3285 started to convulse on the gurney. His screams which had been inaudible previously – now ricocheted off the walls of the observation room when Haywood pressed the wrong button on the wall. "Weinstein, you'd better move it. We're losing him."

As Weinstein rushed through the door, tiny pools of blood started to fill the prisoner's eyes. The whites of his teeth turned pink, then turned bright red, as blood poured from his mouth. What started as a small spot of crimson on the white sheet below the restraint circling his waist had grown to the size of a pie plate. Weinstein jammed a large needle into the patient's neck and blood splattered his biohazard outfit. The prisoner convulsed and within seconds went limp.

Weinstein looked to the people on the other side of the glass, frowned, and shook his head. They still hadn't gotten it quite right. Cardin spoke into the intercom and ordered a technician to prepare to circulate air from the prisoner's containment room into the baboon's container suspended above 3285.

Weinstein told his audience that he would also employ an ingestion test to track the potential pathogen. He walked to the small table near the dead prisoner's head, removed a banana piece, spread blood and spittle on it from the dead man's mouth, reached up, partially opened the cage door and fed Millie. Weinstein approached the glass and motioned for Haywood to turn on the speaker.

Weinstein spoke clinically: "Time of death, fourteen hundred hours. Patient died from hemorrhagic fever from a yet-unidentified pathogen. Patient bled to death internally, went into shock and drowned from the blood that pooled in his lungs."

Cardin stared at the dead prisoner and spoke matter-of-factly. "As head of this biomedical research facility, and under the Homeland Security Act, I am recommending that with the concurrence of the Westchester County medical examiner and the Westchester County District Attorney, this corpse be immediately cremated. I further state that with the medical examiner's authorization, no post mortem examination be performed in order to contain a potential pathogen of unfamiliar origins."

Haywood cleared his throat, swallowed the phlegm, and said, "I concur."

"Agreed," Diaz said.

Cardin said to Weinstein: "Take some blood samples and get out of there. Obviously, this one was far less successful than the others."

Weinstein did as ordered, and then moved the gurney to the wall where Cardin had previously disposed of the syringe. He opened the steel hatch that was secured with a small turn lock similar to ones used on submarines and swung the door open to reveal an intense flame. He unlocked the seat belts that held the rubber cot to the gurney. He then stood at the foot of the gurney and pressed a button that lowered the head end. The body, and the rubber cot underneath it, slipped quickly into the flames.

"Do you need me any more?" Weinstein asked .

"No." Cardin shook his head curtly.

After Weinstein left, Warden Walker leaned close and asked Cardin in a low voice, "By the way, can you spin another one for me later?"

"Of course," Cardin replied.

"What's that about?" Haywood asked after the warden left the room.

Every so often, Cardin explained, Walker would send him a vial of blood from a new young prisoner to see if he was HIV-positive.

"If the blood is clean," Cardin said with a small shrug, "I am told the newbie will be put in isolation where he'll be worked over by Walker until someone newer or younger comes in. At which time he will release his old b**** back into the general population where he will be walking wide and gurgling from his intestines."

Diaz guffawed. "Now that is what I call Lady Justice."

Westchester County is a land of wealth and poverty, a decisive contrast of the powerful, who knew it, and the powerless who resented it. It is, in all ways, truly American.

While three-piece suits like Dr. Cardin, the M.E. and the County Executive were meeting in the darkest part of the night in the bowels of a government-sponsored, privately owned building mid-county, another meeting of quite a different kind was taking place to the south in Yonkers, the fourth-largest city in the state.

Yonkers was the first city to greet you when you traveled north from New York City on the west side- the Hudson River side. At some places along the Bronx-Yonkers border the differences between the two counties were seamless; the urban sprawl of the city spilling into the once coun- trified suburb. While many of Yonkers' neighborhoods with names like "Cedar Knolls" and "Bronxville Glen" typified the affluence that became Westchester's hallmark, some neighborhoods on the border mirrored the squalor of the Big Apple. Two of the five cities in Westchester lay on the border: Yonkers the largest and Mount Vernon, one of the states's most densely populated. This led to a very porous situation. It is what drove the crime numbers up, and it was what most people felt kept Westchester, ranked the fifth wealthiest county in the country, from being number one. These were the few areas where the demarcation line between The Bronx and Westchester often blurred. These were the areas where the suburban- trained police often fell short.

In a small apartment off McLean Avenue in Yonkers, three men had gathered. The average American would have vaguely described them as of Arab descent. The eldest one spoke in a raspy, almost inaudible voice as the radio over his left shoulder blasted music. It was the twenty-third time that the men had gone over the details of their plan. Each time, the dress rehearsal would be at a different location, and without the other two-thirds of the required manpower present.

The elder spoke about the symbolism of the timing. "The action must take place just after their Fourth of July. Their holiday must have passed without incident. They will be complacent and then we will move. We must attack them in their halls of capitalism. That is what America understands."

The Yonkers meeting was held simultaneously with two others, one in a basement of a tenement in downtown Chicago, and the other in an aban- doned factory in Brooklyn. Each meeting was run by an elder. Each cov- ered similar detailed plans but with different targets: the New York Stock Exchange, the Commodities Market, and the NASDAQ trading floor.

None of the three groups had any knowledge whatsoever of the other meetings' agendas, or for that matter, that there were other meetings taking place. Yet the agendas were identical: the infectious ingredient would be delivered to four employees targeted at each location. The pathogen would act quickly. It would not only panic the workers and cut off trading immediately, it would close down the markets – *even* with efforts since 9/11 to duplicate back-room operations for the markets and the largest traders and spread them out in the metropolitan region. The panic would be intense, sweeping, and long-lasting. The 2001 Anthrax incident in Boca Raton, Florida, had closed a single office building for more than a year.

An unknown pathogen with unknown contagion potential would paralyze the financial institutions indefinitely. The state and federal governments would be frantic to identify the pathogen, rid the building of it, stop the spread of the resulting disease and then convince workers it was safe to return. The real dollar losses and the loss of confidence in governmental and public-health systems would be catastrophic.

The delivery of the pathogen would be discussed at a future meeting. However, all knew that the incubation would be swift and the disaster would be almost immediately apparent to the world, within hours of the exchanges opening.

This time, it would not be airplanes into a building. No, it would be – what was the expression? – a whole new ballgame.

"When next we meet," the elder said, "It will be to discuss *the delivery*."

CHAPTER 4

Wednesday, June 30, about 4 AM

Paul dozed upright. His stomach had stopped pumping acid up to his throat and he knew that he should head back to bed and try to sleep. He had recently put off again the full physical he had promised himself as soon as he turned 40. He had struck a deal with himself to keep meticulous mental notes and discuss any and all of his problems with the best doctor money could buy. It occurred to him that maybe it should be with some Dr. Cure-all: It should be at some place like the Mayo Clinic – in a few years, say, on his 45th birthday. Like most funeral directors, Paul knew that when doctors look, they will always find something – something that, inevitably, would land you on the porcelain table downstairs.

Suddenly, the phone that had started this whole, early-morning, memory-lane episode blared once again. It was the private line in his bedroom. Paul jumped. Suddenly, for the first time since being awakened, it occurred to him that a call at this hour didn't necessarily mean it was for night duty for the Funeral Home. He bolted from his chair and ran to the bedroom. Something must have happened to his folks or one of his brothers.

"Arrone Funeral Home," he said, always the professional.

It was Trish, his on-again, off-again girlfriend. Off again, at her recent request. They had been lovers for more than six years. Since Trish was intimately familiar with Paul's nighttime phone rules, just the sound of her voice sent him into a panic.

"What's wrong?" he asked, his legs weak. He settled on the edge of the bed. "Is Keith all right?" A sharp pain radiated through his clenched jaw and started to settle into his head.

"No, no Paul, Keith is okay, and I'm fine, In fact, he's looking forward to spending Saturday with you."

Keith was Trish's 7-year-old son from her previous marriage. Although she and Paul were on yet another break from seeing each other, she saw no need to deprive Keith and Paul of each other's company. That would come soon enough.

"For Christ's sake, Trish, are you crazy? What would possess you to call me like this? Was that you who called twenty minutes ago? Is your mom okay? Wha—" Paul asked, rapid-fire.

"Would you stop for one second, Paul?" Trish said, her voice raised a few decibels higher than her trademark soft tone. "Everyone I love is fine." He wondered briefly if that included him.

"Look, I didn't want to call you, but I knew if I didn't, my boss would call your dad." Trish's governmental career had progressed steadily. She now worked for the Westchester County medical examiner. On call 24 hours a day – thank God for her accommodating sitter, a next-door neighbor – the hardest part of the job wasn't the schedule or the never-ending demands, it was trying to keep her work life separate from Paul and his obsessive contempt for the medical examiner.

She came right to the point. "There was an accident. In Monaco. The body is coming here."

Paul felt his skin prickle with tension, but he forced himself to focus solely on what was to come.

"Senator Rodino's wife was killed when her Land Rover went over a cliff."

Paul sucked in a quick breath.

"The senator has chartered a private jet to bring her back before the news spreads. The county executive has lifted the curfew at the Westchester County Airport so Mrs. Rodino's body can be flown in."

Paul started to speak, but Trish cut him off.

"Something is up," she said in a whisper. She must be at the M.E.'s administrative office, Paul realized. "I'm not sure exactly, Paul, but for some reason the flight was diverted from JFK or LaGuardia so that the body would fall under Dr. Haywood's control."

Trish paused to let Paul process that angle, then went on: "The senator apparently knows your dad. He told the boss to 'call Dominic Arrone.' He wanted to have his wife's body picked up before sunrise to avoid any press. I know your dad's recuperating from pneumonia. I thought it was best to call you directly. Haywood doesn't like it, but he gave me until four to reach you before he calls your father himself."

Paul stayed silent, quickly mapping out the next several hours in a minute-by-minute mental chronology. After the body was at the home, he would have to draw up explicit plans for handling what could be one of their largest funerals yet — if they were given it. There were VIPs to invite in, and the media to keep out.

"Paul," Trish said tiredly, "I know all about your Bat Phone rules. I'm sorry if I startled you."

Paul now felt like the complete ass that he knew he was. "You did the right thing, Trish. No need to apologize." Before she could answer, he plunged ahead. "What time is the flight due to arrive?"

"4:58 AM. The Rodino Cosmetic Company's hangar. No. 12."

"Okay," Paul said, "and tell that schmuck boss of yours I'll be there no later than 4:30. I'll wait until she arrives. I'll take care of everything."

"Will do," she said.

"And, hey, Trish?" Paul continued. "I'm sorry if I …" His voice trailed off; the line had gone dead.

The White House-Six months earlier

Janice Rodino knew the exact place and, the precise moment when the second half of her life began. Not only did she know in that nanosecond that it finally was time to leave U.S. Senator Francis Rodino for good, and live her life — hers, not his, not theirs, not the public one that had empowered and consumed them — but a new life. She would finally discard the woman she had so carefully created, then crafted all these years, discard her as easily as yesterday's leftovers.

The scene where this epiphany took place, most appropriately, was the White House. Specifically, it was the State Dining Room, where the president of France was being celebrated and Franco-American friendship rekindled. Lady Liberty and a fistful of American dollars and promises, Janice thought, had vanquished Freedom Fries. She allowed herself the barest of smiles as she sipped her Dom Perignon. She caught a glimpse of her reflection in a hallway mirror. She performed her series of personal checks and balances that she, and many other public figures did throughout the day. Her Chanel gown fit perfectly on her tall well kept frame. Her deep red hair was perfectly coiffed. Her hallmark makeup was impeccable. She was ready to do the battle of Washington socializing.

She surveyed the spectacle, trying to get a glimpse of George Healey's portrait of Lincoln and the inscription beneath from a John Adams letter, " ... May none but honest and Wise Men ever rule under this roof." She loved the irony. There were no wise men here. With nearly all the wives dressed in Channel or Vuitton, most adorned with Cartier jewels, and the men tuxed in Pierre Cardin, they reminded her of decorated rodents.

Now, now, Janice chided herself, must not start that so early in the evening. It was usually midnight before she began her game of assigning looks, mannerisms and speech patterns of animals to the politicians, their spouses, and the assorted hangers-on. Already, she noted, subdued voices were becoming emboldened by the booze and their own self importance. They were starting to sound like the inhabitants of a dank jungle, with their cackles and caws.

An outburst of honking laughter from a corner caught her own, and most everyone else's, attention. Of course it was Frank. Only the chairman of the Senate Homeland Security Committee would have the gall – or was it Gaul – to belly-laugh at a state dinner as if he were glad-handing at the corner diner. Janice froze. Buoyed by a yuck-yucking entourage, Frank was gesturing to his 22-year-old intern sitting beside him. A thin blonde, she had no breasts to speak of, and the ass of a 16-year-old boy. She was Frank's most recent type, poured into a shimmering column dress.

It wasn't merely that image that seared Janice. It wasn't the senator's flaunting of his peccadillo, and the palpable indifference to his wife's presence. Everyone knew who he was, what he was. Everyone knew where he strayed and stayed, now more nights in Washington than in Westchester, Janice's home base. It wasn't that any of the women in the room were sneaking pitying glances her way – they wouldn't dare. Not because they feared either Janice or Frank, but because they knew instinctively how little either one cared what anyone thought of them. The Inside-the-Belters recognized that the Rodinos were powerful enough to be truly indifferent to the opinions of others.

The skinny intern sitting too close to Frank was no threat to their long marriage. Janice and Frank had stayed in it willingly, for their mutual benefit and often enjoyable mutual enmity. Never for the sex. A selfish slobbering lover, Frank consistently reeked of cigars and stale Jack Daniels. Lying under him – thank God that it hadn't happened for many months now – Janice got through it honing her No. 1 coping skill: finding the irony in her life, or at least in the moment. As Senator Frankie squirmed and grunted, the smell of cigar smoke and whiskey mingling with his body odor, Janice Rodino would remind herself who she was: the woman who had taught American women the beauty and sweetness of "Nature's Scents."

Her attention was suddenly seized by Frank gesturing with his cigar, still wrapped, gold-sealed, and obviously expensive. He leaned in and traced it around the intern's mouth, who playfully pouted. He sniffed it, twirled it and then pointed in the general direction of the Oval Office. The Republican swells around him got it – trying not to laugh too loud, pretending to be sheepish. He was humiliating himself, not Janice. What got to her, though, was the tired, cliché of it – the copy-catting, politically incorrect but-oh-so-archly naughtiness of a cigar and an intern at the White House. The utter lack of imagination of the man. The pathetic bleat of his admirers.

A throb of pain started at the base of her throat and began to move upward. Before it could enter her temple, she willed it to stop. Only someone intently studying Janice Rodino would have seen her take the smallest of breaths, straighten her shoulders, then focus her gaze in the distance, on something well beyond this room.

Janice Calhoun had met the man who would become her husband on a blind date some thirty years ago. He was an attorney in the small town of Eastchester, New York, twenty or so miles north of Manhattan. Janice was an up-and-coming chemist at the Revlon plant in nearby Tuckahoe. Frank, 38, was a town trustee with boundless ambition.

At 29, Janice already was vice president of her division, overseeing the development of cosmetics and perfumes. Back then she was using what was to become a cutting-edge combination of plant extracts and chemicals to produce the most "natural" of oils and additives.

To some, she was that rare woman who had reached the top of her profession. To Janice, her face was squashed against a glass ceiling well before that term was in general use. She was stalled in her ambitions for one reason only: She was a woman. Too many of her projects could not get Food and Drug Administration attention, let alone its approval.

Physically, there weren't two more mismatched people in Westchester. Janice, a statuesque beauty with red hair and flawless ivory skin, riveted Frank. He would later tell her that it was not her large breasts that got his attention but her perfect posture that carried them, along with her stunning, if infrequent, smile.

Frank, on the other hand, stood, at most, five-foot-nine in his wing tips. His waist was already thickening. His head was nearly bald. When he smiled, which was almost always, Frank exposed teeth like a horse, the center top two separated by a large gap. He already was as stooped as a man twice his age.

They were the most unlikely couple to have even a second date, yet alone marry on the four-month anniversary of their first one. They were a classic example of "beauty and the beast." And they played it to the hilt, socially, in business and later, politically. Their chance came quickly, when the then-senior U.S. Senator from New York died suddenly. Clearly, Frank was the underdog, a small Italian man from a small predominately Italian town "upstate," meaning anything north of the Bronx border. His Democratic opponent was a sitting congressman, a Jew from Manhattan.

Demographics alone could predict the outcome – except for the times, and the timing. Politics were changing in America. A media-spinning generation of handlers and pollsters were arriving with the messianic message: That it was no longer so much about what you did, or didn't do; it was how the media experts you hired made you appear.

Frank's future marketing mogul played up his "weakness," billing him as the average guy, and the average guy's candidate. Photos of "beauty and the beast" were plastered throughout the state. Janice did radio interviews at every small station they could find, appeared day and night on local television throughout the state, and walked any district where pollsters told them Frank was in trouble. They made a formidable couple. Even campaign aides were astounded at the campaign's momentum. Rodino for Senate raised and spent a then-unprecedented $12 million-plus.

Frank understood the secrets of his appeal, and Janice's – especially to anti-hippie, anti-feminist, out-of-place, and out-and-out confused white male New York voters. It boiled down to the fundamental fact that if somebody as good-looking and stacked as Janice would marry him, then there had to be a lot more to this guy than met the eye. Hell, he deserved a vote. To the astonishment of every political junkie save Janice, and the ad-sales guys working on commission, Frank won election to the U.S. Senate in one of New York's biggest upsets.

Janice's help was of course to be rewarded. Naturally, in the early Reagan years, a Republican senator from a largely Democratic and liberal state did very well in Washington, D.C. With little effort, "Senator Frankie," as he soon took to calling himself, secured backing for Janice to start her own cosmetic company. As important as the money, he pushed for FDA approvals for the cosmetic and perfume protocols from her former job that had stalled. Shrewdly, before she left Revlon, Janice had accepted no severance pay, only the rights to the projects she had been working on.

Three years after Frank took the Senate's oath of office, Rodino Cosmetics went public. Now it was the third-largest cosmetic company in the United States, with Janice's fragrance line – Irony – fast approaching the sales of Estee Lauder and Chanel.

The perfect match, the ideal political couple, Janice and Frank moved into one of the last farms, and one of the few remaining 25-acre spreads in southern Westchester – Scarsdale to be exact. She painstakingly renovated the main house on Old Mamaroneck Road. The original structure, built in the late 1700s, belonged on the national historic registry. Frank however had other ideas. He had become the "go to" man for business in New York State, and he put an addition on the house that boldly made that statement while costing a small fortune. Frank had no trouble spending either the taxpayers' money or Janice's. She didn't mind, they had plenty.

Visible from the winding drive or slate walkways was Frank's replica of the Oval Office. There he met with clients, contributors and colleagues, often joking that the only difference between his Oval and the one at the

White House was that his was better built. "There was no low-bid govern-ment contract for my office," he would brag.

In recent years, Janice divided her time among her passions: running her company from its Madison Avenue corporate headquarters or, with growing frequency, from "the farm." She sat on boards and raised money for virtually any charity in Westchester, especially the arts council and the county medical center. And, of course, she spent countless hours keeping herself fit. She started jogging before it was trendy, and in the last few years supplemented that by spending daily sessions with a personal trainer. Her image, her body, and her business were inextricably linked one to the other. Now in her late fifties, she was the icon for every baby boomer female from New York to Istanbul.

September 11, 2001, catapulted Frank to national fame. In his third term, the powerful senior senator from New York and a member of every important Senate committee, became, if possible, even more powerful. "Chairman Frankie" was able to target money to upgrade most of New York ports, pleasing both the unions and the bosses. Likewise, most of the state's hospitals were awarded funds ostensibly destined for disaster pre-paredness and specifically for biological attack.

It was amazingly easy for Senator Frankie to secure almost $300 mil-lion for a biotech research center on the Grasslands reservation in his home County of Westchester. There was too much wealth in the northern suburb of New York City to ignore. The research center's CEO and director, Philip Cardin, the senator's longtime friend and contributor, would ensure that the funding would be used to fill jobs, develop antidotes, and eventually produce vaccines against biological agents. If that collaterally helped treat patients at the adjoining county medical center, originally built as a hospital for the poor and destitute, well, fine.

Senator Frankie negotiated a long-term lease of the county's prop-erty for the good Dr. Cardin by promising to take care of a sore point in Westchester County: He would see to it that the nuclear power plant at Indian Point in Buchanan, just a few miles north and west of Grasslands, would be decommissioned. Energy prices were soaring, but the public accepted it. Anything was politically possible, especially when people were running scared.

He had casually explained it to Janice over breakfast one morning: The committee would release funds to subsidize the conversion of the plant from nuclear to gas. He would convince a newer and eager utility company to run the converted plant by having the federal government guarantee a minimum of an 18 percent-a-year profit.

"Best of all," he said with his trademark toothy grin, "certain friends of mine will learn about this stuff just before it happens so they can buy up shares in the utility." It went without saying, Janice knew, that the grateful sycophants would donate to Frank's personal war chest or any political action committee he designated.

Due to such maneuvers and being Senator Frankie, the people's senator, the one who kept their subway fares down and built their local Little Leagues new fields, Frank Rodino kept his seat and his head. His arrogance was unmatched, and people loved him for it. At one recent fund-raising event, a contributor asked him if it were true that he was even more powerful than the vice president. Frank never missed a beat. As if he didn't hear the full question, he slapped the man's back and inserted the first name of the president himself in his answer: "If you mean old George, absolutely!"

Every day, Frank's prize-winning bull mastiffs bounded down to the front gates of his estate. Like them, every day, Frank simply marked his territory. There was no one more powerful in Westchester, New York or Washington. Now with his Homeland Security chairmanship, there was no one more secure. The farm in Scarsdale, the Manhattan condo, the Rodino townhouse off Washington's Diplomat's Row – security bunkers all.

The state dinner was bound to be a bore, and the Rodinos arrived late for it. The room's preferred red-white-and-blue motif had been suspended for a neutral white. Queen Anne-style chairs graced tables displaying, Janice noted, ornamental bronze-dore' pieces, part of President Monroe's gilt service bought from France in 1817.

And now Frank, intern at his side, was waving to Janice. He was taken aback when she returned his wave with a beaming smile.

Mind clear, Janice knew the time was indeed right. Inspired by the French theme of the night, Janice decided she would permanently move to Paris. Why not? she mused. Rodino Cosmetics Company sales there had grown by 300 percent in the last two years, putting a dent in the famous

Sisley Empire. Maybe she would take up residence at the Paris Ritz Carlton, like Harriman's widow, she thought. The wife of the former governor of New York had moved to a suite there, swimming every morning in the pool well into her old age. Her every command was their wish, the staff had joked. One day, she simply had a stroke and died poolside.

Janice signaled with her gloved hand to Frank and his companions. They turned, she frowned gently, shaking her head slightly, and focusing her clear blue eyes on the intern. Visibly nervous, the young woman pointed to the senator and mouthed, "You mean him?"

"No," Janice mouthed back. "I mean you."

Smoothing her skirt over her thigh, pushing her fingers through her hair, the intern slowly approached Janice.

"Yes, Mrs. Rodino?"

"Would you be a dear and ask the senator if he thinks it would be good idea for me to change seating arrangements at the last minute? That's Henri LaCroix over there, and I think he has been lobbying Frank for something in committee. Tell him if he wants me to do some public relations at Henri's table, I would be happy to."

"Public relations" meant only one thing to Frank, horse-trading for funds. A few minutes later, Frank turned up in front of Janice's face.

"Brilliant!" he exclaimed. "I had you moved to the LaCroix table. Remember to tell those frogs with him about my upcoming birthday bash and the new PACs that were started since I became chairman of Homeland Security.

"Just remember, Jan, Henri is no frog," he continued. "We grew up together. Don't go promising him anything on my behalf unless, of course, he brought cash."

The senator let out a loud whoop of a laugh, then kissed kiss wife on the lips, pleased to show the entire room that he could fondle his intern on one side of the room and kiss his wife on the other. Hell, he thought, he was Senator Francis Rodino. He could screw them both on the bar if he so desired.

Janice placed her flute on a waiter's tray and gracefully moved through the crowd. She was content, she had a plan. And never again would she have to taste Jack Daniels.

CHAPTER 5

That same January night, almost four thousand miles away, a woman sat regally in her stiff-backed Louis XVI chair. She courted no nonsense with cushions. As for wheelchairs? Bah. *Que dale.*

The servants had retired, and the bodyguards were supposed to be keeping watch somewhere outside the library, her favorite room. Its closed doors allowed her privacy and an opportunity to relax, to think, to stop pretending she was the 91-year-old doddering matriarch she allowed them to see. She snorted. Barely running the Obiere empire? It was as firmly in her grasp as it had been 40, 50, even 60 years ago. And it would remain in strong hands even after she, and only she, decided to leave this life on her own terms.

Tomaas. She closed her eyes, savoring the thought of his strong, handsome face. Her rake of a grandson, dining at the White House, as casual about it as if it were an American fraternity house. She sniffed. Actually, it was a fraternity house.

Still, she allowed, this was no time to dwell on crassness, no matter how American. After all, her grandson, Tomaas LaCroix, was half American. Even so, at 25 he already was twice the man his grandfather had been. Of course, there was no exponential way to compare him to his American father, who was nothing but a cockroach. At times a useful cockroach, she grudgingly admitted to herself, but only until she, Genevieve Obiere, decided to permanently crush him under her heel.

Genevieve Obiere and the late Charles Obiere had been a legendary couple in European circles. She, of course, still was. Charles, it was long rumored, had been a Nazi sympathizer who had made his money selling munitions to the Third Reich. It had not bothered Genevieve; he had been in good company. Unlike his royal friends, though, who would rather leave their country than denounce the German cause, Charles all too eagerly followed the money trail wherever it took him. When the Allied forces were gaining ground on Hitler, it was Charles, the story went, who turned and sold them vital information to help defeat Hitler.

After the war, the Obiere family, at Genevieve's insistence, invested their German and French money in real estate. By her early thirties, Genevieve had become the first woman to chair the board of the Swiss bank that bore their name. Charles, the fool, had turned to politics. Then, thanks to Henri, he almost destroyed their fortune. Well, Genevieve Obiere had outlasted Charles just as surely as she would Henri. Still, she was 91. Even though she ate well, still adhering to her modified vegetarian diet, her small frequent meals, and kept active, albeit secretly more than they knew, her time was ending. But she would control that, as she had almost everything else.

Enameled nail tips atop gnarled fingers plucked from the ceramic bowl of grapes and cherries she had ordered. Madame Obiere let out a throaty chuckle. Even Charles' death-bed scenes had been under her direction. Her husband had been diagnosed with a severe cirrhotic liver, coupled with renal failure. At best, he had had six months to live.

Knowing that, he had chosen to set his usual single-mindedness on one goal: petitioning his friends in government to bestow the title of "General" upon him before he died. Surely, they had benefited from Charles's generosity and would be all too eager to oblige.

It was Genevieve who derailed his Acela dream train before it left the station. She knew, even if the old fool had not, that anyone delving into the family's past before bestowing such an honor would not only deny making Charles a general, but would probably trigger criminal charges against half the family. She was not about to allow the beautiful tapestry of a life that she had created around them to unravel.

And so, she arranged it. France's president himself came to their town house to pay his respects to Charles. Genevieve took charge. She pulled Chirac and his chief aide into the main drawing room under the pretense of preparing them for the visit to the sick room. She reported the disheartening news: The "pancreatic cancer" had spread to Charles's brain. They were aghast. Charles had told them that he suffered from a kidney ailment.

"You see what these things do to your brain," Genevieve said, head shaking sadly. She pre-emptively apologized for her husband's medical insanity and hoped aloud that he would not burden them with rantings of his "war stories" as well.

She then, she recalled grimly, had gone in for "the kill," as Americans so charmingly put it. She told the esteemed guests that Charles's doctors were upset: The patient would not focus on a recommended treatment regimen that offered the slightest chance of a cure. Rather, he obsessed constantly on some imaginary award he was about to get. If only she could find a way to end his focus on this "award," the entire Obiere family would be eternally grateful.

The men glanced at each other. They told Genevieve in guilty tones, that they were aware of how Charles had asked to be formally designated "General." Now knowing his true condition, they were only too happy to oblige her concerns. Ah, Genevieve, had sighed, "*Quel bon amis.*" With her exquisite lace-trimmed handkerchief, she had dried a tear on her cheek and questioned them demurely about how far Charles's petition had gone in the political machinery. Satisfied it wasn't far enough along to pose a threat of discovery, she offered a "plan."

They went to Charles' bedroom, visited, and then were escorted to her private parlor. All, they assured Madame, would be well. They had explained to her husband that the left wing of the government had blocked their request to bestow the title of "General." Yet all sides had felt that a non-military remembrance would be more significant and fitting for the Obiere name. They decided to rename one of the main exit roads from Charles DeGaulle Airport in Charles Obiere's name. This way, they had told the dying man, everyone who entered France by plane would be first greeted on the ground by their esteemed resident.

"And he took it … ?" Genevieve asked cautiously.

"Like any general of France's army would," the president told her solemnly.

She had kept her composure then, but today Genevieve laughed aloud at the memory. *Men*, she thought.

And so it ended − as Genevieve had wanted and expected.

But things were not as she had expected with her son-in-law, Henri.

She stiffened and curled her gnarled fingers around the scrolled arms of her personal throne. The irritation and frustration of it all was almost too much to bear. How could she have thought that Henri could keep Charles in line? He should have, if only for his own self-interest. Any children he and Jacqueline would have had stood to benefit from the Obiere empire remaining strong.

Yet soon after their daughter married Henri, Charles suggested to her that they invest in Henri's new business venture. Henri's plan was to purchase several funeral homes in European cities with a high degree of tourism. He had researched the number of times foreigners died while on vacation or working abroad. City by city or even regionally, the numbers were not significant. Continent-wide, however, they were potentially significant.

Before he departed Wall Street, Henri had watched with great interest the number of funeral home conglomerates that had formed around the United States. Smart. By snapping up businesses that families had owned and operated for years, keeping the local names to maintain at least the impression of homegrown care, and then buying both equipment and services in bulk, the conglomerates had found the proverbial gold mine. Stocks had soared.

Rather than compete with the traditional funeral homes or try to take on the American. or Canadian conglomerates, Henri decided to take them on as clients, catering to them both. Since no individual can escape death, Henri reasoned, not even in Europe, a captive audience of business travelers and vacationers were hard to ignore. By purchasing funeral homes in key cities in Europe, and offering worldwide shipping service, uniform prices and uniform "products," he could link them all – the conglomerates, the homes and the traveling soon-to-be dead.

He couldn't amass anywhere near the 4,000 or so funeral homes that the large conglomerates had in America. The private funeral industry had gotten wise to the corporate greed and had begun holding out for higher purchase prices. But he could acquire, say, 350 funeral homes, beginning in Europe, using old-fashioned business savvy and the connections he had built. He would offer what no stock-printing U.S. corporation could offer: cash under the table.

Charles was fascinated by Henri's idea and impressed by his relentless determination to succeed. Father-in-law and son-in-law recognized and respected the natural con-man in each other. They developed a jailhouse bond, minus the steel bars. Henri brought out the younger, mischievous risk-taker long dormant in Charles, who enthusiastically bought into the concept of a worldwide funeral shipping company. And Charles prodded Henri to think bigger: form the new company not only in Europe but simultaneously in South America and the United States. Charles pointed out that when it came to burials Americans outspend grieving Europeans 3 to 1.

"And just as Americans die here, European travelers die on the other side of the ocean," he told Henri. "Disney World and all that," he added with a sniff.

Charles bankrolled the formation of LaCroix Worldwide Shipping by using 25 percent of the Obiere family fortune for the initial capital. Privately, Henri thought it was Charles's attempt to stave off his own funeral. The money he lent Henri was secured by mortgages on the properties purchased, along with a twenty six percent share of the company.

The return on the investment started strongly. But just as his U.S. counterparts would, LaCriox's company started to suffer setbacks. The corporate funeral industry worldwide had collectively invested billions of dollars over several decades on the premise that, as the increasingly wealthy general population aged and died off, fortunes could be made. It was a service everybody needed, at least once.

What Henri and the others hadn't factored in was the life-lengthening benefits of modern medicine. Improved lifestyles and better worldwide health care also helped to defer the "death bubble." Companies with huge debts watched their stocks tumble as profits dropped. At the end of the 1990s, the Lowen Funeral Service bankruptcy was the United States' largest to date.

Henri was compelled to return to Charles to request a temporary infusion of cash to keep his company competitive while waiting the death bonanza to materialize. Charles wasn't fazed by the temporary financial setback, but Genevieve certainly was. And now she was ready. After Charles's previous loan to Henri was revealed, Madame had transferred all of their assets into trust accounts he could not invade. And, Charles confessed to Henri that he had acquiesced to losing control of the family fortune after Genevieve threatened to divorce him.

"If we are to divorce" she had said to Charles calmly, "I will divide our assets four ways: I will receive 25 percent, Jacqueline and Tomaas 25 each, and you, my darling, will get the remaining 25 percent." She flicked one bejeweled hand lightly, and handed him a thick set of documents with the other.

"My bank gives me complete power of attorney over our daughter's and grandson's share."

Charles started to sputter. In a typical Genevieve move, she went in for the kill.

The papers Charles originally had signed in making the loan to Henri validated the formula that Genevieve had just described to him.

"With one exception," she said, pointing to a clause deep in the document. Should their marriage dissolve prior to Henri's payback of the loan, Charles had agreed to accept the stock in Henri's company as his 25 percent.

It had never occurred to the fool, Genevieve thought as she watched Charles stalk out, that when they signed off on the deal she would consider divorcing him.

Charles Obiere had become an indentured slave to his wife of more than 45 years. He would be bound until the $3 billion he had borrowed from the family coffers were restored. Charles resigned himself to the life sentence.

Forced to seek financial help elsewhere, Henri's simmering dislike for his mother-in-law intensified. He blamed her and was furious when he realized he would have to sell a substantial amount of his own stock to raise the needed capital. He, too, like Charles, was being forced into submission. Henri LaCroix had become a minority shareholder in the company he had founded. In order to retain his position as president and CEO of LaCroix Worldwide Shipping, Henri not only had to kow-tow to his mother-in-law, but also to a new group of investors, predominately businessmen from Saudi Arabia and Yemen. They were from the only part of the world that had not suffered from the recent economic recession. Years earlier, businessmen from Japan and other Pacific Rim countries had been buying up his stock, along with a healthy infusion from the Americas. But the lagging economy, coupled with the turn of events within the funeral industry in the States, left Henri no choice: His Company was becoming another Arab acquisition.

To add to the insult, Genevieve had convinced the board of directors to hire her grandson Tomaas as an executive vice president. The directors liked the idea of securing the direction of LaCroix Worldwide Shipping into the next generation by grooming an heir.

"I won't stand for it," Henri roared at her.

"You will," Genevieve said. "Indeed you will." After all, Henri himself had used Tomaas to close deals throughout Europe and the United States by "negotiating" with widows and adult children several times his age, who had been bequeathed funeral homes by departed spouses and parents but about which they knew little.

With Tomaas aboard, Madame Obiere was meeting two other goals: Grooming the equivalent of her own private spy, Tomaas, with his own vested interest in growing the family fortune, and driving a wedge between the grandson she loved and the son-in-law she loathed. At board meetings, she would direct all her financial questions to Tomaas, drawing Henri's ire. His hold on his board also suffered from ethnic, religious and social differences with some new board members.

Arab customs did not emulate or even appreciate the Western world's ravenous feeding on the bereaved. Many of the new partners would suggest simply selling the real estate of Henri's funeral homes and shipping warehouse to turn a quick profit. As a result Henri found himself spending more and more time lobbying and schmoozing his board of directors than expanding LWS's operations. And Tomaas's skills and power were growing under his grandmother's tutelage.

As his desperation grew, Henri's six priorities emerged. He had to win the confidence of his Arab investors. He had to convince Senator Francis Rodino to use the U.S. Homeland Security Act to require more onerous and thus more expensive shipping to and from the United States. He then had to expand the requirements to other countries, resulting in even greater profit for LWS. He had to purchase back his stock in increments until he was a majority shareholder again. He had to throw his mother-in-law off the board of his company. And he had to fire his son.

All that, of course, over Genevieve Obiere's dead body.

CHAPTER 6

"Janice!" Frank hustled up to her. "You're supposed to be at the LaCroix table." He guided her across the room.

Henri LaCroix and Frank Rodino made a show of it – the usual back-slapping; the faux bear hug. As if he were offering up a special gift, Frank told Henri that Janice would be seated at his table. "You can show all the rest of these frogs how freaking influential you are, Henry, er, I mean Henri."

Henri LaCroix was born Henry Lamella in the Bronx, New York. He and Frank had met while graduate students at Fordham – Frank studying law, Henry, business. Henry went on to work on Wall Street where he made quite a name for himself until he suffered an incident. He claimed it was sharp investing. The Security and Exchange Commission had another name for it. Henry wasn't formerly convicted of any crime, but the plea bargain required that he give up his broker's license.

No problem. He would build his empire elsewhere. He moved to Europe with what was left of the money he had made from insider trading. After a year on the Italian Riviera, he legally changed his name to that of a French national. He took his own personal show – attending charity fundraisers – on the road, from Italy, across France to London and back.

It was amazingly simple to build his name and influence. "Henri" volunteered his business expertise to charities, earning him a reputation as a wealthy philanthropist. Anyone checking closely would have realized that none of his own money left his hands. By the time he settled in Paris, his place in the charity and social circles was firmly established, even becoming legendary. The Parisian aristocracy sought him out for help in running their organizations; local politicians sought him out to help them raise money.

None of his new friends was the least suspicious that Henri was helping them and asking for nothing in return.

By his second year in Paris, Henri had the names and curriculum vitae of every wealthy person in Western Europe, and he had committed the list to memory. These people knew him, liked him and they used him. They trusted the voluble American expatriate. Their requests were his pleasure to fulfill.

Once, Henri was drawn into helping a bewildered wealthy widow whose son was killed in an avalanche in the German Alps. Her son's body needed to be shipped back to Paris and Henri was adept at maneuvering through the governmental and diplomatic issues. That sowed the seeds!

"We have to talk," Henri murmured to Senator Rodino.

Rodino nodded then said in a loud voice. "Henri, would you do the honors of introducing my wife to your table for me?"

"It would be my pleasure," answered Henri. "Mrs. Rodino ... "

Janice interrupted and said, "Please call me Janice."

"Very well, Janice, may I introduce you to Ambassador Dudley and his wife Harriet. Over here is Claude Van Pelt and his wife Cynthia. Mr. Van Pelt is president of my mother-in law's bank."

Janice knew of the Obiere family but she never connected the man who called her husband so many times at their home as someone who had married into it.

As Henri proceeded to introduce Janice around the dinner table, she was aware of an unusually high ratio of men to women. She also noticed that two of the three men who were not accompanied by a spouse or date were out of place at such an affair. Both men were large and looked uncomfortable in their ill-fitting tuxedos. One sat next to Henri's wife, the other was standing beside a young gentleman Henri was about to introduce Janice to. "Janice, may I present my son, Tomaas."

"Tom," responded the young man quickly. "A pleasure to meet you." As Janice approached the seat next to Henri in which she was to sit, Tomaas quickly signaled the large gentleman standing beside him to take that seat. Tomaas then pulled out the chair to his right and motioned to Janice, "Madame." Henri became flustered by the second unscheduled change of the evening and Janice couldn't help but notice the smile that spread across Tomaas's face. As the guests around the room were taking their seats, Janice sat back and observed her table. Henri was a tall attractive man who would have been called "quite the ladies' man in his day" by the old-time Washington elite. At 6—3, he still retained the physicality of a 40-year-old man. Pseudo-French, his facial features struck her as decidedly eastern European. His nose could definitely be described as Roman. Fitting, Janice thought, since it was at home in everyone else's business. His full head of wavy hair, still dark on top, contrasted sharply with the pure white at his temples, giving him an air of importance over most others in the room – no easy feat.

Mrs. LaCroix, who sat to her husband's left, had the looks of a Hollywood legend. She too, had an unusually full head of blond hair for someone her age. Janice guessed her to be in her late 50's. About the same age as she was. It was unusual for a middle-aged woman to be able to wear her hair to her shoulders without revealing the thinning and damaged ends that come from normal age, along with the ravage of years of coloring. Janice had a practiced eye, based on years as an expert in cosmetics and perfumes, and she enjoyed studying other women. She would usually dissect the previous night's party with her office staff the following day. In her board room she would entertain them with horror stories of some of the women in both fashion and cosmetics. She would also discuss the successes of women like Jacqueline LaCroix, who seemed to defy the onslaught of gravity and aging.

It was early in the evening but already apparent that Jacqueline drank too much. Still, only the slightest of puffiness could be detected under her eyes, and it was only when the light shone a certain way. Before the night was out Janice would have to find out what concealer this woman used. Janice then noticed that Mrs. LaCroix reached into her purse for the third time since she was introduced to the table for what Janice could now see was nicotine gum. Janice concluded that the only explanation as to how a woman who was pushing 60, drank this much and smoked, and could still look this good, was that she was a genetic freak. The only thing, if anything, that took away from her beauty was her disengaged mood. Mrs. LaCroix's mind seemed to be further away than most in this room of should-be's.

Janice's attention turned to Tomaas; he was standing next to his father who was talking into his ear. Whatever his father was saying seemed to make him uncomfortable. She studied the two men closely. Tomaas clearly inherited the best of both parents' genes He was almost as tall as his father with broad shoulders and a full head of long black hair that was fashionably slicked straight back. She had imagined that unkempt or uncombed, this mop of hair had the potential of making this exceptionally well groomed young man look like Tarzan. He certainly had the body for it. She could see his back muscles flexing under his tuxedo. That was where his father's characteristics ended and he assumed his mother's more delicate beauty. He had her blue eyes and her childlike nose. The contradiction of the two looks made him so striking a figure that Janice could not take her eyes off him. When Tomaas and his father noticed her staring at this man who was young enough to be her son she flushed with embarrassment.

Tomaas came directly over to Janice, and with a thick French accent, said, "Madame Rodino, I apologize. In my haste to seat you next to myself, I have selfishly denied my parents of your company."

He spoke so uncharacteristically for a twenty-something-year-old that Janice began to actually blush again. "Don't be silly, Mr. LaCroix. I shall have plenty of time during the evening to spend with everyone at this table. I would rather stay right here if that's all right with your father."

Janice knew that if she said she wanted to take a steak knife and carve out the hearts of three or four of Henri's dinner guests, Henri's only response to the wife of Senator Frank Rodino would be, "Certainly." Janice was already beginning to like her new-found freedom.

While the first course was being served, she started talking about her impending move to France. She said nothing of her plans to leave her husband, but rather explained how important the French were to her cosmetic empire. She went on to say that she felt she would need to find a residence for her extended periods of time there and perhaps the LaCroixs' could recommend a good realtor.

Tomaas chimed in, saying he couldn't understand why anyone would leave the U.S. to spend so much time in France. Tomaas had attended Princeton where he had immersed himself in all that an American college had to offer. He studied hard and played even harder. He had an affable manner that both sexes found attractive. He never seemed conscious of his good looks and never spent time on a regular basis in the gym. He had developed and maintained his physique by joining the rowing club, the rugby club and virtually any other sporting activity that his schedule allowed.

It was when he came into his dorm one afternoon with a massive black eye and bruise to the right side of his face that his roommate John Hingle knew that they would become great friends. It was in the third week of school. Up until that point, John thought Tomaas was too "pretty" and standoffish. Then the hockey stick connected with Tomaas's face, and John, who had played football in high school, immediately knew the extent of his roommate's damages and suggested he go to the infirmary. Tomaas declined and apologized for what he thought was his poor English. John, realizing he probably mistook a language barrier for standoffishness, pushed on and told Tomas that at the very least he should lie down and keep ice on it so he wouldn't mar his face. It was Tomaas' remedy that made John know they were about to embark on a wonderful school year. Tomaas said "Forget about the ice. Do you think you can find me a cold beer? I think maybe I should drink the beer and then we should go to the girls' dorm and see if we can find someone there to patch me up." Tomaas' remedy proved to benefit both young men equally. They walked over to Butler Hall, horsing around as they went until Tomaas entered the front door. He then put his arm around John's shoulders and staggered as though he were about to slump to the floor. He whispered to John, "Yell out 'can somebody help my friend here?' Then let the games begin."

Francis Coppola couldn't have directed a better scene than the one Tomaas had scripted. Within minutes the two men were surrounded by half a dozen young women who at first thought he had been in a fight. Tomaas explained that he was hit in a hockey accident and his roommate was walking him to the infirmary when he felt that he was going to pass out. John noticed that Tomaas was now speaking with a slightly exaggerated French accent. He also noticed that Tomaas had managed, sometime during their walk, to unbutton his shirt down to the bottom button to expose a six-pack of abs. It was a masterful performance with Tomaas balancing the rough and tough jock with the scared little boy who was about to faint.

It paid off with a standing room only audience in the dorm room of a young American beauty who spent the next two hours in a pass-the-baton race with several of her classmates. The baton, however, was a cold, wet facecloth from the bathroom, and the race was to see who could get this Frenchman and or his concerned buddy into their bed first. Later, John told Tomaas that his good looks were better chick bait than the pot he normally used. Tomaas seemed both genuinely oblivious to and unimpressed with his chiseled physique.

The only time Tomaas would even acknowledge his attributes was when he ran short of funds. At those times (they were often) Tomaas would borrow John's brother's car and drive into Manhattan where he would always land a day or two of work modeling for one of the fashion houses. John would ask "How is that possible that you can drive over that bridge and consistently come back with several thousand dollars? And you claim you don't understand why people find you good-looking." Tomas would tell his roommate that what was happening had only partly to do with looks. He would tell John that his grandmother kept a close eye on her only grandson and that he was certain she was paying these huge fashion moguls a hefty sum to take photos and act interested in her grandson.

John would push and ask why he just didn't call his grandmother and ask her for the money directly. Tomaas' look was incredulous. "Why would I do something stupid like that? I would be denying a lady who prides herself on being both a great business woman and caring grandmother the opportunity of negotiating a deal with one of the largest fashion companies in order to benefit her grandson. But more importantly, my friend John, I would be denying myself the opportunity of meeting the most beautiful women in the entire world." John could only bow to the master.

Janice had answered Tomaas by saying that it made sense for a young, handsome male to want to be in the U.S. because this country catered to young men. Europe, she went on to say, catered to older women. To which Tomaas answered, "Then why are you going there?" Janice tried to control a blush at this blatant and welcome flirtation by quickly asking: "So why did you leave Princeton?"

"Gennie had an accident" Tomaas answered. Tomaas was the only person alive who was able to call his grandmother by that name. To everyone else, she was either Madame Obiere or Chairperson Obiere.

Janice remembered reading about the "accident" a couple of years ago, and, of course, hearing the charity-circuit rumors of something more sinister.

Genevieve Obiere hadn't gotten to eighty-something looking and feeling 20 years younger by chance. She never rose later than 5:30, ever. Rarely would she miss her three-mile walk before starting an eight- to 10-hour day running her empire. At 75, she had cut back to only five days a week. Her modified vegetarian diet was her own creation and she found discussions on fad diets to be the utmost in boredom. She had one of the finest wine cellars in Europe. She never ate past 8 PM and never missed her evening glass of red wine.

Her fastidiousness with her diet paled in comparison to the parameters she set with regard to her many residences. Her Paris townhouse typified this. She chose a house that was in the Sixteenth Arrondissement. Her late husband had suggested something in a nearby neighborhood that offered a more "neighborly" feel. He explained that the location she was considering required that you drive almost everywhere. One could not simply walk to a local market if you needed last minute groceries. Her response was as simplistic as it was revealing. She told him that she had no intention of ever entering a grocery store. That is why they had servants. She also told him she loathed the idea of having overbearing Parisian women out on a shopping spree passing by her home. Or worse yet, finding themselves compelled to stop by to say hello. No, Genevieve wanted privacy above all else. Security came in a close second. Ever since the Lindbergh baby kidnapping over in the states, Genevieve became obsessed about security.

The house she chose was one of the few townhouses in the area. It was attached on only one side. She uncharacteristically paid a premium for this particular house because the house that was attached on the opposite side had a mortgage that was both held by her bank and was tremendously in arrears. Before Genevieve closed on her house, the bank had foreclosed on the neighboring property and razed it to the ground, leaving Genevieve with one of the few free standing mansions in the district.

In addition to the house being free standing it was constructed before World War I by a contractor who had built much of Paris's apartment buildings. The house was constructed of rough cut granite stones. The walls were nearly two feet thick. Genevieve had all the windows replaced with bullet proof glass. She had the property enclosed with a six-foot wrought iron fence. When Jacqueline was a child, Genevieve would work out of her third floor office. The office had a distant view of the Seine and a bird's eye view of the back yard garden. There with her governess Jacqueline would play and be schooled amidst one of the finest gardens in Europe. There was no such thing as surveillance cameras so Genevieve relied on a posted guard at the front of the house and attack dogs at the rear. German Shepherds at first, Doberman Pinschers when Jacqueline was a child and Pit Bulls as Tomaas was growing up. From the very first day her bank attorneys had advised her that attack dogs were not the way to go. If, for instance, a child from one of Genevieve's wealthy neighbors had inadvertently wandered into the property and Genevieve erroneously gave the order to attack, she would be facing an untold amount of lawsuits for pain and suffering caused by her mauling hounds. Genevieve's response to her lawyers was the same each time a new set of dogs were trained. "First off" she would start, "no *child would* be able to scale the six foot fence. If it were an adult," she continued, "they would be able to read the *no trespassing* signs posted every four feet around the perimeter of her property. And lastly" she would continue without as much as an octave change in her voice, "if somehow someone did indeed make it over the fence and past the guard then I would certainly not be facing any 'pain and suffering' lawsuits. This I can assure you of gentlemen. The one thing I can't assure you of is that I won't be sued for a wrongful death." She would end the discussion with the same logic as she employed each time. "We all know that a wrongful death suit is far less costly then any pain and suffering suit and we also know that I can well afford several of these suits. Period."

The accident happened at her townhouse, once hers but now occupied by her daughter and son-in-law. She arose at her usual time. Just as she neared the top of the stone staircase, she simultaneously felt something soft at her shins and what felt like a hard rubber bat at the small of her back. She crashed down eighteen steps to the marble floor on the main landing. Genevieve remembered little else – except that Henri had been the first to reach her. She had broken a hip, several ribs and her right wrist. Doctors were amazed she survived at all. She scoffed at their fussing.

After several days, she called Henri, Jacqueline, her attorney and several other lackeys to her bedside. "I have survived a murder attempt," she said calmly, circulating her gaze around to all of them, finally resting on Henri. He tried to joke. "Surely, Madame, you have been reading too much of Hercule Poirot."

"I never jest," she replied, steely-eyed.

"Perhaps you are starting now, in the twilight of your time with us," he said smoothly while looking suitably woebegone. "Or maybe that fine mind of yours … "

"Enough," she snapped, ordering them all out.

She knew the act well, having practiced it on her late husband. It was when her only daughter sided with her husband and told her mother that she was speaking irrationally that Madame Obiere put a series of changes into effect. She would no longer visit at the townhouse. She would use her own residence in France only when her son-in-law was out of town. She had quietly acknowledged the loss of her daughter to her son-in-law but had not yet accepted it. She kept an eye on Henri and insisted that her daughter have a bodyguard around the clock. When Jacqueline refused, her mother said, "Fine. You may, of course, live however you wish. Not, of course, in any of the family's properties."

Jacqueline acquiesced, and came to call the men her chauffeurs.

Tomaas recalled: "I was instructed to leave Princeton and sent to Verbea, where Grandmother has a ski chalet. I finished my studies nearby and visited her often."

She later took up residence at her Geneva mansion and hired private detectives, bodyguards, and several thugs – a network of protection she liked to think rivaled the Duvalier family's Ton Ton Macutes when they ran Haiti.

"I had to go home to help Gennie recover," Tomaas told Janice. "It was supposed to be for a few months but these things sometimes take on a life of their own."

Or, Janice thought, the life that Old Lady Obiere dictates. Janice now realized the oversized men at the table were Jacqueline's and Tomaas's "chauffeurs."

Tomaas was the member of the LaCroix family who was designated to meet Janice at the airport in Paris and see to it that she was settled in her hotel. While on the ride from the airport Tomaas volunteered to introduce her to a realtor and to accompany her on her search for a new home.

Within two weeks of her arrival in Paris, Janice and Tomaas became lovers. Janice had known that sex with Tomaas LaCroix would be fantastic. What she didn't know was that it would be tender. Physically, she could match him in endurance and in imagination. And he loved her for it. There are few 25-year-old men who know that their match in sexual appetite often are older women who are far more interested and experienced in satisfying themselves than are younger women busy plotting relationships.

In the weeks and months that followed the state dinner in Washington, Tomaas LaCroix and Janice Rodino sexually devoured each other. Both great lovers of fine food and wine, sumptuous décor, and luxurious hotels, they began to spend money and time with each other, indiscriminately. They alternately had ferocious sex in the most daring of places – including Henri's office at the shipping empire's headquarters, *sans* cigar jokes, of course – and made tender love in romantic suites in several Paris hotels.

From the first, in silent agreement, they never talked about their age difference. Of course, they each got a different kind of thrill from flouting social rules. Tomaas had been raised in Europe. Nudity, at least breast-baring by women and girls on beaches, did not throw him into paroxysms of drooling as it did sophomoric American men. But "I do love your breasts, Madame," he would murmur to her as he peeled away her clothing. "Well," Janice would whisper, "they are real." "They are that," he said, nuzzling her.

She valued his body for its youth and strength. Unselfconsciously, she would explore it inch by inch, mounting him as he lay flat, stroking her hands across his hair, running her fingers through the curly strands and deep into his skull, stopping to nuzzle his bronzed neck. She would trill her lips down his spine and playfully sink her teeth in his buttocks, and he would groan in pleasure. 'What are you doing?" he murmured once as Janice stroked his thighs, then ran her tongue down each thigh. "Oh, touring," she said airily.

As for herself, Janice had little worry about her aging body. She was comfortable with it in a way that Tomaas admired. In fact, she was unlike any woman he had ever had sex with. Not that he made comparisons. But Janice was, in her own quiet way, fiercely focused. He didn't know exactly on what, but the intensity and surety she brought to sex excited him in all kinds of new ways, heightening sensations beyond anything he had experienced before.

They enjoyed each others' bodies, and used them enthusiastically. Their age difference, never a problem, allowed them to move past the purely physical. Not only did their tongues and pelvises entwine, but their minds, and, to their astonishments, hearts did too.

After sex, they would talk. They would talk intimately, again unlike anything Tomaas had ever experienced. He trusted her and was able to unburden himself. He spoke of his father, their business and his own ambitions. She spoke of her rise in the business community and of her unhappy last few years with Frank. They both found a common bond in the stories each knew about Tomaas's grandmother.

CHAPTER 7

Wednesday, June 30, very early

Paul threw off the boxer shorts he had worn to bed and headed for the bathroom to begin damage control. With each motion, he silently sketched the upcoming scenario: It was 3:45 AM. He had to get from New Rochelle to the county airport in North Castle, a 20-minute drive, by 4:30 AM. Providing the plane was on time, the crate that would contain Mrs. Rodino's casket could be unloaded and put into the hearse by 6 AM. Paul assumed the Senator would have someone there from Customs to clear the special cargo and extra aides or special hires to help Paul load her into the hearse.

He made a mental note: *Call an "extra man."* In the industry that could be an off-duty cop, firefighter, strong retiree – really anybody willing to react at a moment's notice to help with house removals, file the death certificate with the local registrar, be a pallbearer or, in cases like this, get a cumbersome, crated casket, which could weigh as much as 1,000 pounds, into the hearse, then unload it back at the funeral home.

His mind still on the run, Paul paused, turned and stood naked before the mirror. He needed to lose 10, maybe 15 pounds. The lack of sleep stared back at him; the rings under his eyes were darker than usual, raccoon like. He knew he had to at least shave the heavy swath of overnight beard. If he were held up at the airport, he wouldn't be back in time to prep and open the funeral home for the De Simone family. The funeral for the beloved husband-father-friend was set for 9 AM.

Paul bent over the sink, doused his face, shaved. "Bag the shower," he said aloud, then ran some gel through his still full but beginning-to-gray hair. If he got back early enough, fine; he would jump in the shower then. Otherwise, he would stand in the reposing room for prayers – near a floral arrangement with the most stargazer lilies. Nothing, not even he, could smell stronger than stargazers.

As he hurriedly brushed his teeth over the sink, he paused and tongued his chipped tooth. He really should get that chipped eyetooth taken care of. He had lived with it for – what? – almost 30 years?

He and John had been horsing around. Johnny wanted to see if the twins, and their hockey sticks, would fit inside a casket. After all, Pop had told them that people often bury things in caskets, things the dead people, or maybe their families, had loved in life.

They went down to the basement of the old Georgian mansion, to the casket room, which at that time was next to the embalming room. Both were off-limits to the Arrone children until they reached high school.

"Come on," Johnny whispered excitedly to Paul from one of the caskets, "get in."

Sure enough, the copper casket John had selected was ample for the two of them, their hockey sticks and even, John pointed out, their friend Joey Hinkey. "We'll try to get Hink in here the next chance we get," Johnny said excitedly. They froze. A hearse was pulling up, the tires even with the window above and to the left of them. It was their father and a dead body.

The twins scrambled to get out of the casket at the same time. The lid started to fall, and the hockey stick jammed into Paul's mouth, cutting his lip. He grunted, squirmed, and heard a crack and then a "ping" as a piece of his eyetooth went flying.

Holed up in their room for the next week of punishment, Johnny would say over and over to Paul, "That was the coolest thing we ever did."

"You looked like a vampire," John would recall, always with his loud guffaw. "With all that blood coming from your mouth, and your tooth chipped. That was great, that was *so great.* I can't wait to bring Hink inside."

Paul shook himself. What was with him tonight? He didn't have time for Memory Lane detours. He threw on a dress shirt and one of his always-ready blue suits, efficiently knotting his tie on the way to the hearse. He started it, noting with satisfaction that he would be on the Hutchinson River Parkway within the thirteen-minute time frame he had allowed himself.

Despite his years of experience, Paul was a bit uneasy at the implications of arranging a funeral for someone as powerful as the Senator's wife. He had met Senator Frankie several times at a fund-raiser, a parade, wherever all the top-notch Republicans gathered. Even a lowly, rebellious Westchester County legislator couldn't be immune from the party's de facto head in New York State- or politics. The stupidest thing he ever did, Paul reflected as he drove to the airport, was to add politician to his resume. It had been just a few short years after John died and after he had taken over the Funeral Home.

The spring after John's death, Paul had moved into the Funeral Home and taken on more of the day-to-day responsibilities. His father started coming to work less and less. Paul had felt as though he was in vocational limbo. He had taken a formal leave of absence from the New Rochelle Police Department knowing he wouldn't be back. He was determined to like being a funeral director. He respected the familiarity of the family business, although it didn't feel much like his.

It was painful to see how much his father was missing his brother. The old man was drinking way more than he should and his tutorials with Paul were perfunctory. But business was, if not booming, growing steadily. Every family that walked through the Arrone Funeral Home door looking for guidance could take comfort in knowing that their intense pain was shared by the owners and operators. That unique bond of funeral director and aggrieved family couldn't have been more bittersweet. If misery loved company (and Paul had to admit that his misery did), the Arrone Funeral Home was filthy with it that year.

About five months after his brother's death, Paul swung open the Home's heavy door expecting to find a shocked, bereaved client. Instead, he found Sergeant Ian Cullan and a plain-clothes officer standing in front of him.

"Do you have five minutes for us, Paul?" asked Cullan. His sullen companion was the head of the Westchester County Police Union.

In a funeral home consultation room, the cops spent the next hour telling Paul what little respect the politicians had for police in general and the county officers in particular. With Ronald Crimmons retiring from the county Board of Legislators, Paul would be a natural: "Run for his seat in November's election," they said in hushed tones. "We need one of our own."

It was the beginning of a month-long lobbying effort. Everyone in a uniform within 20 miles of New Rochelle got to him: through phone calls, stopping by, at funeral processions, escorted or not.

It was his father who pushed him over the top.

Dominic Arrone was a former councilman in New Rochelle. Except for lawyers, he would tell his boys proudly, "funeral directors were the most elected officials in the United States."

"You should do it," he urged Paul. Friends, relatives and neighbors would help him with money and their time. It was the first spark of enthusiasm Paul had seen in Dominic since that call from the diner. Finally, even his mother got involved reminding him how much Johnny had wanted to run for city office some day, ultimately, for Mayor. That sealed it, of course. With one signature on an application at the Board of Elections, Paul could honor his brother, lift his father's spirit, and cheer the police colleagues he had abandoned. A good bargain: A person's not dead if his dreams are kept alive.

Paul ran and won. It would prove to be a short but very educational stint of public service. Being a Republican in Westchester, the land of the Rockefellers, had its advantages. So did the frequent and large donations his father and brothers had made to the local GOP. In his first year on the Board, Paul was seated on three committees. The most influential was the Board's Budget Committee, where Paul saw how money made policy, and where and how he could make a name for himself.

Yet Paul served only one short term. In those two years, he learned lessons that would last his entire life. In Westchester County, "Them that gives gets" and "Them that gives big, gets big." The Republican Party was dominated by fat, old, white, alcoholic men whose priorities were quite clear: fat, old, white, wealthy, alcoholic men in this land of gentry.

The county budget, even then in the late Eighties, was larger than those of eight states. The sons of Irish immigrants were beginning to share power with the sons, grandsons and great-grandsons of the Italians who once were banned from good housing and neighborhoods but were good enough to break their backs as laborers and stonemasons on projects like the Kensico Dam in the early 1900s.

Westchester County's government had evolved by the late Eighties into a one billion-plus enterprise run by a County Executive in the administrative branch and 17 legislators representing the so-called bedroom communities from inner cities in southern Westchester to the horse country up north.

The chairman of the legislature was "elected" by his peers; there wasn't the slightest question whom they should nominate. He and the County Executive blurred together, running the county the way Paul's grandparents had told him Mussolini had run Italy. They were bookends, he would tell Dominic in the quiet of their kitchen after late board meetings. Their act was similar to Edgar Bergen and Mortimer Snerd, although Paul wasn't sure which one was the dummy. Both were obese, with red faces deepened by alcohol blotches about the cheeks and nose. Many of the 12,000-person county work force got their jobs through a web of local and county party connections. The Democrats and Conservatives had their own smaller fiefdoms, and were thrown bones of money and influence to keep them in line.

Paul didn't do well, certainly not in the traditional Westchester sense of what politics should be. He did succeed in befriending disgruntled employees, disaffected women, and Democratic legislators. After all, there was a caste system in this empire. You just had to study it and work it. Republican men ruled. In their wake stood the Democratic men with whom you could always cut a deal, followed by Republican women who wouldn't complain about them. The Democratic women were at the bottom of this caste and complained a great deal. Then there was Paul who was a virtual untouchable.

Paul's arrival meant his fellow untouchables had their leader. With emboldened comrades, Paul had just enough votes to become the biggest pain in this kingdom's ass. When the establishment did something unusually outrageous, and that was fairly often, Paul would collect his small gang to erect roadblocks.

For Paul, one particular appointment crystallized Westchester politics in the early eighties. Robert Walker, commissioner of the county youth department, was being quietly accused of molesting young boys. Once the first accusation came out, several other boys and their parents came forward to tell their stories of molestation. Paul learned of it while sitting on the Personnel Committee. "There would *have* to be a police investigation," he'd update Dominic. "You sure of that, son?" Dominic had asked him. "Of course," Paul had said in surprise. "I don't care how great a Republican loyalist Walker is."

The stories grew, and so did Walker's exposure. In addition to his predilection for little boys, talk was that Walker was making his staff run fund-raisers for the County Executive, the Chairman of the Board, and key legislators. He also was caught diverting money that had been raised for youth programs in order to fund trips to Europe for those who sat at the top of the county caste system.

One night, at a closed-door meeting on "what to do about Walker" on the eighth floor of the County Office Building, the discussion centered on the fund diversion. *"Justice will be served,"* Paul had thought grimly, humming to himself as the leadership was reaching their verdict; there was no way this guy could possibly last.

Paul and his small band of followers were more shocked than the general public or the press at the outcome. The County Executive and the Chairman, with the blessings of other top Republicans and the Democratic and Conservative leadership, docked Walker four weeks' pay and removed him from his post in the Youth Department. They declared the other allegations "spurious rumor."

With that, a stunned Paul realized, *was that.*

But not quite. Walker immediately was named Commissioner and Warden of the county jail. He was simply too good a soldier to leave wounded and alone out in the field. Besides, in their perverse way, the more conservative legislators felt that putting a pedophile in charge of a jail would act as a deterrent to criminals in the county. At one caucus, Paul heard someone say: "Who in the county would have the balls to commit a crime knowing that you would be sent to Walker for a working over?" There was scattered laughter, followed by uproarious appreciation when someone asked, "Who in the county would have any balls left after being sent to Walker?'

Walker proved to be degenerately true to form. Shortly after his arrival at the warden's office, he was running several small businesses out of the old penitentiary building. Using the prisoners as free laborers, he started a small tailoring business. Walker also found that he could sell much of the meat and other foodstuffs being delivered to the jail to local restaurants.

It wasn't until the second budget of his first and only term as a lawmaker that Paul knew for sure he would never make it in Westchester government. That year, the new warden was asking for money to purchase two more meat grinders for the commissary. There was a shortfall of meat, the corpulent, pale-faced pedophile said in answer to Paul's pointed questions put to him in committee. Prisoners, he said blandly, deserved adequate nutrition, too.

"This line of questioning, this level of detail is unnecessary, Mr. Arrone," the Budget Chair had intoned smoothly. "Let's move on," and Walker's budget additions went through.

A disaffected corrections officer met Paul at a secret location to explain the reason why. Walker had petitioned for the new meat grinders. It seemed that in order for Walker to make up for the shortfall of meat to feed his prisoners he would have to grind up what was left of the delivered goods into ground meat with filler. The warden had stumbled upon a bonanza of a supply of filler and had made an under-the-table arrangement with the medical examiner to purchase the human viscera of autopsied bodies from the county hospital that was located next door to the prison on the county reservation. When this was added to the meat which he had not sold to the local restaurants and other food scraps he had already had in stock, the end product was more than ample to feed the prison population. The supply was so ample that Walker was able to cut a deal with a dog food company in upstate NY to sell by-products for dog food. That was the specific reason he needed two more meat grinding machines. It appeared that the dog food company required a larger percentage of "real meat" in its batch than was necessary for the prisoners. This was how the corpulent, pale faced, pedophile was planning to provide quality control of his merchandise.

Paul fought this and other similar issues with other commissioners with more anger than he knew he possessed.

At the end of an exhausting budget season, conveniently caught in the end-of-the-year holiday rush, Paul was beat. He had concluded that it wasn't that people were unconcerned about the way their government was being run in the "Golden Apple." His county was a mere geographical step-child to New York City, its closest southern neighbor. The problem was that it was impossible to gather a sympathetic ear about the goings-on of a couple of potentially corrupt commissioners golfing on the greenest fair-ways when, in the city, an employee from a besieged parking authority was stabbing himself to death in his car on the Brooklyn-Queens Expressway with a kitchen knife to avoid prosecution.

No matter how large Westchester's budget was, or how much of it was being diverted to the coffers of political parties, Paul realized, it paled in comparison to the heady budget numbers being tossed about in the nation's largest city, which had just teetered on bankruptcy.

Paul the politician, no matter how successful he was in garnering con-stituent support at the same time as needling the Westchester big wigs and annoying the party bosses, soon lost the ultimate battle in the easiest way. It was a redistricting year in Westchester. The hands of Paul's fel-low Republican colleagues, even though they were mindful of how much money Old Man Arrone had given to the cause, were tied. There wasn't much they could do about the new districts being carved. Larger political forces than they were in play.

A new district, part of which slithered down North Avenue, encom-passing Paul and the Funeral Home, would become part of one currently represented by a ten-term Republican from Bronxville. So in the swift click of computer mapping, Paul's political career was ended. A Republican pri-mary was out of the question, his father told him.

Later, if he turned the district map upside down to study the nooks and crannies of the Eastchester district he was thrown into, Paul saw that Patrick Miller, the Chairman of the Legislature, was giving him a farewell extended middle finger.

CHAPTER 8

Paul's anger would subside in direct proportion to the time spent away from politics. And his fans quietly loved him; years later, he still would get the quiet nudge now and then to run again. Besides, he frequently reminded himself, had he not served he wouldn't have made so many rank-and-file friends in government. Nor would he have met Trish.

Trish Morrison worked in the Budget Department of the County Hospital, which had jurisdiction over the medical examiner's office, Paul's favorite target. As the first budget season neared, Paul prepared a litany of questions on how the taxpayers' money was being misspent, particularly when it came to tending to dead people, his own forte and Haywood's bastion of power. The M.E. and other commissioners, though, quickly learned about Paul's rabid style from others who had gone before the Budget Committee, so they sent low-level employees to face the public humiliation that Paul would try to inflict. When it came time for the hospital's budget, he was ready with a dozen pages of typed-up questions. For starters, why were all these contracts being given out to companies without going out for bid, as required by law? How could you justify increasing your work force by 10 percent when there was a decrease in patients this year? He couldn't wait to ask these questions.

With nearly half of Westchester's 12,000 civil service jobs, the county hospital was a hotbed for political patronage; patient beds, too, of course. After all, it was started as a hospital to serve the poor. Now it did a better job serving politicians.

In his behemoth of a budget, the hospital commissioner included money for medical research when the hospital had no such research facility.

In this particular proposal was also a hefty salary increase for the medical examiner and money for two new positions – people to assist the Medical Examiner Office's staff in doing night removals.

Of course, for Paul it was a natural place to make his irrefutable stand about county waste. Unlike everyone else elected to any county government post, Paul knew all too well that Dr. William Haywood never made *any* night removals. He relegated that task to the local funeral homes. In exchange, he would give them $50 for their troubles. If time were a factor in getting one of the bodies ready for viewing by 2 PM visiting hours, the grateful Dr. Haywood would keep the viscera, which needed disposal, at no extra charge to the funeral director.

There was no way Paul could imagine that Dr. Haywood would misstep on this one.

The doors of the legislative conference room opened, but it wasn't Haywood stomping his way in. Trish had been sent to the committee to present both the hospital and the medical examiner's budgets. Wearing a gray tweed suit, her blonde hair pulled back off her face and up, she was lovely and, Paul realized, as smart as they come. The ever-verbose Paul sat speechless throughout her one-and-a-half-hour presentation. She reminded Paul of that actress, the one in Alfred Hitckock's "The Birds." But he couldn't remember the actress's name. The fact was, right then, he could barely remember his own.

Trish spoke in a soft, almost childlike voice. When a lawmaker was recognized by the chair and asked a particularly difficult question, she would tilt her head back and bite her beautiful lower lip. When stumped, or at least appearing to be, she would appear flustered, then ask the board if she could get back to them with that answer.

"Sure you can," Paul wanted to shout to the chairman, and then to Trish. "Take all the time you need. Come back anytime."

But Paul could barely swallow, let alone speak. He couldn't believe it: He was tongue-tied by a tiny woman who worked for one of the biggest slobs in county government. He did not ask a single question that day. Even if the chair had recognized him, he realized later, he probably would have stumbled over his words. Instead he shot off his questions in writing to the commissioners themselves. They did the only politically smart thing they could do: they sent Trish back to the front lines to defend their greed.

Paul would never forget the second time he saw Trish.

She walked into his office unannounced, holding the list of questions he had sent her boss. Paul inhaled, then gave an awkward squeak. "I'm sorry for startling you," she said with a gentle smile. "May we go over these?"

They spent the next two hours going over the hospital and medical examiner's budgets, and Trish knew every twist and turn of every line. Paul was not only taken by her looks, but her acumen and, he grudgingly admitted to himself, her loyalty to her boss.

Paul had lost track of time. The county office building had closed. He glanced over her shoulder and saw the maintenance crew working in the hall. "Would you like to finish this discussion over dinner at the restaurant across the street?" he said, amazing himself. He usually planned such dates days, sometimes weeks in advance.

Trish looked away from him, tilted her head to the side and then bit her lip. "Paul," she said quietly, "that really is a very nice offer, but I have to get home. My husband and I have dinner plans. He is a resident at the hospital. His shift will be over in about a half-hour." With that rejection, Paul had one more reason to dislike county government.

She gathered her material. At the door, she paused and turned. He stared at her. "It's Tippi," she said.

"What?" Paul said.

"Tippi," Trish said smiling as she began to close the door behind her. "Tippi Hedren. You know – "The Birds.""

By the time Paul saw Trish again several years had passed. The Westchester County Funeral Directors Association had invited the medical examiner to speak about "Long Bone Donation of Cadavers" at their annual dinner. Dreading Haywood, Paul cheered when he saw Trish directing other county employees in handing out literature and working the projector that augmented Haywood's presentation.

After dinner, Paul spotted her at the Rye Town Hilton's crowded bar. She was sipping a cocktail. Flustered again, he realized who this woman was. Her hair was now shoulder-length and wavy and she frequently ruffled her bangs. Other than that, Paul thought that time had stood still for her.

He avoided her, though, heading to the bar for a beer. He was exchanging pleasantries with some of the funeral directors from the Sound Shore area when he felt a hand on his shoulder. He spun around on his bar stool and was face to face with Trish.

"Paul?" she said. "I thought that was you. How have you been?" She searched his face more intently than usual in a bar exchange.

"I am well, Trish," he all but stammered. "I have to say you – you look great. You haven't changed one bit." *Gee, how suave*, he thought. He was annoyed at his boyish meltdown

"I'm sure you're just being kind, but thanks for the compliment. It's been tough getting back into shape since I had my son last year." Paul actually felt a stab of physical pain at that news.

"We miss you at the county, Paul," she continued. "Things certainly have been dull since you left."

A Haywood employee approached, telling her that the M.E. wanted to see her right away. "It was nice running into you." She turned, stopped and moved closer to him. "You know, I thought about calling you, Paul, and catching up on things. But this past year has been crazy for me."

Surprised, Paul watched her go. He glanced around, then slipped out to the parking lot and spent the night on his cell phone, seeing if any of his contacts knew the latest about Trish. It didn't take long to learn from a former County Attorney that she had handled Trish's divorce about six months earlier. When he pressed for details, all the woman would say was, "She got full custody."

It never ceased to amaze Paul that an affluent county like Westchester a population with close to a million, managed to retain a small-town mentality. Here he would put out the word less than 24 hours ago that he was looking for information, and it was picked up by a friend who knew exactly what he wanted. He thought that, in this instance, it was a good thing that information was such a "hot commodity" in this corrupt bedroom county.

He called Trish at the office first thing the next morning on the pretext of telling her how informative the previous night's talk had been. "Yes," she said hesitantly. "You never picked up your continuing credit certificate after it was over. Nobody knew where you went."

Asshole he said to himself. Nothing like starting off with a disappearing act, followed by a lie. They were silent for a moment. Finally, Trish spoke quietly. "Listen, I was thinking ... " She drew a short breath. "I was thinking that maybe we could meet for dinner sometime. I could personally deliver your certificate to you."

When he didn't answer, she said teasingly, "You better than anyone know how efficient we are in county government." Paul could think of no other word than that old-fashioned one his grandmother would have used. "Smitten." He was actually smitten.

They went to dinner that weekend and soon started dating in earnest. Trish accepted Paul's long stretches of silence, and something hard within his chest started to thaw. They loved each other. They said it regularly. They rarely fought; Trish because she had had enough of that during her marriage, and Paul because, as he would say, "There aren't that many things that important to argue for."

The sex between them, when their schedules matched and Trish could rely on child care or a play date for Keith, was weirdly satisfying. Trish was a refuge for Paul, a place to hide. Paul was an enigma to Trish, a kind one, a driven one, but an enigma. They filled holes in each other, but was it enough?

Despite strong feelings, things between them cooled over time. If anything, Paul, under the warmth of the covers, stroking Trish's fine skin, bringing her to orgasm, was further away from her than ever. Often, Trish would hold Paul yet feel he was elsewhere in the room, maybe above them, looking down, watching.

She didn't know it, but Paul felt that way too. She had no way of knowing that he was incapable of acting any other way.

They arrived at that get-married-or-break-up place that's inevitable in most relationships. Paul was unable to make a full commitment and that mystified him as much as it did Trish. He should have been able to. He should have taken responsibility for his feelings. In fact, in some ways, she understood his reluctance – actually his *inability* – to commit. She understood it better than he ever would.

But she was no martyr. Twice over the last six years, she had called a halt to their relationship. Each time, she had hoped that the time apart would make it obvious to Paul that they were meant to be together. She always went back to him after a couple of months.

"I won't enable your lack of commitment any more, Paul," she told him. If he looked at her skeptically, it was her own fault. And frankly, she didn't trust that she wouldn't cave in again just as she had the last two times.

This time it would be different. She knew she wanted to be married and wanted her son to have the permanence that he deserved. She refused to enable Paul's lack of commitment. She also didn't trust that she wouldn't give in again as she had the last two times. She had decided that this time – with no recriminations – she would give this split six weeks and then she would move. She was now in week seven. She knew she couldn't afford to raise her son in Westchester County if she hoped to give him a good life in normal surroundings. With the median home price topping $600,000, her dream of a small house with a yard for Keith to play in would be just that, a dream.

She had applied for and landed a job in upstate Troy. While she wouldn't make as much in their budget department as she was making in Westchester, the lower cost of living more than made up the difference. She was vested in the state pension plan; so as long as she worked in a municipality in New York State she would receive a pension that was based on her highest three years (those in Westchester). She had sent the real estate broker two month's rent and one month's security on a four-bedroom house that had cost the same as she paid for one month's rent in her Yonkers waterfront apartment. She wanted to make certain that both she and Paul accepted this stalemate in their relationship for what is was – without placing any blame.

That is why when Paul pleaded with her to breach her security trust at the Medical Center in order to get him information, she agreed. She had not told Paul that she was less than a month from leaving his life forever. She rationalized that when she did, she could point to this last selfless act to show him that she wasn't moving as an act of revenge but as one of self-preservation. She loved him and would do anything for him except diminish her or her son's potential of living a normal happy life.

Paul and Keith had developed a deep bond, almost as if they were father and son. In fact, Trish knew as she watched them play together, that ending their friendship would be a great danger for Keith. She had never liked staying over at the Funeral Home, but Keith loved it. What seven-year-old boy wouldn't? The chills and thrills of dead bodies below them, yet safe in the rafters above. Keith would pepper Paul with the kinds of questions about his profession that grown-ups were dying to know but only a child would ask.

As Keith grew sleepy, Paul would take him upstairs to his old bedroom, and they would swap stories until Keith nodded off. "I'm always going to sleep in your bed, the one you had as a kid, Paul." Paul would exchange a sad smile over his head with Trish as Keith would rattle on. "I want to do everything you did."

Paul would lie or sit across from him on the other old twin bed, and they would talk about what was really important in the world. "Paul, can a body sit up after he is dead? Billy Morton said that their hair and nails keep growing, is that true? Paul what's that noise?"

Paul would tell him it was the air conditioning compressors mounted just outside their window. One recent night he told him: "When I was your age, they were bigger and louder, and nobody could hear us whisper. John and I would sometimes spend the whole night talking," Paul said. He paused. He had forgotten that.

He told Keith about the first time the compressors were turned on and how frightened he was. "I thought it was a spaceship landing."

John had calmed him down though, he told Keith. Flashlight in hand, he had shown Paul where the breaker switch was so that he could disconnect the units at any time. Paul didn't tell Keith that John had taken him out on the ledge to show him.

Keith nodded, understanding. "How 'bout we see *Star Wars* next weekend," Keith whispered, "so you can get over being scared of spaceships?"

Paul got up and hugged Keith, vowing to always be honest with his little friend. He winced though as he tucked Keith in. He had already deceived him. The bed he loved to sleep in really had belonged to his dead brother.

A few nights before Trish's call, she had had to work late so Keith had slept over, an unusual mid-week treat. They had followed their usual routine. Paul had sat across from Keith until he fell asleep. Paul had gotten up quietly, turned down the nightlight, and then kissed the boy on the forehead. He had whispered, "Goodnight, Bro."

CHAPTER 9

T he sign, "Westchester County Airport Next Exit," glowed in the reflection from Paul's headlights. There would be no other signs marking the airport. Paul thought to himself how this typified the arrogance of both the Westchester government and the neighbors that bordered the airport. This was the only public airport in the nation that got away with imposed flight curfews, a fact which epitomized the wealth and influence of the central Westchester area. Paul sat on the airport advisory committee in his first year as a legislator. It would never cease to amaze him that people would buy multi-million dollar homes directly under the flight paths in both Westchester and nearby Greenwich Connecticut, and then show up a week after their closing to try and shut the facility down. It wasn't that they didn't know about the airport before they bought their homes, or that the noise was louder than they expected. No, they tried to shut the airport down because they felt entitled enough to believe they could.

The situation was a huge contradiction to Paul. The New York metropolitan area had three major airports, two of which were 20 minutes from each other. Geographically, there was no need for another airport. Yet the many Fortune 500 companies that relocated to the "platinum mile" a few miles from where the airport sat, along with the more affluent county residents who had their own jets, demanded a more convenient place to take off and land without having to deal with the New York City air or vehicular traffic. To those residents and businesses that crammed meetings of the county legislature the solution seemed clear. Allow them to use the airport for their enjoyment and business and exclude everyone else. Damn the federal money the county received for improvements. Damn the commercial airlines that wanted to provide convenient service to the general public. Damn those who insisted on flying over the county at inopportune times. For Westchester politicians this was a bonanza. They would threaten to take the feds all the way to the U.S. Supreme Court if anyone messed with this unique national curfew. At the same time the county was able to reap large profits from renting hangars to private companies and gate space to public airlines. The icing on the cake for the political elite was to be able to steer to their friends' no-bid construction contracts that amounted to tens of millions of dollars for airport upgrades without having a single increase in traffic. For Paul, the height of arrogance and the lust for control was never more apparent than when the county executive and the board of legislators promoted a $100 million bond referendum for a new much larger terminal, ostensibly to accommodate many more passengers. The county in turn would charge the airlines and private corporate jets larger lease fees.

Yet at every public hearing held on this subject prior to the vote, county officials publicly stated that there would be "*No Increase In Traffic.*" In any county other than Westchester, the residents might have questioned this logic. If it were any other county, the referendum would have failed. But it was Westchester. The referendum passed overwhelmingly. The construction industry built the county a premier terminal, and the county continued to restrict all traffic to the same patterns as before the referendum.

As Paul drove the hearse up an access road to the corporate hangars at Westchester County airport, he noticed far more cars than usual lining each side. With their darkened windows, their drivers had to be cops, likely FBI and God knew who else.

As he slowed down, a man got out of a county police car and waved him over. Paul grinned when he saw that it was Lieutenant Peter Parish. Pete had been on the New Rochelle police force when Paul first started. Then he transferred to the county force while Paul was a county legislator. If anybody knew what was really going on, it was Ferret-the-Parrot Parish, one of the nosiest cops marking him as a good cop.

"Hey, Lieutenant, what's doing?

"Arrone. How have you been?" They shook hands as Parish walked him around to the passenger's side. "Long time no see. Ever since you left county government, you forget about the peons."

"Not true, I think about the peons and assholes practically everyday. It's the good guys and friends like you I never get around to calling."

They drove to a plane on the tarmac behind Hangar 12. "What's going on?" Paul said. "Is that her plane? They're early."

"Yeah," Parish said, "but they're on time. The plane landed at 2 AM and is just about ready to take off back to Monaco."

Paul frowned. Trish was fastidious with work details; she would never have been this far off on the arrival time. He started to get out, but Parish put a restraining hand on his shoulder.

"Wait," Parish said. "We gotta talk. This is freakin' huge. We have been briefed by Secret Service, FBI, the Senator's staff, you name it, and I've been talkin' with everybody."

"Spill," Paul said.

"Get this." Parish lowered his voice even though there was no one within yards of them. "Rodino's old lady went off a cliff in Monaco. It's not clear what the hell she was doing there. She was dead at the scene."

Paul nodded, waiting for Parish to continue.

"Hang on, hang on," Parish said with relish. "We're hearing that Senator Frankie pulled out all the stops on this one. Apparently, he called Prince Rainier himself, and the Prince must have seen to everything personally. The Grimaldi family doctor pronounced her dead at the site of the rollover. We heard CIA wanted the body taken to the American Hospital in Paris for an autopsy, but the Senator wouldn't hear of it.

"How is that possible?" Paul asked. He knew full well the amount of investigatory and bureaucratic work that had to be done on any case, but particularly one of this magnitude.

"Here's where it gets freaky," Parish said. "It turns out Janice Rodino drove off the cliff at the exact hairpin turn where Princess Grace did."

"Are you kidding me?" Paul said. If that was true, how long did they think they could keep the media off of this one? God, "Entertainment Tonight," and every sleazy tabloid in the country would be crawling all over Westchester – and his Funeral Home too – if he got the service.

"Yup," Parish said. "Looks like the Senator wanted his princess to be spared gutting by some French pathologist. Guess the royal family felt if

Grace, who'd lived there for decades, couldn't make that hairpin turn; it wasn't strange that Janice Rodino couldn't."

Paul still couldn't get over it. "No autopsy? On a U.S. Senator's wife? And she dies abroad? How is that possible?"

Parish shrugged. "Word has it the Senator called your pal Haywood, who got some surgeon over there to take the body to the palace infirmary and do a mini-autopsy. He determined the cause, and she was shipped home to Westchester."

"Oh? And just what was the official cause?"

"They tell me that it took about ten minutes for him to figure out that her spleen had ruptured when the steering wheel went into her gut on the first tumble."

A refueling truck pulled up to the plane. They got out and walked to the fence that cordoned off the hangar and runway. *Christ, I feel like Louie and Rick at the Casablanca airport*, Paul thought. The sky was just starting to lighten. He squinted and leaned forward. "What's that?" He asked, pointing to markings on the side of the plane.

"The royal crest of the Grimaldi family," Parish said. "Seems they were so shook up at the spooky circumstances they had her flown back on the principality's official jet."

The day was already getting hot. Paul wiped his brow, then hooked his fingers into the fence.

"But why come here instead of JFK?" he asked, almost to himself. Once the chain of evidence was this far removed, no autopsy on this end would mean anything. Also, once Monaco, or for that matter any other country, signed off on a death, that was it. Insurance companies would have to accept the cause of death according to the investigating coroner, not at a place of entry some 3,500 miles away from the location of the demise.

Parish was getting bored. "We figure that the Senator's in a panic. He calls Haywood. Haywood takes control."

"Meaning he does nothing," Paul said through gritted teeth.

"Yeah," said Parish, "And then when the dust settles, the M.E. will hit up the Senator for big bucks for that new research center up in Valhalla."

Damn. Rodino had some clout, Paul thought. "Homeland Security, my ass. County cops, Medical Examiner, FBI, Secret Service, CIA. Hell, why didn't they just send Air Force One to pick his wife up? And what the hell was Haywood up to?"

"What else has been going on, Pete?" Paul asked. "And what about that research center?"

"Hell, man, where you been? You're medical. Well, sort of… . Listen: guys moonlighting up there are saying that some sort of infectious disease broke out in the county jail recently. About a dozen or so prisoners were taken by the Haz-Mat team to that research center of Dr. Skeletor – you know, Cardin. Word is, three or four of them died and were cremated on the site – you know, to avoid contamination. Maybe they're tryin' to run you funeral guys out of business."

Paul could not hide his surprise. "They built a crematory on public property?"

"Yeah. I swear to God, there's some sort of the mad-scientist crap going on up there. They're supposed to be doing 'government research' and coming up with ways to deal with biological weapons. Only it sounds more like that island guy."

"Dr. Moreau?" Paul asked, trying not to smile.

"No kidding, man. Rumor says that freaky Cardin is using monkeys, apes, gorillas in his experiments. Sometimes pigs."

Paul interrupted. "Leave the County Executive out of this."

"Nice to see you're not bitter," Parish said without missing a beat. "Anyway, my guess is, they're messing with big-time bio agents, like Level 3 or something. When something goes wrong, those animals are routinely put down and cremated right there on the spot."

"Yeah, sure," said Paul as he looked around impatiently, trying to cut Parish off now. *Where the hell is the casket?* he wondered.

But Parish was on a roll. "Our union reps are pissing mad that they make us escort the Haz-Mat team; most of them are private. Can they force us to do that?"

"Hey, this is Westchester County, Pete, my friend. They can force you to do anything. But if I were you," Paul said with a wide grin, "just remember not to eat their meatloaf or any liver dishes while you're up there."

Parish paused, processing Paul's words, and then said, "Aw, screw you, Arrone."

His car radio crackled. He was ordered to escort the hearse down to the hangar doors.

Paul got in and followed Parish's car. As they hit the tarmac, two black SUVs with police flashers on flanked them. Probably special agents from the FBI's regional office in White Plains, Paul figured. Maybe CIA.

He glanced into the rear-view mirror. More blue-and-white lights. Two more SUVs had fallen in behind the hearse. With the exception of the Royal 727 outside Hangar 12 and the activity near it, the airport was desolate. Except for Senator Frankie the curfew on all aviation between the hours of 11 PM and 6 AM was still in place.

The hearse and its escorts came to a stop just outside and under the famous RCC logo in the arch frame of the hangar. *Rodino Company Cosmetics must be one hell of a lucrative company to afford digs like these,* Paul thought.

Two FBI agents approached, flashed ID, and asked Paul to step out so they could search the hearse. "And we need your license," one said gruffly.

As they worked, Paul looked around. He'd had the same sensation on that first night removal on I-95, and had it occasionally since then. He was somewhere, in the middle of something that everyday people just never experienced. He looked out past the runway at an airport 50 acres larger than New York City's LaGuardia – owned and mis-administered by one of the wealthiest counties in the country. In a couple of hours, this runway would be filled with commercial, corporate and private jets, all coming and going to important places. Yet he was standing here on their turf, and nothing would move until he did his "official duty" for a dead VIP.

He started when the FBI agent patted him on the shoulder. "All clear. Follow us." Paul got back in the hearse, the agents alongside it. Two ground men using hand wands were guiding the royal jet back and onto the runway. Paul could see into the cavernous hangar now. At least two-dozen people stared back at him. Most of them dressed in dark suits.

The casket containing Janice Rodino's remains had been unloaded from the jet and placed on an airport baggage transport. Paul raised his eyebrows and shook his head. Her shipping container had been draped with the American flag, both unusual and improper. That honor was supposed to be bestowed only on those who had served in the armed forces and were honorably discharged. Not quite as unsettling but equally unusual, the shipping container for Mrs. Rodino was flanked by uniformed soldiers. Paul guessed that someone at the top had arranged for Army personnel stationed at nearby airports, and maybe Indian Point, to leave their posts for this, a more important one.

The hearse was waved in, then guided back within two feet of the crate. Paul alighted and was met by yet another agent who identified himself and displayed Secret Service credentials. He handed Paul a sealed pouch, then raised a small recorder to his mouth.

"Special Agent Harold McGowan. 0510 hours. I have placed the sealed pouch with Mrs. Rodino's wedding ring, bracelet and authorizing paperwork into the custody of one Paul Arrone who is to take the pouch and the crated remains back to the Arrone Funeral Home at 12 Weyman Avenue, New Rochelle, until such time as the Westchester County medical examiner, Dr. William Haywood, is able to obtain custody of the same.

"Please state your name and confirm the accuracy of my statement into the recorder, Mr. Arrone."

For a split second, Paul considered responding, *"Yes, I am Paul Arrone, and I am making this removal because the Westchester County* M.E. *is probably too drunk to do so. I am also doing this because the odds are better than even that he probably can't even be located since his most recent divorce. I am doing this because if anyone wanted to find said* M.E., *they need only go a few miles to the Westchester Country Club, where Dr. Haywood could probably be found getting a blow job from some black whore he badgered at the county clinic earlier in the day."*

Paul leaned into the microphone and said, "Yes, I am Paul Arrone and the entire statement by Special Agent McGowan is true, and I agree to all of it."

During the exchange, he heard the back door of his hearse open. He watched out of the corner of his eye as Mrs. Rodino's shipping crate was slid in. The hearse sagged a good two to three inches from the weight. An Army officer approached McGowan and Paul, saluted, and spoke directly to a man standing to McGowan's right. "Special cargo all loaded and ready for transfer, Sir."

The man nodded to McGowan, who said to Paul, "You're all set to go. The county cop – Parish I think his name is – will escort you back to the funeral home and assist you in any way you need. He's been told to stay there until the medical examiner arrives."

As the hearse exited the airport and turned onto Interstate 684 South, Paul dialed the phone number of one of his firm's funeral directors. It was now 6:15 AM. If what he'd just witnessed at the airport was any indication, he had better clear his morning schedule so that he could handle any issues that might arise concerning his "special cargo."

"Joe, I'm going to need you to take care of the DeSimone funeral this morning. I'm just heading back from the county airport with the body of Senator Rodino's wife."

Joe gave a low whistle, and then swung into professional mode. Paul wouldn't tolerate anything less. "No problem. I'm actually at the funeral home now. And listen, that pre-arrangement you made last Saturday died in her home about an hour ago."

"Katherine Jones over on Laurel Place?"

"Yes. Hospice pronounced her, and I'm embalming her now. I figured since you met with the family originally, you would want to see them today. I scheduled them to come in today at 12:30. If you think you're still going to be tied up by then, I can get Ron to come in early."

"No," Paul answered. "I'm pretty certain the M.E. will be down very soon on this call. Just be sure the front door is unlocked, and all the lights are on. And Joe, don't forget to check Mr. De Simone. He had a bruise on his forehead from when he fell at the nursing home. You may have to touch that up if the bruise bled through last night."

"Will do."

"Okay, Joe, see you in about a half-hour. Oh, and one more thing. The family wants his wedding ring to be returned to Mrs. De Simone, along with his war medals. They're in the casket. Leave his wrist watch on, and let the photos of the grandchildren stay inside."

"Gottcha," Joe said. "You'd better take 95 back from the airport. I heard on the news there was an accident on the Hutch."

Paul watched Parish's police car in front of him pass the Hutchinson River Parkway's south entrance on I-287 and head for I-95 south toward New Rochelle. With an escort, he figured, either road would do.

Paul's mind moved back in time. What a wise decision it had been for his grandfather, Dominic Arrone Sr., to move the business to its current location. He had started the business in the ethnic west side of the city some 90 years ago. Just as now, the west side hosted whatever immigrant population landed in the metropolitan area.

At the turn of the 20th century, New Rochelle was mostly a summer retreat for wealthy Manahttanites. During the 1930s, the city became the wealthiest community in New York State, earning the reputation and then the nickname, "Queen City of the Sound."

Almost fifty years ago, Paul's grandfather made his move.

In the early Fifties, with the building of I-95, the major federal interstate that would unite Boston, New York City, and Washington, D.C., and eventually the entire Eastern Seaboard, New Rochelle was bisected between north and south. Those who were wealthy and once lived in the south end of town, moved to the more exclusive north end, or to Connecticut to avoid the increasing urbanization of the downtown. The mansions along the Long Island Sound were converted either into apartment complexes and later condos, or into beach clubs. The Neptune Park section that had housed the city's rich and famous, including early movie actors Eddie Foy and Lillian Gish, was being vacated. It was there that Paul's grandfather decided to relocate. He foresaw the changing of New Rochelle's west side. Once home to German immigrants, then Irish, and at that time, Italians, Dominic Arrone Sr. was witnessing a subtle change. Colombians started to move into the housing in his old neighborhood. Dominic, who also had earned a living as a mason while building his funeral business, found a property that struck most prospective buyers as a white elephant. A very large brick Georgian mansion, along with its carriage house, had once sat on the rolling hills of southern New Rochelle. It required too much maintenance and was too close to the Main Street and the Thruway to tempt a large family.

The Arrone Funeral Home sat on the corner of Main and Weyman avenues just two blocks from an entrance ramp of I-95. It was diagonally across the street from St. Jude Roman Catholic Church, in a neighborhood that had become filled with middle- and upper middle-class Italian Americans and Irish Americans. Its proximity to the major highways of allowed the Arrones easily to draw business from Italian neighborhoods in the Bronx. What Dominic couldn't have anticipated was a new and affluent clientele from Pelham Manor, half of a mile west southwest, and Larchmont, two miles northeast, who would come to use the Home.

It either was his foresight or dumb Guinea luck, Paul thought, but however it happened, Dominic Sr. had left his decedents a solid legacy. A living one at that, he thought wryly.

Paul changed lanes as he came within a few exits of his destination. The hearse, now with an additional passenger, moved more solidly than when empty. His mind started to replay the events of this morning and tried to figure out what all this meant. His cynical side was just beginning to wake up as the sun came up over the horizon.

CHAPTER 10

As he pulled off the Thruway, Paul watched the sun rise, his thoughts focused on the day ahead. It promised to be a hell of a day. He was already tired.

Approaching the Funeral Home, he signaled Parish to turn down the first driveway and go straight past the circular drive. As the hearse approached the rear of the building, Paul saw his father's Towne Car parked in front of the carriage house. Paul pulled past the back of the house facing the carriage house, then backed the hearse up to its right-hand corner which was labeled "Funeral Cars Only."

"Give me a hand, Lieutenant," Paul called. "I want to bring her down to the embalming room area."

"Why not just leave her here?" Parish said.

"First off, I have no idea when that lazy bastard of an M.E. will show up. Secondly, I don't want to leave her in the parking lot because Murphy's Law dictates that as soon as the DeSimone funeral breaks, the M.E. will be unloading her right in front of a crowd of people who won't understand what's going on. They'd probably think we're taking Mr. DeSimone back for lack of payment. And if the M.E. doesn't show until this afternoon, I don't want this hearse tied up for the entire day."

Paul went to the corner of the building and pressed a bell that rang in the prep room, signaling whoever was there that help was needed to bring in a new case. Joe appeared at the bottom of the ramp that ran the entire length of the house, from the bottom front right where the entrance to the basement was, up to the back right of the house where Paul and Parish stood. The ramp was shielded from cars entering the parking lot via this driveway by a row of neatly trimmed arborvitae.

"Joe, we need a church truck." It was brought up and positioned about two feet from the opened hearse. Paul said to Parish, "Stay by the truck and make sure it doesn't roll. Joe and I will slide her out onto the truck."

Paul and Joe lifted the crate, which was much lighter than either expected. They looked at each other with surprised expressions. Paul called out to Parish, "OK, now stay in front as we go down the ramp. If Joe loses his grip, and you're not in front to stop her from hitting the wall down there, you'll be back walking the beat at Glen Island Park. That's a promise."

"Yeah, yeah, yeah."

The three men maneuvered the large crate through the double doors at the bottom of the ramp. They were now below street level and in a large anteroom beneath the main entrance foyer above. To the left, Parish noticed rows of locked cabinets with yellow signs that read, "*Danger—Chemical Storage.*" To the right was another set of double doors that read, "Private—Funeral Personnel Only."

The room's structural columns were wrapped with some sort of padding that Parish guessed prevented caskets or bodies from getting bruised. He sniffed and frowned. The pungent smell of formaldehyde, along with the bright fluorescent lighting and stark white walls and floors, made him feel closed in. He felt like he was in some sort of institution. The windows were painted black for privacy. The only noise he could hear was coming from a radio in the distance.

The sudden hum of water through the pipes overhead put him over the edge. "What the hell is that?" he blurted out. "Who the hell is using the water?" forgetting that more than just dead people occupied the premises. He involuntarily shivered. "How the hell do you guys do this crap?"

"Relax," Paul said, "It's probably just my dad taking a piss upstairs. Don't you guys flush at headquarters?"

"Yeah, we do," Parish answered, "And we all breathe there, too."

It never ceased to amaze Paul how a guy like the lieutenant could go out on the street every day and risk his life without a second thought but then be reduced to mush in a situation like this, when nothing but your mind and your imagination could hurt you.

Paul paused. Guess he just answered his own riddle.

"Paul, did you notice these?" Joe touched something under the crate. "They used thumb screws."

"They loaded her in the hearse for me. I didn't see anything."

"What are you guys talking about?" Parish asked.

"If you ship overseas, or they ship here, most countries have a ton of requirements," Paul answered. "One is that the casket has to be placed in a zinc-lined outer box and soldered shut. The fact that there are thumbscrews on this crate means that either she was shipped in an airtight casket or that both the shipping and receiving countries waved protocol." He turned to Joe. "How far along are you in the prep room?"

"I just started to aspirate her when you rang the buzzer,"

"Aspirate?" Parish asked.

"That is the part of the embalming process where we empty the contents of the organs using suction" Paul answered.

"Go cover up Mrs. Jones, Joe. Lieutenant, you give me a hand. I want to wheel her into the prep room." Joe went ahead of the other two. He removed the trocar from Mrs. Jones, ran water from the slop sink over it, and placed it on the porcelain table next to the body. He then covered her with a sheet, leaving nothing but the universal outline of a human figure.

"All clear," Joe yelled from the embalming room.

"Let's go, Pete."

"Do you really need me in there? What exactly are you going to do, anyway?"

"There is nothing on the other side of that door you'll see that's inappropriate," Paul said. "I just want to remove Mrs. Rodino and her casket from this crate. There's a lift in the prep room I may need."

Paul opened the double doors and with himself at one end and Parish at the other, they started to wheel the crate into the preparation room. Parish was surprised by how large the room was. He had seen the medical examiner's autopsy room, but never an embalming room. He couldn't imagine why all this space was needed.

Parish's eyes first went to the far wall of the gray-tiled room, where he saw two porcelain tables, one with a covered body. Both tables straddled a sink. The table with the body on it had what he guessed was an embalming machine next to it. The fluid in the machine was an orange-reddish color.

A tube snaked from the machine and vanished somewhere under the sheet. Like the room he had just left, this one was lit by fluorescents.

Along one of the walls were glass-paneled cabinets containing bottles of different colored liquids. Below the cabinets was an array of labeled drawers. He could make out *Cotton, Ligature, Tissue Fill, Eye Caps, Mouth Forms,* and *Gloves.* On the wall hung what looked like gas masks.

Paul asked him to bring his end of the crate around to the opposite side of the room. Parish noticed multiple signs warning of hazardous conditions and materials. There was an emergency eye wash station and even a shower, the reason for which Parish didn't care to ask, especially before breakfast.

They removed the flag from the casket and folded it in the traditional triangle. Paul noted that there were no seals from the consulate general's office securing the casket.

With the last of the thumb screws off, Paul and Joe removed the bottom of the box so they would be able to slide the casket onto a church truck. As Paul wheeled the church truck close to the crate, he mused about how the funeral industry used more euphemisms than most industries. "Church truck" was the genteel name given to a piece of metal, which had wheels attached that could move anything from a chair to a piano. House movers called them dollies, the UPS man called them lifts. Here in the inner sanctum of a funeral home they were called *church trucks.*

"What do we have here?" Paul asked as some sort of foam rubber bunting fell to the floor.

Neither Joe nor Paul had ever seen anything like it. Intrigued by what appeared to be a new shipping method, they examined the foam as they removed the rest of it. With a much thicker density than foam rubber, it was more pliable than solid rubber.

There's no way it would be cost-effective to load a shipping crate with this stuff, Paul thought to himself. In fact, it was redundant. "Joe, do you see any benefit to this?" Joe shrugged. "Not really."

"What do you mean?" Parish asked.

"The body was placed in a casket," Paul said. "The casket is required to be air and water-tight. The casket was placed in the shipping container so it wouldn't be damaged in any way during shipping. If this followed normal protocol, there would have been a zinc liner inside the wooden box. If there was a zinc liner inside the box, then when they soldered the zinc liner shut, this stuff would most probably melt and possibly catch fire. Also, if you're the only piece of cargo on a private jet owned by a kingdom, what are the chances of you being tossed around?"

"Then why do you think they did it this way?" Parish asked.

"I'm not sure,"

"What's that stand for?" Parish pointed to a logo.

"LWS stands for LaCroix Worldwide Shipping. It's a European funeral home chain that mostly deals in the shipping of remains."

As Paul lifted one last large piece of foam fill, he exposed the foot end of the casket. "What the hell ..."

The casket looked as though it had been shrink-wrapped in some kind of opaque rubber material. He could make out its silhouette and could tell it was a metal casket. He could see the outline of a rubber gasket under this greenish rubbery material so he knew it was an air- and water-tight casket. In funeral lingo, that was a "sealercouch." As he examined the wrapping, he said more to himself than to the others, "What is this?"

Just then he heard the double doors at the bottom of the ramp slam open against the inside walls of the basement. Seconds later, the double doors to his embalming room were thrust open. One of the doors slammed against the tiled wall of the prep room, the other struck Lieutenant Parish square on the shoulder.

In the bright fluorescent light of the lower level of the Arrone Funeral Home, Dr. William Haywood, chief medical examiner of Westchester County, lunged into the room. Behind him were two African-American males whom Paul knew from the same office. Rich and Tyler drove the vans and made the removals during the day; at night, it would appear, they lifted weights and moonlighted as bouncers.

"Arrone," Haywood shouted, "what the hell do you think your doing? Everything you have your filthy mitts on is official investigatory evidence. I can have you arrested. Who the f*** gave you permission to open that casket?"

Paul straightened. "And good morning to you too, Willy."

Few in the greater New York area ever called the M.E. anything other than "Doctor." Some also referred to him as "Professor." He was, after all, the longest sitting medical examiner in the state. Appointed during the Rockefeller days, some said as a personal favor to the then-governor, he had served fewer than four county executives and eight Board of Legislators chairmen. His closest friends called him William, as did his previous three wives. No one ever called him Bill. Certainly Willy was unthinkable.

"You think this is funny, you stupid s.o.b.?" Haywood roared. "I can and will have you arrested today and sent to the county jail where you'll be wearing a belly shirt and braiding some nigger's hair before your daddy can make bail."

"No need to sugar-coat it, Willy," Paul said maintaining perfect calm. "Why don't you tell me how you really feel?"

The face of the now-shaking medical examiner turned bright red. Rich and Tyler stood frozen at his side. Lieutenant Parish looked pained. Paul wasn't sure whether it was because of the impending battle or his bruised shoulder.

Joe had moved casually to the corner. Damn. If he could get to a phone, he could take action on this formidable match. The odds probably would be 8-to-1 in favor of the nearly 80-year-old doctor whose dentures were now clicking ridiculously in his mouth. Joe's money would be on his boss.

He fantasized about describing it to all who had taken a piece of the action. *Ladies and gentlemen*, there was an awkward moment of silence while each man chose his weapon for round one. Paul, looking tired but confident on one side of the embalming room, dressed in a $2,000 Armani suit. The M.E. on the opposite side, sporting a lab coat and oversized black trifocals around his nearly bald head and beet-like face prepared themselves for battle.

Joe was forced back to reality by the screaming Haywood: "Get me the district attorney on the phone."

Paul pulled a trademark move, glancing quickly over each shoulder, then spinning around to see if there was someone behind him. He then looked directly back at Haywood and asked, "Are you talking to me? I thought you were talking to someone who gives a crap."

Haywood sputtered, but Paul continued. "Why stop there? Why not call the attorney general? And when you get whoever the hell you want on the phone, be sure you tell them that I have a transit permit in my hand with a certified cause of death from a country that doesn't see you as anything other than the pathetic piece of garbage you are," He fanned himself with a sheet of thick paper.

Haywood visibly tried to calm himself, then changed tactics. "What if I call your old man's buddy, Senator Frank Rodino? What if I tell him that I was concerned about verifying how his beloved wife was killed – but when I got to the funeral home where she was taken, some punk-ass hotshot former cop, former politician, dead-end mortician, decided he would screw up the chain of evidence all by himself?"

"Well, Willy... . ." Paul started slowly, "I would have to call the same Senator and explain that I had to drag my ass out of bed in the middle of the night because some alcoholic medical examiner was probably too busy with a black prostitute to go to the airport himself." He grinned into the older man's face.

"And then Willy, I would have to explain to the Senator that while I held a certified copy of how his wife died, written by someone who was actually there on the scene, that you, Willy, just wanted to gut her. And I would explain to the Senator that because his wife was moved by several people, including a funeral home in Monaco, a shipping service, Secret Service, and God knows who else, there was, in fact, no chain of evidence that was worth a crap. And that you just wanted to use the scalpel for sport. No, better yet Willy, I would tell the good Senator that after you got through with his wife he'd better not feed his prize bull mastiff any "Lucky Boy" dog food for a while unless he wants to see his beloved in the bottom of that dish." *It was a stretch*, he thought, *but what the hell. Even Haywood must have heard the dog food rumors at the prison.*

Knock out! Joe thought.

Haywood shook with rage. "Arrone, I am telling you. You are going to get screwed someday because of that smart-ass mouth of yours. I only hope that I live to see it or, better yet, that I play a part in it. "Either way, you'll get what you deserve."

Paul smiled. "I hope so, Willy, because nice things happen to nice people."

Haywood had dropped his cane. As Paul went to pick it up, he said formally, "OSHA regulations dictate that if anything falls on the prep room floor, I have to sterilize it."

Haywood stomped on the cane, just missing Paul's hand.

"You touch anything of mine, Arrone, and I will kill you myself." Paul straightened up slowly.

Haywood exhaled sour breath. "You want to know something, Arrone? Ever since you showed your smug face in county government, a bunch of us always, always felt that the wrong brother had gotten shot that day at that restaurant."

Joe couldn't look. He was sure Paul would pick up the trocar from the embalming table and run it through the old man's heart.

Paul took a few steps back. His face showed no anger. Calm had come over him. The acid churning in his stomach had subsided. For the first time in almost two decades, someone had said out loud what Paul had believed all along. He felt oddly relieved. And to think he had Haywood to thank for it.

"Hey, Willy," Paul all but whispered, "screw you and the black horse you rode in on." Then he said quickly, in an apologetic tone, "I'm sorry, there was no need for me to bring your girlfriend into this."

Haywood turned on his heel and hit his nose on the prep room door that had swung back from its initial thrust. His glasses fell to the floor. "Pick those up, Parish," he snapped, and then turned to Rich and Tyler.

"You two get that crate into the van and to my office in 20 minutes. I want an inventory of everything."

Haywood snatched his eyeglasses from Parish, "You will stay here until she's loaded," he told him in a deadly tone, "And you will escort her to my office. If anything is out of line in the chain of evidence, it will be your ass in a sling."

Haywood stormed from the embalming room. Rather than exit through the ramp door which he had come through originally, he stomped up the stairs to the main floor of the Funeral Home. It probably was Haywood who had called his father, Paul figured, and now he was on his way up to spew some more venom.

The two men who had stood guard like granite statues heard the door at the top of the stairs slam shut and then they doubled over in laughter.

Tyler turned to Paul. "Seee-itt, man. You gotta have the biggest pair of balls in the county."

"I can't freaking believe you made him drop his cane," Rich crowed.

"I was trying for his dentures," Paul responded. "Did you hear those puppies clanging around in his mouth?"

They began to beg Paul to stop. "We gotta work for the s.o.b.," protested Rich. "Yeah, any more trash talk and we'll crack up right in his face."

Paul smiled, "I only spoke the truth."

"Yeah, yeah. Word up, brother." They tried to pull themselves together. The pair reassembled the shipping container and was about to exit with Janice Rodino's casket when Paul yelled, "Hey, Tyler, why don't you stop at the drug store on the way back and pick up some extra-strength Polligrip."

Both men broke into laughter. Tyler shot back, "Now you've done it, you crazy nigga.' I won't be able to keep a straight face all week."

As the two men exited up the ramp past what used to be windows but were now exhaust fans for the prep room, Paul could hear them howling with laughter. "Blackhorse," one said, "His freaking cane on the embalming room floor," the other answered between hiccups of amusement. Their laughter grew dimmer as they got to their van. Joe turned to Paul and asked "How could you be sure Haywood wouldn't have you arrested?"

"No way. This battle, like most of them, was won before it began. What did the doctor have in his arsenal? A few political big-wigs who would sell him out in a heartbeat? Anyone who would listen to that crazy old man has to be as corrupt as he is. I, on the other hand," Paul said with a deliberately false tone of modesty, "have an arsenal, thanks to my dad and brothers – an arsenal that can't be beat in Westchester County. The three most important things: Money, money and money."

He stared thoughtfully at where Mrs. Rodino's casket had been, and spoke more to himself than to Joe. "That old fart was shooting at me with a bow and arrow. I returned fire with a Lars Missile launcher equipped with nuclear warheads. I was – how do they put it? – shamelessly over-equipped." Paul turned and cocked an ear to the M.E. van pulling away. "And you know what? I felt no shame at all."

Joe's eyes widened. He was surprised to hear Paul share his own feelings.

"Finish up in the prep room, Joe, while I open up the chapel for the De Simone family. And thanks."

Joe studied his boss thoughtfully. One thing Paul hadn't acknowledged: Haywood's remark about his dead brother.

CHAPTER 11

Rather than go down the basement hallway to the stairs leading to the main floor as Haywood had, Paul went out and up the ramp door. He did that once in a while to assess the grounds as if he were seeing them for the first time. Current and past employees never dared deride Paul's core principle that little details are extremely important in this industry. They're what separate a good funeral director and home from the others. It's very easy in this and any business to get comfortable with less than the best."

You may not think anything of leaving the outside trash cans uncovered, he would say, *but if your wife was laid out here for visiting, and you saw a pile of garbage being blown around the side yard, you might say to yourself, "I hope they take better care of her than they do this."*

The same holds true for how you place the flowers, do the makeup, dress the bodies, he would continue. *All the things that you may think are OK for you, may not be OK for the family. You're only living with the surroundings for a few minutes. But for a family that is sitting there for two to three days in grief, staring at their loved one, items become magnified a hundred times.*

As Paul walked the ramp, he thought it was a shame that Haywood didn't leave this way. He could have captured him and his anger on the surveillance cameras.

Paul had cameras installed at every entrance and mounted on the building to scope out the entire driveway. One-way monitors had been set up in the embalming room, Paul's office, the employee lounge and the upstairs apartment. If someone walked into the Home, a quick glance would tell whether it was a first call by a family or simply the gardener heading to the water cooler. Likewise, deliveries, whether they were flowers, caskets or anything else, were immediately apparent.

Joe looked up at the embalming room monitor when he heard the buzzer ring. He saw Paul waving what must have been a piece of newspaper he had found in the parking lot. There wasn't much sense in trying to convince Paul that that paper wasn't there when Joe pulled up earlier. Joe inhaled deeply; it already was *one of those days.*

Paul walked down the driveway toward the front of the building. He stopped at the end and turned around to get an overview of how things looked this morning. The driveway bifurcated upon entry. One could either go straight to the rear, to the parking lot, or bear left onto the circular drive to the front door. When Paul looked straight down the driveway, he saw it was clean all the way to the carriage house. The arborvitae, he nodded approvingly, was neatly trimmed. He looked left up the circular drive. Placards with "Family Car Parking Only" on them were clearly displayed.

As he walked up the driveway's slight incline, he thought of his grandfather again. He had shown great vision when he raised the driveway to eliminate the need for three steps that used to lead to the flagstone veranda. Paul stepped onto it, making a mental note that a couple of flags would have to be balanced in a year or so. He probably would do that, along with some re-pointing of the red brick front and repainting of the white columns. He heard a satisfied buzz. He might get rid of the rose bushes that lined the sides of the veranda and replace them with some sort of evergreens. Paul couldn't count how many bee stings he had received over the years because of those damn bushes.

He unlocked the large front door and stepped into the foyer. He was greeted by that universally recognizable funeral home smell. Most people thought it was embalming fluid; some thought it was the dead bodies. Paul knew that it actually was the ever-present flowers that were decomposing at a far faster rate than his clients.

He flicked a switch, lighting three chandeliers hanging in the center hall colonial. He looked around; all the Chippendale furniture was properly placed and polished.

Down the hall, past the first door on his left, was the former front parlor that now served as a reposing room for smaller funerals than the

DeSimone's. This was known as Chapel A, the Gretchen Loretel chapel. To Paul, this like the other chapels belonged to a particular memory of a person or a family that occupied his mind. It was here during his first month at the funeral home that he was called out of the office by Marge to "handle a situation" in chapel A. As Paul entered the chapel, he was greeted by a woman who had been standing over the body of her deceased sister. She was holding in her hand the blouse he had previously dressed the decedent in. It seemed that Gretchen had thought she saw her sister breathe. She thought her sister was still alive. She also thought her sister was the Virgin Mary.

Paul's job as the newest and youngest employee was to get this situation under control, get the clothing back on Gretchen's sister who now lay half dressed in the casket, and to make sure that Gretchen Loretel didn't disturb the three other families that were grieving in the other chapels. Paul had come to realize much later in his career what he tried to comprehend during the day he sat in chapel A with Gretchen. *This woman was not crazy*, as he first thought. She was not uneducated nor was she in financial need. Quite the opposite. She was a highly educated, sane woman from an extremely wealthy New Rochelle family, who simply was in the throes of severe denial over her sister's death. She was acting irrationally because she was uncontrollably and completely in the first stage of grieving. Paul sat with her long after the episode was resolved. He stayed in Chapel A with her for the entire time of the visiting hours. He comforted her and they became friends for the remaining 16 years of her life, until she herself was reposing in Chapel A, or as Paul knew it, The *Gretchen Loretel Chapel.*

He went into the second room that used to serve as the main living room. Chapel B, to Paul known as the Billy Johnstone Chapel, was the most frequently used reposing chapel, with caskets placed in front of the old fireplace. Paul could still see the nick in the ornate door molding made when Billy's casket hit it as he and his father rolled him into the chapel. Billy Johnstone was just a few years older than Paul. He had graduated from New Rochelle High school five years before Paul and was drafted into the army to serve in Vietnam. Billy's father was an accountant in town who took care of the books for many of the local businesses including the funeral home; his mother was a nurse at New Rochelle Hospital. Billy was in Vietnam for just three months when his platoon was ambushed. Most of his comrades were killed. Billy suffered both physical and mental damage from the battle and was sent back home.

Paul's dad told Paul and his brother that Billy suffered from "shell shock" and that we should be grateful that he came home alive. Gratitude was not quite the emotion that Paul and his fellow high school buddies showed Billy. The more withdrawn Billy became, the more the teenagers would taunt him. They called Billy "Boo Radley," and would throw fire-crackers in his path and watch as Billy became catatonic. The only time the neighborhood kids treated Billy with any kindness was when he accompanied his parents to Sunday mass at St. Jude's Church. Here, the kids would greet them with "Good morning Mr. and Mrs. Johnstone; good morning Billy" in their best "Eddy Haskel" voices.

The first call about Billy's death was taken by Paul's dad who still received all the first calls personally. He, in turn, called Paul at two in the morning to help with the house removal. Paul and his dad arrived at the small clapboard colonial house on Pintard Avenue around three that morning during a torrential downpour. They were greeted at the door by Mr. Johnstone who expressed gratitude for the two of them coming out "on a night like this," as if it weren't their job. Mr. Johnstone then, very methodically and somewhat clinically, explained that his son had hanged himself in his bedroom. "I heard his music playing later than usual. When I went upstairs, I found him."

Paul's father knew enough to ask Mr. Johnson where his wife Claire was, so that he might extend his condolences to her. They were escorted into the living room where Mrs. Johnstone sat fully dressed in her nurse's uniform on the very edge of an overstuffed easy chair. She was talking to police officer Shehan who was first called to the scene. When she saw the two of them enter the room, she immediately got up, and before either of them could say anything, kissed Paul's dad and said "Thanks so much, Dom, for coming out." She then turned to Paul and said "My dear, let me get you a towel. You are soaked to the bone." All Paul could think was how horribly he and his friends had treated Billy years earlier.

Shehan led them up three sets of stairs to Billy's bedroom. He told them that the medical examiner would release Billy as soon as Paul's father called him. Paul's father opened the door to the attic bedroom that Billy had moved into after he came back from the war, and Paul entered first. The large room was lit by a single bare light bulb at the center of the ceiling. Music from a tape recorder played on a continuous loop – Elton John's "Ticking."

... An extremely quiet child they called you in your school reports
He's always taken interest in the subjects that he's taught.

The greenish linoleum floor was polished to a high sheen. The odor of stale cigarettes seemed to ooze from the walls. To the left was a single bed void of any bed spread, its white sheet and army blanket tucked perfectly neat and ready for inspection. At the foot of the bed lay battle fatigues folded neatly with perfectly polished boots lying directly next to them.

... At St. Patrick's every Sunday, Father Fletcher heard your sins
Oh, He's unconcerned with competition he never cares to win.

On the wall to the right directly opposite the bed was the American Flag tacked up fully opened. Further down that same wall, mounted on peg board, were rifles, bayonets and other paraphernalia clearly marked from WWI and WWII. Wars, Paul thought, where homecoming soldiers weren't vilified.

... Now you'll never get to heaven Mama said
Remember Mama said
Ticking, ticking
Grow up straight and true blue
Run along to bed
Hear it, hear it, ticking, ticking.

Directly ahead of them in front of the palladium window was a desk with a phone. The officer told Paul's father to call the M.E. but not to disturb any of the "stuff" on the desk. The other stuff on the desk was comprised of two guns, an automatic weapon, four grenades, a tear gas canister and an invitation to Billy's ten year high school reunion party.

> *… They had you holed up in a downtown bar screaming for a priest*
> *Some gook said "His brain's just snapped" then someone called the police.*

As they stood at the desk and looked to the alcove under the sloped ceiling of the finished attic, they could see an open closet door: Billy's naked, twisted feet were visible at the bottom of the door. Paul walked over to assess the situation as his father dialed the medical examiner's number. Billy was lying on the floor of his closet in his bathrobe with a broken clothes rod and strewn clothes all around him. He had hanged himself with a leather belt. Sometime after he died, the weight of his lifeless body finally broke the rod and whatever clothing was left on the rod now covered him.

> *… Don't ever ride on the devil's knee Mama said*
> *Remember mama said*
> *Ticking, ticking*
> *Pay your penance well, my child*
> *Fear where angels tread*
> *Hear it, hear it, ticking, ticking.*

The stench of nicotine now gave way to the smell of urine and defecation, a byproduct of Billy's muscles going limp. Paul shifted his stare to the wall to the left of the closet where framed photos of Presidents Nixon, Ford, Carter and Reagan hung proudly in a row. Of all the things that ran through Paul's mind as he stood there waiting – for what like seemed an eternity – for his father to end his conversation, was whether or not there was still time, somehow, in someway, for him to apologize for his behavior years earlier.

... , You've slept too long in silence mama said
Remember Mama said
Ticking, ticking
Crazy boy, you'll only wind up with strange notions in your head
Hear it, hear it, ticking, ticking.

Paul, his father and officer Shehan made their way down the three flights of stairs, out into the rain drenched morning, past the daffodils and into the hearse. His father went back into the house to set up a time for the Johnstones to come in to make arrangements. When he got back into the hearse, Paul could smell scotch on his breath. Paul felt the need to sit closer to his father and to talk. Talk about anything. "Pop, why do you think Mr. and Mrs. Johnstone were so unemotional tonight?" As the hearse drove through the dark wet streets of New Rochelle on its way back to the funeral home, Paul's father gave his take on things.

"Son, almost everyone who suffers from some loss goes through five stages of grief: Denial, Anger, Bargaining, Depression and Acceptance. You are going to have to learn that there is no time table for this. Some people will take months to come to closure, others may take years. Some may never get to acceptance. Your job is to try to understand where the families are and help them along as best you can."

"But Pop, how can anyone get over their only son's death in a matter of hours?"

Paul's father pulled the hearse over to the curb and looked directly at his son. " I don't ever want you to judge anyone who comes into our home for help. There just is no right or wrong way that people will grieve. I suspect that the Johnstones did *not* get over their son's death in a matter of hours. No sir, if you want my opinion, those decent parents lost their only boy a dozen years ago in a rice field in Asia. And now they are probably relieved that he's in a better place."

"What about you? Do you believe that he is in a better place?"

His father's answer both surprised and upset Paul. "I absolutely do son, because he is not here."

For the entire time of Billy's wake in Chapel B, while the community paid their respects to the Johnstones, Billy's friends stood honor guard at either end of his casket. To the right were three World War II veterans who used to drink with Billy at the American Legion Post 8. To the left were two soldiers who served in Vietnam, the effects of Agent Orange and torture painfully apparent on their blotchy faces.

So from that day forward Paul thought of Chapel B as Billy Johnstone's Chapel.

Just outside Chapel B rose the grand staircase to the upper floors. Paul's grandfather had left this and the Juliet balcony above it untouched when he renovated the old mansion into a funeral home. He had opted to close off the second floor by putting up a sheet-rocked wall with an oak door beyond the line of vision from the first floor. A small sign hung from a blue velvet rope strung across the bottom of the staircase stating "No Admittance."

The first set of doors behind the staircase led to what used to be an inordinately large oak-paneled dining room with a fireplace. This room had two service swing doors on either side of the fireplace that had provided separate entry and exit for servants to avoid colliding with and breaking any fine china. The part of this room closest to the French entry doors now served as an arrangement room, where families made decisions around a dining table and six chairs near the fireplace. On the oak-paneled wall opposite hung the Arrone history, or as Paul called it, the "I Love Me Wall." All the Arrone men's funeral directing licenses were hung there, including John's.

Client families who asked, or those who welcomed a distraction, would be shown, for example, his grandfather's two licenses. In those days he would tell them that you received a license to embalm and a separate license to direct funerals. Today, the two are incorporated into the one funeral director's license. Invariably this would prompt people to ask Paul, "You mean you're licensed to embalm, too?" Or the ever-popular, "You don't actually embalm yourself, do you?" Paul always loved visualizing embalming himself.

Interspersed with the documents on the "I Love Me Wall" were photos of Paul, separately and together, with politicians and sometimes members of the public through the years.

Beyond the arrangement room was Paul's private office. Through the swing doors off the arrangement room was the casket display room where tiny cross-sections of caskets were laminated to the wall. The old casket room, now used less frequently, sat in the basement where full size caskets sat gathering dust. Next to the new arrangement room was the flower room, which in the Home's glory days was a kitchen.

Through the swing door off Paul's office was an employee lounge. Both the employee lounge and the casket display room lay adjacent to the flower room, which used to be a breakfast room, because the plumbing was on that side of the building. Paul's grandfather built a ladies' room/sitting room on the opposite side of the hall past the back door. Adjacent to the ladies' room, old man Arrone converted the then powder room into a men's room.

Heading back to the front from the men's room was a service area. Half of this space housed an elevator that brought caskets and bodies up from the basement. Next to this area was an office that was used by the part-time bookkeeper, Marge Anderson. In front of the service room heading toward the front of the building was what used to be a music room, and which was now Chapel C. It was diagonally across from the staircase.

From chapel C all the way down the rest of the hallway and back to the front door lay chapel D.

When the house was originally built, this room was used as a formal ballroom. It had ornate colonial dental moldings and trim. The room had eight ceiling to floor windows, four of which opened onto the veranda; this Chapel was used for very large funerals and for religious services that were held in the funeral home rather than at a church or synagogue. Paul thought to himself that the senator's wife should be laid out in Chapel D – should they get the funeral.

Paul could hear Frank Sinatra music coming from his office. If "old blue eyes" was playing, it always meant his father was in the building. Paul passed through the arrangement room and into his office. His father sat at Paul's desk with a family worksheet in front of him. Paul figured he should take the offensive to mitigate any gripes his father had about the prep room episode with Haywood.

"What are you doing out of bed? Mom told me you weren't to leave the house for another week."

"Blah, blah, blah," answered his father. He leaned forward. "What the hell did you do to Haywood downstairs? What were you thinking of? Do you have any idea how good the county was to me when things were not as good as they are now? For Crissakes, the public administrator kept food on our table by giving us business we would have never seen."

Paul answered in an annoyed tone. "I'm not looking to argue with you Pop. I may have been born at night, but it wasn't last night. How can you sit there and look me in the eyes and act as if this family ever needed a hand out? It is beyond ludicrous. And even if you did get business that put food on our table from those sleazebags, I'd bet you a brand-new hearse that if I added up the business they *may* have given you and put it opposite all the money you have given them, I am sure the scale would tip in *their* favor."

Paul was angry, something he rarely showed his father. "I'm sure Mom is going to love to hear that she couldn't feed her family."

Dominic interrupted. "I never said they put food on the table. I said they were good to us."

"Well, I heard 'food on the table,' so who do you think mom is going to believe?"

"One thing we all can agree on," Dominic said, "is that you can be one pain in the ass when you want to be."

Paul was sick of Haywood and wanted to focus on the far more pressing issue.

"So, Pop, do you think you will be able to hold onto this funeral, or should I send the apprentice out to help you?" Paul reached over his father's stomach for the bottle of Maalox he kept in the desk drawer and gestured at the local newspaper, *The Standard Ledger*, one of the few independent papers left in Westchester that had not become part of the Gannett chain. It also was owned and operated by the treasurer of the Westchester GOP, which accounted for its hefty list of advertisers and its scoop on the day's major story. The *Standard* had devoted the entire front page to Janice Rodino's death. "Senator Rodino's Wife Killed in Car Accident" blazed the main headline. The subtitle read, "Westchester's princess killed on bizarre coincidental curve that killed Princess Grace." The shameless and yet resourceful editor had found an old black-and-white photo of Mrs. Rodino that showed her hair pulled straight back and had run it next to a similar picture of the late Princess Grace.

"You're not going to goad me into a fight like you did Haywood," his father said. "We both know the answer to that question."

Indeed Paul did. He glanced over at unopened bottles of Jack Daniels and Grey Goose that his father had gotten ready and which, Paul knew, would soon make their way to the Rodino farm in Scarsdale. Nobody this side of the Hudson River could outsell his father when it came to funerals.

"I spoke to Frank a half-hour ago," Dominic said, rising and getting his suit jacket. "I told him we would be up to his house by 10."

Paul said sarcastically, "I know you're probably getting too old to make arrangements by yourself, but if you don't mind, I would rather you go alone. There are a bunch of things I need to do here today." His father grunted, waved him off, and picked up the booze.

"Hey, Pop," Paul said as he took his place at the desk, "D.F.I.U."

Dominic looked up with raised eyebrows. "D.F.I.U." hadn't been used around here since, well, since he used to tell Johnny and Paul that in their early training days, as they took on more responsibility. His shorthand for Don't Frigg It Up soon became his son's as well. Funny, he had forgotten that.

"Smartass," his father said. "I'll call you from the car after I meet with Frank."

Paul started to leave, then caught himself. "Hey, by the way. I have a question for you: Why would someone ship a body overseas in an ordinary container when they could have sold a zinc liner?"

"That's easy," his father answered. "They wouldn't."

Exactly, thought Paul, *exactly*. Dominic left and Paul sat at his desk, turned to his computer and started asking questions using new software made especially for funeral homes. With this software a funeral home could take care of routine matters, like logging in vital statistics that would be used as a permanent record, write an obituary and fill out the death certificate. It also could print prayer cards and chart casket sales and funeral expenses. It allowed cross-referencing of families a number of ways. One could enter a surname, or any name of a sibling, or a maiden name, and the computer would list all matching families that had done business with the Arrone Funeral Home since its formation. The most arduous task was entering data from past decades. But once that was done, the program allowed a home to spot trends in the industry that would normally go unnoticed.

Paul began inputting queries of all clients either shipped to another town or country, or shipped to Arrone's from another part of the United States or country altogether.

Names started to appear on the screen. Paul searched, made notes, then sat back staring.

He buzzed Marge on the intercom. Marge Anderson, in her late sixties and by appearances the stereotypical librarian, had started working for Paul's father 40 years ago. She handled billing of families, paying salaries, and ordering and tracking supplies for the Funeral Home. She coordinated Paul's schedule as well as the staff's and would pitch in as a receptionist to greet a family should all licensed staff be out of the building. She did all that while working only part-time.

Marge's office was across the hall from the arrangement room, next to the service elevator. Although small, it was the brightest room in the house, not only because it was painted yellow, but because she kept plants everywhere. She had removed the drapes and blinds from the large window and always kept the plate glass spotless.

"Marge," Paul spoke into the intercom. She could hear tension in his voice and something rare for Paul, a pitch of excitement. "Could you get Ron to meet the Jones family for me at 12:30? And I need you to set up a lunch with Gerard Bianco from Alverez Funeral Home. Tell him it's important. I can meet him anywhere in Mount Vernon that's good for him." He clicked off before she could answer.

CHAPTER 12

P aul parked the Funeral Home's service vehicle directly in front of Angelo's restaurant on Arthur Avenue in the Bronx, just as Gerard was walking through the front door. They had met when Gerard served his apprenticeship at the Arrone Funeral Home. Gerard went on to work for a large funeral home chain in Manhattan, and then was recruited by LaCroix Worldwide Shipping when it purchased the Alverez Funeral Home.

The stock options that had once been the bread and butter of job retention for the large conglomerates had long since dried up. Company stock that Gerard had in his 401k account five years before LaCroix approached him was valued then at 78 dollars a share. Now it was being traded on the market for 75 cents. It took little effort for the LaCroix team to recruit Gerard and many others of the conglomerate's employees to work for their firm. It was a win-win for both sides. The employees had the opportunity to feed their greed with new unproven stock, and LWS had the benefit of experienced licensed personnel to run their ever-expanding funeral empire. The conglomerates paid top dollar for every available funeral home that came on the market. They were able to outbid almost everyone else because, much like government, they would buy their prey with over-priced stock rather than good old-fashioned hard cash. When LWS approached the Arrones years ago to try to purchase their funeral home and cemetery, they employed Gerard in hopes that a friendly face would tip the balance in LaCriox's favor.

Gerard and Paul remained friendly. In addition to seeing each other at the Westchester County Funeral Directors Association dinners and continuing education classes, the two occasionally helped each other when a casket was needed or an extra man required for a house removal.

Gerard was corporate all the way, which in the funeral industry often resulted in uncomfortable complications. Many who made it to management were faced with the emotional and ethical conflict of working in an industry that is based on personal contact, family comfort and local home-town connections. In an impersonal corporate setting, commissions were paid on casket sales and employees were forced to sell future funeral arrangements to grieving family members. These people also had the dilemma of working for companies that paid them better than any local funeral home could, while at the same time denying them future ownership of their own business. In his forties, Gerard had begun to realize he had little hope of owning his own funeral home – while having to meet the ever-increasing financial demands of "Corporate."

Paul had noticed Gerard's disillusionment when he visited him at his office a few months ago. The phone rang. Just before actually answering it, Gerard blurted out, "Alverez Funeral Home, how may I hump you?" He then picked up the phone and asked, "Alverez Funeral Home, how may I help you?"

Paul entered Antonio's a few seconds after Gerard to find him already at the bar. When he saw Paul, he put a big grin on his face and said, "Hey, Goombah, how have you been?" They exchanged more pleasantries, shared a couple of beers and sat down to lunch.

"So how has corporate been treating you?" Paul asked.

"Same old crap, just different assholes," Gerard answered. "How is business at the Arrone establishment? Are you guys finding it slower than usual this year?"

"Yes," Paul said. "I heard from the association that the death rate is off so most places are seeing fewer cases. Are you full management now? Or do you still get your hands dirty?"

"Management" Gerard said. "But it doesn't really matter much up here in Westchester because all the embalming is done out of the Park Chester branch in the Bronx."

"No kidding? You mean to tell me you guys don't do any preparation at all?"

"No prep, no dressing, and no cosmetics. We're as close to being white people as you can get."

Clearly, Gerard was comfortable with divulging his company's policies, so Paul figured he would dig for dirt immediately in case either of their beepers were to drag them away.

They plunged into the meal. "I've been wondering, Gerard, how the hell do you guys ship those cases back to Colombia so inexpensively? I would lose money if I met your prices."

"I'm not certain of everything," Gerard said between bites of eggplant parmigiana, "but I will tell you this: Out of the eight employees here in Mount Vernon and the fifteen in the Bronx, I am only one of two licensees that the company employs."The big honchos hire more 'illegals' than my uncle's landscaping company."

"How do you guys get away with that?"

"Combination of things. Somehow, whenever a state inspector is about to pay a visit, corporate transfers licenses from their other branches and they open up our prep room, and it all looks good. Once in a blue moon, corporate messes up and they pay a fine. Bottom line is, I don't think anyone in this state gives a crap about how, why, or where any spic dies, or how we bury them, or how much it costs to rid them from the area. Dead or alive," Gerard said, "as long as they leave."

He wiped his mouth and threw his napkin into his lap in frustration. "I tell you, man, if you had the time, I could show you something that would make you embarrassed you went into this industry."

Bingo, thought Paul. "Gerard, I have all the time in the world. Drink up."

When lunch was over, Paul followed Gerard the short distance from Arthur Avenue to the Alverez Funeral Home in Parkchester. They pulled up to what used to be the largest Jewish funeral home in the metropolitan area, before the opening of Co-op City emptied the neighborhood and turned it into a Spanish ghetto.

Gerard braked at the curb with Paul behind him. After they got out, Paul asked why they hadn't parked in the home's enormous lot.

"Wait till you see the circus going on back there," Gerard said glumly. "Then you'll understand."

As they walked down the driveway, Gerard told Paul that this branch was where they prepared all the bodies for shipment out of JFK airport for all ten of LaCroix Worldwide Shipping's metropolitan funeral homes.

When they turned the corner to the back of the building, Gerard saw what he had anticipated: five gray vans with the LWS logos and their drivers seated nearby on overturned milk crates drinking beer and shooting the bull.

"Paolo," yelled Gerard, "what have I told you about this? Do I have to make a call to Paris myself to keep you from screwing up?"

"No, Mr. Gerard. This is just our coffee break."

Actually, Gerard didn't care either way. He knew that if he made a stink, or simply raised his voice, the odds were slim that Paolo would tell anyone of his visit to this branch. Illegals seldom brought attention to themselves.

"All right," Gerard said, "But next time I'll have no choice but to call LaCroix himself. You know, he always asks me about you and I always stick up for you."

"Thank you, Mr. Gerard."

"Let's keep things moving," Gerard said, pushing away Paolo's words with a wave of his hand. With that, the men rose, opened the rear doors of the van closest to the building and with one man on each side, slid out a stretcher.

"Is that a conveyor belt?" Paul asked in surprise.

"Sure is," said Gerard. He went on to tell Paul that everyone in the organization knew you could only show up at this location with a two-man stretcher. No collapsible legs and nothing too cumbersome for this system.

"We also take bodies right on the belt here in a body bag or a disaster pouch. Follow me."

As he and Paul walked down the other side of the steps that held the conveyor belt, Gerard barked, "Keep 'em coming, guys."

Gerard kicked the swinging door open. The stench and cacophony from within assaulted them. Paul, so used to death, actually reeled. He quickly shook it off and entered one of the largest preparation rooms he had ever seen. Completely tiled from ceiling to floor in light blue tiles, it must have been one hell of an embalming room in its day, Paul thought. Today, Salsa blared from a boom box whose handle and knobs were covered in dried blood.

It smelled and looked to Paul like a slaughterhouse; worse, in fact. Filth and blood were on almost everything in sight. Embalming chemicals, which under OSHA regulations had to be in storage cabinets with proper labels, were in cartons strewn about the huge basement floor. One of the embalmers was actually standing on a case of cavity fluid to work on the corpse that was assigned to him.

"Why don't they turn on the exhaust fans?" Paul asked. "Don't they work?"

"Sure they do," Gerard replied, "but then they can't hear that crap Spic music they listen to."

"But what about the fumes?" Paul asked. God, didn't they even know the risk of septal cancer?

"Hey," Gerard answered with an exaggerated shrug, "If they weren't here, they probably would be doing cocaine somewhere. I figure we're doing their noses a favor."

As they walked, Paul took out a handkerchief to wipe his face and surreptitiously cover his nose.

"So now let me show you how we can undercut you independents," said Gerard. "You see these eight men stationed at each embalming table? Of these eight men and the ones we saw upstairs, there isn't one with a funeral director's license. Paolo's the only one who went to school to study mortuary science, but he couldn't pass the national boards. So he's their recruiter. Now here's where it gets hinkey."

Can it get more hinkey than this? Paul asked himself.

"Each of the eight people you see here is trained to do one or two specific tasks," Gerard continued. Esteban at table number 1 is trained to raise arteries and, should the body be posted, err.... . I mean autopsied." Gerard feigned a professional voice, "Esteban would tie off the arteries and veins and move on to the next table. Jose is trained to inject fluid, and then he moves to the next table to do the same thing. Juan treats the viscera if the body is autopsied, which they almost always are down here. Jose number 2 only does suturing. Alphonso removes the bodies from the conveyer belt and washes them down at the end of the process. Chavo here dresses them. Julio puts on the cosmetics and Chico floats around to help whoever needs him. If any one of them runs into trouble, they call Paolo."

Paul tried to interrupt with a question.

"Hold on," said Gerard. "Now as day laborers, LWS pays these 'experts' $50 cash a day. No benefits. No health plan. No retirement. No stock options. There is no way you guys can compete with this.

"This," he said crossing his arms, "is as brilliant as Ford's first assembly line."

This is obscene, Paul thought. "Why not just train them to do a complete case and try to bring them into the job legitimately?"

"First off, legitimate costs money. Corporate doesn't want to spend money. Secondly – and this is where I think they were brilliant – by only training them to do one or two things in a prep room, they're useless to any other funeral home. So there's no risk of losing a worker to a competitor. Third, should one of them go to the state inspector to complain, or get hurt or sick in this room, corporate would deny that they ever worked here. If the employee was asked to explain the aspects of embalming, not one of them would be able to tell any more than one-eighth of what an embalming job requires.

"Hell," he said with a laugh, "that's less than you can find out watching *Six Feet Under*."

Paul searched for something to say. "What a frigging disgrace," he finally muttered.

They continued to look around. The workers ignored them.

"Don't tell me what I see over there on that shelf is what I think it is," Paul said, pointing to a jar. It was sitting next to a pair of pliers, three-quarters filled with pieces of gold and white.

"Christ," said Gerard, "it's really amazing. These guys can barely speak English but they could tell you what gold is trading at on any given day, at any half-hour interval." The dentists in Bogotá had not yet discovered the benefits of amalgam fillings. This coupled with the resurgence of gangs and its associated ghetto fashions in the metropolitan area gave the workers at Parkchester their one and only job perk. There was little doubt that the gold in this jar would be turned into rings and necklaces to support the "bling" craze.

"Why the blue toe tags on two of those bodies" Paul asked?

"Very observant. The autopsied bodies that have blue tags are only to be prepped and put in the holding room next to the embalming room. It means that someone from corporate will be down to personally finish the job. I think these are the bodies that are going to be viewed at a Colombian branch of LWS.

"I even have seen this treatment for bodies prepared for shipment to other countries as long as they are going to one of the corporate chains. Rather than risk one of these $50-per-day cowboys screwing up the treatment of viscera, I assume they prefer to ship a body with the least amount of organs so that they won't suffer embarrassment at the other end."

"What do you do with the viscera?" Paul asked.

"Most of it we toss over there." Gerard pointed to the red medical waste barrel. "Some of it, mostly organs and some bone matter, corporate sells to some lab."

Paul was astounded, at the ethical issues this raised, but also because he knew how much it costs funeral home operators to dispose of their medical waste.

He wondered why corporate would give up the opportunity to dispose of the viscera in the most cost effective way, which was to bury it with the body. Paul decided to press Gerard on this issue: "Does that make any sense to you?" he asked.

Gerard thought for a moment and shrugged. "Maybe there was an incident where hardening compound wasn't used, or the chest cavity wasn't sutured properly, and when a family overseas saw their loved one with a chest full of decomposing guts, maybe, just maybe, they threw a hissy fit."

"How the hell would I know?" he added in exasperation. "Look around yourself and you tell me the odds of having an incident when you're paying 50 bucks to a guy who will process ten to fifteen bodies a day. All I know is, the ones that are blue-toe tagged get special care. That means we dry the body cavities with carbolic acid, seal every possible leakage point and leave them overnight in the side room until corporate picks them up and finishes the job themselves at their uptown headquarters.

"It's the same process we follow when a shipper comes in from overseas with a blue acrylic paint on the tiny casket key cover. Once you see the blue, you call headquarters and put the casket in the side room. They do everything from there. I assume the same rationale applies. If someone is shipped from Rome or Bogotá to LaCroix, I wouldn't think that their 5th Avenue funeral branch wants some coked-up spic to handle the remains. Like they say, it's not rocket science we're talking about here."

Paul knew that all too well. He just hadn't figured out what "it" really was.

CHAPTER 13

Thursday night, July 1

I n between duties Thursday, Paul made some calls, trying to find out what he could about Janice Rodino, her body, and any other news. In the afternoon, his father walked into his office. "We got it," he said.

"The service?" Paul asked.

"Yes," Dominic blurted. "It will be Sunday, July 4th, appropriately patriotic. That will allow time for officials to arrive in Westchester. And with Monday the official holiday, that still gives everybody a three-day weekend. Except us, of course. We have a lot to do between now and the service."

"Where's the body?"

"Still at the morgue. We get it tomorrow. I hear they'll autopsy her tonight."

Paul watched his father leave. He knew the old man worried about the crowds, the press. He wanted to help him more, but Paul needed to talk to Cullan. He had a lot of questions that needed answers.

That night, they met for their usual first-Thursday-of-the-month dinner at Mama Tenore's Italian Restaurant on Post Road just east of the Larchmont border. They liked to think of it as their own private Kiwanis Club.

The tradition had started a few weeks after Paul's first night call, the jumper from I-95. Something had changed between them since that night. Maybe, he reflected, then-Sergeant Cullan had started to understand and even respect the "new" Paul. After all, a new life, and new responsibilities, had emerged after John's death.

Gradually, over time, the pair fell into the first-Thursday pattern. Although they would see each other on other occasions, the monthly dinners had become their private taking-stock, a time for "what-would-have-been-could-have-been."

Cullan was already seated at their usual table, in the back far right corner where they could talk without being overheard. Paul had arrived on time but noticed that Cullan was already half-way through his vo. As retirement got closer, his old friend was drinking more and more.

"How's it going, Cappy?" Paul said. He'd been calling Cullan that since he made captain some 15 years ago. It was what Cullan had aspired to his whole life and what Paul knew he deserved. Being made police commissioner three years ago seemed anticlimactic to both men. "Cappy" stuck.

"I put you down for the forensic seminar next month at the Tarrytown Marriott," said Cullan. "It's supposed to be about how mistakes are made with close kin DNA."

Even though Paul's temporary leave of absence some 20 years ago had become a *de facto* leave of the department, Cullan had included Paul in most of New Rochelle's police training.

"Thanks, Cappy. What am I going to do when you retire for a cushy consulting job in a few months?"

"Who said I'm retiring?" shot back Cullan. "Is Bridie bothering you again?" Bridie was Bridget Cullan *nee* MacNamara, Cullan's wife of fifty-two years. She had grown fond of Paul over the years and would call him to discuss family matters concerning her husband or their two daughters. Like Cullan, she considered Paul to be the son they never had.

"No, no, Bridie didn't call me. And it would be none of your damned business if she did, you old bastard. I just figured you're getting too old to be able to carry all the graft you take around town. I bet you can't even count it anymore."

Cullan responded with a leprechaun's smile. "Sure, it's so much I don't count it anymore. I weigh it," he said in an exaggerated brogue. "And you know what, you smart-assed bastard? I don't even have to water it down. I can weigh it dry these days."

Paul kept goading him. "I bet you're a day away from taking a private job on the Point." Premium Point, a peninsula on New Rochelle's waterfront, jutted into Long Island Sound. There were only 30 or so mansions out there, but the area was so well monied that they had no municipal services. Plutocrats like John Kluge and Page Morton Black lived on Premium Point and footed the bills for private garbage collection, snow removal and gardeners. Even the mail never made it past the guardhouse, whose security was provided by retired NRPD – The Barney Fifes for the Mayberry millionaires.

"Keep it up, Digger, and you will be eating dinner by yourself. The only way I am leaving this job is when you come to carry me out of my office on a stretcher," Cullan said. "And I am telling you now: I want to be buried in your cemetery, not that Mick one next door."

Paul's grandfather had opened Sycamore Cemetery 60 years ago. It sat between Holy Rood, the Catholic cemetery, and Coutant, the Protestant one. When Paul's grandfather was new to the business, Catholics were forbidden to be buried in anything other than a Catholic cemetery. When Gramps would purchase a grave for one of his families, he noticed they were always placed at the back entrance or on the property that abutted the railroad tracks. Then, when gramp's mother developed cancer, he went to the cemetery office to purchase a large family plot in the middle of Holy Rood Cemetery. The middle section was the highest ground, where private mausoleums were built by New Rochelle's Catholic elite.

Old Man Arrone went to St. Jude's rectory because the church owned the cemetery. Monsignor Fitzpatrick was sorry: There was no room but the back driveway. Undaunted, Dominic Arrone Sr. visited Angelo, the cemetery foreman, whom he knew as a fellow member of the Casa Calabria. The foreman told Dominic that it was impossible to buy a grave in that section of the cemetery. He had pointed to a map hanging on the wall. In all 24 sections except the two that bordered the rear driveway 'N.W' was written in large letters.

"I don't understand," Dominic had said. Angelo had answered simply: "No wops."

Within six months, Dominic had purchased a house in neighboring Pelham whose backyard was wedged between the two cemeteries. The house sat on six acres, more than the other two cemeteries combined. With the help of Monsignor Fitzpatrick, who was all too glad to rid his cemetery of these new immigrants, Dominic applied for and received permission from the state to open a cemetery.

Dominic's mother had died two months earlier and was resting in a receiving vault at Woodlawn Cemetery in the Bronx. She was the first burial in the Arrone cemetery.

"I want to be buried anywhere by the road," Cullan said, lifting his glass, "so I can be certain that you will kick the ass of any foreman who doesn't cut the grass above me."

Paul chuckled.

"*And* I want to be taken there in a horse-drawn caisson," Cullan added with a grin.

Paul studied the older man's face. Dry skin, deep wrinkles about the eyes, and age spots had obliterated the freckles. Paul didn't mind death, his occupation and daily routine, but he very much minded his old Sarge getting old.

They were quiet for a moment. Both men knew that with the election of a new, progressive 28-year-old mayor, Cullan's tenure as New Rochelle commissioner probably was ending. They also knew, and wouldn't say it, that if Cullan didn't have as demanding a job to go to every day, he likely would die sooner than later.

The talk, spoken and unspoken, made Paul uneasy. "Save your breath, Cappy," he said. "Only the good die young, so I figure you'll to be around far longer than I'll be in business." He hesitated and then said, " I need to pick your brain about something."

Cullan grimaced warily. "I figured I was being set up."

Paul gave a summary of what he had seen at the Alverez Funeral Home the day before. Lowering his voice even more, he told Cullan of his suspicions.

Cullan listened, took a long drink, then put down his empty glass none too gently.

"Paul, I think you've been spending way too much time with dead bodies – and, obviously not enough time doing detective work," Cullan said quietly.

"But—"

"No," Cullan interrupted. "You don't need to go in that direction. It's true that caskets and even urns have been used to bring in all kinds of things, and there's no end to stories about drug mules. Christ. Earlier this year, the DEA busted a ring in Chicago for bringing in cocaine and heroin using baby formula cans – and real live babies rented to women posing as their mothers. But Janice Rodino's casket? Are you kidding me?" He sat back, shaking his head, and then leaned across the table. "Your hatred of the corporate funeral chains has blinded you. Not to mention your dislike for Haywood; he'd have to be in on this, wouldn't he? Anyway, it's all clouding your judgment."

He paused, and Paul stared at him.

"God almighty," he said with a snort. "What are you thinking? Why on earth would LaCroix risk messing around with the casket of a U.S. Senator's wife?"

"That's exactly what he would think people would say. Who would ever suspect anything? Listen," he said eagerly, "think about it: Why else would Haywood take an extra day to do the autopsy? You don't leave a Senator's wife lying in a refrigerator for an extra 24 hours because you just don't have the time. Trust me, Cappy. I am on to something. I can feel it. I need you to find out that information. Can you do it??"

"I'll say it again. You are way off-base on this one."

They sat quietly. Finally, Cullan sighed.

"I'll see what I can find out," he said resignedly.

With those words, Paul knew he had hit the mother lode. Cullan was an old-time cop who did things the old-time cop way – in other words, his way. He knew Cullan had no problem accessing the New York Statewide Police Information Network for his own personal use. Had Paul asked any of his other police friends, as he had occasionally tried to do in the past, he would have gotten the usual, tired response: "Any unauthorized access of NYSPIN or any improper use of the information may be subject to criminal prosecution under NYS *Penal Law section* 156.00 *subsection* 6 *Pursuant to* 28 CFR 20.3 Law enforcement officials can only access information available through NYSPIN for the administration of criminal justice."

Paul knew he could depend on Cullan to come up with the information that he needed. More importantly, Cullan was one of a very few people in a position of power in Westchester whom Paul trusted.

They moved on to other, less dangerous topics, at least for Paul.

"How are the plans for Sunday's fireworks going?" he asked. One of the year's biggest events for New Rochelle, the July 4th celebration, tended to consume Cappy's time and attention. As police commissioner, he had all the headaches and none of the fun. This year with the holiday falling on a Sunday a bigger crowd than ever was expected, since most people had Monday off from work and could party later than usual.

"I don't know," Cappy said with a shrug.

"You don't know?" Paul asked, surprised.

"Well, all the plans are in place, for the pyrotechnics, extra cops – that'll cost a bundle in overtime – all that," Cullan said. "But between you and me, we actually might cancel this thing."

"You're kidding!"

"Nope," Cullan said, "We're getting word already from the feds that a higher terrorism alert may be in place before the week is out. And that might include canceling major events, especially fireworks displays. Or," he added with a snort, "they'll leave that call up to me. That's a real crowd-pleaser. It's like canceling Christmas."

"What's in the pipeline?" said Paul. "Is this just another phony alert?"

Cullan frowned. "Dunno. But I got a bad feeling about this. The Internet chatter, Washington said, is more intense than ever – different, more sure of itself. It's a little spooky, nothing substantial. And frankly, the guys I talked to down there sounded shakier than ever. They're worried about something, but they wouldn't say what. In fact, maybe they don't know themselves." Cullan stared into the amber of a fresh v.o.

"Usually these things, these alerts, are timed to distract people from other bad news, or to justify a hike in gas prices. Or some sort of bull. But this time? I don't know."

"You think it's the real deal?"

"Real deal, how? How the hell are we supposed to know what the real deal is? How do you prepare for what could be anything, of any size? Christ. This county can't even agree on an evacuation plan for the nuke plant at Indian Point – yeah, right, evacuating about a million people. To where? And all that Homeland Security money and equipment that the force was supposed to get after 9/11. Where is it?"

Paul glanced at his watch, then faked a yawn and stretched. "Well, it's time we hit the road, Cappy."

Cullan grumbled. "It's not that late."

"You know," Paul said, as he gently pulled him to his feet, "you should be spending more time with Bridie and less time with funeral directors."

"You're right, Paul, and since you brought up the subject, you shouldn't be wasting your time having dinner with old men like me." His voice had taken on a pronounced slur.

As he staggered a bit, Paul caught him and they exited Tenore's arm in arm.

"You had better not screw up your chance with Trish," Cappy said, pointing his finger at Paul's chest. This may well be your last shot at holding on to the best thing that ever came along in your life."

"And what would that matter to a person who was buried in Sycamore Cemetery?" Paul shot back, anxious to end this line of conversation.

"Frigging smart-ass kid," Cullan said with a grin. "Always has been your problem. Probably always will be."

CHAPTER 14

Later Thursday night

Paul left Cullan and drove in his BMW to the county hospital. If he had taken the hearse or any of the home's business cars, someone might recognize the Arrone FH 1—6 license plate. He deliberately parked in the front lot to hide his car in the rows of those employees and visitors that crowded this late night parking area. He then walked toward the back of the building to get to the morgue.

It was nippier than usual for a late summer night. He should have taken off his suit and thrown on a pair of jeans and sweatshirt. As he turned the corner of the main building, Paul thought about the irony of how practically every hospital in America placed its morgue entrance in the same area as "Receiving." *If hospitals were forced to place the morgue next to admitting*, he wondered, *would there be any better care for the patients who came in? For that matter, would they even come? Maybe they'd take better care of themselves.*

Better yet, he thought, sardonically, an emotion that was consuming him more and more each day, *what would be the effect if, when the hearses pulled up to the intercom, the corresponding doctor's name came over the hospital loud speaker: "Dr. Smith, please come to medical records to sign a death certificate for another of your former patients." Would Dr. Smith start treating his patients with greater care?*

Aversion to death, Paul concluded, *is just another extension of the American psyche preoccupied with youth and beauty.*

What would the country be like if we talked about death from an early age? Paul thought. *We should confront it more directly everywhere. Maybe show the tiger that sells all that crappy cereal to kids as a victim of a hunting escapade. Imagine parents explaining to their children why three men with rifles stood around the dead carcass of their breakfast friend; each with one foot up on the dead animal's body. Taken to its logical conclusion, children then would learn about the politics and trauma of replacing someone they loved, or whether it was even possible to replace their friend.*

What would Madison Avenue do? Would Snap, Crackle and Pop chip in and sell the cereal while there was a search for a replacement tiger? Would Mrs. Tiger and the cubs show up on "Oprah" and discuss how they could no longer pay their mortgage and were being evicted from their den?

Kids ought to know, from an early age, Paul thought, *how tough it was out there. OK,, so killing the tiger may be extreme, but at the very least, kids should be shown that the old, fat black syrup lady who has been force-feeding them cholesterol filled-pancakes for years had finally suffered a stroke and was in Burke Rehabilitation center learning how to walk and talk again. Then the next time they went into the supermarket, their parents could show their children that the syrup bottle which now came in the shape of a wheelchair.*

Maybe I'm just jealous, Paul concluded. *Jealous that there actually are people who can go through a good portion of their 78 years of life expectancy without having to face their mortality on a regular basis like he had to.* As a final negotiating gesture with himself, he thought, *All right, the tiger doesn't have to be killed. But couldn't they just show him getting fat and old and losing his shiny coat? Let's see him on* TV *forgetting his lines just once or twice.*

Paul was about 100 feet from the back corner of the hospital. He slowed, then hid in the shadow of the building and peered around the corner. The three receiving bays were empty, just as he thought they would be this time of night. The space next to the receiving bays, to the left of the ramp, which provided for hearse parking, also was empty.

He walked up to the top of the ramp and pressed the intercom buzzer. Like every other funeral director in the area, Paul knew that Kenny Browne worked most nights. Kenny was a 70-something black man who had worked for the medical examiner's office his entire adult life; first as a janitor, then as a morgue assistant and now as a night watchman.

If any other voice but Kenny's responded back from the box, Paul decided he would simply walk away and come up with some other plan.

"County morgue," Kenny's voice shot out from the box. "What can I do you for?"

"Kenny," Paul whispered, "it's Paul Arrone. Can I speak with you for a minute?"

"Hell, my man, you got as much time as you need," Kenny said as he buzzed Paul through the glass door. Paul walked a few steps past some elevators and came to a wall. The hallway ran perpendicular to the entry door. In front of him was a sign that read "Westchester County Medical Examiner," and under that: "Autopsy Room."

The arrows beneath both pointed left. Paul went to the right.

Had he gone left, Paul would have been captured on the surveillance cameras that the county had installed after 9/11. This too, he thought, was done in typical Westchester County-government style. A $4 million dollar no-bid contract had been given out under the pretext of post 9/11 "Emergency Terrorist Security." The owner of the Yonkers contracting firm that was granted the contract was none other than the husband of the Westchester County district attorney, Rosemarie Diaz.

Senator Francis Rodino had been instrumental in getting half of the contract funded by the federal government in the same package that enabled the Cardin Biotech Group to develop the bio medical facility. Security at the county morgue was touted as a safety measure to contain any contaminants of residents who may have died in a chemical or biological attack.

Aside from surveillance cameras, there were three isolation bays added to the room where autopsies could be performed on victims. The bulk of the money, however, was spent on an elaborate refit to the main entrance of the autopsy room. Here, as in other areas of the hospital and the research center, they installed an airlock system. Unlike other locations that ran automatically, the medical examiner had insisted that this system be manually activated if there was a suspicion of foul play.

Haywood's theory was that if there was a terrorist act, the medical examiner would know long before anybody showed up at his door. He also would know that the ten minutes to enter and ten minutes to exit would make life unbearable for him – and that was if the sensors detected no hazardous materials. If the sensors went off while someone was entering or leaving, the side doors would open into a bay ready for decontamination.

Paul remembered watching the local Channel 12 news cover the ribbon-cutting of new security features installed around the county. During the news conference, the sensors detected embalming fluid on Dr. Haywood's lab coat. The entire entourage was delayed for 40 minutes until the decontamination process could be overridden.

Paul was convinced that if taxpayers were aware of such an elaborate system installed by the husband of their district attorney that could be easily deactivated by the M.E.'s office, they would conclude it was a waste of their money. And if that weren't enough, and Paul was certain it was, he wondered what the taxpayers would think if they knew that there was a back entrance to the autopsy room that was left completely out of the security loop except for a lone desk with an old black man sitting there intermittently. Dr. Haywood insisted on having his own private entrance so that no one in county government would be able to track the hours, or the shocking lack of hours, that he worked.

Paul figured that Haywood also needed his "back door," to continue his thriving viscera food exchange with the prison warden.

The rear entrance had a steel windowless door with a panic bar and alarm. Haywood had the only keys, and should anyone enter or leave without his key, the alarm would sound. This, Paul thought, was the type of good old-fashioned security that served the taxpayers well.

Paul turned right down the antiseptic-smelling, darkly-lit hallway. He could see the light of Kenny's television dancing on the wall 100 feet or so in front of him.

At the end of the hall, situated in a little alcove, was a small desk containing surveillance monitors, a television set that was turned on to a baseball game and a cut-up apple. Standing next to the desk was a large black man dressed in surgical greens that had the initials WCME on it. When the man spotted Paul, he held his stomach and let out a laugh. "Lordy, Paul, Tyler tells me you put on one hell of a show this morning. The old man wasn't worth a crap the entire day, thanks to you."

"The old man is never worth a crap any day," Paul said.

"You're right about that."

"Listen, Kenny, I need a favor. I need to get into the autopsy room for two minutes to see Mrs. Rodino."

"You know I can't do that. They would have my ass."

"Nobody will know, I promise. We're handling the funeral anyway. I just need to find something out before they do the autopsy. Which brings up an interesting question. Why didn't they do her autopsy yesterday?"

"Don't have a clue, we were all talking about that earlier. We just figured you shook the old man up so much he couldn't work the rest of the day."

"A possibility."

"Why don't you just tell me what you're looking for and I'll go in and see if I can find it for you."

"Thanks, but no, Kenny. I need to get in there."

"That's a lot of heat you're asking me to take."

Paul fished a fifty-dollar bill out of his wallet. "Would fanning yourself with this cool you down at all, Kenny?" he said in his best Bogart imitation.

"Paul, my man, normally I would say sure. Hell, you've always been good to me, but if Haywood finds out, I would be out of here quicker than I could eat that there apple on my desk."

Paul drew out another fifty and two twenty-dollar bills from his wallet, folded them lengthwise and put them between his fingers. "I hope this cools you enough, Kenny, because this is all I have."

"OK," Kenny said, looking around nervously. "But I am telling you, if anyone catches you in there, I'm going to have to say that you went in without my permission while I was on a bathroom break."

"Agreed."

"Take my flashlight," Kenny said. "You can't be turning any lights on once you're inside the Autopsy Room. Otherwise someone from maintenance may see you from the front entrance."

"Fair enough, I'll be out in ten minutes. You're the man, Kenny."

"I will be dog meat if the boss catches us," Kenny muttered under his breath.

He unlocked the private entrance to the morgue and turned on the light. Paul entered what he assumed was Haywood's dressing room. There were two open lockers and a bench to sit on. One locker contained two suits, some shirts hanging in dry cleaners' wrap, and two pairs of shoes. The other locker contained surgical scrubs, two lab coats, and rolled-up operating room booties. Paul walked past the lockers to the glass door at the other end of the room.

With the dressing room light coming over Paul's shoulder, he could see Dr. William Haywood's private green-tiled shower. Paul opened the glass door and stepped inside. It smelled of antiseptic cleaning products. He walked past the shower head to the closed vinyl folding door separating the shower from the back of the autopsy room, switched on his flashlight and slowly opened the folding door.

Paul recognized the back of the L-shaped autopsy room that held bodies left unclaimed for long periods of time. It was what his colleagues called the M.E. Deep Freeze.

The right side of the hallway was a ceiling-to-floor green-tiled wall. On the left side were stacked ten stainless-steel freezer doors, five atop five. Paul had come here more times than he liked to count to pick up someone for burial in a welfare grave.

He walked slowly down the hallway, examining each nametag on each door. He came to the end of this section of the morgue, which turned at a right angle to the main section. Above his head was a nightlight that stayed on in perpetuity.

For as many years as he'd been in the business, that lone fluorescent light would flicker. For Paul it was a symbol of government bureaucracy. Left stranded, not important enough to get fixed, and yet too important to disconnect.

Tonight, he thought, *the fixture might just be the beacon all the lost souls passing through these corridors would need to find their way home.*

He shook himself. I must be really nervous, he thought. *Get a grip.*

As he turned and faced the main autopsy room, he was flanked by "double-decked" stainless-steel refrigerator doors marked in numerical order. Twenty through one, in descending order on his left, then forty through twenty one on his right. He would start on his left and check the nametags until he found Janice Rodino.

He automatically skipped Door No. 20. Like the flickering light, it had broken some ten years ago. The door handle had simply snapped off during a transfer of remains one day. No repair; it was held shut with gray duct tape. Paul reached Door No. 1. Again, there was no name of Rodino. He crossed to the other side and started looking from No. 21. Before he knew it, he was standing back under the flickering light. Drawer number 40 held no Janice Rodino. What had they done with her?

He looked down the hall to the four autopsy tables that stood in the main operating room, on the off chance she may have been left on one of the tables. By the light of the flickering fluorescent, he could see that all four stainless steel tables were empty. The subtle warps in the tables alternately appeared bright, then black.

Peering into the black hole of that room, Paul couldn't help but think that the tables were smiling at him, their teeth in the mouth of death. He shook himself. *What the hell is wrong with me*, he wondered, as acid started to regurgitate in his stomach and up his esophagus. *Aren't I the wizard of whimsy?*

He glanced around, knowing he was running out of time. He was about to run backward through the refrigerators, opening each one, when he remembered the holding bays. They were off to the right of the autopsy room designed to hold bodies deemed chemical or biological threats. Just possibly, Haywood had done one decent thing in his career and had placed the senator's wife in one of those never-used rooms rather than in the dirty meat freezers his staff called the *Hall of Drawers*.

He took one last look around before turning off his flashlight. He knew he couldn't risk being seen even as a shadow through the main frosted doors of the Autopsy Room. With the little light that did shine into the room, Paul made his way to the four doors that held individual isolation cases. He pulled open the first, stuck his head in, cupped his hand over the lens to minimize the light and turned on the flashlight for a second. Empty. He did the same with the second, then the third. All empty. When he got to the fourth door, it wouldn't open. It must have been locked.

He turned around and froze. To the right of the door a red light flashed, signaling a potential chemical or biological incident on its other side. He had to take the chance. He shone his light directly through the glass panel port hole into the room. He wasn't prepared for what he saw. On the other side of the door lay the casket of Janice Rodino, still wrapped in that strange green rubber cocoon he had seen yesterday. The only difference now: a yellow and red Bio Hazard sticker was pasted to the foot end of the casket.

Paul thought of going outside to see if he could barter with Kenny – maybe he could barter his Breitling watch for the combination to this room.

Suddenly, a red light flashed behind the frosted double entry doors to the Autopsy Room. Three seconds later, a loud siren blast signaled that someone had entered and triggered the room's bio-lock.

Paul's mind raced with various scenarios that would get him safely out, all implausible. His only choice was to go back the way he came and hope that Kenny wouldn't give him up. He bolted past the autopsy tables and down the long corridor of refrigerated human remains. He stopped at the flickering ceiling light fixture and looked carefully around the corner to see if anyone was entering from the shower room. There was no sign of anyone.

He moved quickly past the "Deep Freeze" section to the vinyl sliding door that led into the shower. Without hesitation, he pushed open the accordion doors to find himself blinded by light pouring onto him from the shower room.

He heard Kenny's voice raise several decibels as he slid the door nearly closed. He peeked through the remaining crevice. There, beyond the shower room, he could see Dr. Haywood's broad back as he faced Kenny. He couldn't hear Haywood but he did hear Kenny answer him loudly enough to give Paul notice of impending disaster: "No, sir, no one has called about Mrs. Rodino."

Paul looked around and noticed a bio hazard suit hanging from the shower head. His first thought was to hide in one of the empty containment rooms. But there was no way he could get past Haywood, stationed at the tables just a few feet from those rooms.

Panic crawled through him. Once again he felt tightness in his chest, just as he had when Trish had called him about Janice Rodino. This time, the tightness squeezed a little harder. He broke into a cold sweat.

An alarm sounded. Paul jumped. It was signaling that someone had entered the biohazard chamber leading to the main entrance of the autopsy room. Unless sensors had detected some lethal element, the alarm could only mean that someone was about to enter the lab.

The vinyl accordion door rustled. He was sure he was moments away from being charged with breaking and entering and God only knew what else. Two men entered the autopsy lab from the main entrance. Both were fully dressed in biohazard suits that bore the emblem CBG. They nodded to Dr. Haywood who waited by the first autopsy table in his bio-hazard suit. One of the men wheeled in a large machine. Attached to it was what looked like a vacuum hose. A technician pointed to a panel of green lights.

Paul's vantage point wasn't very good but he dared not loosen his grip on the tail end of the duct tape attached to the outside rim of Drawer No. 20 of the refrigeration unit. No one would notice that the bottom half of the duct tape was missing from the door, he assured himself. It was, after all, at the far end of a dimly lit hall where the county's rich and famous, poor and downtrodden, had lain.

He was acutely aware of the cold and the stale smell of the metal, wet from condensation within the unit and mixed with dried blood and body fluids that had caked along the inner crevice of the tray just under his nose. But he couldn't slide back and away from the odor. If he did, he surely would lose sight of the situation outside. Equally important, he would lose his grip on the two inches of duct tape. That duct tape in turn was maintaining his privacy, and keeping his ass out of jail.

His chest, jaw and head throbbed. Claustrophobia snaked up his leg. Fear of being caught crept over the rest of him, suffocating him. The only light inside his cold tomb was coming through the sliver of the opening for Paul's eye. Teeth clenched, he breathed in and out through his mouth. He had to focus. He had to try to find comfort in the darkness. He tried to imagine that he was in a very large standup freezer: only on its side, he thought grimly. He found minor comfort in the knowledge that he controlled his release from this cave. At any moment, he told himself, he could throw open the door, and jump out, and face a prison sentence.

He lay face down on the tray. His left arm was up against the damp plastic wrapping of a very large person who was lying face up next to him. His or her stomach rested against the elbow of Paul's new Armani suit. He could tell by the smell escaping from his cellmate's mouth that it wasn't long since he or she had been brought there. The body was still pliable; the organs and tissues did not appear firmed up by the refrigerator's cold temperature. He was thankful that his roommate to the right suffered from apparent emaciation prior to death.

Paul's brain started to hum. He had to focus his mind away from this dark crypt if he were to hold onto what little control he had over his mental state. He blinked, then refocused on what was happening in the Autopsy Room.

The two men with Haywood had opened the containment room door and wheeled Mrs. Rodino's casket out, placing it next to the silver autopsy table. They angled the large machine they had brought in with them next to the casket. One of the men removed the hose and waved it over the entire length and width of the casket. He looked up, shook his head *No*, then moved back.

The medical examiner approached the casket. With a scalpel Paul figured that Haywood had probably used earlier that day to cut open someone's chest, Haywood slit the green rubber casket's covering from top to bottom. The man who had put down the hose collected the rubber material and stuffed it into a red medical waste garbage bag.

Haywood held a casket key. He stood at the foot end of the casket and prepared to unlock the seal that kept the casket air- and water-tight. As he started to turn the key, the other man placed the same hose at the middle of the casket, right where the lid would open. As Haywood turned the key, the man looked steadily at the machine's green lights. Again, he shook his head *No*. The casket opened. Again, the same man waved the hose nozzle over the entire inside of the casket, repeating the process of alternately looking at the machine, then Haywood, then shaking his head *No*.

Haywood moved to the head end of the casket and inserted the key. He started to crank the bed and the body on it into a higher position, to Paul's eye level across the room. Paul could see the outline of a woman's body.

He watched as the two men lifted Mrs. Rodino out of the casket, placed the body on the autopsy table, and removed the sheet. They passed the machine's wand over each other as Haywood looked on.

Paul started when Haywood turned on the full bank of operating room lights hanging over the autopsy tables. The brilliant light of the operating room-strength bulbs washed away many features. But even they weren't enough to dilute the trademark red hair of Janice Rodino. The bluish tinge of her taut body could not hide the delicate beauty of her features. In fact, in this light, she looked much younger than a woman of her age.

She must have died instantly, Paul thought, *for her body's physical integrity to remain intact*. And yet Brian had told him at the airport that she went over a cliff in a car. But there didn't seem to be any trauma or external bruising to the body. Paul leaned forward and stared intently at the still form. From his vantage point, at least, the chest cavity hadn't been opened, or even touched.

He squinted. There appeared to be two incisions; one by her carotid artery, apparently used for injecting embalming fluid, the other in her abdomen. Yet that incision was lower than where any embalmer he knew would insert a trocar to aspirate her internal organs. It was also much too long an incision for that.

Janice Rodino's stomach was slightly distended. Maybe the aspiration had been foregone until after Haywood does his autopsy? Paul marveled at the possibility that Haywood actually held enough clout to be able to tell an embalmer on the other side of the Atlantic only to inject a body and do nothing else.

Haywood raised a scalpel. As the other two men held the wand over the work field, the medical examiner opened the incision on Mrs. Rodino's lower abdomen. Fluid oozed from the incision as Haywood moved his gloved fingers, then his hand, into her intestines.

CHAPTER 15

Suddenly, a piercing, whooping sound screeched from the machine. It seemed to ricochet around the room, clanging metal inside the refrigerator. Paul's nerve endings ignited. Staring back at the machine, he could taste his own stomach acid. A dozen lights turned from green to flashing yellow. Two lights stopped flashing and went to solid yellow. One of those then glowed red.

The three men stood frozen, staring at the machine. After what seemed an eternity, the man closest to it walked over and read something on the display. He looked to the other two, shrugged his shoulders, and shook his head *No*. He appeared to re-set the machine. No sooner did it turn on, than the same sequence of green to yellow to a single red light reappeared, along with the blaring siren. Haywood, whose hand was in Mrs. Rodino's intestines and the biohazard-suited man whose hand held the wand over it, stood like manikins as they watched the man working the machine. The man moved suddenly, and then looked around the room as if he had an idea. He said something inaudible to Haywood. The doctor pointed to a cabinet. The man walked slowly over and took out a bottle. Paul recognized it as formaldehyde.

BioMan gestured to WandGuy to move away from Mrs. Rodino. He was silently instructed to wave the wand around an area in the corner. The first man reset the air-monitoring machine; it restarted and this time, all lights stayed green. He then opened the bottle of formaldehyde and waved his hand over the open bottle to send some of the gas in the direction of the wand.

Within seconds, the same exact sequence Paul had previously witnessed repeated itself a third time.

This time however, the man operating the machine inputted something on the machines keyboard. The lights went to all-green status. He then moved the bottle of formaldehyde directly under the wand and all the lights still stayed green. He gave Haywood the OK sign.

Haywood slowly maneuvered his hand deeper into Mrs. Rodino's intestines with the same degree of care as if she were alive and able to feel the pain of his movements. Paul's mind raced. None of this made any sense. He had snuck into the morgue thinking that if he got to Mrs. Rodino's body and she had been autopsied, then her chest cavity would be emptied. Now he was witnessing what – God almighty – he would swear looked like a post-mortem appendectomy.

Paul was finding it difficult to breathe. He sipped air, as if he could use his lips and teeth to screen out pathogens and microbes he was certain were circulating all around him. Paul knew that the average person died with two trillion microbes on their body that multiplied by a factor of ten for every hour they were dead – refrigeration or not.

He started shivering so violently that he worried the metal ice tray he was on would rattle, exposing his hiding place. Body temperature plummeting, Paul still felt pellets of sweat cascading from his forehead, around and into his eyes.

He couldn't stand it. He moved his left hand, pinned under the edematous slowly decomposing belly of the corpse next to him, to get the handkerchief out of his suit's breast pocket. All he could focus on was the tightness of the space and the panic. In a split second, the engraved pen that his father had given him almost twenty years ago when he went into the business, tapped the side of the tray he was lying on, bounced to the side of the tray below him, and hit the steel floor of the refrigerator. In the hollow coldness, the sound was deafening to Paul. He held his breath, reached, then pulled the refrigerator door shut.

He was holding the tape so tightly that his right arm started to cramp up. He was convinced the door would be opened any second and three men in bio suits would stare in at him. But nothing happened. After a few moments, he realized that they either hadn't heard the noise with their suits on, or they figured it was part of the refrigeration compressor kicking on. He let the refrigerator door open a few centimeters and looked out. He almost gasped aloud. Something silver was poking out of Mrs. Rodino's corpse. The man with the wand was making circles close to her abdomen. Paul could see the lights on the machine were all green.

Haywood drew the object from her body. Paul squinted with fierce concentration. It was some sort of metal cylinder. The medical examiner picked up a hose attached to the table, turned on water, and washed off blood and body residue. Meanwhile, one of the other men was opening what looked like a large platinum coffee thermos. Haywood carefully placed the cylinder into the larger container, turned, and extracted another identical cylinder from the body, then another. They too, were placed in the thermos, which was put in a briefcase sitting on a nearby table. The briefcase was lined with gray foam rubber with an indentation identical to the thermos.

Paul stared as Haywood sutured the incision closed. Haywood then covered Mrs. Rodino with a sheet and pushed the wheeled table into the walk-in single freezer. All three men then exited the autopsy lab through the main entrance decontamination lock.

Paul had no idea what he had just witnessed, but he did know that whatever it was had to be potentially dangerous for Haywood to forgo his usual personal exit. As soon as Paul heard the whooping of the siren, he knew the air-lock system was engaged and he had about ten minutes before the three of them could leave the building.

He slowly opened the freezer door, looked around, then jumped to the floor below. The terrible taste in his mouth and the tightness in his chest took a back seat to his desperate desire for a shower.

He decided to check for any information from the sensor machine that had lain next to Mrs. Rodino. Paul knew that the expensive air-lock system had two stages to enter and exit. Once someone entered under an activated system, they could leave only the same way. Therefore, the three men, barring any contamination, would have to spend five minutes in the anteroom and five minutes in the sensor room beyond it. Once the yellow flashing lights went out, Paul knew he would have five minutes to get whatever information he could before Haywood would be free to re-enter through his private entrance.

Paul moved slowly. The stench of death from the refrigerator lingered in his nose. His body was starting to warm up, but his pants and part of his shirt and suit were still soaked from the water in the tray. He looked down. Crap. He was dripping water onto the Autopsy room floor. He reached the machine.

Suddenly, deafening sirens sounded, indicating that someone had re-entered the airlock. What was going on? Who was coming in now? He thought wildly. Had Kenny given him up? If so, why didn't they just come in the back door?

Paul was paralyzed. For a split second, he thought he might be dream-ing the whole episode. As in his old dreams, his legs were stuck to the floor. He was becoming lightheaded and finding it more difficult to breathe.

He looked around in panic. If he bolted out the main exit, he could become trapped in the air lock. If he went out the back door, he might run into Haywood himself. Then he remembered Kenny's warning earlier that evening just as Haywood arrived. Paul's best chance would be to go out the back door and hope the Kenny would be able to distract Haywood long enough for him to get out of there unseen.

Paul ran down past the refrigerated corpses, stopping short at the now infamous Drawer No. 20. He inched his head around the steel corner of the refrigerator wall to see if Haywood was on his way in from his private entrance. The deep freeze corridor was quiet. No light peeked through the accordion door of the shower that led to the dressing room that would, he hoped, lead him out of there.

The siren from the second airlock started to blare, giving him about five minutes to make his getaway. Paul sneaked up on the brown accor-dion door and slowly opened it. Darkness greeted him. He fumbled for the flashlight that Kenny had given him and turned it on. He saw nothing through the shower room glass door, nothing in the dressing room.

He stepped into the shower and through it, entered the dressing room expecting any second to run head-on into Haywood. The stillness was unbearable; a sense of vertigo overwhelmed him. He walked up to the exit door and put his ear to it. He could hear the now-muffled siren.

"Kenny," he whispered. He waited. No response. He spoke his name aloud, clearly. Again, there was no reply. He slowly opened the door but could see nothing but the flickering lights of surveillance monitors dancing on the green tile walls and twirling on the back of Kenny's empty chair.

Paul decided to make a run for Haywood's private exit. He knew that doing so would trigger an alarm, but he figured once outside he could get lost either in the evening crowd of patients' families coming and going for visits, or maybe he could find refuge somewhere on the 400-acre reservation. He was afraid to head to his car and risk discovery just yet.

Nearing the exit door, Paul's peripheral vision caught something. A figure was slumped on the floor in front of Kenny's chair. It was Kenny, lying flat on his face. Paul reached him and gently shook his shoulder. He moaned. Paul could see a large bump rising on the back of the night watchman's neck. Spit and chewed apple bits oozed from his lips.

Paul's eyes flew to the center monitor. The three men who had been in the Autopsy Room were rushing out of an elevator with the briefcase that contained the thermoses. The monitor was labeled "Sub-Basement." Paul watched them next appear on the monitor labeled "Tunnel to Cardin Research Lab."

If those men were in the tunnel, he wondered, *who was entering the autopsy lab?*

Paul looked down at Kenny, uncertain of what to do. The siren stopped, signaling that whoever was trying to enter the lab had been successful. He hesitated, then turned and ran for the exit door. As he hit the panic bar on the door, a different and far louder alarm sounded. He left quickly, but then forced himself to walk slowly so as to not bring any attention to himself in case anyone was near the back entrance of the medical center. He walked past Haywood's fire-engine red Jaguar with its familiar license plate, ME60 – 60 being New York State's county code for Westchester.

He decided to head toward the rear entrance of the hospital where he had entered only an hour or so earlier and then simply walked around the building to the front entrance where he could mingle with other hospital visitors. If he could make it to the men's room, he reasoned, he could dry his clothes using the hand dryer.

His head whipped around. Three police cruisers were speeding down the hill to the area where he stood. He darted into the bushes of the lush periphery that ran in concentric circles around the government buildings on the reservation. He hunkered down as his mind raced to figure out what to do next. The crouching of his body dizzied him and he vomited into the dirt between his feet. He tried to calm his pounding head and heart.

Then he remembered the Indian shrine. Erected when Paul was in office some 15 years ago, its ostensible purpose was to express sympathy for a tribe of upstate Indians whose burial ground, Valhalla, was taken by the local government several centuries earlier. Paul knew the actual reason was to get the upstate tribal chief to sign off on the quit-claim deed so that the county wouldn't face a protracted legal battle over who held title to use the land. The Indian tribe, after all, had burned through Upstate New York, taking back land to open future casinos.

The spot was the highest point on the reservation. From there, he reasoned, he would be able to see not only what was happening at the rear of the hospital but whether anyone was near his car in the front parking lot.

Paul was shaking, chilled in his cold wet clothes. He tried to hold himself in check. He glanced furtively around for the clearest path to the top of the hill. Crouching, he ran for it. When he got to the trees, he stood up and ran full out like he was back on his high school track team. In those days, there was a clear finish line. In those days, too, he would have been free of acid pumping into his throat and his heart pounding in his chest.

Ironically, Paul realized, he was more concerned about being caught than dropping dead from a coronary.

He was now making good time up the hill. But then he started to involuntarily retch. He paused to give himself a few moments' rest when branches snapped to his left. This was insane. Would the county police chase someone up a hill for going out the wrong exit door of the morgue?

The rustling of branches sounded closer. Paul took off full speed up the hill, figuring he at least had home-court advantage. He had served on the committee that built the burial gardens and could still remember most of the layout. *Maybe*, he thought, *I could hide behind the monuments, totem poles, or even the gazebo.* But he had to get there first.

The tightness in his chest was becoming unbearable as he scrambled up the wooded hillside. He remembered learning tracking while on the New Rochelle police force and used some of these lessons to try to elude his pursuer.

Yet someone was close on his tail.

Then he heard rustling to his right. Either his pursuer had overshot his mark and passed him, or someone, likely another cop, was closing in from the other side. Paul knew he had to ignore everything and reach the top. Finally, he was there. He made his way to the reflecting pool, deciding to hide behind the bushes that bordered the benches next to it. There he would regain his breath and recoup a bit of strength.

The bench at the far side sat almost at the edge of the hilltop. From that vantage point he could see the entire reservation. There were now more than six police cars at the receiving bays next to the rear entrance of the hospital. It took a bold stretch of the imagination to believe that the county would mobilize that kind of force so quickly for an opened door, or even an intruder, if they suspected one. The only thing the county did quickly was spend taxpayer's money.

He heard a sound that seemed to be coming closer. He threw himself on the ground and rolled under the stone bench. The dampness of his shirt against the bare cold dirt of the garden bed made him shiver again. He froze as he heard the familiar beep of a Nextel phone signal. He listened intently. A burly man was whispering into a phone. Unbelievably to Paul, the man walked to the bench and sat. He could see little but was sure the man was not dressed in a police uniform.

The man whispered again – in French.

His heart froze. He just remembered that every evening at 9 his answering service called his own cell phone to check in before turning the phone lines and any new calls over to his staff for the rest of the night.

Paul knew that he had left Cullan at about 7. It could very well be almost 9, but he couldn't risk breathing, much less searching his pants pocket for his cellular phone. Even if he could get to it, turning it off would trigger the silly sign-off song. They'd grab him.

A mild electric jolt went through his thigh into his groin. His damn phone was vibrating. He must have changed the setting during that morning's funeral.

He rolled ever so slightly, forcing the cell phone in his pocket, into the earth, muffling the sound.

A sound cracked above him. Paul's eyes widened but he didn't move. A moment later, an arm slumped over the bench near him, the hand almost on the back of Paul's head. His thoughts a jumble, he considered jumping up, launching into a tirade of how he was only guilty of stopping by to say hello to Kenny, and this whole thing has been blown out of proportion, when he stopped and stared. The hand almost upon him was motionless. A dark streak was lazily coursing down the hand.

Warm liquid dropped onto the nape of Paul's neck. His nose twitched. Blood. He knew the smell well, all too well.

He rolled from under the bench, scrambled to his feet and bolted toward the gazebo. As he did, he heard something he usually was too late to witness. The death rattle of a man.

CHAPTER 16

Friday morning, Paul was uncharacteristically late in coming down from his apartment. A note that had been taped to the back entrance of the Funeral Home the night before informed him that the DeMelia family would be in at 8:30 to make funeral arrangements for their mother. At 9:45, the family was leaving just as Paul entered his office. His father, who had come in to the office to handle Janice Rodino's funeral arrangements, had met with the DeMelias.

"Why didn't Joe or Ron make the arrangements, Pop?" Paul asked

"Why didn't you tell anybody you wouldn't be available?" Dominic said, frowning. "And what's with you. You look like hell. You sick or something?"

Paul looked at him blankly.

"Anyway, don't worry," Dominic smiled. "I needed the overtime."

But that wasn't the big news, he told Paul. For starters, Senator Frankie wouldn't be coming in this morning after all.

"Dr. Haywood had told him that Janice was pretty beaten up by the car crash. There's no way for her to be viewed, and Haywood recommended she be cremated."

Paul stared at his father, trying to keep his face composed. Before he could say anything, Dominic added, "Haywood even took her body to Ferncliff Crematory himself out of respect for their long-time friendship. I'm going up there later to sign the paperwork. We'll be handling the memorial service Sunday."

Paul wanted to contradict the M.E. but caught himself. He walked to the window, unclenched his fists and turned to his father.

"Doesn't it make you suspicious that Haywood, who barely takes the time to do his own job, is now doing ours?"

"Stop looking in the shadows, Paul," his father said gruffly. "Haywood actually did us a favor. There was a huge mess at the Medical Examiner's Office last night."

"Oh?"

"Someone broke in and shot Kenny."

"What! What are you talking about?"

Paul's father picked up the newspaper and turned it so Paul could see the headlines. He stared at the story and photographs, obviously taken outside the morgue.

He skimmed the news: "He's *dead*?" Paul almost shouted. "But …" He stopped himself and read on. Dominic watched him closely.

Kenny apparently had stopped a foreigner who had stolen morphine from the hospital pharmacy. Kenny confronted the man, who shot him in the head. The suspect ran out a door that triggered an alarm. The county police, along with private security people from the Cardin Biotech Group, chased the man into the woods. There was a brief shootout, the paper reported. During it, someone shot and killed the man in the Valhalla Memorial Gardens. Pending ballistics tests, the bullets probably came from the gun of a Cardin Biotech Group security guard. County police also found what appeared to be the missing vials of morphine. They were searching for an accomplice, officials said. An arrest was imminent.

"Did you hear what I said?"

His father's question jolted Paul. He drew in a deep breath and tried to focus. He looked at Dominic, his expression blank. "What was that, Pop?"

"I said you should probably call Commissioner Cullan and see if we can get some police support for the traffic and crowds that will be here Sunday. I'm already fending off media calls."

"Yeah, sure, that's a good idea. I'll take care of it." Paul's voice trailed off. Dominic looked at him strangely. A delivery man appeared at the office door with a clipboard. "I just delivered a casket spray," he said. "I need a signature."

Paul reached for a pen in his breast pocket. A chill skipped down his spine. His pen. He had lost it in the freezer last night.

It took no leap of faith: Haywood would immensely enjoy connecting Paul to last night's incident – whatever it was. He had tossed and turned all night, and he still couldn't make sense of what he saw in the morgue and what happened afterward. It was significantly bad, even by Westchester standards.

What in God's name had been inside Janice Rodino? What was Haywood, and likely a whole slew of officials, up to? Who killed Kenny? When he left, Kenny was knocked cold but still alive. Who had chased him through the grounds? And God, he thought with a shiver, who was on that bench?

The delivery guy coughed impatiently. Paul grabbed a pen from the desk and hustled him out.

The intercom on the phone buzzed and Paul almost hit the ceiling. He took a deep breath, and ran a hand over his face. "Your brother Anthony is on the phone," Marge said.

"Hey, Ant, how'd you make out?" Paul said, forcing a calmness he didn't feel.

"I got most of the info you asked for yesterday afternoon. I'll be able to get the rest as soon as the market opens. But listen, man, I understand the funeral home questions, but I'm not sure why you need all the info on that bio medical company. If you're looking for an investment, why don't you come out to the island this weekend? Karen and the kids would love to see you, and we can go over everything I find out then-after I kick your ass playing tennis."

"Thanks, Ant, that sounds great, but I need this today. I wouldn't even bother you if it weren't so important. I will take a rain check, though, and get out there for a long weekend soon."

"Not a problem," Anthony answered. "Call me anytime after two today. Just tell Barbara that I'm expecting your call. How is Pop doing?"

"Good," Paul said. "He's here this morning, in fact. Do you want to say hello?" Paul glanced around, then yelled down the hall. "Pop, pick up the phone. There's someone selling junk bonds. He wants to speak to you."

Marge interrupted again. "You have a visitor."

"Hi, Paul," the soft voice said. "You wanted to see me?"

"Trish," Paul said, looking at her as if he'd never seen her before. He forced a smile, sensing that his reactions were a beat behind where they should be. "I'm sorry. Come in, come in."

He went to the door and tried to put his arm around her. She stiffened.

"What's up?" she said calmly.

Paul looked her in the eyes. He was losing her. He knew it as sure as he knew – what? As sure as he knew he loved her? As sure as he knew what he was getting into with this Rodino thing? As sure as he knew where his life was going? As sure as he knew *what*? He didn't know anything.

He frowned, and then stared off. Until recently, he realized, he'd been certain he knew almost everything. Now he was certain of nothing.

Trish eyed him in surprise. He could occasionally be preoccupied or distant or (the memory touched her with sadness), boyishly bowled over when he saw her. But rarely – actually she couldn't think of a single time had Paul Arrone seemed lost.

He drew a breath. "I need a favor," he said handing her some papers.

She glanced at them and then back to his face. "A favor?"

With little explanation, he outlined what he wanted her to do; to get for him.

Trish walked to the window. She stared out, feeling the heat of Paul's impatience on the back of her neck.

She turned and stared at him searchingly. He was surprised at what he read in her face. She seemed downcast, resigned – not even close to the reaction he had expected.

"You want me to breach my security trust at the medical center in order to get you information," she said flatly. It was a statement, not a question.

Paul shifted uncomfortably. Trish walked toward him. He flinched inwardly but met her gaze.

She reached up, started to place her hand on his chest, over his heart and then brought it briefly to his cheek. She stood on tiptoe and kissed him lightly on the lips.

It tasted good, Paul realized. It also tasted like good-bye.

He wanted to stop it, that good-bye. He wanted to pull her close, and shut out the whole outside world, and all the worries, and all the memories.

He sighed. His thoughts shifted, his mind racing again down simulta-
neous tracks -one trying to figure out what the hell had happened the last
few days, the other trying to plan the Janice Rodino service. He wanted to
jump the tracks, maybe toward Trish, maybe with Trish to a better place. He
was amazed at himself. He had never once wanted to be any place but here,
in New Rochelle, at the Funeral Home. But now the tracks beckoned.

She looked up at him. It was in his eyes, all of it; the distraction, the
obsession, the paralysis.

She gave an imperceptible shrug. *Why not*, she said to herself. *Why
not get him the records he wants.* In less than a month she would leave his
life forever anyway. Later, after she did, she could always point to this last
selfless act. The thought had a bad taste to it. But after all, leaving wasn't
an act of revenge. It was one of self-preservation. Paul of all people, would
understand that. Besides, she reminded herself, compromising her work
ethics paled in comparison to having to tell Paul and her son of the move.

"I'll get back to you as soon as I have something," she said, and walked
to the door. Paul restrained himself from asking her to come back; from
asking her to hurry.

Trish spent the better part of the morning at a county records warehouse in Elmsford combing through the financial disclosures of the list of
politicians Paul had given her. Her presence there aroused no suspicion.
The storage facility also contained many of the county's budget records so
it was natural for her to log herself in at the security desk.

There were two piles of papers in her briefcase: a list of local politicians
and copies of the politicians' Board of Election campaign financials next
to them. Trish had asked a friend from the Sierra Club to pull the list that
morning. Paul had figured that a request to the Board of Elections from an
aggressive environmental organization would raise no eyebrows. They routinely pulled campaign-finance filings with donations to see what politician
was being influenced by whom.

Paul was right. The Board of Elections seemed nonplussed at the
request. They had the package ready by the time Trish's friend showed up,
only an hour after she called it in.

Trish placed her briefcase in front of her; a wall of budget documents to
serve as a decoy in case someone happened by the small work cubical. She

had two sets of documents – money raised and assets. After she matched them, she would walk over to a nearby copy machine, make two copies of each, return to her work spot, then repeat the task some two-dozen times; once for each of the seventeen Westchester legislators, then once for the county executive and once for the district attorney and Senator Rodino.

Elected officials have to make full disclosure of contributions to their campaign chests. They, as well as certain appointed officials, also are required to fully disclose their income, assets, and debts.

Because only elected officials and not appointed ones have campaign committees, the four county commissioners on whom Paul had asked Trish to pull files were the ones that filed financial disclosures solely.

By the fourth set, Trish had not only noticed a pattern but was beginning to think that Paul's theory could be right. The politicians who had declared stock ownership in Cardin Biotech Group had received no campaign contributions from Cardin himself.

Trish was about to put District Attorney Diaz's file away when her eye caught a section on her disclosure form: "spouse's assets." Listed under Diaz's vast holdings was a 20 percent share of CBGWC Realty LLC. Trish was familiar with the company because she regularly posted rent checks from it as income to the county hospital. She also recalled getting Haywood to sign off on expense checks that went to the corporation for services it provided the medical examiner's office.

The district attorney's husband, Luiz Diaz, was along with his many business interests, the contractor who built the bio medical research center. He apparently took the 20 percent share as part of his payment for the work.

Trish's last mission before leaving the record building was to make her way to the grants applications. Because the county was the landlord for the Cardin Biotech Group, it had on file all the grant applications that CBG had made. She pulled the applications and found that CBG had listed some 300 pathogens it was currently working on. Such a medical facility is required by federal regulations to submit a detailed list of projects being worked on.

Trish drew in a sharp breath. Cardin Biotech Group was researching five Bio Level 3 contaminants for the Army; all high level and dangerous.

She shivered. *This research is giving me the heebie-jeebies*, she thought. *I need to get out of here and call Paul.*

That night, at around 11:30, the buzzer to the flower room at the Funeral Home sounded. Paul looked up from the kitchen table, where he was eating warmed-up pizza, to the video monitor bank that was cut into one of the kitchen cabinets. Someone was waving to him.

Paul was used to people showing up to make funeral arrangements without calling first. Seldom, though, did anyone come by at such a late hour.

He turned on the outside spotlight, and then made his way down the back staircase that led to the old kitchen area, now the flower room. At the bottom of the stairs, he opened the door with little regard to who was on the other side. Even though a visitor was unusual, he hadn't heard of anyone showing up at a funeral home with any intention other than to declare an end to a life spent in the community.

As he flung the door open, only the night air greeted him. He stepped out to check if whoever had waved to him had walked over to the prep room ramp. Nobody. Maybe the person, caught up in grief, had gone around to the front door to see if it was open.

Paul walked around to the front. The hum of traffic on I-95 a few blocks away grew louder; it sounded like a long squeal. Paul shook himself. He drew in a deep breath and let it out slowly. What was with him tonight? He had been feeling spooked ever since yesterday. Yesterday … at the morgue. A chill shot up his spine. How had he let it drop from his mind for even a moment?

Christ. He had left the flower room door open.

He started to trot, heading to the back of the building by way of the opposite side. That way, if someone legitimately needed his service and was wandering around his property, he would have made a complete circle.

He turned the corner of the left rear of the old mansion. Again, no one. No person and no vehicle. The light from the opened flower room door fell on the concrete ramp leading to it.

Paul decided to get to his office and replay the surveillance tape to see if he could recognize the visitor. He walked up the ramp then stopped short. A beige envelope was taped to the glass of the flower room door. He glanced around, grabbed the envelope and locked the door behind him; he hurried through the Funeral Home to his office.

He turned the burglar alarm system onto "Monitor" so he would be able to hear a beep if someone had entered the funeral home while he had walked the perimeter. There were enough motion detectors and electric-eye beams in operation, that once there were no sounds from the alarm keypad, he felt secure that he was still alone.

He sat at his desk, heart thumping, and turned on the security cameras to view all the settings to make certain that no one was lingering. He also replayed the surveillance footage on the computer DVD to see if he could recognize who had dropped off the envelope and to check if anyone had entered the building.

"Gotcha," he said, trembling a bit. He slowed to the spot on the tape where the man – it was a man, he decided – had rung the bell and waved to him. The man had boldly looked directly up into the camera. Paul froze the frame, enhanced the image and magnified it by fifteen.

A stocking covered the face.

Paul fast-forwarded the frames. Damn. He went over the tapes for about forty minutes but could only make out that the man had long hair, tied into a small ponytail that stuck out from under the cap covering his head.

He arose and walked to the alarm keypad. A tone rang. Paul jumped. "Asshole," he muttered to himself. The motion detector in the office had only picked up his movement. He reset the keypad to the "Off" mode and turned to shut off the office lights. He stopped. The envelope. He had been so rattled he'd almost forgotten about it.

He reached for it then hesitated. He spun on his heel, went out to the flower room, and opened a supply cabinet. As he walked back to the office, he pulled latex gloves over his fingers. He took a letter-opener and large envelope that contained a register book from his desk drawer. He dumped the register book on the floor. Carefully picking up the envelope by its corner, he laid the envelope on the desk. He slit it and shook it gently. A piece of paper wafted to the desk. He placed the envelope into the larger register book envelope, sealed it, and wrote the date, time and how he found it on the outside of the packet.

Using one gloved finger and the letter-opener, Paul unfolded the piece of paper. It was a lab report of a blood sample. The page contained some fifty items with check boxes next to each, under headings of "Yes" and "No."

His eyes scanned quickly. Alcohol, No. Barbiturates, No. Cocaine, No. Prozac, Yes.

At the bottom of the page, two items were asterisked. The specimen, it stated matter of factly, contained 10 ccs of curare.

"Damn," Paul muttered. He remembered a case he'd read about when he first joined the police force. A man murdered his wife with half the dose of the same drug. Even though the body had been exhumed ten years after the burial, toxicology studies found the drug and convicted the husband.

Paul gave a short whistle. "Whoever's blood this is must have died in about 15 seconds," he murmured. "Maybe less."

He flipped the sheet over. A yellow post-it note with a phone number was attached. Under it was written, "I can be reached at this number until noon tomorrow." Attached to the bottom of the page by a paper clip was one of Paul's own business cards. Written on it, in Paul's own handwriting, using his now missing pen, were his cell phone number and his New York Athletic Club audit number.

"What the hell," Paul said out loud. Obviously, he'd given this card to someone. Who?

Paul hadn't had any business or personal meetings at the NYAC in midtown Manhattan for several months, a habit he had started during his stint in politics. The Central Park location not only offered a sophisticated midtown place to do business but assured a level of unparalleled privacy. You had to be a member to get past the front door. The club offered twenty-six floors of different sports venues, two restaurants, a bar, and eight floors of hotel rooms for overnight stays or conducting business. Up until the early 1990s, it was a men's-only club.

Paul thought back to one of his more colorful political meetings. He had agreed to meet with two representatives of a company who complained to him that they were excluded from bidding on the multi-million-dollar Westchester County garbage contract. The two men said: "The fix is in. Youse guys is corrupt." It took a while for Paul to assimilate the charge.

Two mob bosses from competing crime families in the greater New York area were saying that the county was crooked.

Six hours after Paul agreed to meet the men, his funeral home office was occupied by four agents from the Yonkers office of the Federal Organized Crime Task Force. They told Paul that the men he had agreed to meet the following week were members of one of New York's notorious organized-crime families.

The agents' request was straightforward: Would Paul agree to wear a wire to the meeting since the men would surely try to bribe him? Paul called Cullan for advice. He began to brief him, but Cullan couldn't help but stop Paul to rib him: "You mean the Gambino crime family thought *Westchester County* government was crooked? Now *that* tells you something."

Cullan then got serious. If Paul were a law enforcement officer, he would recommend helping the OCTF. "As a friend, though, I'm telling you to stay out of this."

There's too much risk for you, Rookie. If these guys catch you wearing a wire, you're dead. If they bribe you and they get caught, you're dead. If they do neither and something goes wrong soon after they meet with you ..."

"I'm dead," Paul finished for him.

As with most of Cullan's advice, Paul took it very seriously. He called the garbage contractors and told them that the only time he had available was on the following Wednesday, after his swim at the Manhattan branch of the New York Athletic Club.

Knowing that the contracts would be discussed that Thursday morning, Paul figured that if the men were serious, they would say "Yes" to the meeting.

It turned out that the attorney for the garbage carters was a member of the NYAC and was delighted with his choice of location. The following Wednesday, they met poolside, then lunched bare-assed to discuss business. Clearly, Paul was wearing no wires. Clearly, Paul could see, the only thing these guys were carrying was about 50 extra pounds apiece. A bribe never came up. Everybody, except OCTF, was happy.

This was the beginning of Paul's habit of meeting downtown for business. And while the club had since changed to allow women members and to end a century of nude swimming, it kept all its other security benefits.

Besides, Paul thought, he never had the same level of concern with any of his subsequent meetings and had doubted he ever would. Until tonight.

CHAPTER 17

CIA *Headquarters, Langley Va.*

Early in the morning of June 29th, the chatter reports had sat in front of a head analyst, who was marking his first month under the newly formed Homeland Security Department. The question confronting him was what to do with the report's information. It was no longer enough just to obtain information as it had been years earlier. Now if you hoped to succeed, or for that matter even keep your job, you had to know when the information was pertinent. Even though the chatter that had come across his desk had been 7 percent greater than normal, was that enough to kick this information up to his boss? As he'd sipped his black coffee, he had tried to weigh all the options and rationales for what would be his ultimate decision. There was the death of an elected official's spouse, and that along with the slight increase in chatter could mean something. On the other hand, there was no clear connection between that death and any reported terrorist activity. If he started the "chain reaction" of an alert, he could cause official embarrassment and lose his job. After all, the only person higher to whom his boss could appeal was the director of the CIA, who in turn answered only to the President. No, he said to himself, I can't let the terrorist fever cloud my judgment. He had decided to e-mail a CYA memo to his boss which would be reviewed in the morning. After all, the 4th of July weekend was coming. He already knew he would have to speak with his boss several times before this high alert weekend ended.

The same head analyst, who just two days earlier had questioned whether to call his superior, had no doubt about his decision to do so tonight. He was no longer sequestered in his small office, but sat now with other of his contemporaries in a bullpen of sorts just outside the main conference room of the director of the CIA. Nearly every senior analyst had been called into work today as the terrorist chatter had risen to an uncomfortable level. Even when the July 4th holiday was factored out of the equation, there was still an unusually high amount of noise. The ground troops that had infiltrated many of the known cells had confirmed that there was indeed something afoot in both the New York and Chicago metropolitan areas. The mission of the roomful of agents was to come to a consensus recommendation to the director. Should the agency recommend a rise in the terrorist level? Should the department leak this information to the media? Should the President and the Hill be notified? This would be the discussion for the next several hours.

Paul racked his brain to try and remember what business meeting he would have made at the club in the past few months. Nothing came to mind. He logged onto his computer and pulled up his calendar. Just as he thought: The last six months had no scheduled meetings at the NYAC. In fact, he had had no business meetings in Manhattan at all. *Could my life have gotten so mundane that I haven't even gotten into the city in the past six months?* He asked himself. He hadn't even taken Trish there?

With a sigh he went back, meticulously looking at every date. Nothing piqued his suspicion. He had met with his accountant and his attorney for a dinner meeting at the end of last year. He had met his older brother and sister-in-law there for several lunches and dinners around last Christmas. He had had a series of appointments with a personal trainer almost two years ago.

Then just as he was about to call it quits, he saw the calendar entry from three and a half years ago. This appointment stood out because it was the first one logged into what was then his new computer's calendar. He had scrolled back to the very first entry of his electronic date book: Lunch with LaCroix re: cemetery.

LaCroix was the same company that had shipped Janice Rodino's casket stateside. A company owned and operated by one Henri LaCroix. But the appointment, Paul remembered, wasn't with Henri, who had tried to purchase the Arrone Funeral Home almost 20 years earlier. It was with his son, Tomaas, a character Paul found hard to forget. Tomaas had been sent by the company to see if Paul and his family would reconsider selling their cemetery. The first meeting between the two funeral-owning families had ended with Henri chalking up one of his biggest business upsets to a then twenty-something Paul, and Paul knew he hadn't made a friend. No one, least of all Henri, could have guessed Paul to be so aggressive about keeping the family business in the family. All of the "intelligence" Henri did prior to the meeting led him to believe Paul would seize the opportunity to shed the funeral business. The private detective Henri had hired all but assured him that Paul would jump at the chance to return to the police force. Henri was not the only one to be surprised that day some 20 years ago. Paul's parents and remaining brothers all of whom sat around the conference room table sat in disbelief as Paul submitted a higher, last minute bid. He did this by collateralizing his dead brother's stock in the funeral home; stock that Johnny had willed to him. Stock that everyone at that table had long forgotten about.

The next, recent meeting more than three years ago with the younger LaCroix had been to set a different tone. And different it was. Paul had booked a suite at the NYAC and left his business card at the front desk along with a guest pass for Tomaas. Paul had drinks set up in the living room of the two-room suite, alongside a stack of documents, the last three years of financials on the cemetery his family owned. He had told his accountant that the meeting should last about a half-hour – after which he and Tomaas would have dinner in the main dining room. Both men agreed to keep to the time frame.

Paul had been on a speaker phone with his accountant when he heard a knock on the door followed by a hearty *"Bon jour"* as Tomaas burst in, with each arm slung around a model's neck. In each hand he held a bottle of Cristal.

Introductions were made. Paul recognized one of the women from the swimsuit edition of *Sports Illustrated*. Feeling decidedly awkward, Paul introduced his absent accountant via the speaker phone, then told Tomaas that he had planned to spend some time going over the documents, followed by dinner downstairs.

"That won't work," Tomaas said in all seriousness, "because I made reservations in 20 minutes at Giraffe." It was then the hottest spot in Manhattan with a six-month waiting list, and, Paul knew, harder to get into than Raios.

Tomaas spoke to Paul but projected his voice to the speaker phone. "Besides, it is better that you talk directly to my accountant, no?" he asked, his French accent thickening. "He will go over every detail with you so that you can bill Mr. Arrone, and he can bill my father for several days' worth of work, not this measly thirty-minute thing. Is this not better?"

From the other end of the phone came: "It sounds good to me. Have a great time, you guys." Tomaas and the two models already were. They passed the Cristal around and drank from the bottle as if it were Evian.

That night, Paul learned three things: Tomaas could spend his father's company's money with Olympic speed, Tomaas had a deep dislike for his father, and third, there was a part of Paul that wanted to be in this life and not the on-call 24/7 drill of dealing with death and the end stage lives of the community he grew up in.

Paul smiled to himself. Even years later, he remembered the feeling of celebrity he had experienced seeing his name and photo on Page Six of a New York tabloid. That evening, Tomaas had ordered champagne and caviar for the entire table.

"None for me, thanks," Paul had told him, "I'm happy with my scotch and I don't care for caviar tonight."

Tomaas had turned to the eager waitress. "Bring a bottle of Cristal and two ounces of your best caviar for each person at this table, and just keep it coming until we leave."

Paul opened his mouth, but Tomaas turned to him and stopped him. "If you don't feel like drinking the champagne or eating the caviar," he said seriously, "just toss it."

"Why order it, if we aren't going to consume it?" Paul asked.

"Because," Tomaas said very slowly and deliberately in his thick French accent, "the amount of the expense account I send to my father will be how successful he judges my meeting with you. I intend to make this weekend one freaking outrageous successful meeting. You are more than welcome to join in. You are equally welcome to take the champagne bottle by bottle, and pour it down the sewer if you like."

Paul wanted to get past the cavalier talk. "Then why did you meet with me? You certainly could have enjoyed this weekend partying without having to baby-sit a prospective client of your father's company."

Tomaas's answer intrigued Paul.

"Listen, *mon ami*. To my father I am more of an excuse than a son. He needs me because, as an only child, he can use me to get what he wants from my mother and my grandmother. He has been having a tough time with his company."

Paul knew what Tomaas was talking about. Large funeral home conglomerates were all suffering from too-fast expansion and, like it or not, too-slow death rates.

"So," Tomaas continued, "my father sends me out into the wild to buy the properties he feels are critical to his firm. This way, if any member of the board of directors complains about the price, he can tell them Tomaas negotiated the deal."

"Why put yourself through that?" Paul said. "Do you do everything your father tells you to do?"

"No, I certainly do not," he answered. "In fact, I agreed to this meeting because my grandmother asked me to."

Paul lifted his scotch and said with a laugh; "And I suppose you do everything your grandmother asks you to do?"

Tomaas leaned away from his model toward Paul and said earnestly, "I most certainly try to." Then Tomaas lowered his voice so that only Paul could hear him. "The entire family knows how embarrassed my father was when he was bested by you all those years ago. He never figured a 24-year-old would be able to compete with the deal he presented to your father and brothers. As Tomaas continued to talk, Paul realized that he was far less tipsy then he let on. "Stock options and cold cash were being offered to a family who had a son sitting on the Stock Exchange, who must have advised your parents of what a deal this was. My father also hired a private detective who told him you weren't interested in staying in the business. And my father figured if one day you wanted to go back into the business, your family could have bought you any other funeral home with those proceeds."

"Well," Paul said, "he figured a lot of things wrong."

Tomaas looked at him with new respect then raised his glass to silently toast him.

"So now that you brought it up, Tomaas," Paul said nonchalantly, "where does the LaCroix empire get all that cash to pass under the table?"

"Ah," said Tomaas, "when it comes to my father's dealings, I have adopted the same motto as your American military: Don't ask, don't tell. As for his *empire*? Just like that conglomerate here in America and the one in Canada, he has been overextended for several years now. In fact," Tomaas lowered his voice to a conspiratorial whisper, "he has lost the bulk of his company to my grandmother and Arab businessmen."

Paul tried to remember more of that night and the details of that conversation. He recalled asking why, after so many years, the LaCroix Company had become interested in the cemetery his family owned.

Tomaas had been a bit vague on the details. He said he knew only that his father had earmarked several cemeteries in metropolitan areas for acquisition and that the Arrone cemetery in New Rochelle had significance to Henri because of some connection with the area's Colombian population. "I don't know," Tomaas said with a shrug. "I never fully understand my father's motives."

None of that had made sense to Paul, then or now. What could be the relevance of the ethnic population of a community and the rate of return on a cemetery?

Paul looked down at the business card. Was it possible that Tomaas LaCroix had sent this card? Did he know something about Janice Rodino?

Well, he knew he certainly wouldn't find out anything else going through his computer. Also he was running out of time. Even though it was just after midnight, Paul knew that whoever had left this package for him was probably sitting in a car nearby, waiting for his call. He was about to dial the number on the card, then stopped. He walked to Marge's office and looked through her desk until he found the tape recorder she often used for dictation. He attached the recorder to her phone and made the call.

It was answered on the first ring. A woman with a throaty voice said, "Mr. Arrone?"

Paul was so taken aback by the female voice that he didn't answer. *"Allo?* Is there anyone there?" came the heavily French accented voice.

"Yes, this is Paul Arrone here. To whom am I speaking?"

"Please, Mr. Arrone, if you are going to waste my time, we might as well hang up now," the woman said curtly. "Do you think I would go through all the trouble of getting you to contact me in this manner only to give you my name?"

"Why don't we start there? Exactly why did you go through all this trouble to contact me?"

There was a pause at the other end. Then the woman spoke slowly and matter of factly. "Mr. Arrone, you just happen to fit into my plan very neatly. I am sure that, after we meet, you will agree that I also will fit into your situation, given the events of the last few days. If the document left for you regarding Mrs. Rodino is of interest to you, then you will be at the Essex House Hotel at 6 AM this morning. You will go to the front desk and tell them that you are Mr. Wood and that you are there to see Mrs. Carlin. A security guard will escort you to my suite. You are to come alone.

"If, on the other hand, I have miscalculated and the document I sent you does not interest you enough to embark on this journey, then you are free to hang up the phone, throw that paper away and go about your business. My offer to meet with you will remain intact until 6:05 AM. Good evening, Mr. Arrone."

"No, wait!" Paul shouted into the phone. "You can't just expect me to walk into a possible ambush without getting at least a bit more information."

"Mr. Arrone, I don't haggle. You will either be there, or you won't. I am already tremendously unimpressed with your detective acumen. Look closely at the phone number written on your old business card. It was written with the pen you lost the other night. Good night, Mr. Arrone." The line went dead.

Paul started to panic. "Who the hell is this woman?" he said aloud. He paced the room. *Janice Rodino's blood work. What does it mean? And how did this woman get the pen I dropped in the M.E. office. Oh my God.*

He reached for the phone and called her back. He was met by a dial tone. He started to call Cappy, but stopped. Cullan had gone above and beyond the call of duty too many times. Whomever Paul was meeting probably had a criminal record or was about to acquire one. Cullan could lose his pension trying to save him.

Paul stopped the recorder, removed the tape, took it back to his office and placed it in the same envelope it had arrived in that night. He took stationery and wrote down in police-report fashion the events of the last few days, including this last phone call and ending with his plans to go into the city in the morning. He placed the envelope inside a Fed Ex one, and addressed it to Commissioner Ian Cullan.

He attached a post-it: "Joe, please give this to Cullan when he comes to Mrs. Rodino's service. Only then. Should he not be here, then call Fed Ex to have it picked up for next-day delivery. Even with the holiday."

If something went wrong, Paul figured, then at least Cullan would be able to piece together what Paul was missing. If things went okay at the hotel in the morning, he would simply come back and lock the file in the Funeral Home safe.

Bleary from so little sleep, Paul arrived at the 57th Street exit of the West Side Highway at 5:30 AM Saturday. He parked his BMW in a garage a block away from the Essex House, the same one he used when he stayed at the NYAC nearby.

The choice of the Essex House for the meeting heightened Paul's curiosity. Whoever arranged this meeting knew Paul's habits.

He entered the lobby of the hotel at 5:52 AM, went to the front desk and told the young lady behind the counter that he was there to see Mrs. Carlin.

"Your name?" she asked.

He hesitated. "Mr. Wood."

"One moment, please." She turned her back to him and spoke into a cell phone. Within a few seconds, a tall, burly man with a bristle cut appeared next to Paul. The clerk behind the desk said to Paul, "Laurent will escort you to the suite."

Paul, and the escort he immediately dubbed "The Gargantuan" entered the elevator, which rose to the top floor. They exited the elevator and passed a suite with a placard that read "Presidential Suite," then stopped in front of Room 2402.

Laurent opened the door and motioned to Paul to enter. He saw three other men who made Laurent look malnourished.

Laurent gave a small bow. "With your permission, we would like to search you for weapons or recording devices."

Paul thought, then said, "If I say 'No,' what happens?"

"Nothing, sir," Laurent said smoothly. "If you decline, I am to take you downstairs to the dining room, pay for your breakfast, and send you on your way."

Paul had to hand it to somebody. He had never seen so polite a hired goon in all his years at the periphery of police or government work.

"Okay, knock yourself out," Paul said. He placed his hands on his head and spread his legs apart in the typical search position.

The men went immediately to work. One patted Paul down. Another ran a device that looked like an airport scanner wand around his entire body. The largest of the men was checking Paul with a device he had never seen in any police seminar or crime scene.

Once the quartet seemed satisfied that Paul was clean of any weapons, recording or transmittal devices, Laurent nodded to Paul and said, "Let's go."

They stepped out of the room and headed for the presidential suite. Now this is more like it, Paul thought. As he stepped inside, he was greeted by yet another bodyguard who stood like a Beefeater at the entrance to the suite. This one was much less muscular and far better dressed than the others and perhaps more lethal. Laurent motioned for Paul to sit on the sofa in the enormous living room that overlooked Central Park.

Paul sat waiting for the mysterious Mrs. Carlin to appear but he could hear a man's voice coming from what he assumed was the master bedroom.

Finally, the door swung open. Tomaas LaCroix entered.

CHAPTER 18

(Still Saturday)

Tomaas extended his hand. Paul tried to keep the surprise out of his face and compose his thoughts. He knew he would need all his wits about him in the negotiations to come.

Paul studied Tomaas' handsome face. He was older by a few years, of course: they both were. But Paul saw something deeper than maturity in the Frenchman, something more essential than businesslike acumen. What Paul detected happened to be his expertise: appreciating the etching that the loss of someone you love leaves on the face. Noticing the subtle carvings, the lines of shock, hurt, abandonment, and sometimes rage. Pain was beginning to cling to his face as a mask.

Paul saw it every day. He saw it in the faces of the never-prepared visitors to the Funeral Home. He saw it daily in his own mirror.

Paul didn't wait for the usual opening courtesies. "Clever," he commented.

Tomaas looked at him quizzically.

"To have a woman call. It threw me a bit, as you intended."

Tomaas didn't acknowledge the remarks. "How are you this morning?" he asked, offering Paul a handshake.

Paul returned it coolly. "I am well," he said. "And I'm hoping that I will be even better once you tell me why you called me here for this cloak and dagger act."

Tomaas started to answer, but Paul interrupted. "And while you're at it, what's with all this security? What could I possibly do to you? Embalm you to death?"

Tomaas smiled faintly. "The security was not my idea. We will just have to leave it at that for the moment."

He walked toward the window where he stared at the view. Then wheeled around

"As for why you are here," he said slowly in his thick French accent, "that I can explain." The fact is I need your help, and I am willing to pay for it. I believe Janice Rodino was murdered. And I believe you can help me bring the one who killed her to justice."

Paul said, "If you think there has been a murder, then you should go to the proper authorities, not stand here telling me about it. Furthermore, if you tell me something that indicates there was a crime, or even something highly irregular, then I have no choice but to go to the authorities myself."

The bodyguard interrupted. Unlike the other men that ostensibly guarded Tomaas, this one was older, smaller and dressed formally. He wore a gray pinstriped suit with a boutonnière. He spoke with a British accent. "Please calm down, Mr. Arrone. Why don't you just listen to what Mr. LaCroix has to say? If, after he is done, you feel you don't want to be part of this, or you feel compelled to go to the 'authorities,' or you simply feel like jumping off the Brooklyn Bridge, then no one here will stop you."

"Ah," said Paul, "a veiled threat so soon? How disappointing." The bodyguard glowered.

Paul turned to Tomaas who stood impassively.

"All right," Paul said, "What do you have in mind?"

Tomaas inhaled, and then let his breath out slowly.

"A few months ago," he began, "Janice and I," he pronounced it John-eece – "um, met and became 'involved.'" Paul could here the quotes around the word.

"He's talking about Janice Rodino" inserted the bodyguard.

"Got it," Paul said dryly.

Tomaas continued. "A few months ago, well, more than six months ago, I met Janice in Washington." He hesitated then said almost proudly and a bit defiantly, "We became lovers. She moved to France, my permanent home. She leased a suite at the Ritz Carlton. She was planning to divorce her husband. You know," he said, looking at Paul, "the Senator."

He paused. "Our affair naturally created a stir in my parents' circles. Janice and I only briefly considered – what is the expression? – cooling it.

She said that she could not care less what people were saying. That this was the first time in years she was happy."

He stopped pacing and quickly ran a hand across his face.

"It was the first time in years that I was happy, actually," he said so quietly that Paul had to strain to hear.

"Then my swine of a father forbade me from seeing her," Tomaas continued, more angrily now. "He said that this was affecting both our family names – and his longest and closest friendship with Senator Rodino. And then he threatened to have me removed from my position in the company, which," Tomaas said derisively, "was such a joke. He barely controls his own company. Hell, the bastard barely controls his own bladder."

Certainly, Paul thought, *Tomaas's hatred of his father had matured along with the rest of him.* "Anyway," the young Frenchman continued, visibly pulling himself together, "we started fighting regularly about this. Then one day, he called me to his office. He told me that all of this fighting is foolish, that his objection was not so much that I was screwing – his word," Tomaas said with clear distaste, "his best friend's wife, but that I was doing it so publicly as to embarrass him. He suggested that Jan and I move into the family's summer villa in Monaco where we could enjoy each other's company away from the Paris social scene."

He paused. "I am so angry with myself that I didn't suspect something was wrong." His shoulders slumped, but he went on: "Of course, I told Janice. Her first response was indifference; 'I don't care,' she told me, 'if the whole world knows we are in love with each other.'" Tomaas swallowed with difficulty.

"Then that same night, after dinner at the hotel, we ran into one of your U.S. Congressmen. Janice knew that it would take only as long as dessert to arrive before someone contacted her husband, who in return would call my father. We talked. She said to me that it probably would be better if we moved to Monaco. The irony of this was that, most of all, she was concerned for my well-being." Tomaas stared out the window. "She was concerned for me," he whispered more to himself than others.

"Soon thereafter I moved to Monaco. She was to wait another week or so as to attend two important fund-raisers, then join me at the villa."

He paused, pain etched on his features. "I was out on the terrace the night she was to arrive. She never did."

He walked over to Paul and said evenly, "She was run off the road."

They looked at each other, Tomaas visibly shaken, Paul genuinely empathetic. For one of the few times in his life, Paul connected with a man in grief as a man, not as a professional funeral director. Something passed between them, an agreement, leading, perhaps, to solidarity.

Paul began to speak, but the ring of his cell phone stopped him. Tomaas turned away.

Paul looked at the caller ID line. It was Cullan's number.

"I'm very sorry," Paul said, "I really must take this call."

The smaller bodyguard started to protest, but Tomaas waved him off. He walked Paul to the bedroom. "Take your time," he said, closing the door.

"Hey, Cappy," Paul said, "how's it hanging in the Queen City of the Sound?"

"Listen, son," – uh-oh, thought Paul – "we have a problem here."

It wouldn't be good news. The only other time he had heard that tone and that greeting from his old Sarge was when his brother was killed.

"Go ahead," Paul said quietly.

"I got a call from the D.A. about five minutes ago. She was about to issue a warrant for your arrest in the killing of Ken Browne at the morgue. She said she only called as a courtesy to me and your father."

"That's insane – *Kenny*? Come on." He drew a breath and sat carefully on the edge of the enormous bed. "Cappy, I swear ..." he stammered. "What is going on? Can they do this?"

Paul's skin was clammy. Pain in his chest was squeezing his breath away.

"Listen closely," Cullan said. "They lifted your fingerprints from the inside of the morgue refrigerator and matched them to your funeral director's license."

"Come on, Cappy, mine *and* just about every funeral director's fingerprints are all over that morgue. That is what we do."

"I know. But they also pulled a print from under a bench in the hills of the reservation" He paused. "A second man was killed there."

"Cap, it's a public park, anyone—"

"I know, I know. And we have to talk—"

"We will," Paul interjected, but Cullan went on.

"Here's the deal: I can't stop her from arresting you but I told the D.A. that to arrest you today, on such circumstantial evidence, would not be in her best interests. I also reminded her that your arrest will make front-page headlines all weekend, including the very same day the world will be descending on your funeral home for Janice Rodino's memorial service, and it's too late for your family to pull out. How embarrassing will it be for the Senator to be doing business with someone accused of murder, however flimsy the evidence?

"Diaz agreed to hold off for 48 hours. That brings us to tomorrow night. Now listen closely, Paul. I am going to need you to let me know exactly where you are going to be Sunday. I will personally take you into custody here in New Rochelle. If she has you arrested tomorrow and brings you up to county, you'll sit there the rest of the holiday weekend. You won't be able to post bail until sometime late Tuesday."

"If they give me a shot at bail at all," Paul said, trying to relieve the pressure in his chest.

"The thing is," said Cullan, "I can't have you go to the county pen, son. We both know that can't turn out well for you. I don't trust her and I don't trust those other bastards at the county government. You're under everybody's skin, Paul. You have been for a long time. They're gonna eat you alive."

"Why won't she just have me transferred tomorrow night herself?"

"I have already spoken to Judge Belserene. She won't be around to honor any transfer that the D.A. may present to the city. As for me, I simply won't let you out of my jail."

Paul drew a long breath and ran his hand over his face; he was tired.

"I can't let you take the heat for me, Cappy. They will crucify you. This new mayor has been looking for a reason to dump you. And this would be the perfect reason."

"Don't you worry about me," Cappy said. "This old war horse has carried eight mayors into battle over the past 40 years. I know this mayor would love nothing more than to see to it that this is my last battle, and you know what. Maybe it will be, but I guarantee you this; this old war horse may go down with this battle but as I do, you can rest assured that the last kick of my hoof will land right smack in the middle of the Mayor's head before I fall on top of him and smother that mother f***er."

Paul hadn't heard Cappy so energized in years. Despite the worry, the old man was enjoying himself.

"I won't let you jeopardize your pension or your future, Cappy. Or Bridie's, for that matter."

"Sorry, this is non-negotiable. I have spoken to Bridget and she is in complete agreement. She's even planning on making you a baked ham and apple pie for Sunday dinner. She says she'll even dine with you in cell No. 8, 7 PM sharp. That's it, end of discussion. You and I will talk. In the meantime, stay out of trouble. And quit the detective work. That's *my* job."

Paul hung up. He was shaking. He held his head in his hands. Forty-plus years and his life was unraveling around him … He, who had always been so in control, well, he was out of control now.

A familiar friend was in the room and for the first time Paul named it: *despair*. That's what he had recognized so easily in Tomaas earlier, despair; as familiar as breathing. Each of them were members in the brotherhood of misery.

Suddenly, Paul slumped. Fear evaporated. He didn't care what happened.

Or did he? He stared numbly. Then it came to him. This was the same pattern that allowed him to grow apart from Trish; the closeness, then the despair, followed by withdrawal, then numbness.

And Cappy. His eyes welled up. Cappy had been and still was a devoted and true friend, and how one-sided Paul had let that friendship become.

He heard a cough from the other room. *Why am I here?* he asked himself. *Now what shall I do? And what will my father, both of my parents say? How will they react to my very public troubles? They'll look at me as if they don't know me. And they don't. And I don't know me either.*

Paul knew he had to pull himself together if he had the slightest chance of getting through the meeting on the other side of the door, and through the day ahead of him.

He dug deep to fight off his funk. He called up the only other dependable emotion that he did well, anger. There was nothing like disgust and outrage to get focused.

He walked to the bathroom, ran cold water over his face and into his hair. He straightened his tie in the mirror, avoiding his own eyes. He returned to the living room and joined Tomaas at the window. Traffic was stirring bumper to bumper. "Where were we?" he asked quietly.

"I was telling you that I was standing on the terrace of my villa in Monaco. It looks down on the sharply curving road. A white Range Rover was coming up but was run off by a truck. I saw the Rover go down, but it didn't look so bad." Tomaas shook his head. "I wanted to go for my binoculars, but I didn't want to look away. I know it was pretty far off in the distance but I thought I saw the passenger get out of that truck, go to the Rover and the driver's side and do something. I don't know. He seemed to be checking on the driver but then, nothing. Whoever it was quickly went back to the truck and it sped off. By the time I called the police, they said they already were on their way."

Paul saw a tremor go through the younger man. Tomaas muttered in French. "Excuse me?" Paul asked.

Tomaas turned to him and Paul saw fury in his eyes. "My father made the mistake of calling me to offer his condolences on Janice's death *before* the ambulance had even made its way to the hospital."

"Maybe someone in the local police called him from the scene," Paul suggested.

The bodyguard jumped in. "Not likely," he said, in a stuffy British accent. "The villa is owned by Tomaas' grandmother, Mrs. Obiere. Mrs. Obiere is, not to be unkind, somewhat paranoid since an unfortunate accident some time ago. Today she has in her employ, at least on a part-time basis, nearly forty percent of the local police department. The same holds true for every town where she has a home."

The Englishman stood beside Paul. "What did you say your name is?" Paul asked.

"I didn't," the man said abruptly. "There is more: The local police led us to some conclusions. When they heard who had died in the accident, they pulled video surveillance tapes from the villa's cameras. The captain himself had overseen their installation. That included surrounding the residence itself and cameras on the rooftop eaves to cover the approach roads.

"Mrs. Obiere always has them review all the tapes prior to each of her arrivals at the villa. The captain would be responsible for telling her of any suspicious activity or anyone out of the usual approaching the house before her arrival."

Hell, Paul thought, *this Mrs. Obiere sounds like she would put Howard Hughes to shame.*

The bodyguard walked to the penthouse's elaborate electronic media center. "Madame had all the tapes pulled from the house, duplicated, and secured. This is what we have come up with."

He sat down nearby and reached for a laptop computer. He expertly began the demonstration. Tomaas turned his back.

"This, Mr. Arrone, is where the camera caught the accident. If I back the tape up, you will see over here that the truck was lying in wait for Mrs. Rodino." He fast-forwarded a bit. "Right here is where the two vehicles hit. If I freeze the frame and enhance the image, you can see that something is covering both the license plate and, we have discovered, a logo on the truck.

"A private detective hired by Mrs. Obiere already found a truck in the LaCroix Worldwide Shipping fleet with duct tape residue on the vehicle and its license plate. Also, white paint had been scraped across the front right bumper."

"Why didn't anyone turn this over to the Monaco police?" Paul asked.

"Because Mrs. Obiere has no interest in convicting the driver of the truck of an accident. Now, if I may finish, Mr. Arrone. If I move the frame forward an increment at a time, you can see a man get out of the truck and run to the car, as if he means to help the driver. But he has something in his hands. If the image is magnified by 100, we can make out a slim article in the man's hand. As you can see, the man's face is partially covered by a baseball cap and glasses. However, there are enough facial features for a tentative identification. And with sophisticated software we have acquired, we believe he is one Carlos Ramirez."

"Ramirez is a hired assassin from Colombia," Tomaas said. "I am told he has been associated with over seventy-five drug-related murders, perhaps two political assassinations, and God knows what else."

A mug shot of the man was now displayed on the screen. A line below indicated it was a CIA photo.

A bodyguard, Paul thought, studying the man at the keyboard. *Right.*

"I recognized him," Tomaas said shortly. "This man in the picture met regularly with my father."

Paul looked at Tomaas. He was beginning to see the kind of family, and world, he moved in.

"What is more disturbing is this: That man, your Senator Rodino, and someone else, a friend of Rodino's from his home town, I believe, visited my father at his home the week before Janice was killed."

Paul looked at him thoughtfully. "How can you be certain that this assassin actually worked for your father? And would you be able to recognize the man who came to your house with the Senator that night if you saw him again?"

"Definitely," Tomaas answered.

"I can answer your first question," the bodyguard said. "Look at the screen again please. The next series of photos are from the security cameras at LaCroix Worldwide Shipping headquarters. The building is, of course, owned by the Obiere family.

"All of these photos are of the same man. They were taken at different intervals over the last six months. All photos show this man going into Henri LaCriox's office. In two of them, we have both this man and Henri walking out of his office together.

"True, the man looks different each time, but we have determined each is of the same height and build. Even with different disguises, facial identification software shows positive identification: Carlos Ramirez.

"And he was not shopping for a coffin," the bodyguard said with a small, frightening smile. "At least not for himself."

The trio was silent for a moment as the room turned yellow from the rising sun.

"Okay," said Paul. "So how do I figure into all of this?"

Tomaas looked at him thoughtfully, and then said, "We believe that what you saw at your Medical Examiner's Office last night can be of great help to uncovering what really happened to Janice, and nail my father for her death."

Paul paused, and then asked quietly: "What makes you think I was at the office that night? Or that I can help?"

"Well," Tomaas said, "we can play this cat-and-mouse game for the better part of the morning, or you can look at the pictures inside that envelope and we can agree to work together."

Paul riffled quickly through the photos. Here he was, entering and exiting the office on the night that Kenny was killed. *Wouldn't Haywood & Co. love these*, he thought angrily.

"Perhaps," Tomaas suggested, "there are additional photos that could exonerate you in the death of that man that evening. Or the other death."

They had him, Paul thought.

"Before I agree to cooperate," he said, "tell me something: Why do you suspect your father, other than the fact that he disliked your affair with Janice Rodino? Running her off the road? That's an extreme length to go to, don't you think?"

"I'll answer that," interrupted the bodyguard as he put his hand up to Tomaas in a manner that was more like an attorney-client rather than a bodyguard -protectee relationship." First, I want to say, Mr. Arrone, that you appear to be less, how shall I say, informed than we had been told. We have reason to believe that Henri and this assassin have had an even longer history together. We have traced the assassin to several drug-related deaths and we feel that Henri could have been using his company to smuggle the drugs back into the U.S. in some of the bodies that his firm shipped."

Paul suddenly got it. The wheels of his mind spun into overdrive. *Holy crap*, he thought. *That could explain so much.* Not just what he had seen in the last few days: Janice Rodino's casket at the airport, then the morgue scene, but other things that hadn't made sense to him for so long: LaCroix's corporate push into the metropolitan region. Alverez's bizarre operation.

Crap, thought Paul, what a — a *sacrilege* was the only word he could come up with. *Using death to make obscene amounts of money. Using deaths to make more deaths. Hopping borders easily, distributing drugs like prayer cards. Coke and heroin flooding the streets. It was a sacrilege*, Paul thought *and it was brilliant.*

"I'm in," Paul said. "But we have a lot of work to do. And we had better do it carefully."

He turned to Tomaas. "Do you have access to LWS's computers?

"Yes, of course. I have everything we need right here or will get it quickly."

"Good," said Paul. "Order me some coffee and let's get to work." *And then tomorrow*, he thought, *I'll have to help Pop with Janice Rodino's service.*

CHAPTER 19

It was a Saturday afternoon, but still the officials gathered in the Westchester County Disaster Preparedness Room. It was several floors underground, between the Westchester Medical Center and the Cardin Biotech Group research facility. The room was connected to both buildings by tunnels and was built by the Cardin Group as part of the lease requirements with the county. It was intended to be equipped to handle any disaster, with a command center and enough food and water to house public officials for several weeks, if need be. A bunker, actually, it had its own oxygen supply. It was also lined in lead, as protection in case the Indian Point nuclear power plants leaked radioactive material. It was impervious to sound and, officials believed, tracking devices.

Today's officials were meeting here for its secrecy. This would be only the third time, and the last time, this cast of characters would meet to discuss their common concerns. They did not trust even their closest aides or the facility's guards. They certainly did not trust each other.

Warden Walker was the last to storm in and the first to break the silence. "What the hell are we going to do now? I can't have any more suspicious behavior happening at my penitentiary. We've had enough deaths and enough illnesses. People – the press – are starting to ask too many questions. I want to know what we are going to do now."

Droplets of sweat that had been building on the oily forehead and droopy upper lip of the pale-faced commissioner, wriggled then fell, flecking the top of the mahogany conference table they sat around.

Senator Frank Rodino, sitting at one end, began in a very low voice. "What we are going to do now," he said, his voice raising a decibel with every syllable until he was screaming, "is to have you shut the hell up, you fat, fag bastard, and do as you're told!"

The corpulent warden shrunk back as if he had been struck.

"If we decide," Senator Frankie continued, "that your entire prison population is going to get infected with a virus, I expect you to sit there quietly. In fact, the only thing I expect to hear from you is: 'Thank you, sir. May I have another?'"

The Senator turned to the Westchester County executive and barked, "What's the matter, Steve? Can't you keep your employees under control?"

The county executive's face reddened around the eyes, but he said nothing – instead reaching for the glass of scotch that sat in front of him. He looked across the table to the warden.

"Bob, I think it would be best if you wait outside and take a moment to compose yourself. I'll fill you in on the details you'll need later."

Robert Walker drummed his fingers on the table and tried to look defiant.

"I'm not asking you, Bob. I am telling you," Steve O'Brien said firmly.

Walker slammed back his chair, rose and, mumbling under his breath, waddled to the outside corridor. Rodino pressed something under the table and the soundproof door shut decisively behind him.

County Executive O'Brien said: "Bob won't be a problem; he is just, um, emotional."

"You bet your fricking Irish ass he won't be a problem," the Senator said in a deadly tone.

He turned to the medical examiner. "Update me."

Haywood started methodically, as if he were cutting into one of his bodies.

"We know Arrone was inside the building that night. We know we can muster enough evidence to have him arrested. We're not sure what or how much he saw, if anything. Or who, if anyone, he told."

"All of that will be a moot point once he is arrested." District Attorney Diaz interjected.

Haywood turned to her. "You get him to the county pen, and I will personally infect that bastard with the virus."

The Senator said to Diaz, "Do you have enough evidence to bring him in? Don't forget, he's got a lot of friends, especially among the cops and higher-ups. And a handful of judges and a lot of county workers, who still think he's some kind of rebel-martyr. And then there's his father."

Diaz was uncharacteristically nervous as she replied. After all, her mentor, Jeanine Pirro, the first female D.A. in Westchester's history, had schooled her in going after domestic violence cases – which had been her forte. Not former politicians and well-connected ones at that, which looked as if it were to become this current district attorney's forte. This was new territory for her and possibly dangerous.

"I have his fingerprints all over the place" she said. "That, coupled with testimony from Haywood about that exchange over the Janice Rodino body the day before, gives me probable cause to bring him in."

She leaned forward. "I certainly don't have enough to indict him. Even if I did, we could never prosecute him successfully on what I have now."

"What about breaking and entering?" asked legislature chairman Patrick Miller. "And other charges. It might not be murder, but—"

"He'll never see the inside of a judge's chambers," Haywood cut in. "We only need to get our hands on him, and we will, tomorrow, after your wife's service," He turned to Rodino. "We'll wait a discreet amount of time, then take him."

They were silent for a moment. Then Haywood smiled. "Actually," he said slowly, "our other situation can help take care of the Arrone one."

"How so?" O'Brien asked.

"Let's figure Diaz's people pick him up tomorrow night, after the service. He's booked on murder charges and put in the county jail – in a cell alone, given his status."

"I will inject him with the virus that evening. We've perfected the timing. By morning, he will be too sick to go anywhere. Cardin will help keep him alive, even if it's in a coma, until after the Fifth."

"Now here's the good part," the medical examiner said, his eyes glowing with excitement. "The virus is to be released early Tuesday just before the financial markets re-open. There are plenty of workers and traders there even earlier. In the meantime, Diaz makes sure that a couple of laborers – Arabs, we'll say – are arrested. Under any pretext she wishes. I'll make sure they're placed in the same general area as Arrone."

Some around the table could already see where he was going.

"As the stuff hits the fan with the terrorist plot, the Arrone kid will be dead or just about. Between him and the Arabs, who also just happened to get infected too; we'll let the feds, the press and everybody else make the connection. After all, he did get to the casket first."

Only Diaz looked vaguely shocked at Haywood's scenario.

Haywood turned to O'Brien and Rodino. "And since you're worried about our fat friend out there," he said with a nod of his head toward the corridor, "well, Westchester County will lose its warden to the same infection hitting a handful of others."

Cardin broke in, his long face thoughtful. "We will not be able to cremate them immediately. Under The Patriot Act all bodies and records will have to be looked at by the feds and their medical people first."

"Good," Rodino said. "That'll make everything look even more legitimate."

The Senator turned to Diaz. "What about that damn police captain friend of his? The one from New Rochelle. Can he intervene? Can he screw this up?"

"Ian Cullan? He's Commissioner now," Miller reminded him.

"Cullan has already interfered," Diaz said. "He's called in a ton of markers to keep me away from Arrone until tomorrow night."

"What are you smiling at?" O'Brien asked.

"I was just thinking," Diaz said. "If Cullan had minded his own business, Arrone would have already been arrested. We probably wouldn't have to think up the virus time table, let alone use it."

"Just remember," Haywood interjected, "I thought it up."

Diaz rolled her eyes. "Getting back to your question, the Mayor is prepared to fire the Police Commissioner tomorrow if he causes problems. New Rochelle's city charter allows for that as long as the Mayor immediately appoints the deputy commissioner so there's no void. Once fired, Cullan is a private citizen. He can be arrested, if need be, along with his friend Arrone."

The tension had dropped a level in the room. The Senator turned to Cardin. "You're up. What have you got?"

He steepled his fingers. "Let's quickly review," he said, "my lab has perfected a vaccine for an Ebola-like virus. Properly timed, it can inoculate against hemorrhagic fever. In the process of developing it, my lab has discovered or created several important variations: a form that exhibits similar, but less ravaging symptoms and with a far lower mortality rate. We also have a concentrated "super form" of the virus that produces certain, almost instant death."

The officials looked warily at each other and then back to Cardin.

"The incubation period for the last two, we estimate, is twelve to fourteen hours – unlike the week that it can take when spread normally." He leaned forward. "And this, I know, is what you want to hear most. We are relatively certain that we are the only lab in the country, if not the world that has produced a vaccine for such conditions. Given our head start in knowing about it, we are undoubtedly the only lab that has such a large supply of the vaccine."

The politicians smiled.

Cardin continued. "Thanks to my good friend the Senator," he said with a nod to Rodino, "we entered this field at the behest of the White House, which wanted to show its commitment to the African continent."

"How well will it work?" O'Brien said. "People have to need it and want it badly enough, but we can't have them dropping like flies."

"The vaccine we developed has a success rate of 90 percent," Cardin said. "That is far below any acceptable level of success for any vaccine currently in use. It means that, statistically, for every 100 people who are vaccinated, ten will become ill and about five will die. Compared to the smallpox vaccine, where one in one million will get the disease, you can see how dangerous this vaccine is."

"Not to mention the virus itself," Rodino muttered.

"Are you sure the government will allow your vaccine with that kind of record to be used?" asked the district attorney.

"Normally they wouldn't, but under extreme cases it will have no choice. Besides, if there were even the possibility of the virulent form of the virus falling into the wrong hands, and an outbreak threatened to spread throughout a large city, the government would have no choice but to use the vaccine."

"But from what I understand," O'Brien said, "the Ebola virus isn't readily transmitted. It's not airborne like the flu, or touching, right?"

"Correct," answered the Senator to Cardin's annoyance. "However, it's been rumored for some time that the former Soviet Union had developed an airborne form of such a virus during the Cold War for use in a biomedical war. I have also been told by our intelligence agency that three vials of the virus were stolen from what was supposed to be a secure lab in St. Petersburg six months ago. We have reason to believe it has made its way here."

The Senator spoke slowly, envisioning the scenario. "So hypothetically, if there were an outbreak in New York City, and people showed immediate symptoms, there would be no time for the government to determine whether what they're dealing with the airborne kind or the contact kind."

"All that health officials will remember," Cardin said, "will be the 1976 outbreak of the Ebola virus in Zaire. Eighty-eight percent of the 318 people infected died. There is only one lab in the United States that has even studied this virus this recently, and there is only one lab in the world that holds a patent on the vaccine. That would be the Cardin Biotech Group."

They were again silent, contemplating how they had missed out on Afghanistan and the military contracts, how they had missed out on Iraq and all those oil and reconstruction deals. They would not miss out on this one.

Senator Frankie sat back and propped his feet on the table, his hands behind his head.

"Gee, Phil," he said, "what is the stock in your company trading at these days?"

"It closed yesterday at $38," Cardin answered.

"And what was the stock of that European lab that was awarded the contract for the smallpox vaccines after 9/11?"

"Their stock went from $24 to $103."

The Senator looked around the room. His famous horsey grin appeared.

"And that was without a single confirmed case of the disease ever being identified," he said with satisfaction.

"Speaking of stock," O'Brien said, "are we sure the shut-down of the main exchanges won't affect ours?"

"Not a chance," Rodino said. "If anything has backup in this country, it's the stock exchanges."

Diaz had another question. "Why haven't other labs worked on this?"

O'Brien was incredulous. "Think about it," he said. "This is one of the richest counties in the nation and we barely run a bus from the inner-cities to our parks. And you can't figure out why countries aren't tripping over themselves to produce a cure for a disease that hasn't left the borders of Africa? What truck did you fall off of?"

Cardin shook his head. "It's not so stupid a question, Steve. The fact is, many labs, including the governments, are studying such diseases. But only ours has taken on the task of finding a cure. The others have backed away due to the small universe affected. Why cure a disease that strikes a few people every so many years, when you can devote your time and money to larger, more pervasive illnesses. But we're getting off the track." He turned to the chairman of the board. "Pat, is everything in proper order on your end?"

"Yes," Miller said. "Certain officials purchased big blocks of the stock when you first opened up your research center two years ago. It was considered a great public-private joint venture.

"Remember that, at the time, the prevailing opinion was that no company would be able to compete with the research facilities of New York Presbyterian that were then coming to downtown White Plains. It was a natural thing for local politicians to invest some, or in a half-dozen or so cases *most*, of their deferred compensation in a home-grown company. Because the compensation board and not the legislators do the buying and selling, we're all clear of any appearance of wrongdoing. That is, if something doesn't go our way," he added hastily.

Miller looked around at the doubtful faces.

"Look," he said. "I am one of the three members on the county's deferred compensation board. Using standard New York State deferred compensation and pension laws, our compensation board will most likely start to sell some stocks as they double in value, and certainly shed more if the stock triples."

"What if we want to hang on to our stock until it hits a high?" the county executive asked.

"You can't have any say in what the Chairman of the Board of Legislators does or doesn't do with the stock," Diaz said, "Otherwise you could be brought up on insider trading charges. You don't want to be another Martha Stewart."

"That's great for you to say," the County Executive said sarcastically. "You own the most. One million shares of the frigging stock. So you stand to make close to $90 million dollars."

The district attorney rose angrily. "Listen to me, you little prig," she said, pointing her Neiman Marcus manicured nails at the county executive, "we took all the risk. Remember, my husband's company built this piece of garbage building, and he took stock in lieu of payment owed him – all under bid, all so you assholes would look good at election time. None of you had any financial risk.

"And now you, of all people," she blared at the county executive, "are going to sit here and make us believe that we are going to have to run you a fund-raiser because you might not be able to 'get by?' Give me a freakin' break."

"Calm down, calm down," soothed the Senator. "We're talking a long way down the road, if ever. Despite protections, the stock market still will take a while to recover."

"But rest assured," Cardin said, "One of the benefits of the Cardin Biotech Group is that our stock also is traded on the London markets."

CHAPTER 20

Saturday noon

When the hearse pulled up in front of the Alverez funeral home no name displayed in the window. Not unusual for trade embalmers who have no particular affiliations or allegiances. Paul backed the hearse into the nearest bay. A construction company was digging up a trench next to where he parked.

It was just after noon. Gerard would be down on Arthur Avenue for his usual lunch ritual. Paul got out and walked down the ramp to the embalming room. He spotted Jose from earlier in the week and waved him over.

"I did a trade call for Gerard this morning," Paul said. "A body from Bogotá. Gerard asked me to bring the casket here and wait for him to get back from lunch."

"Mr. Gerard didn't tell me about you coming here to drop anyone off," said José.

Paul spoke matter-of-factly. "I'm not sure the body is staying here or going down to the Madison Avenue branch."

He swung the hearse door open. A solid-bronze Model 48 Supra was exposed. This casket always elicited awe, even among the most staid in the profession. It is the most expensive one on the market retailing for $29,000. Usually a funeral home owner will sell one once in his lifetime, if ever. Industry workers treat this piece of merchandise with the reverence given a Bentley Arnarge Red Label at a used-car lot.

"Dios mio," José whispered under his breath.

Paul pointed to the blue-painted knob that covered the casket key hole.

"How about you help me get this downstairs," he asked José, as he slipped a $20 bill in his hand. "I'm supposed to wait with it until Gerard calls me to get it to the downtown office." Like anything else blue-tagged, José knew it wasn't to be worked on at this site.

The two men maneuvered the casket as if it were filled with nitroglycerin. They went down the ramp through the prep room and into the private office area that Gerard had shown Paul.

As they came to a rest, Paul tapped the top of the casket and said, "There you go, baby, safe and sound."

José asked Paul if he wanted him to beep Gerard to find out what to do next. "Don't bother," Paul said, taking off his coat. "It's been a while since I've worked in the prep room. Why don't you let me give you a hand while I'm waiting for Gerard?"

"Thanks, Mr. Paul." José cast a last look at the casket. "I'll be back."

Paul followed him out, placed his jacket on the doorknob and rolled up his sleeves. Then he closed the door that separated the embalming room from the downstairs office/holding room. As long as his suit jacket stayed on the knob, Paul thought, the chance of any blood-and-guts soaked hands of these Hispanic embalmertrons touching that door was nil.

His head swiveled to the window. Jackhammers.

They had been a couple of blocks away from the Alverez funeral home when Paul had pulled the hearse over to review the plan. Tomaas would lie in the casket and wait for Paul to tap twice on the lid. Paul would gently turn the casket key just a hair so that the locking mechanism would not be fully engaged. Once Tomaas heard the taps, he was to count to 60, open the lid and slip out of the casket. If for any reason, he couldn't open the casket, he was to tap from the inside using a cloth-covered hammer that Paul gave to him so as to not dent the precious casket.

Tomaas would then use his LaCroix pass codes to tap into the Alverez Funeral Home data base and retrieve what Paul wanted.

Standing in the prep room, all Paul could hear was that jackhammer. Damn. Had Tomaas heard him? Or worse yet, would he be able to hear Tomaas? He couldn't go back in there; Jose would notice. Would Tomaas be trapped and suffocate?

Paul strode across the room. He took a fifty out of his pocket and asked José to go out and ask those workers to knock it off for ten minutes. "Why?" José said, frowning.

"I'd like to show your staff how to do restorative work by rebuilding the nose of that shooting victim over on Table 3."

Paul knew that the $50 would never make it to the construction guys outside, but he also knew that José would bribe them in some fashion, maybe offering them a few of his gold teeth collection.

A few seconds later, there was relative quiet outside. Paul casually walked by the office door, but heard nothing from inside. Either Tomaas was pilfering through the Alverez computers or he had suffocated inside the Model 48 Supra. Either way would mean Paul was facing felony charges. More of them, he thought grimly.

As soon as Jose came back down the ramp, Paul asked if anyone had ever showed the staff how to do restorative work on a body. Paul knew the answer, and in fact, knew that no one in that room was even remotely capable of embalming a body, much less doing restorative work. Paul went on to tell them that in today's market-place, a good restorative artist could make upwards of $400 an hour. A complete hush came over the room, with all of the half a dozen or so workers' hanging on Paul's every word.

"Okay now," Paul continued "if someone will bring me that container of restore wax, I'll begin to show you how it goes." About three-quarters of the way through, his cell phone rang. He removed his gloves to answer the phone. "Sure, Gerard," he said. "No, it's no problem at all. I'll call you when I get there. José, Gerard wants me to bring that call down to the Madison Avenue Branch. Hell. They're hopping mad that I'm not there already."

Paul took out another twenty, making it look like his last. "Can you help me one more time to get this casket back in the hearse ASAP?"

Paul reached to the nearby counter for a casket cover. He knew that if he didn't cover the casket, Jose might notice it was now unlatched.

"Tell Gerard I'll replace this the next time I see him."

Several minutes and blocks later, Paul pulled over, reached, and tapped three times on the casket.

The lid opened slowly. There was just enough room in the hearse for Tomaas to climb out and make his way to the passenger seat next to Paul.

"Got it," Tomaas said.

The hearse headed slowly back in the traffic on U.S. 1 to New Rochelle. The two men rode in silence.

For the first time in days, Paul had a moment to reflect on the dramatic turn of his life. He was about to become a fugitive from the law. This would be the second time he ran away from the law, he thought ruefully. Both times he was wanted, each time for completely different reasons. He was losing the only woman he had ever been in love with, and had just broken into the computer system of a colleague's funeral home and stolen information.

Depression washed over him. Tomaas finally broke the silence, "When are we supposed to meet the police commissioner, your friend?"

Pulling himself back to the present, Paul said, "In an hour, upstairs at the Funeral Home. That should give us enough time to look over the files you got and see if what we suspect is plausible."

Paul drove the older hearse into the carriage house; he got out and handed Tomaas a baseball cap and a basket of flowers he had placed on the floor earlier. "Here, put this on and use these flowers to cover your face. Go through that door, and stand as far to the right of the room as you can. The cameras shouldn't be able to pick you up. I'll come down the back stairs and get you. Just give me two minutes to get in there and pick up my messages from my secretary."

In Langley, Virginia, at CIA headquarters, the director was in what many referred to as the "War Room." One wall was blanketed with TV screens, another with clocks showing the time in every time zone. Before him was a 20-by-30-foot map of the United States. The highest-tech computers in the world ringed the room.

The director's top staff sat quietly as he spoke into the speaker phone.

"That's right, Mr. President. The increase in chatter we've been discussing this entire week, along with our sources around the world, indicate to us that terrorists are indeed planning a domestic strike on or near this 4th of July holiday."

"Hell, Ron," the voice shouted, "the 4th is tomorrow. That means we could sustain some kind of hit anytime from now through next week." There was a pause, then: "I know it's a horrible time for the head of the Homeland Security Committee, but have you spoken to Senator Rodino yet?"

"No, Mr. President, just the head of the FBI and your people."

"Well," the president said with a sigh, "I guess I have to ask it: What exactly do we know, and when did we know it?"

The director's chief of staff began the run-down. "The chatter picked up a couple of weeks ago. This is the same pattern that we've seen around the 4th of July and other dates such as New Year's Eve. It has become routine. But a week ago, things became more intense. We pushed all our operatives to find out what we could.

Of course, we had much information that did not pan out, or that we felt wasn't substantive enough to act on. We also felt, Mr. President, that the death of Mrs. Rodino added to the chatter. In fact, we had practically every terrorist group trying to claim credit for this and make it into something other than just an unfortunate accident.

"We spent the last three days reconfirming with our sources, along with the FBI and today, we got our first solid lead – from a mole we have inside a cell in Chicago. The best we can make out is that it's a threat of a biological attack in one or more locations, likely our larger cities."

"As we speak, Mr. President," the director broke in, "all local authorities are being notified. We have reason to believe the nature of the attack will be soft targets – maybe shopping malls or fireworks displays."

"Damn it, Ron," shouted the President, "that's worse than having no intelligence at all. How are we going to handle this if you can't give us a more specific target?"

The CIA director responded slowly and carefully. "First, Mr. President, we recommend the terror level be raised to Orange or even Red. We have notified the locals. As you know, they've gone far in helping us capture some of these cells. We will be working around the clock to make sure this does not happen, Mr. President, but there is one more element to this."

"Great," said the president.

"Our informant believes that unlike other attacks that are full frontal and bold for the sake of shock, this one will be more quiet and more insidious; possibly a virus, maybe smallpox, something that will be spread at one of these events, but won't show up until some time later. Something that would give a massive infection rate that would be very difficult to control. But in the meantime, the terrorists will announce it to the world and we will have mass panic on our hands."

They could hear muffled voices as the President conferred with aides.

"Here is what I want done," the President said. "I first want you to first notify every pharmaceutical company that is under contract with this government, then all the others.

By the next time we speak, which should be in the next hour, I want that map of yours to have the location of every single antidote and vaccine that is known to the CDC to be marked out. If we get one whiff of a problem, we'll send the Air Force, if need be, to pick up and deliver the medicine to wherever it is needed.

"After we hang up I am heading to Camp David where our team will mobilize and coordinate with you. The Vice President will remain here at the White House."

There was silence and the director thought the president had rung off.

"Oh, and Ron?" the President said, "this is an election year *so don't screw this up!*"

The line went dead – which Ron figured he would be soon, one way or another.

Chapter 21

Saturday night

Cullan, Tomaas, and Paul sat at the dining room table in the funeral home apartment. In front of each, stood a bottle of beer and a small stack of computer sheets that Paul had just printed out.

"Okay," Paul said. "If you guys pick up the pile of papers in front of the both of you, I will try to explain what I think we have. Given the limited time I've had, some of this may be sketchy, but you'll get the idea.

"The Alverez Funeral Home, and for that matter all the funeral homes in the LaCroix Worldwide Shipping group, use EternaWare software. This software does specific things for the funeral industry – many of which are not important for us to discuss right now. One thing it does do, though, is track all funerals that have taken place both in the individual funeral home and within the funeral network of LWS. This program also helps funeral homes sell pre-need funerals."

"Pre-need?" asked Cullan. "Now that's planning."

"Yup. You see, the repeat business in the funeral industry is higher over the long term than any other industry. Let's say, for instance, that a man was buried from the Alverez Funeral Home five years ago. This software will chart whether the man has a surviving spouse and other relatives. If so, and he's buried in a local cemetery, then the probability of his widow being buried from the same funeral home is in the high 90 percent range. So, the funeral home will send out follow-up mailings from the time of this man's death until the time they bury his widow, or siblings. At that point they move on to the next generation of survivors. After I downloaded Alverez's files that Tomaas obtained today …" Paul continued.

Cullan raised his eyebrows and turned sharply to Tomaas, who made a "Who me?" face before Paul continued.

"I searched the last few years for funerals of *traditional* Alverez clients, where the death occurred elsewhere but the bodies were shipped to Alverez using the parent company, LWS. The first three pages are a list of those deaths. As you can see, 12 of the 13 deaths all happened in South America, which is no surprise since Alverez is a predominantly Columbian funeral home. What *is* a surprise is that without exception all the people on the list died in accidents or under suspicious circumstances while on vacation or visiting relatives in Columbia. If you check further, you'll see that every single body on the list had been earmarked by the main computer as a future client, meaning, as I explained before, that they had a spouse or close relative buried from Alverez and they owned a cemetery plot here in New York. Under these circumstances, there is almost a 100 percent chance that these people would be shipped back here to New York and would use the same funeral home as before."

Paul leaned forward. "I think these people were killed, probably by that assassin friend of your father's, Tomaas, then shipped back to New York."

Tomaas's jaw dropped. He sputtered in French then drew a breath. "You think my father would kill a bunch of people just to get their busi-ness!? I think the man is despicable, but even I don't believe this."

Paul was quiet for a moment before saying slowly, "No, actually I believe there is much more to his scheme: more and worse."

The other two men exchanged glances. Tomaas looked shocked, Cullan, skeptical, but he had a good idea where Paul was going.

"Bear with me for a moment," Paul urged. "If you look at pages 6 and 7, you will see a list. It was faxed to me by a friend at the local newspaper who used to cover me when I was on the Board."

"Board?" Tomaas asked.

"In politics, I used to be in politics." Paul hastily explained. "This list covers all the day laborers – stray immigrants who died in Westchester County over the same time period in accidental or unusual deaths. If you pick up page 8, you'll see what happens when I merge the two lists. Without exception, a few days to a week after the burial of one of those people who died in an accident in Colombia and shipped back here, you will see that some unlucky immigrant fell off a ladder or something and was then shipped back to Colombia."

"Well, I'll be," said Cullan in a whisper. Paul saw a wave of enlightenment cross his face.

"Exactly, Cappy," Paul said, nodding.

Tomaas slammed his hand down in irritation. "Exactly *what*?"

Paul drew a deep breath. "I think your father, or certainly someone high up in his organization, was having people on vacation in Colombia killed. When their bodies were returned via casket, so were drugs."

"Drug smuggling," Tomaas said with a groan. "Why should I be surprised."

"In return," Paul continued, "some poor bastard gets thrown off the Division Street Bridge or something and his remains, or whatever is left of them, are stuffed with money for payment of said drugs, then shipped back."

"His remains? His actual body?" Tomaas looked shocked. "Not merely the casket?"

"Why not?" Paul said with a shrug. "Who would look there?"

He went on. "I'm guessing that if you looked at all the records of all the deaths that LWS handled, you would find similar events with other countries. Think of the possibilities: conflict diamonds from Africa, or maybe small pieces of antiquity missing after the start of the Iraq War ..." Paul continued more quietly, not really wanting to ask. "Tomaas, did your father ever handle bodies of soldiers for Washington?"

Tomaas leaped to his feet and began pacing the room.

"Are you saying, are you actually saying that my Janice was murdered for the sake of shipping drugs?"

"No," Paul said. "I don't think so. I haven't figured out her case yet, but it wasn't for drugs."

He rose, faced Tomaas, and placed a hand on his shoulder. "She was very likely murdered by that assassin hired by your father."

"What's that?" said Cullan, clearly shocked.

Paul had Tomaas repeat the story he had told him earlier at the Essex House. When he finished, Cullan, like Paul, zeroed in on a question: "Could you identify the unknown man who visited your father with Senator Rodino just before Janice died?"

"Of course," Tomaas said grimly.

Cullan turned to Paul, "The conclusions you've drawn from all of this are wild even by your standards. But I have to admit, something *is* going on here. And yet if you go back to that first set of papers, there was a death in Colombia that, according to the software and normal practices of the funeral industry, should have gone to the Alverez Funeral Home. Why didn't it? How do you explain that?"

Paul pulled out a fax of an old newspaper clipping. The headline told of a small plane that was smuggling drugs across the border when it crashed into a home in a small town in Texas.

"Normally, I would say that it would just be the cost of doing business, like this incident here. However, in this particular case, the decedent was the wife of a man who happened to own a printing company in Mount Vernon. There would be no way for LaCroix to know that this man did all my campaign printing when I ran for office, or that we are good friends. So when this man called on me to bury his wife, one would have thought that this would send a panic through the LWS network. Not so. You see, as Tomaas will explain later, LWS had become so formidable a force that it had its own hangars at the major airports around the country, including LaGuardia and JFK. About five years ago, LWS got a contract from the Port Authority to offload and hold all human remains that entered the metropolitan area. So even if they were to *lose* a funeral, there would still be a window of opportunity where they could retrieve contraband. Now you may think that's a stretch, since many families accompany their loved ones home on the same plane, but think about it. LWS could easily open a crate, then open the casket inside, take out the contraband, and put everything back together while, say, as in this instance, the husband was going through customs.

"It may not be the easiest or most ideal scenario," Paul continued, "but it is doable. Now in this particular case, if I'm right, testing the remains of the chest cavity of my friend's wife for traces of cocaine or other drugs that may have been smuggled in could prove positive."

"We don't have nearly enough concrete evidence to get a court order to exhume that woman's body," Cullan said. "But for right now, I want to do some of my own research." He stood and prepared to leave.

"Paul, can you get Tomaas back in here tomorrow without anyone seeing him? In fact, maybe he had better stay here; it's safer for both of you. I want to sit him down in front of those monitors for the entire time of the memorial service and see if he recognizes anyone in the crowd that will be here to pay their respects to the late Mrs. Rodino." Cullan cleared his throat before continuing. "Oh, and Paul, I'll meet you right here in this apartment at 6 PM sharp to take you into custody. Right?"

"Yeah, right, like I have somewhere else to be."

"Give me your word," Cullan pressed.

"You have my word," Paul answered, hoping as he spoke the words that this was the only time in his life he would be forced to lie to his old friend.

It was close to midnight. The two men worked in darkness lit dimly by moon light. Any artificial light at all could cause a neighbor to call the police. The men also could not use any machinery to dig up this grave. They had to do it the old fashioned way, by hand.

Angelo, the foreman, and Joe, his assistant, were aware that what they were doing wasn't right, and possibly even illegal, but they felt a tremendous loyalty to their boss and to the Arrone family. Paul's grandfather had given Angelo's father his first job in this country at a time when Italian-speaking immigrants were unemployable. Both Angelo and Joe knew they would have nothing were it not for the Arrone family. They owed the Arrones. So the fact that they might lose everything if this venture went wrong was no deterrent at all.

The men had been working since dark and had just hit the top of the concrete vault that the casket was placed in. They were sitting to the side of the open grave taking a break when they saw the hearse pull up with its lights off. Four people approached. Angelo could only recognize Paul. Even at that, he wasn't certain since he had always seen him in a suit and tie. This man approached in jeans, ready to work.

Then he heard Paul's familiar voice whisper, "Hey, Ange. How far did you get?"

"We are done, boss," Angelo answered.

"Great." Paul then did the introductions.

"This is Tomaas. He'll help you, Joe and me lift the casket out of the grave. Over there are two forensic chemists. They'll take over when we get the casket into the garage."

The two chemists were private, for-hire, licensed chemists Paul had met on one of his seminars with Cullan. Their record of convictions in court was second to none. They stood by the hearse dressed in black and were almost invisible except for the smoke and light from one of their cigarettes.

When the men got to the grave, Joe was installing a tripod over it. This would be used to help lift off the top of the concrete vault. Tomaas handed Paul a pair of night goggles and said, "I thought we might need these so I charged them, and a case of champagne, to the company this afternoon."

"We're not going to have time to drink."

"Who said the champagne was for you?" shot back Tomaas.

Paul felt exhilarated by the smell of the damp earth that had just been dug and the wearing of the goggles, but most of all by what they were doing. For the first time in two years, the acid wasn't churning in his stomach. He had no signs of an impending panic attack, even though logically he knew this should be the time for one.

After the top to the concrete vault was lifted off, Angelo jumped into the grave. Joe handed him a long, nylon, seat-belt like strap. Angelo straddled the bottom half of the concrete vault and shimmied the strap under the bottom half of the casket.

Once that was done, Joe handed him another strap. Joe and Tomaas lifted the bottom half of the casket with the first strap that Angelo had just secured. With the inch or so of room that the two men created for him, Angelo shimmied the second strap from the bottom of the casket to the top, and then climbed out of the grave.

"Okay," said Angelo, "On three! One, two, three!" The four men lifted the casket buried some three years ago out of what was supposed to be its final resting place, and into the cool summer air that blew from nearby Long Island Sound.

Once the casket cleared the hole, Angelo said, "Hold!" as he kicked a waiting wood plank across the opening and underneath the casket. He did the same thing once again at the other end of the casket and then said, "Now down slow!"

As the casket came to rest on the wooden bier, Paul could hear a slight sloshing inside. He knew that was not good. Even though the grave looked dry and the casket had been placed in a vault, there may have been some seepage of water which would make the chemist's job much more difficult, and perhaps impossible. Paul also knew that if it weren't water from an external force, then the sound he was hearing was due to the fluids of a decomposing body and a byproduct of formaldehyde on its tissue. That would mean that inside the casket they might find broken-down adipose tissue to such a degree that the chemists might not be able to determine anything. Either way, the sound sobered Paul up within seconds and he felt the acid churn in his stomach.

Under the light of the full moon, the four men put the casket on a cemetery "roller" and began to wheel it quietly toward the hearse. They moved in complete silence with the exception of an occasional squeak from the wheels beneath the casket. No one in the unnatural procession said a word. Caskets just don't come back up from the ground.

The finality of death was being mocked here, and it made everyone, including Paul, uncomfortable. They placed the casket into the hearse. Paul got in and told his small band of night marauders that he would meet them at the garage at the bottom of the hill.

He backed the hearse up to the cemetery garage, which on this evening was transformed into a temporary lab. The chemist's team took over from this point. They had brought with them their own assistants so that the chain of evidence would be intact, should they have to testify in court. Angelo and Joe sat in their truck, eating peaches soaked in homemade wine. Tomaas was sitting on the passenger side of the hearse, sipping champagne and text messaging someone on his cell phone. All knew that this could be a very long night.

Paul stood just a couple of feet from the hearse in a reflective mood. He was remembering the day he buried the woman he just exhumed. He thought about the funeral industry buzz word, "closure," and wondered if he had crossed the line and capitalized on it. He knew that his former political campaign printer had never been able to come to closure over his wife's death. He had told Paul at the time of her death that he swore he saw his wife pushed in front of that train in Bogotá while they were on vacation. The official report said she slipped and fell. So when Paul called him earlier and told his old acquaintance of his suspicions, he was not only willing to sign the exhumation authorization, he actually seemed enthusiastic. Paul hoped he wasn't doing a disservice to his old friend with his own compulsive behavior.

The cooler night air felt refreshing to Paul. It was a damp night and Paul could see the moisture that had formed on the gravestones in the moonlight. He was pleased at how well manicured his employees had kept this land. The shrubs as lush as he could remember; perhaps nourished by uncountable tears shed by family members who had loved ones buried here. His mind started to wander as he remembered committal services of various people. His mind could hear the bag piper standing on the hill and playing on so many occasions; the members of the American Legion sounding taps for the military funerals.

Paul felt comfort in the dense quiet of the cemetery. Everything was in its place here. Just as he liked it. No surprises; just the consistency of eternity to comfort himself and all those who were placed here. He wondered if tonight's escapade would result in some condemnation from beyond. Could the souls of those who rested here defy Paul's reasoning and logic and somehow harbor ill will for him for what he was doing?

A smile came to his face as he followed that thought to its conclusion. If in fact his mental follies were realistic, then, too, would be the fact that his twin-brother John's spirit would be among those who watched on this evening. And if that were the case, Paul felt an amused pity for all the other souls who would have to suffer the protective lecturing of his persuasive dead brother.

Paul instinctively turned and looked up the hill to the highest point of the cemetery. There, in the moonlight, stood the private mausoleum of the Arrone family. A small version of the Parthenon, the building was built by Paul's grandfather and his friends, fellow masons who had been imported from Italy to build many of the roads, bridges and infrastructure of the New York metropolitan area. Yes, his brother even had the advantage of higher ground. Paul was enjoying this fantasy when his thoughts were interrupted by the opening of the side door to the garage.

The chemist was dressed in a hazmat suit complete with gas mask. She waved for Paul to come over to her as she held the door open with the heel of her foot. As he approached she took off her gas mask.

"Mr. Arrone, you can go home if you like. We're going to be here for several hours." A smile appeared as she went on to say, "Your instinct was correct. We have positively identified cocaine in this woman's chest cavity."

"Are you certain, doctor?" asked Paul, trying to conceal his excitement.

"There is no doubt. In fact, that's the reason I came out. There is such a large trace of the drug it's going to take my team several hours to document the entire situation. It appears to most in my group, including myself, that whatever container was used to hold the drugs in this woman must have broken upon its removal; perhaps a plastic bag that got caught on a splinter of a sawed off rib. This created quite a mess inside the entire thoracic cavity. Without the proper time and chemicals it would be next to impossible to eradicate the traces of the drug we have found. I will have the stenographer e-mail a preliminary report within an hour. We will photograph and document the rest of the report and await your instructions as to where you would like us to deliver it. We should be done by 4:30, 5:00 at the latest."

Paul leaned in and hugged the woman with such force that she lost her balance, causing the door to shut behind her.

"Thanks, doctor, you're amazing."

Paul ran over to the hearse, stuck his head in and in an excited whisper yelled "*Bingo.*"

Tomaas knew from the smile that this was good news but asked anyway. "Is this *bingo* a good thing for you Americans?"

"No," Paul answered, it is a *great* thing! Wait here. I'll be right back."

He then walked up to the truck where he could hear Placido Domingo's voice coming from a tape deck on the seat.

"Hey Ange, it's going to be a while so why don't you guys go home. I am going to need you back here before dawn, though, to bury her and put everything back in its place." As Paul was speaking, he placed an envelope filled with twenty dollar bills on the dash board.

"No. No, boss, we don't want anything for this."

Paul was about to press the issue by saying buy something for your grandchildren. He often did this when he gave Angelo extra money for the work he did around the cemetery. But this time was different. Paul could tell by the grip Angelo had on his forearm as he pushed both the envelope and arm out of his truck's window, and the authoritative voice in which Angelo addressed him, a voice he had never heard him use before. In a matter of seconds, Paul was able to conclude that these old Italian gentlemen were far more uncomfortable with tonight than even Paul was.

"Okay Ange, thank you very much. I'll call you tomorrow to check in."

Paul knew there was no need to tell Angelo to make sure everything was in its place before people came through the gates to pay their respects to their family members on this holiday weekend. Angelo had been doing it for over 40 years and the cemetery was always impeccably maintained.

CHAPTER 22

Sunday

Paul dressed in his finest suit for Janice Rodino's Sunday service. As he walked toward Chapel D for a final check on the room, he looked around as if it were his first time there. It was a beautiful place, he thought. It was unique because it was a family funeral home, his family's. For decades, they had not only built a business, cemented a reputation, and created a "client base," they had made the Arrone name into an institution and provided a life of service for themselves.

The flowers that had arrived at the chapel were stupendous, befitting, he realized, not just a Senator's wife, but a woman in her own right. A woman whose cosmetic and fragrance lines had become her empire and a woman who would give much of it up for, well, a kid, and maybe something more.

Paul carried the package, but as he walked around, he still made the slightest adjustment to a blossom here, a leaf there. He had to move only a few small baskets. His staff had done well. They knew how particular he was.

He approached the high table, with its simple but elegant linen cloth draping to the floor, awaiting Janice Rodino's urn. He smoothed the swath of lace on top.

Tomaas had loved her. Despite his panache and worldliness and even his cockiness, the young Frenchman was hurt, bereft. Paul had studied him over the last few days. It was no act. Tomaas's push for the truth wasn't merely a macho attempt at revenge. He needed to know, plain and simple, what had happened to Janice. He needed, Paul thought wryly, *closure*.

Paul unwrapped the silver-framed photograph and stood it to the right of where the urn would be.

He wished he had known her, which he realized was unusual for him. When he had not met the deceased, even after he had been told their life's highlights to prepare the obituary, he rarely felt a longing to meet them, to know them. They were gone and the most he could do was help to ease the pain of farewell.

Had he felt that way at John's service? He wasn't sure. It was impossible for him to remember.

He stopped and sat, also something he never did. But as he often did, he allotted himself a few minutes to think of John, and to his surprise, instead of the ice-cold shock that usually took a hold of him, he felt – what? He searched his mind and his heart. Actually, he thought he felt sadness, but in fact, he felt grateful. Grateful for having known John, grateful for what his brother's life and, yes, even his death, had taught him.

In a few moments, this room would be filled with mourners, fake or not, curiosity-seekers, politicians and a handful of celebrities. Paul was glad he and Tomaas had arrived first.

It was a half hour before the service was to begin and a crowd had already formed at the main entrance as those who mourned and those who wanted to be counted as one who mourned, jammed their way into the funeral home. While most parked in the rear lot, those who showed up in limousines and government cars either parked in the circular drive, or doubled parked on Main Street. There was a contingent of local cops, state troopers and secret service agents on hand to secure the site of the memorial service for the wife of the head of homeland security.

The caravan from county government showed up together in several cars. Cardin, the county executive, and Haywood got out of their limousine as Walker and the district attorney were waiting in line to get into the front door. The fact that there was a crowd jamming into the funeral home along with the sweltering summer weather, helped to camouflage the injection Cardin gave Walker.

"Hey there, commissioner," Cardin said as he patted Walker on the shoulder, on the veranda of the funeral home. The virus was placed in a ring syringe in the palm of Cardin's hand. However it could just as well have been a dart gun and nobody would have noticed with all of the morning's distractions. As Cardin surreptitiously dismantled the weapon in his hand,

Ian Cullan appeared out of nowhere. He leaned into the group and grabbed hold of Walker's arm as he said, "Can I have a word with you in private?"

The two men walked down the veranda of the old Georgian mansion and took a seat on the wicker chairs that were placed outside, so that funeral home visitors could smoke.

As the two men sat, Cullan shooed away a couple of bees that had wandered from the rose bushes. "Damn bees, I got stung a few minutes ago," he said as he rubbed his neck where a welt had risen.

"Me too," responded Walker as he rubbed the spot on his shoulder where Cardin had injected him. "Listen, Walker," Cullan said, "I'm not going to mince words. If Paul Arrone ends up in your jail, I expect you to keep him out of the general population. Should any harm come to him, I'll hold you personally responsible."

Walker, whose body just barely fit into the large wicker chair, was now sweating through his blue suit. He tugged at the collar of his shirt that was hidden under the fat of his chin, trying to gain some breathing room before he spoke. "Now you listen, Cullan. I don't tell you how to run your jail and I won't allow you to tell me how to run mine. Arrone is suspected of killing a man and I take exception at you insinuating that anything other than proper treatment would be given to anyone at my penitentiary."

Cullan got up from the chair, "Just remember what I said, Walker." He then leaned over and whispered into his ear, "Otherwise I'll personally feed *you* to the dogs."

Paul assisted his father throughout the service but remained in the background. He hung back, allowing Pop to "take his leave." Paul did approach Senator Rodino when he first entered the back of the chapel to offer his hand. Senator Frankie, dressed in a black pin-stripe suit, gave him his. He had to. There were too many watching, but Paul felt the ice and saw the hatred in his eyes.

All the local politicians and representatives were there, of course. Some had even brought their wives. Paul mentally ticked them off as they came in. The governor had sent his regrets, but the junior senator from New York was there, the state's Republican Senate majority leader, the Westchester County Executive. They were all accounted for. Yes, even all 17 of the county legislators, including the Democrats. *Of course*, Paul thought wryly, *they knew enough to sit toward the back.*

Finally, it was over and Paul was free to let Tomaas out of his "jail." He entered his office. Tomaas had his back to him, staring at the image he had frozen from the surveillance camera's tape.

"That's him," Tomaas said. "The man who met with your horse-faced senator and my horse's ass of a father."

Paul stepped forward, bent to the screen and stared. It was the chairman of the county board of legislators, Patrick Miller.

"And this is … ?" Tomaas asked, pointing to the man.

Paul identified him. Then Tomaas strode to the door.

"Wait!" said Paul. "Where are you going? What are you … ?"

"We have a different agenda now," Tomaas said calmly. He paused, walked back toward Paul, and extended a hand. "Thank you," he said. "Keep me posted."

Paul sighed as the door closed. He had more problems of his own to face.

He went to his office safe and removed the report from the chemist Tomaas had hired to analyze last night's evidence. He placed it, with some other evidence and a note, in an envelope, addressed it, and left it in the center of his desk. The note would explain to Ian Cullan why he had broken his promise, and where he would be.

Paul had decided that it was time in his life to stop leaning on his oldest friend. Rather than let Cappy take the fall for him, he would go down to the city marina, get on his boat and sail across Long Island Sound, where his older brother, an attorney, was waiting for him.

They had worked out a plan. He would turn himself in to the Suffolk County Sheriff's office by the end of the day tomorrow. Like Paul and their father, his brother the stock wizard, Anthony, and the eldest, attorney Dominic III, had developed their own political clout. Theirs was out on Long Island. Even on a holiday weekend like this one, they could count on their connections in the Sheriff's Office.

As much as he hated leaving Cullan in the lurch, the one thing Paul was certain of was that his brothers would never leave him hanging or let him spend a night in harm's way. Paul hoped that Cullan's anger at what he had done would not prevent him from viewing the video he had left him describing his theories of what was going on in the dirty world of Westchester politics and the somewhat dirtier world of LaCroix Worldwide Shipping. Sure, Cappy would be preoccupied with making certain the annual New Rochelle fireworks display went off well, if it went off at all. And, as Paul just heard on the radio as he drove to the marina, the unusual raising of the terrorist level to red would only compound his responsibilities. Still, Paul was relying on his belief that Cullan was the single best detective he had ever met.

As he set sail, he looked back at the City of New Rochelle and wondered if he would ever see it again. While he stared directly at the shoreline, he had the sensation that he was looking at his city in the rear view mirror of a speeding car.

He knew he would *not* see Trish. The last message he retrieved was from her, telling him she had left for the weekend in Troy. And also, he was sure, for good.

Paul wasn't accustomed to sailing the 50-foot Hatteras motor yacht by himself. He had purchased it two years ago, ostensibly as a business expense for his funeral home to do burials at sea, and to scatter cremated remains. It had an extended hard-enclosed aft deck which made it ideal to hold several bereaved family members and a minister on what would usually be a two hour jaunt out onto Long Island Sound. While the boat was large enough to allow Paul to write a fair amount off as a business expense, he chose this particular size because it was the largest vessel that could be maneuvered by himself if need be. Normally, the funeral home hired a captain and a first mate when a family requested use of the boat; otherwise Paul and one of his fellow yachtsmen from the Huguenot Yacht Club would take out the *SS Anubis* for an afternoon of sailing through some of the most affluent waters in the world.

Paul named the ship the *SS Anubis* after the Egyptian God of Embalming. Anubis was the son of Ra and his duty as the guide of the dead in the Underworld on their way to Osiris had been legendary. He had the body of a man and the head of a jackal. Paul could not count how many times he had seen that image in connection with his brother. John even had the image engraved onto his signet ring.

On this day Paul sailed his ship solo. He wasn't traveling far; just about two nautical miles for a quick stop and then across the Sound to Long Island. His brother Anthony was a member of a Yacht club in the Hamptons; and he and Paul would routinely tie up at each other's club for short visits. Paul knew the crew at Anthony's club was familiar with the *Anubis*, and he also knew there would be no problems or questions about it tying up there for a few days.

In the helm, next to the radar screen, sat the pile of information that Tomaas had gotten for Paul. While Paul did not ask Tomaas specifically where he obtained this information, he knew it was not acquired by some amateur. This information was as complete as Paul had ever seen. It must have cost someone a fortune too, he thought, but between what Trish had found out in the archive room coupled with what Tomaas had provided Paul knew that he was in possession of enough information to cause a crap storm in Westchester.

The "Golden Apple" was about to become severely tarnished, thought Paul as he pulled the boat along the south side of David's Island. This was the side of the island that was not visible from the mainland. A couple of miles off the New Rochelle mainland, David's Island had been used by the army for over a century until the early sixties. Then it was decommissioned and sold to Con Edison which sought to put a nuclear power plant there. When the proximity to New York City and the outcry of local residents put a halt to this plan, the island was sold back to the city for one dollar. These days the old deserted island had become fodder for developers who wanted to build high end condos. No one ever went out there except a few kids looking to get drunk in the old barracks. It was the perfect place for Paul to make his rendezvous.

Paul anchored the boat about 30 feet from an old beach where he and his father used to fish. With the tide going out he knew he had to meet up soon or set sail alone. Paul started to re-read the documents that lay in front of him as he rubbed his sore arm.

At Tomaas' insistence Paul had allowed a private doctor to give him several vaccines – one of which was for anthrax. Trish had identified the pathogens that the Cardin Group were working on; they were on file with the federal government. It was Tomaas, however, who stepped up to the plate and deployed his people to breach security at the medical examiner's lab to see if there was a connection to what was being worked on by Cardin and what was removed from Janice's abdomen. The team hired by Tomaas took samples from the morgue box that Paul had hidden in, as well as from virtually every other nook and cranny in the lab. The doctor that Tomaas brought to Paul's apartment earlier that day explained that 99 percent of the pathogens that were identified could be present in virtually every medical examiner's lab. "In fact, these pathogens are probably incubating in the embalming room two floors below us," the doctor had nonchalantly told Paul.

The only thing that they could not discuss was the information that had been taken from the air sensor in Haywood's lab. The lab that Tomaas had hired could not identify these items so they had to be sent out to another for more sophisticated testing. The doctor recommended that Paul be given whatever pathogens he could safely vaccinate him for: "Just to be on the safe side." And as a result, both Paul's arm and left buttock were now swollen and sore from the afternoon's barrage. To add insult to injury a welt was rising on Paul's neck from an apparent bee sting from that damned rose bush in front of the funeral home. He vowed that that bush would be the first thing to go if he was lucky enough to get out of this mess.

Paul was becoming anxious. The task was an easy one, he thought. *Go to the Cameron boat yard, rent a row boat and row the two miles to David's Island and meet me. What could be simpler?* He decided to take one last look from every vantage point of the *SS Anubis* for the lone row boat. None was there. Just as Paul was about to weigh anchor he heard a shout from the port side of the boat.

"Ahoy mate! Permission to come aboard?"

Paul was so startled he let out a yelp. As he looked over the side of the boat he saw Tomaas floating on his back spitting salt water into the air like a fountain.

"You asshole, you scared the crap out of me," Paul shouted. "Where is your boat?"

"What boat? This is such a short swim. You need to get into shape, old man," Tomaas said, laughing.

Paul lowered the ladder and Tomaas jumped on board. Paul noticed that Tomaas was in his underwear. Paul figured that the swimming idea must have been an impulse and that he had left his clothes on shore.

"What would you do for clothes if I forgot to bring your bag?"

"I've only known you a short time, but I know there is no way that you would forget such a thing" answered Tomaas. "It is not your nature."

"What about those test results?" Paul asked, trying to change the subject. He had become uncomfortable with the fact that he could be so predictable even to a new acquaintance like Tomaas.

"They are supposed to e-mail them to me. I expect to have an answer soon. If you give me my bag and show me where I can change, I will get my laptop and see if the information has been sent."

Paul led Tomaas below deck to the mahogany-paneled master cabin where he had put Tomaas' travel bag.

"Make yourself at home. I even made sure I picked up the absolute necessities for your journey." Paul pointed to the ice chest that he had taken from the galley and placed on his dresser. In it were crushed ice and several bottles of Dom Perignon. As he pointed he realized that perhaps he too had come to know more about his new friend than one would expect in such a short time. Shared tragedies had a way of doing that. Paul had certainly seen his fair share of those at his funeral home.

He went top side to weigh anchor before they got bogged down in low tide. As he worked, he realized that it had been good idea to feign his goodbyes to Tomaas earlier atop the funeral home. Paul had figured if his apartment had been bugged, at the very least he could spare his new friend some of the horrors of retribution from the Valhalla mafia, as he called the Westchester politicians.

As Paul maneuvered the yacht away from the small island and into the deeper waters of Long Island Sound, Tomaas reappeared next to him with his laptop in tow.

"That's odd. What do you make of this e-mail?"

Paul read the e-mail on Tomaas's laptop. It confirmed that no other pathogens, other than those previously found, were detected in the air monitors. The memo went on to read that the technician did however examine the CD of the air monitor's computer memory that Tomaas had lifted from the medical examiner's lab. The computer indicated that the monitor had been prompted to specifically ignore formaldehyde gas at the same time it was prompted to test specifically for anything in the Ebola family. The author of the memo went on to say that the Ebola virus wasn't an airborne virus and would only show up on such a piece of equipment given two circumstances: First, if the virus were to mutate and become an airborne virus. Second, if in a lab setting a large volume of the virus were being studied or worked with. The date and time of the log coincided with Paul's episode at the lab.

"What does all this mean, Paul?"

"I am not sure, but this can't be good."

"Why don't we call your friend the police commissioner and see what he thinks about this."

"Sorry Tomaas, I won't involve Cappy in that sort of mess. From the time I set sail I became a fugitive."

"But I'm sure he would help you."

"I have no doubt he would and that is precisely why I won't contact him. I'm not going to bring him down with me. He's a law enforcement officer and I can't have him breaking the law at this stage of his life."

"But isn't that a decision for him to make?"

"Now are you sure you know how to sail this boat?" Paul asked, determined to change the subject.

"I have been sailing all different types of boats since I was 13," Tomaas sniffed. "My grandmother keeps three of the four she owns at her place in Monaco." His voice trailed off as the mention of that country brought back memories of his lost love.

After a moment's silence, Paul said, "Remember, as we get close to my brother's yacht club, you'll have to take the boat in by yourself. I don't want you involved in aiding and abetting. I'll stay below deck until later; then I will meet up with my brothers. I know the people we're dealing with are after me big time. I just need to buy myself some time so I can sort out all of the events of this last week. Anthony has a 45-foot cigarette boat that is being fueled up in New Rochelle as we speak. He hired a friend to take that speed boat on a ride as far north as he can get before he's intercepted."

"I see," said Tomaas. "It will look like your brother came to New Rochelle and dropped off his boat and sailed back here to his yacht club, while you took the boat that could out race almost any Coast Guard or private boat. Hey, wait a minute. How come I don't get that job?"

"Because even though you're a mere child, you seem to have as many connections as Cappy. I need your help here where I can communicate with you. Anthony will put us up some place where we'll be safe until we unravel this mess. Oh, and I don't know anyone else who can drink all that champagne down in the master cabin."

"Good point. *Oui.* Very good point," Tomaas said laughing.

The late afternoon sail to the Hamptons was far more cumbersome than Paul had anticipated. The sound was filthy with sail boats, luxury yachts and various power boats – all out enjoying the 4th of July holiday. Tomaas went atop to the fly bridge while Paul stayed out of sight in the helm. The blinds on the windows were all but completely closed. Both men left the boat's internal phones on speaker so that they could talk casually as they made their way across the Sound. At the start of the trip, several of the boats they had passed recognized the *Anubis* and blew their fog horns to signal hello. As they were getting closer to the Long Island side of the Sound, Paul's anxiety rose. He knew that this would be the most dangerous part of the trip.

As soon as Cappy or the County Sheriff realized that he was not around to be taken into custody, an all-out search would begin. Paul only hoped that the decoy ship would work. Without a Plan B, he began to feel very vulnerable. Just then a fog horn blared as a speed boat made a direct line to their yacht.

"Who is that?" Paul asked.

Tomaas was looking through the binoculars at the boat coming to them. "It looks like a boat with just a few very good-looking ladies aboard."

"Get rid of them, Tomaas. We can't afford any slip ups."

"What is this *we can't?*" Tomaas joked. "I will take care of this."

The sleek speed boat, which was larger, faster and more expensive than Paul's brother's, pulled up next to the yacht somewhat recklessly. Paul could see through the slits in the blinds that there were three women on deck, none of whom looked to be older than 18. Paul knew he was tired and suspicious from the week's events, but even so, he could not believe that these three girls would be sailing what he estimated to be close to a million-dollar Ferretti speed boat all by themselves. Remembering that the phone was still on speaker, he whispered "get rid of them." Paul's patience was inversely proportional to the increase in the size of the welt on his neck. He couldn't believe what happened next. Tomaas threw the girls a line from the bow, laughing and speaking to them in French. Paul could make out only a few words but he certainly knew the signs of flirtation that these young girls were transmitting.

Tomaas pulled their boat closer until it gently made contact with the rubber buoys on the *SS Anubis*. The girls kept asking Tomaas something to which he kept answering no in French. Paul was mentally kicking himself for not taking Trish up on her offer to teach him to speak French. *I'll never need it, we don't bury French people here*, was the answer that now seemed so parochial and so ignorant that it hurt him to even recall it. Paul was thinking that perhaps the girls were asking Tomaas for permission to come aboard and he was saying no. But if so, why had he allowed them to tie up to the Anubis?

And then all of a sudden Paul heard Tomaas yell out a loud, "*Oui*." "*Oui*," yelled back the girls.

"*Oui*," confirmed Tomaas.

Paul jumped up and looked out of the windows to see the three girls standing with their bikini tops off, breasts bared for Tomaas to see. Tomaas leaned over the rail of the *Anubis* and handed the girls a bottle of Champagne with a note attached.

"Merci," was all that Paul could make out of the short conversation that ensued before the girls threw the line back and sped away giggling as they spewed salt water all over the port side of the ship.

"What the hell just happened?" Paul barked into the open intercom. "Get down here." Tomaas entered the helm and started talking before he was through the door.

"Nothing just happened. They said they spotted me with their binoculars and wanted to come aboard and party. I told them that I was simply making a delivery of this boat for a client and couldn't risk losing my job by allowing them aboard." Tomaas paused and grinned. "I also told them my boss was an insane old man."

"This is not funny," Paul said. "What if they tell someone they saw you? What if they saw the name of the boat? What if they give your phone number to the police?"

Tomaas responded in an authoritative tone that Paul had never heard from him. "First off, I don't think *this* is funny. Murder rarely is. What I do think looks suspicious to me is a bare-chested young man ignoring the flirtations of three oh-so-beautiful girls. I also figure, so what if they tell someone they saw me? Your story still stands and is probably more believable that your brother hired someone to sail both boats rather than risk his trading license over such a felony. And lastly, so what if they give out that phone number? I gave them a phone number from next to the console that was marked crematory. I am a hot number? No?" Tomaas's mood changed suddenly as he continued sternly: "And furthermore, you of all people should know that people don't act this way on the day of their loved one's funeral. You should have realized I was doing something to help, not hurt."

Paul had been very impressed with this young man long before today. But this speech, clever and yet delivered with a light touch, reaffirmed how mature he was, and how determined he was to find out what had happened to Janice.

"Sorry," Paul started to say when Tomaas interrupted him. "Are you okay, Paul? You look like hell. You are all pale and your eyes are bloodshot."

"I am fine. Would it be possible to speak to that doctor you brought over earlier to give me those shots? I'd like to ask him and the chemist who sent you that e-mail some questions."

"Sure, I'll get each one on the phone for you." Tomaas picked up one of the four disposable cell phones he had packed in his bag and dialed the number of the doctor. Paul disconnected the call when he saw 666 appear on his pager. Paul called his brother Anthony, who told him that a swat team was stationed at the yacht club. Anthony was being very careful by talking in cryptic messages.

"Paul, the police know you skipped out on Cullan. They also know you have my cigarette speed boat and are heading toward the Hamptons. I suggest you turn yourself in. I'll meet you at the place we went when you and John turned ten. The police are tracking my cigarette using GPS that the radar and safety instruments onboard are giving off, so don't try to hide. They know you are speeding past Montauk right now and they're sending the Coast Guard out to get you. Even though they won't be able to catch up with you, you will be out of gas in about six hours."

Paul threw the disposable cell phone into the water.

"What does this mean?" Tomaas asked.

Paul responded slowly as his mind pieced together the information. "It means that somehow Anthony found out about the police and tipped off the person racing his boat to change course and head out towards him. He also wants me to go in the opposite direction. When John and I turned ten the entire family spent a weekend at an Inn in Watch Hill, Rhode Island. He clearly wants me to go there and wait. We can tie up in the Watch Hill harbor or we can go across the bay to Stonington Harbor in Connecticut and tie up until Anthony pages me again."

Tomaas started turning off all electronic equipment on the boat.

"Exactly, Tomaas, no signals. And we have about six hours to get to a safe haven. You had better be as good a sailor as you say you are!"

Tomaas looked at Paul and smiled as he said, "Well, at least we both know I am a good swimmer."

Tomaas and Paul made it into Stonington Harbor just after night-fall. The channel was lit with what remained of the fireworks display from ashore. They had decided they would anchor there and take the dingy across to Watch Hill where they would rent a room at the Ocean House Hotel. Once there, they would contact Anthony and piece together their information. Paul was confident that whatever his brothers had found out coupled with what he, Cappy and Tomaas had found, would shed light on what was going on back home.

What they had not figured out yet was where and how they would all meet up to brainstorm. Paul was now physically weakened from the series of vaccines he was given earlier. He was running a fever and figured that his ulcer had finally given up in that he was beginning to taste blood in mouth.

Before Paul climbed to consciousness out of a deep sleep he heard voices talking in whispered tones. The first thing he remembered when he opened his eyes was the searing pain in his head that the small amount of light coming in from the window caused. He lifted his head off the pillow in a start to get up but was rebuffed by the vertigo that followed and his head fell back onto the pillow as if it were attached to a 50 pound weight. He stank of alcohol and vomit and could remember nothing after talking to Tomaas on the boat.

"Where am I?" he asked the backs of the two men who were transfixed on a small TV set in the corner of the room. One of the men, Tomaas, turned around quickly and said, "Good morning! How do you feel? For a while there I thought I was going to have to call my father to have you shipped back to New Rochelle in one of his custom caskets."

The man standing next to Tomaas said. "You're at the Ocean House Hotel in Watch Hill. It is Tuesday morning. You had a bad reaction to one of the vaccines I gave you yesterday."

As Paul's eyes focused he recognized the man from yesterday afternoon as the doctor who came to his apartment. "How did I get here?"

Tomaas, now sitting on the edge of the bed, explained, "We were about to put the dingy into the water and you started to vomit blood and collapsed. I carried you down the ladder and put you in the dingy myself. You could stand to lose a few pounds by the way." He winked and grinned. Anyway, I rowed to the shore and when I got close I poured one of the last two bottles of champagne over you. I then asked some local guy to help me get my friend who had drunk too much at a fourth of July party up to the hotel. I offered him the last bottle as a thank you. He was more interested in getting back to his girlfriend to drink the champagne than in who you were. I called the doctor, who happened to be on holiday in Newport, Rhode Island and he came right over. And here we are. "Two more things," Tomaas said. "You Americans are very festive about the 4th and you owe me 2 bottles of Dom Perignon."

Paul became more alert as the IV drip began to re-hydrate his body. Of all the things that he should have been thinking about in the first moments of consciousness, the only thing that came to mind was: *what are the odds of this doctor being a half hour away from a place where neither Tomaas nor I even knew we would end up?*

His suspicions gave way to fear as his eyes focused on the television the two men had been watching when he awoke. While the TV was too low for Paul to hear anything, the headlines behind Wolf Blitzer's head spoke volumes. "Terrorists Attack! Ebola bleeds financial institutions."

The doctor interrupted like a co-conspirator allowing Tomaas to fill in Paul. "I'm going to leave you two alone now. If you need me, just call my cell number I left with Tomaas. I gave you something for your headache and nausea. I would leave that IV in until the bag empties and then you should be good to go. Just try to take it easy for a while. Either of you gentlemen know how to remove the IV needle?"

"Don't worry Doc," Tomaas said, "we will make believe Paul is embalming himself. We will be good. Merci beaucoup." Tomaas walked the doctor to the door. They spoke French in whispers.

Paul was now sitting up, his vertigo subsiding as his anxiety rose. "That is it!" he shouted. "That is what they brought into the country. You were right, Tomaas. They did kill Janice! We have to go. Now!"

"Relax," said Tomaas, in a voice that Paul thought was uncharacteristically calm for a person whose worst fears about his lover's murder had just been confirmed.

"Don't you get it? Don't you see what's happening?"

"Paul, I got it long before you did. Remember, I was the one who came to you to tell you she was killed. But we have to figure a way to alert the authorities without getting ourselves killed too. All the airports are closed. The television said that the government has stopped all commercial traffic to try and contain the disease. There is a curfew on all automobile traffic in or out of New York City and Chicago. All the ports have been shut down. Even if we *could* get to Washington, who would listen to a fugitive and a Frenchman?"

"We can head back to Long Island," Paul said. "I doubt that anyone would be interested in looking to lock me up out there when they have this catastrophe on their hands." At that moment his heart sank. Anthony! What about his brother? What if he went to work today only to be killed by this attack? "Did you bring your bag with us last night, Tomaas?"

"Of course. You did not think I would pay for this room with a traceable credit card."

Tomaas handed Paul the bag. Among the clothes and the cash lay two of the four cell phones they had packed. Paul was able to reach Anthony who laughed off Paul's concern. "What the hell is wrong with you, little brother? Like I'm going to hop on the L.I.E. and go trade stocks while you're being sought for murder. Jeeze, Paul, get a grip."

"Tony, I need you to find out about Trish and Keith. I want to be certain they're okay. Can you find out where they are so I can call them?"

"Easy there, Paul. Already done. They're both well and in touch with 'Three' every hour to see how you are doing. "Three" was what Tony called their brother Dominic Arrone III. "'Three' will handle all phone calls from this point forward. He insists that you not speak to anyone but him. This will protect all the people involved. They can evoke attorney-client privilege as the crap hits the fan."

Paul knew exactly what kind of people he was dealing with and didn't question the legal wisdom of his older brother. And because he knew who he was dealing with he was afraid that they might try to harm Trish and Keith.

"Do you think they will remain safe?"

"No doubt in my mind, Paul. Everyone is well. Mom and Pop have opened a "New Rochelle Hilton" of sorts. Trish, Keith, Bridie Cullan and her daughters along with a division of New Rochelle's finest retirees are all enjoying mom's cooking as we speak. It's a fortress up there. They have more fire power than the time Nixon came to town in the seventies. By the way, I don't think even they are that stupid to harm the old man. Anthony was referring to their father who, even in retirement, had more high-powered friends and held more political chits than any living person he knew.

"Just for the record, Tony. Trish had nothing to do with this. Tell Dom to tell Trish that I love her," Paul said in about as awkward a manner as one could.

Both men refocused on the issue at hand. Anthony confirmed that there wasn't a police officer around who wasn't on terrorist duty. He told Paul that he could sail right into the club and that he would pick him up himself. Which was his way of saying that the world might be about to end and nobody gave a rat's ass about the Arrone boys. Before they hung up, Anthony also told him about the progress that he, Dom and Cullan had made through the night. All that they needed was the information Paul was transporting.

CHAPTER 23

Tuesday morning, July 6

The New York Stock Exchange opened after the long 4ᵗʰ of July weekend under tighter security than anyone had seen since 9/11. Even the maintenance workers and their lunch containers had been doubled-checked.

Despite the security, trading was down both there and on the NASDAQ, mostly because of the insecurity the nation felt as it experienced the first red terrorist alert ever. On balance, George Meekham, the head of the Exchange, was pleased that things seemed to be going relatively smoothly.

In Chicago, Craig Donohue, the CEO of the Mercantile Exchange, was less optimistic. While the alert started off smoothly, one of his vice president's secretaries had been rushed to the hospital in a Hazmat truck. She had developed severe bleeding from her nose.

Donohue was on a conference call with the CDC and the CIA when his own secretary barged in to tell him that the Exchange vice president and another gentleman who shared a ride in with him had both collapsed with the same symptoms.

It was exactly 9:11 in the morning when the Department of Homeland Security suspended all trading. The building was quarantined.

Back in New York, Meekham was informed of what happened in Chicago earlier and was watching stocks plummet on the Big Board. While he was upset about what he anticipated for Chicago, he was relieved that the Big Apple was spared.

He was reviewing the directives issued by Homeland Security when he noticed droplets of blood speckling the report. The last thing he remembered was kicking the panic bar installed under his desk to summon Security.

A short time later, the Hazmat team entered Meekham's office suite. They were greeted by his secretary, a pale-faced woman of about 60 who was dressed very conservatively with the exception of her red lipstick. She was about to tell the Hazmat team what happened when the team noticed that as she spoke there was no delineation between her red lips and her teeth and gums.

At 11:09, the Office of Homeland Security closed and quarantined the largest stock exchange in the world. The NASDAQ was closed within an hour.

The pandemonium that followed was unlike anything New York had ever experienced. As news spread, hospitals were inundated with healthy people clamoring to be tested. For what, they didn't know. Pharmacies were ransacked for any and all over-the-counter medicines.

Then as quickly as the panic came, so too came the quiet. By the end of the day, the fear of infection by an unknown pathogen confined New Yorkers in their homes. The normal rush on food and water in supermarkets during other crises never happened. The streets were deserted. In 98-degree weather, police patrolled in full bio-hazard suits. The news channels, usually scrambling for news, now had a real catastrophe, but they were mute as reporters, cameramen and anchors refused to risk exposure.

There was a quiet in the city that is usually seen only during a blizzard. This quiet was enhanced by the fact that businesses and private residences had turned off their air conditioning units. Windows and doors were sealed closed to keep out any potential airborne virus. Oddly, the quiet of this attack was far worse than the chaos of 9—11. Then, even during the height of the calamity, New Yorkers found comfort in seeing their Mayor working the streets. This time, there was no Rudy Giuliani. This time, the mayor of New York City worked from a hidden bunker somewhere on the island. There were no heroics by the NYFD or NYPD to watch on television; in their place were pictures of dead bodies being removed by anonymous people in haz-mat suits. This time New York wasn't paralyzed by a physical attack as much as it was by an unknown and unseen enemy.

The Center for Disease Control had ordered that a makeshift morgue be set up on a lower west side pier. The concept was a simple one: Wrap the bodies in airtight morgue bags and cremate them as soon as practicable.

There remained a distinct possibility that, depending on how severe the outbreak was, these bodies sitting out over the Hudson River in human-sized zip lock bags might never be identified. The priority of the morning was "Contain and Burn." Anyone who entered a hospital anywhere in the nation, and all who were currently in hospitals, would remain there quarantined until given permission to leave by the CDC. In a further effort to contain the outbreak, the New York State Bureau of Funeral Directors contacted all 1,965 funeral homes in the state to inform them that no bodies were to be removed from hospitals or private homes until further notice. Any funeral home in violation would lose its license to operate and the corresponding funeral directors would be subject to arrest.

A nation that had a need for instant gratification when it came to news, found itself in a virtual blackout. CNN could only report on the number of bodies its helicopters, spying safely from the skies above, could spot being brought to the makeshift morgue.

Anchors lamely interviewed whatever doctors they could reach to discuss various unknown pathogens and scenarios with the accuracy of a child playing pin the tail on the donkey. One network tried to provide a community service by interviewing a series of doctors and health officials who explained that those locked in their homes on this summer day had a higher probability of death due to heat stroke than of contracting a disease.

The streets in the financial district, particularly those near the stock exchange, were littered with bodies of people who had jumped from their offices. Their bodies and or body parts and fluids were doused with household bleach before being shoveled into airtight containers and shipped to the pier. Psychiatrists would later say that many of these people suffered from post traumatic stress syndrome from the first attack and simply could see no other way out other than diving to the pavement from their offices. According to the psychiatrists, those who jumped had lived in quiet fear and desperation since 9—11 and had anxiety levels higher than prisoners of war.

New York City was under attack again. This time, there was no smoke, no noise, and no heroes in the street to guide them. This time, there was no tangible beginning or end to the attack. The city that was known for its motion and vibrancy was about to be taken down by sensory deprivation.

It was a senior doctor from the federal Centers for Disease Control and Prevention that was the first to confirm symptoms as similar to the Ebola-hemorrhagic fever. At 2 PM, at the command center of the CIA, its director was being briefed. Five more people had come down with the symptoms, bringing the total to fifteen. Seven people had died, two from heart attacks brought on by the stress of the situation.

The only good news on the dark horizon was that, so far, the infections seemed to be limited to the three institutions. The director swung around in his chair at the head of the conference table in the bunker of CIA head-quarters. He looked up at the map on the wall and barked, "Who on this map is capable of handling Ebola?"

A voice from the other end of the table spoke. "Sir, probably no one. There is no known cure for typical Ebola virus. Worse, the CDC has deter-mined that this may be a hybrid of the disease, one that was stolen from the former Soviet Union."

Someone pointed to a spot on the map just north of New York City.

"The only lab in this or any other country that has even worked on this virus is the Cardin Biotech Group's research center in Westchester County, New York."

"Who runs that place?" demanded the director.

"A Dr. Phillip Cardin."

"Get him on the line."

In less than a minute, Cardin was on the speaker phone telling the group assembled around that table of his work with the disease. "And, of course," he said calmly, "my-our-development of the vaccine ..."

Everyone listening began to talk. "Quiet!" barked the director.

He leaned toward the speaker. "Can this vaccine halt the spread and contain the illness?"

Cardin was very matter of fact. "We certainly believe so."

But he did have to inform the group of the higher-than-normally accepted mortality rate associated with a vaccine. "Still, I am confident that once it is administered widely, the virus will be held at bay."

Cardin also assured them that as long as the virus wasn't a mutation that could be transmitted via the air, the affected buildings would be safe to occupy within a few days.

The director asked what would happen to three of the most important financial institutions and the population in general, if the virus was indeed some mutant that could be spread by air. Cardin's answer was chilling even to those who were used to hearing such news.

"You all remember after 9/11 the anthrax incident in Boca Raton, Florida? That building remained closed for over three years. If we have an airborne infectious agent, then our first priority would be to contain it, but the usability of any of those buildings in the foreseeable future would be remote."

He heard the murmurs of disagreement.

"Even if it isn't airborne," Cardin asked quietly, "would *you* go back to work there?"

There was silence, then: "How quickly can you mobilize your team, Dr. Cardin?" the director asked.

"I can have a team ready with enough vaccine for the two New York sites within two hours. The Army would have to administer the vaccine in Chicago. I just don't have enough staff for that type of operation."

"You got it," said the director.

"Also," Cardin continued, "I'm going to need a 'hold harmless' agreement from the government that keeps me and my company away from any and all liability stemming from this particular vaccine in perpetuity. I will not risk the ruin of my company on someone getting sick 20 years from now and suing me for helping you guys."

The director turned to the secretary of state who was online with the president, who himself had heard the entire conversation. The secretary of state nodded his head.

"You got it," the director said again. "We will send as many Army choppers as you need to transport your team to ground zero. A second set of army medics will arrive at the same time to pick up the vaccine to take to Chicago." He paused. "This country owes you a great debt, Doctor."

CHAPTER 24

Wednesday, July 7

The district attorney, her assistant, and three Westchester County Police officers pulled up in two separate police cars in front of the small police station in Southampton. Diaz led the team into police headquarters and demanded to see the chief of police.

Behind the railing that separated the pedestrians from those who protected them in this small sleepy summer village sat Ryan Smith, the chief of police, the Suffolk County sheriff, Dominic Arrone III, Anthony Arrone, and what looked like several plain-clothes detectives.

Diaz handed Smith the transfer papers and said in a very officious and impatient manner, "Where is my prisoner, Chief? It is bedlam out there with everything going on. I don't have time to waste out here in the boonies." As she spoke, she straightened out her Chanel suit.

Smith was a portly, red-faced man who had gone through the police academy some fifty years ago with Ian Cullan.

While the two lived at different ends of the metropolitan area, they went on several fishing trips each year with other officers of their generation.

Smith got up from his chair slowly, and playing off of Diaz's boonies comment, started talking in an exaggerated southern drawl. "Well, now, Missy Diazzz, is it? Well, folks out here in the boonies don't move as fast as you all up there in suburbia. Now let me tell you the little problem we got us here. You see, I got me a prisoner who is telling some pretty tall stories. So I figure I got me two choices. I could either ignore him, or I could call the United States Secret Service and wait for them to get here and sort this all out. So while I'm trying to make this decision, I get a call from my county police, who tell me they ran into you an hour ago out on the highway.

"So," he said, stroking his chin, "I figure what in blazes would be important enough to bring a purty little D.A. and her henchmen out of their perch to my small town on a day when the rest of the world is sitting in fear. It certainly can't be no itty-bitty mortician accused of a possible murder. *No, Ma'am*. It had got to be something far more important, so I called the Secret Service, and they are on their way here as we speak."

Diaz, furious with Smith's good-old-boy act, shouted, "Save the hokum for a judge, Chief. I am taking him now." She motioned to one of her police escorts, who started to push past the chief.

Diaz looked up, stunned as Chief Smith pulled a 12-gauge shot gun from the top of his desk and aimed it directly at the district attorney.

"Don't anyone move," he yelled. "Connor, do me the pleasure of taking this police officer who tried to push past me into custody for assault."

"You have got to be kidding me," yelled Diaz. "Do you know who you're dealing with?"

Chief Smith lost the Southern accent. He spoke clearly and angrily.

"Indeed I do. I may not be as bright as your garden variety police chief in Westchester County, but one thing I can tell you is this: Sitting out here on these sand dunes all year leaves us a lot of free time. And with all that free time a good portion of it is spent checking on and maintaining the multi-million-dollar summer mansions of some of Hollywood's biggest producers and some of New York's television brass. So you now have a decision to make. You can either wait here a few hours until the Secret Service is through with my prisoner, or you can take him as soon as I get him ready."

He leaned toward her and spoke grimly.

"But I can tell you that before he leaves this building, I will have a television camera from every network outside that door. You do the math, lady. We're in the midst of the largest act of terrorism we've ever had. No reporter will go into ground zero to cover it. I make a few calls to the guys whose houses I care for and tell them I have an angle on the biggest story ever and their reporters can do it in the safety of my beach community. You tell me what will happen. Either way, *this* story is being told. It is your call."

Diaz was no fool. She knew that she could push and get Arrone into her custody before any news coverage would get here. She wasn't convinced the media would even come, given the terror alert that the country was still under.

But she did have to concede to herself that if she took Paul Arrone, and something happened to him while in her custody, it would be her ass in the sling. So she figured she had better leave, regroup with her compatriots in Westchester by phone, and come up with a Plan B.

CHAPTER 25

It was Friday night. Paul sat in his cell in Southampton watching CNN on a portable TV that Chief Smith had brought to him two days ago. Latest reports indicated that the infection appeared to be coming under control. No new cases had been reported in 24 hours.

At the bottom scroll of the TV was a running total of those infected and those dead. There had been 400 infections reported with 280 deaths. Dr. Philip Cardin's interviews were being played every 15 minutes as were those of the county executive who was crediting Cardin and the research facility with saving the country.

Paul's head was in his hands. "At least Trish and Keith must be safe," he muttered. He then stared at the television, talking to himself under his breath. He couldn't believe what crap he was watching, how those assholes were getting away with murder. He was so engrossed that he hadn't noticed that Cullan had appeared at the bars of his cell.

"Why am I not surprised that you would react that way?" Cullan said.

"Hey, Cappy," shouted Paul with the glee of a child. "What the hell has been going on?"

Cullan swung open the unlocked jail cell, pulled a chair in from the hallway.

He placed the chair opposite to where Paul was sitting on the bunk and scratched the back of his neck as he started to tell Paul how he thought things would wrap up.

"First off," Cullan started, "before I forget to tell you. That was both the most brilliant piece of detective work and the stupidest thing I have ever seen you do. That being said, let me fill you in on what's been happening. I know you're going to get all excited about some of the things I say – but for crying out loud don't interrupt me till I finish. We can do the post mortem afterwards. You were right on target about the smuggling. The official story is that three vials of a variant Ebola virus were stolen from a lab in the former Soviet Union. Two vials remain unaccounted for, but the third was smuggled in using LaCroix Worldwide Shipping. The feds believe that it was the virus from one of the other vials that was used to create this terrorist outbreak."

Paul couldn't contain himself. "Jesus Christ, Cappy, I told you I saw Haywood remove three vials from under Janice Rodino's belly. Whoever is telling you otherwise is trying to protect Haywood and those other county pricks. It is a cover-up damn it. I knew it!"

"Look," said Cullan, "I'm giving you the official story. If you keep interrupting, we're never going to get through this. And worse yet, if you can't accept what I'm telling you, then I am not sure what will happen here." Cullan looked Paul directly in the eyes as he said this.

He paused for a moment, stared up at the ceiling of the small cell and began again. "As I was saying, Senator Rodino now claims that LaCroix contacted him about a vial that was being smuggled in Mrs. Rodino's casket. The Senator told a former Army General, who is working closely with his homeland security committee, and just happens to consult on security for the Cardin Group."

Paul moved behind Cullan and began to pace back and forth like an angry dog in a kennel. "Real freaking convenient, wouldn't you say, Cappy? A damn Army General on the payroll. Hell, why not tell me the Vice President was employed by those assholes. Oh, wait a minute. Stupid me. You haven't finished your fairy tale yet. I am sure that is what you *will* tell me next."

Cullan chose to ignore Paul. When he was on one of his rants, it was best to pay no attention to him. To do otherwise would be like dancing in a mine field. Still staring at the ceiling Cullan took a deep breath and continued: "The Senator, Cardin, and the general all say that the Cardin Group cooperated in an elaborate sting operation that now has yielded two terrorists living and working out of a basement apartment in Yonkers. The feds believe – at least they're being led to believe – that the terrorist cell was trying to double-cross Cardin and get the vial but not pay for it. That is what they said went down on the night you were playing popsicle in the m.e.'s freezer. The deal went bust, and members of the cell ran, killing Kenny and a private detective on their way out. The detective worked for one of the major stockholders of LaCroix. It was his body that was found on the garden bench that night."

"Impossible," Paul said. His tone now took on that of a prosecutor before a judge, refuting exculpatory evidence of a criminal. "All anyone has to do is pull the surveillance footage of that night and you'll see those governmental rats scurrying through the tunnel to the Cardin Lab. Remember, Cappy, I was there and I saw that on the monitors when I left Kenny – *alive*."

Cullan spun around and stepped in front of Paul to stop his pacing. He pointed a finger directly into his face and said, "Exactly, son, you were *there*, and that is only one of the many crimes the authorities can charge you with. Now if you just give me a damn minute of your time to hear me out, everyone may end up being the better off for it. And you may end up out of jail." Cullan tossed his hat onto the prison cot and backed up so he could lean against the bars of the jail. He began to scratch the nap of his neck as he slowly picked up his story where he left off.

"Once that attempt to get the vial failed, Cardin negotiated the sale of the vial. He used the authority given to him by the powers-that-be under the Patriot Act. That went down on Sunday evening and, according to the district attorney, the two men were arrested that evening for attempting to buy a dummy vial and place in the county jail. The *actual* vial is in safekeeping at the Cardin lab, and will be either removed or destroyed there. As for the two men arrested, this part will explain why the feds believe the other vials are in this country.

Paul yelled, "I know they are, for Christ's sake! I saw them!"

"Settle down," Cullan said. "Otherwise I'm going to let you cool your heels here for another couple of days, then try to talk some sense to you next week." He took a deep breath and then continued. "The feds believe that these men working with accomplices were able to bring the other two vials in under other means. This, they tell me, is typical behavior with these cells. You never place all your eggs in one basket. You never tell one cell what the other is doing.

"The feds believe that these terrorists – probably on or about the same day they killed Kenny in their failed attempt to first get hold of the virus – obtained the virus through a yet undetermined source and used it to start the terrorist attacks. We know they employed a known assassin who the feds believe actually killed Kenny. He has since been sent to a prison in Colombia, where he's wanted for more than 70 kills. I don't think even *you* can argue that the feds did the right thing here. He will be executed in jail by a rival drug lord faster than we could have set a date for his trial. And there will be no appeals.

"The two men Diaz captured on Sunday showed signs of the disease as early as Monday and subsequently died. They worked at JFK, and in fact a few years ago, worked at the LaCroix terminal. The feds are quite certain they were not acting with any approval or knowledge of anyone in county government because – get this – the prison warden, Robert Walker, contracted the disease, and he, along with the suspected terrorist, died Tuesday night. Because each agency in the government still hides information from the others, the feds are tremendously grateful that you tipped them off to the original, albeit erroneous plot.

"Your work enabled the CIA to mobilize the forces necessary early on and stop what could have been a catastrophe. With the help of your brother, Anthony, the Securities and Exchange Commission was able to catch Pat Miller, the chairman of the Board of Legislators and conveniently a member on the compensation board, selling stock in the Cardin Group today when the markets reopened. He'll be charged with 144 counts of insider trading at least.

"And, oh, I was able to convince the FDA to test that famous dog food company of yours that you always complain about. They did this last week before any of this crap happened and they found traces of human DNA. Haywood blames this completely on Walker – dead men tell no lies. And you will love this. Haywood has submitted his retirement papers at the request of the county executive. LaCroix, who might have gotten off if you hadn't uncovered the Alverez plot, he's being held on income tax evasion for his role in not declaring the cash he used to buy all those funeral homes years ago. There is no statute of limitation on fraud. His mother-in-law, Mrs. Obiere, the largest single stockholder of his company, has signed a complaint and has ordered a forensic audit of LaCroix Worldwide Shipping. That should keep Henri behind bars for most of the rest of his life. But if he does get out, he'll be facing similar charges in France and seven other countries."

He was silent.

"That's *it*?" Paul shouted. "These bastards get away with murder? I know what I saw, and I saw three vials coming out of that body!"

"Paul, the script has been written, and it ain't going to change," Cullan said heavily. "I have known you your whole life, and what I'm going to tell you is something that I know you're not to going to like to hear, but I'm hoping you listen for a change; for your sake.

"The U.S. Attorney's Office has had all charges against you dropped. Even though you were dead right, you still could be charged with breaking and entering, grand larceny and a bunch of other charges. The district attorney is willing to go along but the story has to end here and now. The moment you walk out of here the narrative is as I just told you. Nothing more, nothing less, now and until the end of time. This is not easy for me to say, son, but I think it is time for you to let it go."

"But, Cappy, these people are frigging animals. And by the looks of things they are beginning to eat their young. Where does it end? When is the time to take a stand and say *enough*?"

"Son, I am talking about the bigger picture. Sometimes bad people get away with things. Sometimes good things even happen to bad people. And – what's that book? Sometimes *bad* things happen to *good* people. All I know is that you can't spend any more of your life being angry and unhappy. It has ruined your relationship with Trish, it distanced you from your dad, and it kept you out of a profession that you were born for. These politicians are bad and they may or may not get away with it.

"Your twin brother was a good person, and he got hit with a stray bullet. You can spend the rest of your life trying to right what is wrong, or you can accept what's out of your control and move on. You can be happy. You deserve that. Your brother would have wanted that.

"You did a good thing this last week. You did a good thing for your dad when you went into the family business. You did a good thing for your brother to run things the way he would have wanted you to. Why is it that you feel you can't do a good thing for yourself?"

The question went unanswered as both men awkwardly avoided looking at each other, and instead began to stare at the institutional pale green concrete walls of the cell. Paul was thinking that while he never dreamed he would end up in jail, this place held for him a weird sense of security. This cell housed him safely through this terrorist attack. This cell taught him that his world and even the larger picture, the entire world, would go on without his help, his anger and his guilt. There was something liberating in having all the decisions, albeit minor ones, made for him in the last few days. Paul's thoughts were interrupted by Cappy.

"Look, son, all I am suggesting is that you try to change the way you allow things to affect you. You don't have to change who you are. None of us would want that, but it might be a good time to try a fresh start. Think about it. I know I have, and that's why I handed in my papers today. As of next week I'm going civilian."

"I don't believe what I'm hearing, Cappy. Don't tell me they made you retire as part of this *sick deal*. What are you going to do?"

Cullan couldn't help but chuckle. "You are a tough one. No, nobody made me do anything so you can stop looking at that grassy knoll for conspiracy. I'm the lone gunman, if you will, in this decision. Nothing more. I think it's the right time to give it up, period. As for what I'll do, I'm not sure yet, but fishing will be part of it. Hell, maybe I'll even buy a black suit and be a professional pallbearer for you. It is time for some changes in my life. That is all. It is not all that drastic. I still plan to meet you the first Thursday of every month, so you can buy me dinner. I may be old, but I'm not crazy. I figure I have about ten more years of dinner bills to soak you for before I'm comfortable that you've spent as much on me as Bridie will on my casket."

Paul stood there for a few moments speechless while he tried to sort out the information that was just given to him. Even though he was the younger of the two men, in the jail that morning he was the one who had the bigger problem with change. And if this past week or so did anything, it was to ensure that his life would not stay the same. He had to accept a *deal* of an altered reality of this past week's happenings. He had to deal with Trish moving away from him both physically and emotionally.

And now he had to go back to New Rochelle where his mentor and friend would no longer be in charge of a department that had held his dreams for so long. His safety net back into the world of police work was being forever yanked out from under him. Certainly, the odds of his ever going back on the force after so many years were virtually nil, but he liked the comfort of knowing he'd had that option as long as Cappy was commissioner. It seemed too much for a man whose primary decisions over the last few days had amounted to whether he chose chicken or meatloaf for dinner.

"All I am asking is that you spend some time thinking about things, son. I will stand by you whatever you decide. You know that. But once you leave this cell, things will be different for the rest of your life. Things *have* to be different as far as I can see. Take your time. Smitty will call me when you're ready to check out of this hotel and I'll come and get you. It would be an honor to escort you back to New Rochelle as my last official duty. I will be waiting to hear from you."

Paul went over and embraced the older man. "Thanks for everything."

Cullan put on his raincoat, opened the cell door and even though it was not locked, purposely pushed it open wide until the steel door clanged against the frame of the cell. He strode down the hallway with the military posture of a man half his age. *The last of a breed*, Paul thought. He heard the younger Suffolk County officers greet him as "Commissioner," as they saluted him. Paul suspected that those officers also knew, particularly after this week, that men like Ian Cullan were fast vanishing from this planet.

Three months later

A heavy scrape of metal jarred Henri LaCroix from his bunk.

"Visitor," growled the guard. "Senator Frankie himself."

LaCroix was taken to a small, private room next to the warden's office. Senator Francis Rodino walked in briskly and began just as abruptly.

"Listen, Henry, we've been friends for a long time, but don't you ever again send your flunky lawyer to my office to tell me you *demand* to see me."

"No, *you* listen," Henri replied angrily. "I am *not* doing time in this hell hole, period. I want you to arrange some sort of minimum-security gig like Pat Miller got for pleading to insider trading. My people checked: He'll even get to go home some weekends. I'm also told that his electrical contracting company has been awarded $6 million in county and state no-bid contracts while he's doing time. It all smells like a payoff for keeping quiet. It smells big time. If it's good enough for him, it's good enough for me."

Rodino flicked a piece of lint from the sleeve of his pinstripe suit and shrugged. "There is one little problem, Henry: He doesn't have a mother-in-law showing up every other week with enough evidence to convict him on a dozen charges. Oh, and Henry, another small detail. Unlike Miller, you weren't in charge of 40-some odd politician's pension funds for Westchester's greediest in which each and every one made millions. So from where I sit, your situation doesn't even come close."

LaCroix was livid. "Look here, Senator Graft, I took that fall 30 years ago for you, and I'm not doing it again today. I lost my trading license and had to move to Europe because of your greed, you pig politician. Er-excuse the redundancy, Frankie."

"My, my *Henri*," Rodino said with a sneer, "it seems all those years you spent around those frogs have turned you into an ingrate. What is it with you French people? Let me give you a piece of advice, my Bronx buddy. If you're going to play chicken, you had better take the side of the road closest to the ravine and cut your brake lines and steering column. That's how I do it!"

Henri sat back in his chair and looked at the Senator, his eyes slits of contempt. Then a broad smile came across his face as he started to mimic the Senator's characteristic speech pattern. "Well, Frank," he said smoothly, "let's talk hypothetically, shall we?"

LaCroix leaned forward, allowing a burst of his prison breath to hit the Senator full-face. "What if, hypothetically, that is, what if your wife isn't dead."

"You're insane," whispered the Senator. "They saw her body."

"Uh-huh," LaCroix said. "They saw *a* body. They never saw her body." The two old college friends stared at each other. "Which has since been cremated," LaCroix added thoughtfully.

Senator Frankie put his head in his hands.

"Allow me to continue, hypothetically of course. Let us say that your wife, the late Janice Rodino, who built an empire using your connections, wanted to end her marriage. And let's say that your wife, hypothetically, knew all your secrets. Of course she would: They are the very same secrets that made *her* rich and famous."

Rodino looked up sharply, his face tinged with purple.

"Of course Janice also knew that being the person you are, you would never allow her to leave you in any way whatsoever," LaCroix mused. "So she moves to France to sort things out and, just for the fun of it – and the fun must be emphasized – she takes up with a young stud. Now, going from living with the epitome of corruption, you, to the epitome of naiveté, my son, she also must confront the devil herself, who just happens to be my mother-in-law. And let us say, hypothetically, of course, that this Satan convinces your wife that she could get her out of her marriage and get me out her life all in one fell swoop. In the hypothetical process, Janice has an attorney tell me, your best friend, all your dirty secrets, including the numbers of your offshore accounts. We all know that you would ultimately screw me. Therefore, I had to be armed for such a fight. She had the ammunition to help me fight back.

"As for your wife? A little plastic surgery and a move to Switzerland, all to start a new life under the protection of that old crone, who naturally will leave everything to my son."

LaCroix reached across and lightly fingered the lapels of the Senator's jacket. "And you, Senator, will find your accounts empty," he tightened his grip, "unless you get me out of here."

Senator Rodino gathered his composure and leaned within a half inch of Henri's ear and whispered "You have gone insane. Even if your hypothetical game is even half true, why would Janice tell you?"

"Ah.... Frankie, you of all people should recognize the first credo of politics: the enemy of my enemy is my friend. I can only imagine that your wife was purchasing a fair amount of insurance by having that whore of a mother-in-law and her attorneys give me such information. Sitting here in prison gives a man time to think. My guess is that when your wife empties your joint account in that Swiss Bank that bears that devil's name, she'll need something to prevent you from taking action. Or maybe ..." Henri continued, as he now leaned back and started to grin at the pain he was causing his boyhood friend, "just maybe she wanted to preclude an examination of the books of the third world charities that would inherit half her wealth upon her death. It is not uncommon for these charities, particularly in small corrupt countries, to have funds disappear. What a catastrophe for her if you, her executor, were to investigate where those monies went."

"But why tell you? You of all people?" Frank asked incredulously.

Henri took his time before answering. He wiped lint off the shoulder of his prison uniform as if he were wearing a five-thousand dollar Broni suit.

"Let us continue hypothetically, shall we Frank? Let us imagine that Janice, knowing who you are, and knowing how you screwed me all those years ago, me, your best friend ..."

Henri stopped mid sentence and started to shout. "I was not only your best friend, I was your only friend and you screwed me during the ensuing years, and now, dammit you're still screwing me!" Henri fought to regain his composure and continued. "But I digress. Let us imagine that Janice knew of your predisposition to screw those who were closest to you. She knows that my mother-in-law with a capital C will have enough evidence to keep me in prison for the rest of my life. So she has this information leaked to me by an Obiere attorney who suggests that I bargain with the infamous Senator for a cushier ... mm ... shall we say, 'a college' where I can spend the rest of my days. We are, of course, speaking hypothetically."

"Take that hypothetical crap and shove it! You stupid frog!" screamed Frank.

"Now, now, Frankie. I hope you have better manners when you horse trade on the Senate floor. So now where was I? Oh yes. So I'm given just enough information to get myself in a better jail and just enough to make sure that you don't bother your beautiful wife. Oh, and Frank, here is where it gets really good. Should something happen to a certain middle-aged woman living on the French Riviera with her young stud, or should I not be moved to a more genteel abode, then I will be visited by the same attorney who gave me this information. I am told that the documentation that I will be given, should either of these aforementioned hypothetical things happen, will be more than sufficient to put you away for the rest of *your* life. I am told that ironically, this information could be used by me to actually broker my release from prison through the United States District Attorney, Manhattan office. So, while my mother-in-law may have my balls in a vice, Frank, it seems that your wife has a piano wire tied around yours – just waiting to castrate you."

The blood had drained from Frank's face as he sat and quietly asked a question to no one in particular. "Why you? Why tell you?"

"Who the hell else," shot back Henri, "you asshole. Don't you see? I am probably the only person, next to your wife, who has such a major hard-on for you. If she were to go to the authorities, she would be right back at that precious Scarsdale farm spending what remains of your viable years fighting you. This way is far better. She gets more money than she can spend. She gets a new life in Europe away from you. She gets to be with her young stud boyfriend who happens to be my no good s.o.b. son. What does she have to lose? Even if for some bizarre reason you chose not to go along with it, you will never hurt her. They all have *plausible deniability* in having a scumbag like me broker this deal. Who the hell would believe me if their attorneys don't back me up? As for money, my son, the crown prince of the Obiere kingdom could take care of her several times over on what that shriveled old whore will leave him. No, my old *friend*, you taught your wife well. Now the student has become the mentor. If it were me, I would have simply killed you and blamed some terrorist organization, but Janice must be a far better person than I am. How ironic is this, Frank? It all comes down to just you and me, once again. This time I am not rolling over for you."

"All right, enough" Rodino said so softly that Henri had to strain to hear him. "I will need a day or so to think about this."

"You can't afford to think about this too long," Henri responded.

As the Senator left the prison his mind was filled with anger and swirling with ideas. He decided he would handle this like a political problem rather than a personal problem. He thought this situation was analogous to the time he was screwed out of the Senate majority leader's job by a group of southern conservative colleagues. Rather than fight them, he gave in and two years later was able to bargain himself into the more powerful head of homeland security. Then, like now, he employed an age old political strategy: "Revenge is a dish best served cold."

He would deal with Henri first off. *Arranging a change of prison venue was of no consequence for a man who had helped the nation with a terrorist threat, and whose only offense was that of tax delinquency. Besides*, Frank mused to himself, *the entire nation is acutely aware since July 4th of what horrible illnesses can befall someone in a prison.* How ironic, Frank thought, that Henri may have solved both of their problems with this request.

What to do with the rest of the information that he was given today was not as easy. Was Henri getting back at him for years of being screwed? Was it possible that the medical examiner could be so sloppy and incompetent as to not be able to identify his wife? Were Henri and his mother-in-law working together to try to extort a good portion of his wealth from his Swiss accounts?

Emotionally, Rodino was furious and desperate to find out if in fact he had been duped by his wife. But politically, he knew he had to leave it alone. In only a few months he had made a fortune on his Bio Tech stock that eclipsed the fortune he and Janice had amassed in their lifetime. As a widower the Senator proved to be an even bigger "Babe Magnet" than as a married senator. The death of his beloved wife during a national terrorist act had catapulted him into an even larger political arena with talk of Frank Rodino as a possible Presidential candidate in the next election. *Political solution*, Frank repeated over and over to himself as he walked to his limousine. *Political solution, not emotional solution.*

The *Genevieve* was moored about a quarter-mile off the most private beaches of St. Tropez. It was already the high season and the St. Tropez regulars had long become accustomed to seeing the 125-foot floating palace. The 'General' brought her down first some 30 years ago. The sizable staff was busy tending to the needs of both the mistress and the yacht, in that order. Additional security hired from a pool of retired United States military men completed the contingent.

Genevieve Obiere sat regally on the aft deck under the awning. Two untouched glasses of iced tea and a china plate of biscuits graced the table before her. A note that confirmed that her package of money had been delivered to the prison in South America now served as a coaster for her drink, sopping wet, the ink no longer legible. Her guest emerged from the darkness of the main salon dressed all in white. A huge straw hat and large dark sunglasses covered the healing sutures of recent plastic surgery.

"Good morning, Genevieve," Janice said as she took the seat next to her. "What a lovely day."

"Yes it is, my dear," Madame Obiere replied. "I must say, you are looking well. I particularly like you as a brunette. It is far more becoming than that red you wore for so many years." Madame paused to reflect on the palette of blues between them and the horizon. "You look well and all has seemed to end well. Do you not think?"

"Of course, Gennie, and I am very grateful to you." She sighed and gestured with an elegant wrist. "But I can't help but miss Tomaas. I don't know if he ever will forgive me for not sharing all the details with him."

"You let me worry about Tomaas," Madame said with a husky chuckle that ended in a raspy cough. "The two of us have been out-maneuvering each other since the day he was born. Remember only this: When I told him you were alive, he cared far more about seeing you than the details."

She glanced at the captain. "I have been told that he arrived on my plane about a half-hour ago. At any moment we should see the transport launch bring him from the docks."

It was fall, and the night air was crisp. The leaves' bright colors could be seen under the full moon that shone above Senator Rodino's Scarsdale farm. The man with a black cap pulled down over his face, squatting behind one of the stone pillars that marked the side entrance to the farm, shivered. This weather was vastly different from that of his homeland in Colombia. And while squatting at this particular gate left him open to the view of passersby, it was the only side of the property the dogs were trained to ignore. It bordered the Scarsdale Country Club and the Senator, ever the perfect neighbor, didn't want to risk having his bulls harassing potential contributors.

This would be the last night of three that the man with a black cap would spend in the affluent town. Intelligence gathering occupied his first two days. This last day was devoted to employing his plan, the last piece having just fallen into place as the Senator stepped out to give his Bull Mastiffs their nighttime treats. As Frank fed and petted his three protectors, the man behind the pillar readied a treat of his own. He took his pocket knife and stabbed the raw meat that lay on a rock before him, creating several small craters in the meat. He took the horse tranquilizers that were tucked into his sock and wedged them securely into the meat. He waited until the dogs barked their displeasure as the Senator went back into the house, then tossed the meat some one hundred feet in their direction. He would have preferred to slit the dog's throats with a straight edge razor that was nestled under his belt next to his gun, but he knew that killing the first would only enable the other two dogs to bark and cause his discovery.

Frank walked back into the house from the garden entrance to his own oval office. On his desk lay a large folder containing the day's terrorist briefings. The fact that the folder was brown and not red was the reason why it had gone unread. Frank had his chief of staff review the daily findings and deliver them to him wherever the Senator might be. If there was an imminent or grave threat, his chief of staff would put the findings into a red envelope. What constituted imminent or grave was a threat against the Senator or his family, his properties or holdings, his contributors or supporters, a national landmark, or a large number of innocent people, in that order. Had the Senator not been typically self absorbed that evening and read the report he would have seen among it the report of a known assassin escaped from a prison in Bogotá, Colombia. According to the report there was no violence involved in the escape and it was assumed that the prison officials had been bribed to let the prisoner out. Canada, Mexico and to a lesser extent South America all enjoyed "privilege status" with the USA. A terrorist suspect would have to be very overt for the Homeland Security Office to single him out if he came from one of those countries. No, Frank was not concerned about what was in the brown folder on his desk; instead he was preoccupied as to why the cable television was out in half his town. He wasn't concerned because the security monitors in his home, which ran off the cable, were out. He was annoyed because he could not get ESPN.

Frank poured himself a Jack Daniels and called the president of Westchester Cablevision on his cell phone.

"Ira, Frank Rodino, how the hell are you?" Without waiting for an answer he continued, "What is going on with the cable? I'm without TV, phone and computer."

"I know Senator," said Ira in an apologetic voice. "I'm going crazy here tonight. It seems some vandals cut a main feeder line that ran under the Heathcoat Bridge. We think it was some kids and we know it was a bias crime because they spray painted anti-Jewish epitaphs all over the place. We should have service back in order by midday tomorrow. If you need to do work this evening, I can send someone from my office with a mobile internet laptop."

"No, that's okay. I am just going to do some reading and listen to some music. But thanks for the offer. And Ira, feel free to send over a check for my next fundraiser. Give my regards to Linda."

Rodino hung up the phone, walked over to his 600-CD changer and typed "Bobby Darrin" into the control panel. Suddenly, "Mack the Knife" was cascading through all twenty eight rooms of the Senator's estate. He turned and headed over to a wing back chair that flanked the fireplace. Had he not been so consumed with self praise for remembering to hit Ira up for a ten thousand dollar contribution, he might have noticed the dark outline of a figure standing next to the rhododendron bush, just 10 feet from where he was about to sit.

The limousine drove down East Main Street in New Rochelle, past gas stations and car dealerships that belied the neighborhood that lay a quarter of a mile south on Long Island Sound. As the light changed to green, the car turned right past the stone pillars that held signs that read *Premium Point, No Outlet, No Trespassing, Guard on Duty* and lastly, as to not seem to be unfriendly, *Bon Repos,* and proceeded down the half a mile long entrance to the guard house that stood at the base of the peninsular and separated the extremely wealthy from the pedestrians. Inside the guard house sat Ian Cullan and Antonio Nunziato.

Nunziato was a New Rochelle Police Lieutenant who had retired two years ago and had landed what many of New Rochelle's finest tried to land – a security gig at the Premium Point homeowners association where the pay was good, the job undemanding and the benefits excellent. Whether it was tickets to a Yankee game from the manager who lived on *The Point,* or discounted airline tickets from the owner of an upstart airline, right down to discounted furniture from the owner of Ethan Allen, the security team would always get thrown some sort of bone from its famous residents. Nunziato and Cullan had worked together for over 25 years.

The limo pulled up to the guard house and opened its window, as the smell of salt air from Long Island Sound permeated the car. The chauffer spoke with a German accent.

"A Mrs. Von Bitter to see Mrs. Iselin."

"One moment, sir, while I call up to the house," Nunziato answered. Mrs. Iselin lived at the very end of the point in a house that was once occupied by the Metromedia mogul John Kluge. There was no answer at either the house or the tennis court which was odd for a home with a household staff of seven. But Nunziato knew that "odd" was customary on the point, and dispatched one of the guards making rounds in his golf cart to see what was going on. "It will be one minute, sir" Nunziato said, and instructed the man to pull the limo out of the driving lane behind the wrought iron gates where his car sat, and over to the side of the guard house next to the brand new Mercedes-Benz. The driver pulled next to the G500 suv that looked like a black, square ice cream truck. He would have no way of knowing that the car was equipped with bullet proof windows and an armored body.

"You know what?" Cullan said, as he downed the last of his coffee. "I have to get these groceries to Bridie, and the house is right next to mine. So why not let me escort them in, and I can check on the Iselin place for you."

"Mighty nice of you, Commissioner, but since you joined the land of the gentry I can't have you doing the work of a peon like myself."

"Your ass," shot back Cullan. "I am just a tenant in that house."

"You can save the bullcrap for someone who believes you, Commish. I saw your application when you went before the homeowners association. That house may be owned by the Obiere Bank of Switzerland, but I know that you and Bridie have a lifetime tenancy there. Hell, just the association fee the bank pays is more than you used to make as commissioner. Oh, and while we're in the subject of pay, I also saw what they pay you for being the head of Obiere Industries Worldwide Security. In the old days, you and I would have called that highway robbery, you lucky Irish s.o.b."

Rather than argue a lost point, Cullan grinned like a leprechaun and said softly, "Didn't even have to go out on the highway to pull this one off."

The speaker at the control panel crackled as the patrol called in to say that everything was okay at the Iselin estate. Mrs. Iselin and staff were out in the greenhouse setting up for her lunch with Mrs. Von Bitter. "You can send her on down," said the voice on the other end.

"Hey Tony," said Cullan, "tell them to follow me and I'll show them the way. A 'Police Escort' that only you and I will know about." As Cullan was about to leave, he returned to Tony and said "By the way, Thursday Paul Arrone will be coming out to have dinner with me and Bridie, and I was wondering if you could do me a favor. See if you can talk the boy into running security with me for Mrs. Obiere. It would be as close to getting back into the police force as he could manage without any of the down side. He could name his salary. He can travel all over the world checking on their holdings. And best of all, no one would call him 'digger' anymore."

Nunziato grinned, not because Cullan was the only one who called Paul "Digger," but because this was about the fifth or sixth time Cullan had tried to get someone in the small "Premium Point Armed Forces" to pry

Paul away from the family business. "I'll see what I can do" Nunziato said as he helped Cullan on with his cashmere jacket.

"Thanks, Tony, I owe you one," Cullan said as he got into his black Mercedes that was parked next to the limo and started to drive through the now opened gates as Mrs. Iselin's guest followed.

7:30 AM – *Earlier That Same Day*

Trish looked out of her kitchen window as she packed Keith's lunch for school. Their backyard stretched back to the woods that adjoined their four acre piece of property. The trees were now bare of leaves, but the abundance of evergreens gave Trish a good feeling about the upcoming winter. This would be her and Keith's first winter in upstate New York, and the much heralded winter nightmares of the Greater Albany region had started playing in her mind following the first signs of frost some three weeks ago. Even if this winter was tough, she figured it would just be one more thing she would have to adjust to. She made a mental note to ask the guys at the gas station she had been using whom they could recommend to plow her driveway this winter. This was just one of the many new responsibilities that came with home ownership that she was fast learning about; this along with the fact that your responsibilities are somewhat directly proportional to the size of the house and property one owns. In this case, hers would be large.

Trish had used the money from the sale of her condo in Yonkers to put a down payment on what she had always visualized would be her dream house: a large white clapboard Dutch colonial which reminded Trish of the Cunningham's house on that sitcom *Happy Days*. Her house even had an apartment above the garage similar to the one that "The Fonz" lived in. Coming from a condo in Yonkers to a house upstate with four acres would have been a major adjustment for most people, but because Trish had always imagined such a place for herself and her son, the transition was easier. Right down to "Scout," their Beagle puppy, who now sat under the kitchen table waiting not so patiently for Keith to drop a piece of breakfast toast her way. The only thing missing from Trish's "Visualization" was a husband, and specifically she was missing Paul. His visits (he was coming up tomorrow) were making it more difficult for her to move on with her life. She was always happy to see him arrive, but his departures left her feeling empty and questioning whether she had made the right decision. She knew that ultimately she would have to stop seeing him completely in order to gain some objectivity about the situation. She had starting dating, although very infrequently, and only very casually. She had not given it a time frame but made up her mind to broach the subject with Paul this weekend.

"Are you going to see David anymore?" Keith called out from behind her. She figured Paul's impending arrival prompted this question. David was a doctor at the local hospital. Just like Keith's father, thought Trish. *Old habits die hard.*

"I may. I'm just not certain," she answered.

"Well, I don't like him! Why do you have to see him?"

"Now that is silly," Trish said. "You don't know him well enough to say something like that. As far as *why* I have to see him, it's not a matter of why, it's a matter or whether I *want* to see him again or not."

"Then why do you have to want to see him again?"

"There are some things that you just don't understand about women yet," Trish said, trying to dismiss the issue. Then so as to change the subject, Trish asked what he and Paul had planned to do this weekend. "Are you guys going to the zoo?"

"No," answered Keith. "The zoo up here is nothing like the Bronx Zoo. Miss Babcock told us at class that there is going to be a dirt bike race on the Pella farm Saturday. Me and Paul are going to go there and ride dirt bikes."

"Oh, Keith, Paul isn't the type of person who likes to ride dirt bikes."

With a sly grin Keith said, "There are some things you just don't understand about men yet."

Trish smiled and thought that her baby was growing up faster than she wanted him to. "Go get your coat. Otherwise you will be late when the school bus gets here." Keith bolted to the mud room closet just off the kitchen and returned with his new coat. As Trish connected the Velcro closures, she thought how nice it had been to be able to buy Keith all new clothes this school year. Even though her salary was comparable to what she made in Westchester, the cost of living was so much lower that Trish found herself in the same financial category as the local doctors and other professionals. Granted, the only department store in this small town was a three story "Robertson's" on Main Street. The store boasted "The only cosmetic counter in the county on the premises," in their advertising. Trish figured she could never again afford to live in any county that had a Neiman Marcus. This suited her just fine because she was able to give her son the things she had growing up. Things that transcended even the obvious financial benefits, like being able to send Keith out this past Halloween with his new friends minus the feelings of fear and dread; the kinds of things that give you inner peace. The kinds of things you can't buy.

While house hunting for several months, Trish was drawn to a small town like this because the realtor (there was only one in town) knew everyone and everyone knew her. While Trish normally did not care for this type of familiarity, she knew that this was the type of town that was fast vanishing in America. She figured that if she didn't bring Keith to a place that had no malls or multiplexes then the chances of him ever experiencing such a lifestyle would forever be lost. And while there was a small part of Trish that did indeed miss the sophistication that came with living in one of the wealthiest counties in America, along with the proximity to NYC, she was beginning to become very comfortable with the "lending hands" way of her upstate neighbors. To have her lawn mowed by her neighbor's son or the groceries dropped off by the owner of the Reliance Market on his way home was a lifestyle that she was beginning to enjoy.

On an educational level, the schools seemed good enough to Trish. They in no way had the money or the programs that Keith was used to in Westchester, but they also lacked the drugs and the alcohol that accompanied the wealthy adolescents of the "Golden Apple." The free time of their Upstate counterparts was occupied with earning extra money for simple sports equipment that most Westchester kids take for granted. No, thought Trish, the kids up here were preoccupied with getting by, and not with getting Prada.

Even Paul had commented on the difference in media coverage just a few miles away from Gotham. The newspapers carried the kind of stories that both he and Trish had remembered from when they were kids – when there were such things as local papers. You would often see or read stories about how people lived in their community rather than how people responded to real or imagined disasters. Paul also noted how the local newspaper carried detailed obituaries of the local population. He would say that was the way things were when he was growing up and New Rochelle had its own newspaper. Now a person's death was relegated to just so much space and at a cost that was becoming prohibitive to all but the wealthy. Paul had told Trish that the last death notice he inserted in the *New York Times* for a family cost $3,700.00 for one day. Paul commented, after reading a half page obituary about the life of a local waitress who worked for 30 years at the breakfast counter of the drugstore, that a person's life (and death for that matter) became increasingly insignificant the closer you got to New York City. Paul added, "That was just for a death notice, mind you. The *New York Times* would never do an obituary on a person unless they were important enough to have made news in their paper while he or she was alive."

As Trish watched Keith get into the school bus and wave goodbye, she had a warm feeling about the future. While this move was disruptive and came with a rollercoaster of emotions, she felt at home. She smiled, threw her head back and chuckled out loud as she remembered a quote from an interview she once saw with Katherine Hepburn, who had said, "The trick in life is not getting what you want but learning to want what you get."

"Absolutely." blurted out Trish as she blew a kiss to her son and went back into her new house to get ready to go to work.

6:00 AM *that same day*

Paul got out of his BMW and was hit by the cold salt air of early November. Even though Glen Island Park was officially closed on Labor Day, the park turned into a passive paradise for those who wanted to walk by the water, launch their boats or as Paul would do this morning, jog. As he began his stretching routine, he admired the yachts docked at the Huguenot Yacht Club that sat just across the water on the mainland. Paul walked down the ramp for two reasons: one was to get a better look at the boats; the other was to put some distance between himself and his warm car so as to avoid giving in to his urge to get back in the car and forgo this morning's jog. Paul had performed a "Should I jog or should I go for doughnuts and coffee" dance every morning since he'd started this new exercise routine. The jog always managed to win out, and now after two months, Paul was noticing the physical and mental benefits of his morning workout.

He adjusted the volume of his iPod as he started his run on the lower half of the 80-acre Island. He was listening to Usher and knew the lineup of music would be followed by Eminem, Lincoln Park, etc. While Paul hated this music, he knew that Keith was always impressed by his knowledge of music that all the "kids" were listening to.

As Eminem's *Cleanin' Out My Closet* started to play, Paul started his run along the lower part of the park near the now closed beach. He weighed today, as he did every morning on his new regime, whether it was better to get and stay in shape so he could live a long life, or whether he should simply become sedentary so he could help his arteries clog up and be done with it. Thus, a new list would be made today, as a list had been made each of the last 60 or so days, outlining the pros and cons of his existence.

He would see Trish and Keith this weekend. That was always a good thing. Although now he had to drive two and a half hours upstate to do so, it was still a very good thing. He had not realized how important Trish was in the scheme of his life until she was no longer available. Paul had come to realize over the last few months that this was a clear pattern in his life – not knowing what you had until you were about to lose it. As with Trish, Paul had somehow slighted the importance of his family business until he faced losing both his license and his business. While he ran his business with all the care of the perfectionist that he was, his heart was absent with Trish. The fact that 20 some odd years after he entered the funeral business he was now finally able to put his passion behind his work ethic was a good thing. Even recognizing that he would never reenter the world of professional law enforcement was a good thing in that it enabled him to pursue that desire as a hobby, the way it should have been for some time.

As for Trish, Paul would reach the same conclusion today as he did on many of his early morning runs: unlike the inanimate object that was his business, his being a disaffected lover/significant other had more serious consequences. To be an absentee soul mate was equivalent to making Trish date one of the corpses that passed through his business. Something she had dutifully done for longer than Paul figured he deserved. The solution would not be easy, but Paul was determined to win back her love. No, win was the wrong word, Paul thought as he picked up his pace and was now running full out. He would try to earn a place in Trish's life and then hopefully back into her heart.

Paul's mind now focused on his trip upstate tomorrow. He would have to be certain there would be coverage the three days he was away from the funeral home. That was a wash, both good and bad, but certainly more good than bad. Good, because his dad had now re-entered the funeral business, actively covering for Paul while he took time off. Both Paul and his mother recognized the enormously positive benefits this had on the elder Arrone. Bad because Paul knew the odds of a hysterical Italian family (Paul chuckled out loud at the redundancy) walking in upon the death of a loved one and demanding to see only him was directly proportional to how far away from New Rochelle he was. But now there was a third category, a category that until recently his psyche was unable to comprehend; the "There is-nothing-I-can-do-about-this, it-is-out-of-my control-and-I-have-to-accept-it" category. This category, new to him, had been ironically absent for a good part of his adult life. It stunned Paul that he was making a living comforting people through their losses, and yet could not deal with his own lack of closure. "Had to be low blood sugar," Paul said out loud as he started to ascend the hill by the Glen Island Casino. He was a mile or so into his run and his legs had begun to feel the affects of his not stretching them properly.

The Casino in its earlier day was home to the legends of the "Big Band Era," with such notables as Glen Miller and Tommy Dorsey playing there. Today the newly refurbished building was a catering hall that paid rent to the county. The fact that the rental contract was awarded without going out to bid ensured that all the local politicos held their fundraisers there at a largely reduced fee. This brought to mind another aspect of his life that had both good and bad items on his mental ledger. His recent run-in with the local Westchester politicians brought him a great deal of discomfort. When Anthony and Cullan fully explained the "vaccine for money" scheme that had transpired, Paul was dumbfounded. He knew how corrupt Westchester was, but never imagined the depths to which Westchester had sunk. Another item on the negative side was discovering that his family had themselves bought the Cardin stock. Lastly, and most significant, was the anger that he held for those people who had gotten away with these tragic happenings. It was too soon for Paul to assess whether this would ever make it into the "acceptance" column or whether there was still something that he could do to right the situation. The plans he was recently making to disrupt the political status quo in Westchester would have to be put on hold until he stabilized his personal life.

Paul quickly refocused his thoughts elsewhere. He knew all too well that if he dwelled on the perfidy of Haywood and the others, he was capable of being consumed by it. Hell, he was the master of it. After all here he was a middle-aged man who had lived and enjoyed less of a life than his dead brother who had lived half as many years. Paul wondered how two such close people – brothers who shared the same DNA; brothers who lived in the same environment; brothers who spent most of their waking hours together – could end up so different. The answer, or at least the answer for today, came to Paul as the natural opiates from his morning run started to kick in.

The single biggest difference between him and his brother was that John hadn't had to live through the murder of his brother. For the first time in over two decades, Paul felt grateful for something about that dreadful morning. Grateful not only that he was alive, but grateful that his brother would forever be spared the agony of grieving over someone he loved. While this was a shallow victory, it was one that Paul would take on this day, nonetheless. He then moved on to other pressing issues that needed his conscious attention.

Tie up loose ends. That is what Paul needed to do. He knew that at this stage of his life he could be happy growing old as the local funeral director for his home town. He knew that he wanted to win back Trish. He knew that he had to reconnect emotionally with many of his longtime friends who had stuck by him for so long. He also knew he had to resolve what to do with the job offers that LWS and Cullan were tempting him with.

Tomaas' grandmother, Mrs. Obiere, had been lavish with her compliments about Paul's talents and had made a generous job offer. Each month since the past summer's events she would send a note along with a gift. The letter and gift would arrive on the first Wednesday of the month. No coincidence that this fell the day before he would meet Cullan for their monthly dinner. Paul knew he was being tag teamed. Yesterday Paul had received a first class ticket to Paris along with a letter from the new chairperson of the board of LaCroix Worldwide Shipping, Genevieve Obiere. The letter outlined how the company wanted him to run the North and South American divisions in concert with Tomaas LaCroix who would run the European and Asian divisions. She was very persuasive in her approach, outlining how a young man like Paul could turn around the "faulty" mindset of the corporate funeral conglomerate to mirror the values of a family-run business like his in New Rochelle. The values and success of the Arrone Funeral Home, she carefully explained, could only be enhanced by the success that she was sure he would bring to the industry nationwide.

She continued to lure him with a lucrative consulting contract that included apartments in New York, Paris and Rome – which she craftily noted would be a good opportunity for a young man like himself to "court" a particular young lady. *"Court"-do people even use that word anymore?* Paul thought as he read the letter. Lastly, she enclosed a Cartier solid gold pen with a note attached that read "I know you have a problem holding on to these." Paul smiled, thinking, she is one sharp woman.

But did he want to start a new life when the one he was living still needed so much work? Paul was now rounding the northern tip of the island. The highest point. The Sound, while not known for its pristine qualities, glistened as he had never remembered. He jogged past the old cannons that were placed on the island during the Revolutionary War to protect New York City from a sneak attack. Beyond the glistening waters he could see the old red brick barracks on David's Island.

His mind shifted to the day he met Tomaas there, and he started to wonder how his new friend was doing. Oddly, it seemed that he heard more frequently from Tomaas' grandmother than he did from Tomaas. *He would call rather than write. His last call was a month or so ago and his French friend had sounded – what? Paul grasped for a word to describe his mood. He was certainly happy, but it wasn't just that. Content. Yes, Tomaas seemed content beyond his years.* Paul made a mental note to track down his friend when he got back from Trish's and do some serious "catching up."

He now was coming to the last leg of his morning jog. He passed the part of the park where sculptured animals stood guard. The lion and the horse had served as childhood friends for him and his brothers. Behind the animal garden was a path that led to an old wood cottage that looked as though it belonged on Nantucket Island rather than Glen Island. A small sign was posted above the door: "Police."

Paul thought about Cappy. *It would be good to see Cappy and Bridie tonight.* Paul had been certain the two of them would feel out of place living in a mansion on one of the most exclusive peninsulas in the world. But when he went there the first time for dinner and found Cullan, Bridie and the grandchildren horsing around in the indoor pool with a sterling silver ice bucket filled with beers by the lounge chairs, he knew he was wrong. He was happy that his friends were making up for lost time. He was particularly pleased that Bridie was getting a shot at a life she so deserved. Their age meant little to Paul in the scope of happiness. Paul had seen many a married young couple have their happiness cut short by death. The one thing Paul knew for certain: it was the ability to obtain a degree of happiness in life that was important. No one was guaranteed a quantity of that time. Age was insignificant to a funeral director who had buried people in virtually every age group from infant to centenarian. And while Paul would acknowledge the statistical data of the odds of living a long life, he knew with certainty that death could drop in for a visit in anyone's home like a crazy relative who comes by without calling. Whether Bridie and Cappy had one week, one year or one decade remaining to them, Paul knew their time would be rich with good times and happiness. Good for them!

Paul would never have guessed that Cappy would have fit so well into the corporate world. "Well" was an understatement. He was thriving in his new position. Paul figured that it must be exhilarating for Cappy, who for the better part of his life had been bound by bureaucratic restraints, to run security for a multinational corporation with a free hand. To employ the latest and best in the world of security, with the added benefit of the company's multinational "safe haven" status was the wet dream of every law enforcement agent around the world. To Paul, his old friend seemed

15 years younger. There was a piece of Paul's soul that wanted to accept Mrs. Obiere's offer so that he too could "play" with Cappy and the many toys that her corporation offered. But even though Cullan was close to three decades his senior, Paul had the odd feeling that he would be holding Cappy back if he made such a move. Or maybe it wasn't so much holding Cappy back as it was that he saw himself taking a step backwards by toying with such an idea. Whatever – he shrugged – he didn't have to make any decision on this morning's run. He would just go and enjoy dinner tonight and take it from there.

At the same time, on that same day, Paul was jogging in New Rochelle, the *SS Genevieve* was about to weigh anchor and sail to yet another port on the Riviera. A servant wheeled a cart of a lavish lunch and secured it outside the master cabin next to the breakfast cart he had left there several hours ago. He then wheeled away the untouched breakfast cart. Inside the cabin Janice lay in Tomaas' arms, thinking to herself that staying up all night drinking and having sex with her lover made all the tangible things in her life pale by comparison. Tomaas had his thick arms wrapped so tightly around her midsection that she could barely breathe. She had noticed that since they reunited, he held her a little tighter and sat a little closer than he had before. She spoke softly. "You know if we keep up this pace, there could be a problem."

"How so?" Tomaas began to kiss the back of her neck.

Janice continued in a rather clinical voice. "Given the age difference, this type of activity could prove harmful in the long run." She paused and then jokingly added, "But hell, if it kills you, it kills you."

They both laughed, and Tomaas started tickling her. It didn't seem as though they could be any happier. There was, however, one dark cloud that seemed to follow their relationship; and while neither of them spoke of the details of what had happened several months ago, they knew that they would soon have to confront them.

Tomaas was so happy to have his Janice back that at first he didn't care what brought her back to him. She, knowing most of the story, still felt she had betrayed him by allowing him to think she had died. If the shoe were on the other foot, she thought, she wasn't sure she would be so forgiving.

Tomaas's grandmother was very specific on *never* uttering a word about what had happened to anyone, *ever*. They shouldn't even discuss it between themselves. Both knew that Genevieve had their best interests at heart, and probably would have honored her command until the end of time had Tomaas not been so much like his grandmother. He had to know. He tightened his grip around Janice's waist and began to beg in a whisper. "Only one question ... *please*. And I promise I will never bring it up again."

Janice figured that if there was one person in this entire situation who stood above everyone else, it was Tomaas. She also sensed that he was the one person who deserved at the very least a single answer if not the entire story. "Okay," Janice said softly, "just one question."

Tomaas leaned over, kissed her on the cheek and then began to whisper into her ear. "You are alive, Oui, so whose body was that in the car? I have to know if you or my grandmother had anything to do with the death of that woman. And how were you able to take on a new identity?"

Janice sat upright in the bed and put her finger on Tomaas mouth to quiet him. "That's more than one question," she said as she searched her mind for what she should or shouldn't say. "First, no one in your family killed anyone ... well ... I should rephrase that and say neither your grandmother nor I had anything to do with any killing. Your grandmother found out about my husband's plan from various spies she has in her employ. She had someone in her organization contact the man who was to assassinate me and made him a far more generous offer to kill no one.

"She then sent word out to the hospitals her foundations so generously support. She said she wanted to start a new program for LaCroix Worldwide Shipping. The program was simply to cremate, at no cost to the hospital or government, any indigent person who died without any relatives or friends. Her foundation would pay the nominal costs and LWS would reap the benefits of the huge public relations scheme.

"Genevieve did the math and knew that she could expect several deaths a week that would fall into this category. She also knew that while she was arranging the necessary legal paperwork that four unclaimed female corpses were laying in morgues throughout France. She figured that she would go along with the plan to have the car crash that my husband had planned. The only difference would be that Madame would pay to have the car blown up on impact so no one would be able to identify the body. My husband was, you have to remember, more interested in getting his contraband over to the States than he was in the condition of my body."

A chill went up Tomaas's spine as he uttered, 'That *bastard!*'

"Wait, continued Janice. "Here is where it gets freaky. The night before the accident a young waitress from a local pub died of an aneurism. Her name was Eva. She was in her late forties and had no family to claim her. Pastor LaBrea called your grandmother himself and asked if she would start off her charity drive with this poor soul from his parish. Your grandmother agreed, and assured the pastor that the body would most certainly be cremated at no cost to the church.

"Your grandmother realized that the car didn't have to be blown up; and that the original plan that my husband orchestrated could be carried out – without me, of course." Tomaas moved closer to Janice as she continued her story.

"The plan had changed ever so slightly, but significantly in your grandmother's favor. This woman's body was taken to one of the funeral homes your family owns and her hair was dyed to match mine. After her body was washed, she was given a postmortem manicure and pedicure and her body was sprayed with my perfume.

"I had to drive the car myself, so that the border patrol would be able to identify me. That's when I made my call to you. I then drove down to the sea where this young lady's body was placed in the car. I, in turn, was placed on your grandmother's yacht. One of Genevieve's personal bodyguards then drove the car to just behind the hairpin curve, out of sight of the villa's cameras. He then moved the dead woman into the driver's seat and employed a remote control device that took the car around the curve and down the hill.

"Once the car came to a rest, the driver of the truck ran down to the crash site and retrieved the remote device. Your grandmother called the pastor personally to tell him that the cremation took place the day Haywood drove that body to the crematory."

"How could you two be certain your husband would not identify your body?" Tomaas asked in astonishment.

"I knew Frank wouldn't. He has the most perverse fear of death. He wouldn't even go and identify his own mother when she died. I wasn't sure about the rest of the gang. But your grandmother was right once again. She had told me that greed and fear would blind these men. Haywood met me on only a few occasions and your grandmother figured that given the circumstance, there was a good chance he would think I was the dead woman. She was right.

"Even if it didn't work out that way," Janice continued, "what could they do? Notify the officials that the wife of a U.S. Senator who had been declared dead by *their people* in Monaco was actually someone else? That would *never* happen.

"Look Tommy, I feel terrible about not letting you in on this from the beginning, and I hope you can forgive me, but your grandmother made a very compelling case to keep you completely out of this. Remember, even if no one was killed, we're talking about falsifying papers and possible fraud."

"Can the authorities come after you now?" Tomaas asked anxiously.

"Me … Me?" responded Janice as she looked around the room. "Why on earth would they come after me − Eva, a poor woman from the slums of Paris who just happened to marry a prince?"

They looked at each other for a moment and then laughed and fell back onto the pillows in each other's arms.

5:30 AM *that same morning*

The clock recessed into the marble façade of the Geneva headquarters of the Swiss bank that bore the Obiere name had just turned 11:30 AM. The penthouse boardroom was being readied for a 2:00 PM board meeting. Several secretaries were placing files around the table and filling the crystal water decanters in front of each of the eighteen chairs. The solid cherry board table and matching paneling still had a faint smell of the furniture polish that had been applied by the maintenance crew the night before. Painted portraits of those who served as chairpersons of the bank board adorned the walls with the latest, that of Mrs. Obiere, hanging closest to the head of the table. In a little over two hours, Mrs. Obiere would take that seat and chair the quarterly meeting as she had done for the past 20 years.

Directly behind her chair at the head of the table was a set of double doors that led to her private office in which she had been sequestered with her primary attorney since seven that morning.

William Spence had been Mrs. Obiere's lawyer for almost 40 years. She had hand picked him out of law school after she and the General had gone through many of the local attorneys without success. William had all of the prerequisites that Mrs. Obiere required. Head of his law class, a master's degree in business and most importantly, an impeccable English background. That for Genevieve meant a total lack of emotional availability. William had become as close to Mrs. Obiere's business equal as anyone would ever get. She confided in him on issues that she dare not even tell her late husband. He was an extremely capable attorney and a ferocious businessman who was subservient to no one, save the woman who had hired him some forty years ago. When it came to Mrs. Obiere, William acted as if he were one of her servants. They met this morning as they had every other week for the past 40 years; this pattern was only broken in the last month when they met more frequently.

William stood like a mannequin, his back to a huge hand-carved mahogany desk. He was dressed in his customary gray pinstriped suit, which was adorned with its customary boutonnière. In front of him was a push cart that contained all the important papers of this morning. In front of the push cart was one of the two oxblood leather chesterfield sofas that sat in the middle of the room. This morning, as had been the practice on so many other mornings, one of the sofas had been moved and placed directly in front of the fireplace. On the sofa sat Madame Obiere. The room was dimly lit with only one of the Tiffany lamps turned on. The remainder of the light came from the roaring fire in the stone fireplace that blazed a foot or so from Mrs. Obiere's patent leather Ferragamo shoes.

"What next?" she asked, holding out her arthritic hand that was encrusted with diamonds. He handed her the last of what was a million dollar pile of old German money that sat on the cart. The only difference between now and all the other meetings was that Mrs. Obiere had asked for this one and several others over the last few weeks – in what appeared to William to be an uncharacteristically hurried departure from the practice of forty years. This manner of disposing of "paper work" had pre-dated paper shredders and was the only way Mrs. Obiere disposed of business. Waiting until the last particle of paper was turned into ash.

"How much is left in the safe?" she asked. She was of course referring to her private safe in the sub basement of her bank.

"I would say two or three more of these "meetings" should take care of it, Madame.

"How can I be certain, William, you won't someday double cross me? Or worse yet, wait until I am dead and undo much of what I have done?"

A lesser person would have been insulted by such a question. But then a lesser person would never have worked for Mrs. Obiere for 40 years without missing a day. "Stoic" took on an entirely new meaning when describing William. Mrs. Obiere wanted the perfect unemotional man and that is what she got. William never shared, nor did she inquire about his private life. A few years earlier Mrs. Obiere was informed by her chauffeur that William's wife had died over the weekend. She never knew whether this was true or not. When she arrived at her office that Monday morning at 6:00 AM, William was already there working diligently on her affairs. A lesser person would have taken insult at the old lady's question of loyalty, but William knew all too well that their relationship transcended mere emotional insecurities.

"We can offer three reasons why this just isn't possible, Madame. Firstly, even though I am 25 years your junior, we both know that you will outlive me and most likely everyone on the board of this bank. And secondly, Madame," he started to say as he pointed to the remaining Reich banknotes that were in her hands, ready to be to tossed into the fire, "if 'he' was afraid to double-cross you, what makes Madame think that we have the fortitude for such event. Lastly, Madame Obiere knows that we are not ignorant. Therefore, we fully expect that there are files such as these somewhere in a place that I don't have access to, most likely controlled by your new head of security, Ian Cullan. That should keep us in line. No, Madame?"

"What next?" she snapped to change the subject. William pointed to the middle shelf of the cart on which sat a dozen or so files marked H. LaCroix.

"Return those to the vault, William. I want to use those only if it looks as though that bastard ever has a chance of getting out of jail. Those files flagged with the red tape are to be sent to the parole board should he even get that far."

"We have been told he stands a good chance of being moved to a minimum security prison. Are we to address this?"

"No, I have no concern as to where he's incarcerated, so long as he remains incarcerated. If I wanted him harmed, he would have been harmed while he walked the streets squandering my money. No, I just want him far enough away from Tomaas so as not to influence him or my daughter ever again.

"What do we have next?" she asked in a tone that William recognized: she was growing tired of doing much more today. He handed her a file that read "Diaz." She opened the file, and as she looked down she muttered slowly and softly, "This is one tough lady." William diverted his stare into the flames of the fireplace and mustered all his strength to remain silent. It would take one to know one, he thought to himself.

Mrs. Obiere looked up quickly as if to catch William snicker but she saw only the neutral face of her loyal employee.

"Did you transfer the money?"

"Yes, Madame."

"Do you think there is enough manpower and resources to be able to win a recall election against this District Attorney?"

"Yes indeed, Madame, I do. We have also one of the largest law firms in New York, which has done much work for Madame's companies over the years, volunteering their associates to look over the petitions and support this "grass roots" group in any way necessary. Even if the recall is unsuccessful, the amount of unpleasant publicity that will be leaked to the media will surely prohibit her from ever winning another election."

"Good, that bitch has got to go!"

William was about to say *excuse me?* He had rarely heard his employer use this language or tone when discussing an adversary. There had to be more to this story than he was aware of, he thought as he answered, "Very good, Madame."

"What next," Genevieve asked as she snapped her fingers. William handed her the bill from the cargo company that transported the Ferretti from NYC to Monaco; the speed boat she had given to Tomaas two years ago was now repainted in its original colors. "Highway robbery," she snapped as she tossed the paid bill into the flames.

"How was Madame certain that Master Tomaas would not recognize his own boat?"

"What is the bigger question, William, is how I could be certain he wouldn't recognize the French models from the modeling agency I bought two years ago. Or how I could be certain that he would not see the tracking device I had those young ladies attach to that yacht. And the answer to all these is the same. He is a man. Men are generally stupid animals, William. No offense."

"None taken."

Mrs. Obiere continued. "Flash a pair of ample breasts, and your average man would not see anything else. Because I feel my grandson is above average I raised the ante to three pairs of ample breasts. I could have been behind the wheel of that boat myself and Tomaas would not have noticed." She was now laughing out loud. "You know, William, modern women want equality and that is just what they are getting. The price, however, is that they are giving up their position of superiority."

"While we are talking about that day, may I ask Madame how she was certain that the Ebola vaccine she had the doctor give Paul Arrone would work?"

"Yes, William, as my attorney, you may ask." Mrs. Obiere always prefaced her sentences that way when she was about to tell William something that could cause her to be indicted. By prefacing each statement there would be no doubt that this was an attorney-client discussion. She went on. "My people were only a few hours ahead of that smart young man in figuring out what was going on. The pharmaceutical company that I own in Berlin had perfected a vaccine for Ebola years ago. There just wasn't a market for it so we put it in the freezer for future research."

"How did Madame know it was safe to use on humans?"

"We knew because we tested it on humans. I had them inject that bastard of a son-in-law five years ago, when he went for his annual physical and flu shot." William raised his eyebrows. Obiere continued. "Oh please, it was a win-win situation. Either he would die a horrible death, or we would have a marketable vaccine for the future. And I must tell you, William, my attorney, it is a far better vaccine than that quack Cardin came up with."

William had been with Mrs. Obiere his entire adult life and knew what she was capable of. "Amazing," he said in a whisper.

"I will tell you what amazing is. Amazing is that I have a better vaccine sitting in the deep freeze, and that is where it will stay. You see, I now own LaCroix Worldwide Shipping, which has a large block of Cardin stock under its belt. Said stock is going through the roof, ergo my vaccine stays put."

"As you wish, Madame."

"What next?" she asked as she looked over her shoulder to William. The room was so dark that she had difficulty discerning him from the mahogany paneled walls. He handed her a file marked "Trish" and as he did so, gave his "take" on the contents.

"It appears that the young lady is dating a doctor on and off in her new town, but your people don't think it is serious."

"I don't have to tell you, William, how important she is to the overall plan. There is little to no chance of my getting Paul to work for me if he is jilted by his love."

"But surely Madame can find another person suitable to run the shipping company?"

"No, I most certainly cannot!" Shot back Genevieve. "Twenty five percent of this family's wealth is tied up in LaCroix Worldwide Shipping. I intend to get back every penny, with interest. For that I need good people for the long haul. There is, of course, you and my grandson, who are more than capable. You have the staying power to be *in the hunt for the long haul.* If nothing else, it is my opinion that within the next ten years the property values alone will exceed the individual values of each branch. My grandson will not have the staying power unless I stack the board with people he can work with. People he can respect and people he can become friends with. I don't have time to do a 'Star Search.' We both know that we can expect him to be absent for the near future as he and his new bride "Eva" enjoy an extended honeymoon on the Riviera. When he comes back, we need to hit the ground running and get this last chapter under way."

William cleared his throat and said, "I don't suppose Madame would see that she doesn't really need this business and just be happy to run the remaining parts of her vast empire."

Mrs. Obiere rose from the couch and faced William. "No, Madame *does not* see it that way. Let me tell you a little secret, William. It is not about what I need, it is about what I want. I always get what I want. Now, here is the secret part. I seldom get what I need. This would actually give me both."

"Very good Madame. Then we shall stay the course."

"Good," responded Genevieve as she tossed the last of the old money into the fire. She wiped her hands together and said, "Things are wrapping up nicely, William. Thank you."

This was the first time in his employ that she had actually uttered those words to him. Yes, her appreciation had revealed itself through bonuses and percentages in her companies over the years, but he never heard her say those words.

"I am quite hungry William. It has been a good morning's work."

He walked over to the gold-plated antique phone on Mrs. Obiere's personal desk. "Shall I have them send up your vegetable plate, Madame?"

"No, William," she replied in an upbeat tone that he hadn't heard in years.

"I want you to spend some of that fortune I pay you and take me to that new restaurant down the street. I feel like a steak. A very large, very rare steak. And I think I will have a martini too. How does my grandson order those? You know, like that spy in the movies."

"Yes, Madame, that would be shaken, not stirred," William answered.

"Shall we?" she asked, as she motioned her arm towards the double doors that led to the massive board room.

"My privilege," he responded as he opened the doors. He gave her his arm.

The two walked past the board room and started down the long marble hallway to the elevator bank.

"You know, William, we are not going to rush either. We will get back when we get back. I have started those damn meetings on time for over twenty years. This time, all those stuffed suits can just wait for me."

"Splendid indeed, Madame."